DOC SPEARS

LEGIONNAIRE
ETERNAL

DARK OPERTOR   **BOOK 6**

GALAXY'S EDGE

ISBN: 979-8-88922-048-0

Edited by Lauren Moore
Published by Galaxy's Edge Press

Cover Design: M.S. Corely

Website: www.GalaxysEdge.us
Facebook: facebook.com/atgalaxysedge
Newsletter (get a free short story): www.InTheLegion.com

JOIN THE LEGION

FOR UPDATES ABOUT NEW RELEASES, EXCLUSIVE PROMOTIONS, AND SALES, VISIT INTHELEGION.COM AND SIGN UP FOR OUR VIP MAILING LIST. GRAB A SPOT IN THE NEAREST COMBAT SLED AND GET OVER THERE TO RECEIVE YOUR FREE COPY OF "TIN MAN", A GALAXY'S EDGE SHORT STORY AVAILABLE ONLY TO MAILNG LIST SUBSCRIBERS.

INTHELEGION.COM

FREE SHORT STORY
TIN MAN
WHEN YOU SIGN
UP FOR OUR VIP
MAILING LIST

Who stands as the model of the ideal legionnaire? Who in the storied history of the greatest fighting force the galaxy's ever known shines as their brightest beacon? Who is the template for legionnaire virtue, the person that every leej who ever wore the bucket strives to be?

Only one legionnaire qualifies.

Rex.

The general has become more myth than man. More fable than real. The Legion he led to victory in the Savage Wars followed his example of warrior perfection and absolute duty unto death to save humanity while painting glory across the stars. The Legion was his legacy; it cemented the legend of Tyrus Rex. But Rex also founded another, less well-known organization: a small unit of shadowy covert operators who left only his invisible signature as their calling card.

Dark Ops.

Kel Turner's achievements in Dark Ops could be the stuff of legend too—were they known to any but the few who witnessed them. So when the most respected operator in their ranks leaves the Legion, no one is more puzzled than the very figures of rectitude and honor he draws inspiration from daily: the flesh-and-blood operators Kel admires more than Rex himself.

Convinced he's responsible for a Legion infiltrated by appointed officers, a Dark Ops burned by the light of day, and the suffering of someone he loves above all, Kel finds the battlefronts of Kel's internal war pushing him to step out of the armor.

Until the fateful day when he's reminded that a legionnaire's debt to the galaxy is never paid in full.

It started with a mission to kidnap a conspiracy-obsessed trillionaire; the work to tame a world of insectoid fanatics; a collision with a lost Savage civilization and a technology of cataclysmic terror; an organization researching ancient alien artifacts and the unknown entity that controlled it; a clandestine no-holds-barred operation to destroy a political dynasty bent on absolute control; and finally, a mission beneath the jungle hell of Psydon where an unstoppable plague brewed in the cauldrons of a new conspiracy.

Kel Turner's career has been a thread joining the many events that now threaten to determine life or death, freedom or slavery, and the future or end of the entire Republic.

Rex was the perfect legionnaire. But in a galaxy missing its savior, there's one dark operator worthy of inheriting the title of deadliest weapon in the Legion arsenal.

And his name is Kel Turner.

01

It's a myth that the inner arms of the galaxy are so dense with stars that a night sky viewed from planetfall is as brilliantly bright as day, with skies so thick in blue starlight that their collective blaze rivals a world's sun. The reality is that even this close to the galactic center—the core worlds —the cold gulfs between stars are an unimaginable distance separating all life. The few mortals who have truly tried to contemplate the immensity of the galaxy and the space between the thousands of its life-sustaining worlds were rendered insane for their efforts.

The Mute had done so and reached the conclusion that drove so many others mad. The infinite meant not only as many possibilities, it meant as many cruelties. But succumbing to the madness that came with that realization was a choice—to be either a victim of the galaxy or one of the rare few who would dare fight it.

Everything he pondered about the twinkling canvas of the night was ruled by a math as mysterious as magic—a faith in the science of jump drives and those who mastered their operation. For a ground-pounder like him, it was with puzzling awe that the nature of folded space made the time to travel to the brightest star in the dense sky of the galactic center—so close it seemed you could touch it—a longer journey than to one so far away and so dim as to be an almost imagined dot of light. Star densities, gravity wells, spatial anomalies, all disregarded linear distances as useless concepts when it came to how folded space transited a person from one place to another.

Byblos was the third of such worlds he'd been on, scattered within the vague boundaries that defined the core and mid-core of the galaxy. Unaligned worlds close enough to matter but far enough out of the Republic's control that they harbored the kinds of people and activities he sought.

And though the stars on Byblos *were* close together, even near the bustling spaceport, there was darkness. If you knew how to find it. If you knew how to use it. The Mute did. He'd spent a lifetime making darkness his ally. The math he was the master of didn't calculate the mass of stars or the gravity wells of black holes.

His science decided who lived and who died.

He took a last look at his sanctuary these past nine months. The tunnels beneath the abandoned amphitheater were home to the city's underclass, and the place where the myth of Wadih the Mute was born. Making his sanctuary in the catacombs had been a perfect choice, the pens long empty of the exotic animals and fighters that died for the amusement of all on the sands above. Since the taste for blood and pain had fallen out of interest, the abandoned stadium was a refuge for the undesirables. When it was torn down, who knew where the multitudes of crippled beggars, former slaves, and mentally stunted would end up?

The man would not remain long enough to find out.

He'd sold what he could and destroyed the rest. His weapons he would ditch when he was through with them. The grav container would stand up to a detailed search—his specs, his datapad, and the other smaller pieces of tech all well disguised within. If the sultan's thugs or customs took his container or he had to abandon it, he'd still be able to function. It was a rule. Never be dependent on a *thing*. Depend only on yourself.

He looked wistfully to where the small mass converter had sat in the refuge. He'd disappeared—how many—three bodies into it? He should remember. It was unpleasant work, disarticulating the limbs, separating the rest like a butcher would a carcass, in order to feed the pieces into the machine. But you discarded from memory that which served no purpose. Especially the unpleasant. The same way pain was discarded.

But without the mass converter, there was no traceless way to get rid of a corpse, should he have to abandon his plan to leave tonight. If circumstances prevented him from lifting with the *Siderion Sultan* tomorrow, he'd be sorry he'd no longer have the safehouse to retreat to. It couldn't be helped. The time was now.

All that was left were the many ifs. If he drew attention by having to kill too many people. If he squeezed this next Hool only to find he wasn't higher up the food chain and didn't hold the needed information. If his disguise failed to fool the many layers of security at the spaceport.

If, if, if.

If he didn't make it off the planet by sunrise, he wouldn't come back here to rebuild the safehouse. He'd hop one of the many sub-orbital craft and fly to the spaceport in the northern continent and find another way off-world. He had contingencies for contingencies. However it played out—whether or not the next sunrise brought him a change of planetary scenery—he'd find a way into space and put his time on Byblos behind him. It wasn't hope. It was a certainty. Because he was on a mission.

His life was about the mission. He'd had many. And every one he had held sacred. The preparation. The planning. The execution. He was like the shipwright who poured over every detail, examined each component of the ship to discover the microscopic crack that, if missed, would grow to a fissure under repulsor reentry and doom the craft and her crew to a fiery death. To those like him, to neglect any detail was to ignore the tiny flaw that could give way to catastrophic failure and with it, admit to the galaxy that his honor had concealed a flaw like the missed micro-fissure hidden in a piece of faulty impervisteel plate.

It began and ended with honor. Hard won. Proven by competence. Unspoken, because there was no need. Building honor required believing in yourself. It was more than having the skills within you; it was the absolute faith that you could access them at will to meet the demand of the moment. That you were better than the rest. Because otherwise, it would be impossible to do what he and those like him could do. There were others like him.

And it was for them that he did this.

The tunnels beneath the abandoned amphitheater were full of the usual derelicts found in any underclass, sleeping in illegal ethanol or legal drug-induced states. More of those who called the tunnels home were like him, working the deep hours of night while the high born and well-off slept, then retreating to the stifling shade of the oven that was the underground during daylight. They did the invisible but necessary chores that kept a city functioning. Some were freed men—former slaves in a part of the galaxy where slavery was not supposed to exist. Most were simply without guild or class, from long lines of downtrodden who did the things not even a bot would be wasted on, its efforts more valuable than those of an organic tool.

At this late hour, it was another class of underground dweller he stepped over and around—the professional beggars. Their trade was plied near the spaceport during the high-day and evening. Unlike the derelicts who committed petty crimes to support their dreamflower habits—and got whittled down an appendage at a time by the scimitars of the sultan's constables for each infraction for which they were apprehended—the beggars had a commensal role in this society, and were tolerated.

For the beggar, a credit chit meant another day of life. For the wealthy visitor, dropping a credit in the bowl was more than an act of pity in a galaxy without the quality. It was an act of superstitious warding—driving away the kind of bad luck that might descend like a foul air and force one into becoming a beggar oneself. Sometimes a chit dropped by a clean and manicured hand was not an act of largess, but done to impress the lady on the other arm, a means of providing kind character to further a romantic advance.

Drunken spacers, fresh with new credits won from the tables, were another good mark. The young crewmen especially had pity for a blind or lame child. The older spacers knew the game though, that the subjects of pity had most often been made purposefully so, in order to provide a living for the one who collected the credits dropped in the crippled's bowls.

The galaxy was a cruel place, even where the light of the Republic supposedly outshone the stars themselves.

He'd only had to kill one of the gang who preyed on the squatters taking refuge below the stadium. The twisted corpse of the biggest of the predators was enough to send the message that they no longer controlled the tunnels. That had begun the mystique of Wadih the Mute amongst the invisible underclass and the criminals who made their suffering even worse. The gratitude of his fellow denizens had become a ring of security for his activities. The hidden entrance. The security door. Silence about the tools and amenities he'd secreted inside. And the occasional guest who did not leave.

Short memory is a universal human trait, one shared by a variety of the galaxy's humanoid species. Other gangs occasionally tried to move into the business of extorting the poorest of the poor under the Mute's protection, ignoring the earlier lesson. Those he did not disappear into his mass converter powering the clandestine apartment. Those his fellow subterranean dwellers converted into energy for themselves.

Cannibalism is not a galaxy-wide taboo.

He wove past the last of the fitful unconscious, tented against walls beneath thin sheets of junkyard plasteen or piled beneath cast-off carpets, hoping to shield themselves from the bites of rodents or assault by another gutter dweller. When he was gone, the silent giant who'd protected them would become a larger myth for the poorest of Byblos to remember.

"Wadih the Mute snapped the neck of the strongest of the Strangler's Guild with one hand! The rest he broke and scattered like ash."

"He was mute, but in his eyes was compassion."

"You're crazy to think there was kindness there. He was a murderer who ate his victims!"

"You should talk. Wadih refused to partake in the bounty of nourishment he gave us. And he could speak!—when it suited him. And it was many times that with my own eye I saw him give medicines and food to young Aleyna and her baby. Even the rat catchers knew to leave them alone, for Wadih would punish any who tried to steal from her while she was unable to beg."

It was true, Wadih had dribbled compassion where he could. The only reason the girl Aleyna was no longer considered a child herself was because of the equally malnourished infant she cradled in her stick-thin arms. But he wasn't here on a mission of mercy. Helping the anemic girl had been the best way to get her back to begging on the corner soonest. The one where she'd been so successful in charting the activities around the slave trader's guild and the customers who visited their den.

The opulent offices of the slavers were distant from the actual market and pens, bordering the red-light district where off-world visitors were corralled. Aleyna was allowed there, allowed to ply the trade of a beggar, her spot secured by the bribes he paid the gang who ran the territory.

His first successful lead had come only after months spent waiting for the right combination of alien traffic to appear in the city. The waif Aleyna described the new alien species making appearance at the offices of the slavers. The girl was illiterate, her size and mental development forever harmed by her circumstances. But she was not completely stunted in ability.

She described an agnathian. The purple, spiny alien had turned out to be a Hool. And by the time he finished his interrogation and had fed the last bits of the scout into his mass converter, he knew the Primus Pilus Society was right.

What had been discovered on Psydon was the tip of the iceberg. Destroying the lab there had been only a temporary setback to the development of the plague they engineered. No weapon was ever made without a plan for its use. Who would this one be unleashed on, and why? With Psydon denied them, the peculiar Hool devoted to science—a rarity for their species—were searching for a new lair and a new source of human test specimens who wouldn't be missed. Whatever genocidal plot some unknown cabal was brewing in the galaxy, the Hool were only the technicians, not the directors. The Hool only cared about credits. They were the linchpin to whatever joined the spokes of this new conspiracy. But first, he had to dangle a lure to bring in a Hool higher up the food chain.

He hadn't needed to augment the Hool's procurement report to sweeten the promise of what Byblos offered. A good supply of humans. No questions. No Republic presence. Hool were aggressive, but not without reason. And from what he knew of them, thrifty. When he'd wrested all the information he needed from the scout, he fed the Hool into the mass converter. He sent the actual report along with a doctored message that the scout was continuing on to locate more sources of humans who wouldn't be missed. And waited. Finally, another of his kind had appeared in the city. And this one he felt certain would have what he needed to continue the mission.

Out of habit, he checked his load one last time. It wasn't necessary. He never forgot nothin'.

"You! Halt and present your ident. Where are you going at this hour?" The policeman in the puffy silk trousers and white tunic identified him as one of the sultan's common constables. One hand rested on a curved scimitar, the other held a shock stick.

"Easy, Waseem. It's the mute stevedore."

Wadih recognized the older cop. The younger he did not. A new member of the sultan's force, most likely.

"Off to work early, Wadih?"

It was only in the seclusion of his hidden fortress that he allowed himself to be anyone but Wadih. He made a wet, wordless gurgle like a waste disposal and nodded obsequiously as he pulled the floating tool trunk along.

The younger beat cop curled his lips in disgust at him. "Why doesn't the sultan let us clear the ghettos of all these infirm leeches? Producing more and more defectives is a blasphemy that causes all to suffer more."

"Now, now, Waseem. The Prime Designate reminds us that there's a beast for every burden. Like Wadih, here. Mute, simple as an animal, but useful for its labor. The bots can't do all the work. Many cargo ships require a strong back and a pair of thick arms to reach the deepest spaces. I know it well. I got my start in the yards."

"You were a steever?"

The senior watchman spat. "Don't be daft. That's work for unbelievers and defectives. I was a taskmaster. Being able to knock heads and catch thieves is what got me offer to join the watch. But I've herded and proctored the lot of them. They say this one can jimmy apart a seized container latch without damaging it and lift as much as a loader all by himself, isn't that right, Wadih?"

It was true. Daily workouts in his hidden apartment and the grueling work in the holds of cargo vessels had made him as hard and strong as at any time in his life. There were more aches, creaks, and popping joints than when he'd been younger, but he used the pain. When he needed to feign weakness, a limp wasn't hard to fake when the memory of yesterday's wrenched knee was so fresh. When the bleakness of his surroundings and the human misery he swam in was overwhelming, the strain of his task more unbearable than the heaviest carryall, the pain reminded him of who he was and why he was here. Wadih grinned and gurgled, patting his tool trunk.

The younger cop waved him off. "On your way then, mute."

"It's okay, Wadih," the older watchman offered in apologetic but superior tones, as though speaking to a sickly herd animal. "Watchman Waseem knows you now. He's just learning the beat. Soon he'll know you by sight. Be sure to alert him if you see trouble in the ghetto, yes? I'll be on the day shift soon, thank the Prime Designate."

Wadih made another servile grin with plenty of slurpy assurances as he bowed repeatedly before loping away in the dark. But it was not to the port he was headed. Not yet. And when he left this world behind, it would not be as Wadih.

In an alley he disguised his matted hair beneath many wraps of synth silk, donned the loose flowing thawb, and traded his work boots for sandals. The logo he draped over the tool trunk advertised repairs. Workers from the late shift were dispersing from the spaceport and he melted into the flow of their exodus for homes and beds.

Aleyna had followed this new party of three aliens—two of them a different species than the first—to confirm exactly where they were quartering in the district reserved for off-worlders. A beggar with child represented no threat, whereas a hulking man like him could just as easily be a thug as a licensed laborer, and was prevented from entering the quarter of vice and foreign uncleanliness. She was allowed places where he was not. Two nights in the red-light district confirmed they would be there for a third. Byblos was not a well-traveled world. Only two ships sat at the spaceport, the *Siderion Sultan* and the *Oasis Palm*. Both were scheduled to lift tomorrow.

The Hool's contingent had arrived on the New Jutland registry ship, *Maersk Valhalla*, which had since departed, its stasis chambers stuffed with a load of local fruit. He was glad. Because had the Dansk ship carried unwilling human cargo, he'd make sure the consequences would be severe.

Byblos lay within the supposedly civilized inner galactic belt. Everyone knew the edge was a place of violence, brutality, and mystery. But even close to the seat of the Republic, where the stars were numerous and bright, the savagery that lived here was supposed to be ancient history. The galaxy was so large, the Republic stretched so thin, the traffic of slaves was beyond its ability or interest much of the time.

Slaves dug the endurium out of the desert mines and tended the farms of the floodplains that grew the flower of dreams—off-world intoxicants were illegal, but what was not proscribed by the faithful's law was therefore permitted. Unbelievers could be treated as property. And slaves made more slaves. While the faithful of Byblos cared little for what any unbeliever thought, like the dreamflower, the slave trade was best kept from the attention of the Republic which engulfed everything around them.

Spaceport immigration kept tight control of entries and exits to the world. It was not just to keep unbelievers from defiling Byblos, but to make sure that while on the sultan's world a visitor knew they were tolerated, not welcome. If some meddling Galactic Hugs speciatarian deviated from the itinerary of their stay to disappear into the interior to make trouble with a holocam, they'd find themselves tracked down and in the hold of the next ship lifting.

The hotel Wadih wanted was sandwiched by a gambling house and a brothel. Alcohol was not allowed on Byblos, but dreamflower and non-believer women of many races were available to the unclean, as well as to the native highborn. If it was not proscribed by their book, it was permitted. At least for the rich, and in the quarter where it was confined.

Outside the brothel, two private security guards stood gatekeeper, denying entry to spacers and other off-world visitors to the club reserved solely for the sons of the Prime Designate, one of many in the red-light district. A pair of drugged spacers were roughly turned away and sent off to one of the other fleshpots, where the unclean guests on Byblos could leave their credits behind when their filth returned to space.

As Wadih, he'd not been able to get to know the vice district. Aleyna had been all but useless in describing the layout of the hotel and the location of its entrances. He could scout it himself, but that would be more conspicuous than what he was about to do. He waited until the spacers had stumbled away before approaching, made the gesture of a fellow believer to the guards, who returned it.

"Brothers, I am summoned to do work at the lodging for the visiting unclean." He indicated with open palm to the adjacent building. "I do not work in the vice district or mingle with the unbelievers, but this is an urgency. The environmental system in the hotel is failing and the usual repairman is sick. Is there a service entrance? I do not wish to be seen entering such. The manager gave no instructions. He hurriedly offered me triple my fee to rush to his relief and it was only that which got me from my bed. He raved that the foreign devils could not tolerate even our mild nights without there being proper coolness with which to sleep."

The guards frowned at his speech. He'd practiced the language daily, letting the teaching program and his ear for how the locals conversed guide his diction, but he knew it was not to a native level of ease with which he spoke. He rubbed his jaw. "I was awake anyway. This tooth ails me greatly and I can hardly swallow, my tongue swells so. Tomorrow I will be first at the healer's door. The credits will be welcome, because he will take advantage of my pain to rob me for his fee."

One man chuckled at Wadih's predicament. "Then the opportunity for work so far past the hour of last prayer is not so unwelcome, yes?"

"The Prime Designate smiles upon me," Wadih said as he made a bigger show of his discomfort, swallowing gingerly and rubbing at his jaw with renewed fervor.

The other tough had enough of the discussion as a new group of intoxicated off-worlders moved to attempt entry. "You may pass through our courtyard to reach the alley. Follow around the garage and you'll find it, servitor. The entrance you seek is there. Go with the Prime Designate now. We're working." Both men moved to head off the advance of yet more of the unclean threatening to taint the purity of Byblos.

The low courtyard wall and the urban crevasse of a passage leading rearward beckoned new darkness to conceal his activities away from the lights of the main thoroughfare. He found a niche in a wall and guided the tool trunk in. He creeped cautiously to the alley until he could evaluate the rear of the hotel. Just as the guard had said, the service entrance waited. It would be where he would leave from, not enter by. He moved back to the cramped walk that separated the brothel from the hotel.

He took his specs out of the satchel, released three of the micro drones, keyed his implant, then waited. In the space of a few deep breaths, he was rewarded with a ghostly image beamed directly to his retina. A schematic developed floor by floor as the tiny bots worked up. It wasn't as perfect as it would have been viewed in his bucket, but then again, what was? The world was never clearer than when seen through a HUD.

Translucent lines resolved to create hallways and rooms and red-hot occupants. The drones finished their mapping and the telltales of his target's location became just as clear to him. As it happened, the best route to ascend was from right where he was. He traded sandals for grippers, added gloves, and then activated the masking field. It wasn't as good as mimetic armor, but to anyone who wasn't looking directly at him, he'd be little more than a dark blur, matching the tones of the molded duracrete blocks.

Luxury suites were always on top floors. No one paying the big credits wanted to be robbed of sleep by some heavy-footed guest trodding away above them. Five stories up he climbed, following a path between windows, until a gentle stride across the roof took him to a location just above a window on the other face.

The noises of revelry echoed up from the front street. Down the block, the watch was breaking up some kind of fight, providing yet more distractions from his activities. There was no better time than now. Over the parapet, he scaled down and hung next to the arched window and checked the feed again. The elevators were unused and, except for the end of the hall, all hot forms were in their rooms, horizontal.

The specs sliced into the maintenance program and the window opened at his command. Closing the window behind him, he waited. As if he could see through the walls themselves, around the corner at end of the long hallway, he noted someone big guarding the door to the largest suite. Someone very big. The thermal image was not defined enough for him to identify the race, but by Aleyna's description, and instinct, he already knew.

When he was gone, the girl would be dead within a year. Her infant, sooner.

He checked the pistol a last time, took a deep slow breath, and oozed around the corner like sap running down a tree. The instant the sight settled on the Gomarii's head, he pressed the trigger. Its blue-skinned hand raised too late in a futile gesture of challenge. The magnetic coil sent a 20-gram needle dart silently through the thick frontal skull and out the back, the impact into the wall the loudest noise of all, but hardly much of a sound.

He was moving before the dart left the barrel. He'd called his shot true as he finished pressing the trigger. He didn't need to see the splat of brains and black blood on the wall, or hear the wet collision of tissues against the decorative patterns molded into the stucco to know the tendrilled mouth was silenced forever.

The massive body made a dull thud, the air perforated by the sharp clatter of the guard's blade falling on the tile. He padded ahead. Not a run. Not a walk. A hunter's glide. The glowing specters of sleeping shapes remained unaware as he passed their rooms. He came to a halt in front of the door where the other Gomarii quartered. He watched the rise and fall of its prostrate chest, blinked twice, pushed the door, entered, and dispatched the sleeping guard.

The Gomarii on duty had been complacent, more or less asleep standing up. The one off-shift had been snoring loudly, its mouth tendrils vibrating in time with the chorus of throat noises, when he shot it once in the brain. The bodyguards hadn't expected a real threat, instead depending on their reputation to deter anyone foolish enough to attack their charge. Gomarii, the galaxy's foremost slavers, were rarely seen. He'd helped to make that so. But even to someone who didn't know what they were, the blue-skinned, tendril-mouthed behemoths conjured a warning to frighten away any but the most committed thief.

He dragged the other dead one out of the hall to join his dead partner. Both had the same brand burned into their chest. The clawed hand surrounded by stars. They were clan Gomandii soo-Parka. So much the better he'd erased their existence from the galaxy. Like he had so many of their clan.

It was time for the last door, the elegant suite, and the prize that awaited.

The phantom in his specs was a hue of blue ice, moving from the bedchamber to another room. Variables formed into an equation to be solved quickly. Was it alerted? Was it merely going to the fresher? Let it reach its destination and settle? Hit the door now while it would be distracted by its own movement? Its back was to him. Equation solved. Go now.

The green ready symbol flashed. Two blinks, the painfully loud click of the lock disengaging, and he was a rising tide. The piercing tone warning of his intrusion was futile now that he was the gale force wind filling the room. He tossed the mini-stunner on the move, faded to one side of the sleep chamber threshold, and the super nova of purple arcs beat to life.

The Hool was coming out of the fresher, on its way to the bedside blaster smuggled through customs. The blanket of white sparks finished their dance across its blue skin and like a toppled game piece, the Hool was down. He wore gloves and though its many spines lay flat and limp, he was careful. One scratch, and even a man as large and fit as him would become instantly ill. If careless enough to get a puncture, the envenomation would halt his heart.

It was a worry.

Worry and anxiety were different things. Anxiety was fear. And fear never helped anything. Worry was what his kind called attention to detail. It brought focus. Calm. And control of the only thing that could be controlled—yourself. Whether in an ion storm on the surface of a barren moon or surrounded by Savage Marines with only half a charge left in your blaster, only self-control mattered.

The chrono check said he had no more than two hours. The small window in his specs drew his attention. Someone exited the lift. A staggered gait and fumbled attempts to access the door told him it was an intoxicated guest. Time to get back to work.

He needed to administer the agents. The last and only Hool he'd nabbed had suicided before he could start the interrogation. Not this time. All cnidarians and agnathians could punch their own off switch by self-envenomating. The custodian of the ghoulish prison on Abaddon had done just that as her disembodied prisoners joined their kill team to witness inky black eyes rolling back into her smooth skull. She'd escaped their questions and their justice. As had every other fish face or spiny since the Hool scientist had been captured in the subterranean lab on Psydon.

He plunged the hypo into the stunned alien's neck.

While the drug took effect, he swept the rooms, pocketing the Hool's datapad and credit chip. Both would give him something to tinker with on the trip. He wasn't as proficient a slicer as the specialist on each kill team, but the programs did most of the work. While they worked, he'd pore over the recordings of the pending session. Drug-assisted interrogations left gaps in details that took days, not hours, to assess and verify against the other collected intelligence. And if he couldn't break the encryption of the Hool's devices, it would still provide him with a distraction between the frequent bouts of exhaustive exercise he planned while locked in his cabin on the *Siderion Sultan*.

The neutralizing agent had enough time to take effect. He administered the inhibitor and finally, the stimulant. The Hool opened its eyes.

"You've been given an antivenin, Hool. The nanos neutralized your poison. You can't harm me with it and you can't suicide. I also gave you an inhibitor. You're going to find it impossible to move. Or to resist my questions. If you try, you will feel a great pain."

To complete the planted suggestion, he touched the stunner to its chest and delivered a brief shock. The drug hadn't paralyzed the agnathian, but its mind was critically weakened to suggestion. The physical pain of the shock would plant the suggestion deeper. If the Hool resisted, his own mind would ally with his interrogator to deliver white pain.

"With every attempt at fighting me, your brain will punish you worse for resisting. Give me your name."

Not realizing the contradiction that allowed it to speak though rendered paralyzed, its voice croaked the sibilant noises as ordered. The suggestions had taken root.

He addressed the Hool by name with the ease of one who knew the language. "Skasz-na Shellas-ska, why are you on Byblos?"

"Slaves to be bought. So few sources available. Must avoid notice. Byblos best." The speech was slippery. Every syllable wet. Even in its drugged state, the sharp tongue and rows of pointed teeth were menacing.

The dopamine release he got from the admission made the ache in Wadih's knees evaporate. At last, he was pulling on the first thread that would unravel to reveal who was beneath the disguise. It was why he'd had to be Wadih for so long. Why he'd suffered these many months living like the destitute souls he'd surrounded himself with. It was confirmation.

There was a wide conspiracy, and the gathering subjects involved more than just the Hool.

He knew the Gomarii and their humanoid trafficking rings well. The Hool also tested their bio-mods and genetic manipulation therapies on all sorts of non-sentient lifeforms. They bragged to their customers the stringency of scientific method they used with which to test the safety of their products. And for the customer desiring bio-prosthetic enhancement, revitalized youth, or exotic cosmesis, did it really matter if the products were tested on the living tissue of animals? What mattered was that they worked as advertised. The cost was great, and the Hool had a well-earned reputation for delivering on the promise of their biologic improvements.

And now he knew for certain what he'd long intuited. What had been discovered in the subterranean lab hadn't been stopped on Psydon. And the Gomarii were not muscle for hire, but they were muscle. If they were joined in this, then it meant the Hool were bringing something special to the table.

"How many slaves did you purchase?" It was an order large enough to fill the holds of the *Siderion Sultan*. That meant a large lab. It also meant the Hool were anticipating a long and difficult process, not near completion. Maybe there was enough time to stop them before they achieved success.

"Where are you taking them?"

His specs recorded the interrogation, each answer waiting to be transcribed by the datapad hidden in his trunk for review during the trip. The chrono flashed an alert in his specs that two hours were gone. Without hesitation, pity, or malice, he administered the last agent to the Hool. What he did wasn't personal. To him, the agnathian was the same sort of lab specimen its kind consumed out of necessity.

But it wasn't wrong to take pride in a job well done. It was a lesson learned early in life, one that the craft of the sniper taught him best. Hidden for days at a time, mind strained and brittle, the hunter waiting for the hunted, he'd learned a great lesson.

Patience is bitter, but its fruit is sweet.

He watched the Hool as its own venom brought waves of spasms, until the tremors ceased, leaving the creature frozen in tortured rigor. He left by the elevator, then weaved through the labyrinth of the first floor service areas meant to be accessed by staff only.

"What are you doing in here? You are not a guest." Dressed in the silken robes of the hotel staff, the man wore the red sash of a boss.

"Eh?" Wadih cupped a hand to ear to feign deafness. Naturally, the night manager drew close, sucking in a breath as he did, ready to shout with doubled indignation. Not only was there the annoyance of a trespasser, the man was a defective. Deaf!

Wadih's hand shot out with its knife edge to strike against the side of the neck with sharp focus. The carotid blow dropped the unsuspecting man like a lightning strike. It was a faster way to resolve the encounter than by going through a back and forth while playing the part of repairman. Stuffed into a closet, the knocked-out manager wouldn't be discovered until long after he was gone. Exiting by the service entrance and taking a course back along the path, he retrieved his items, the sounds on the street fading as the staunchest of revelers surrendered to the fatigue of the late hour.

With the trunk in tow and on the main concourse again, he made the sign of respect to the guards next door, both of them too weary to respond after a long shift of fending away the unclean. With purpose, but unhurriedly, he strolled back in the direction of the main port entrance. Foot traffic was rare now. There were few watchmen on the streets, but none were so diligent as to stop and question him. It was nearing the hour when even one accustomed to a reverse schedule ached irritably with the fatigue, yearning for an end to the last dark hours before first prayers and the meal and bed that waited.

On the way he found the clothier's shop, let the specs work, and soon stood in the owner's private fresher.

The depilatory removed all the stubble on his face and the greasy tangle of hair on his head. With a few splashes and a wipe of the towel, he was smooth. He cleaned himself as quickly as he could, selected outfits suitable for off-world life, donned the jewelry over both ears and inspected the result. Wadih was gone. Samar Burstead looked back at him.

To any who could place it, the name was Plenaxian. Plenax was a world quarantined after a genetic weapon was unleashed on its population. The tale of the Plenaxian eugenics war was fodder for conspiracy theorists, holodrama writers, and outrage. Until interest faded. The cultural cycle shifted. The need for information—from which to be entertained, outraged, or made anxious—replaced the fuzzy incident from the edge with seamball stars, fears that jump space travel was destabilizing the fabric of the universe, and endless political scandal by the House of Reason.

It took less than a few generations of comfort to erase most any unpleasant truth from the common history. With virtually no records leaving the proscribed world of Plenax and the entire incident suppressed by the Republic, even their own machines for bureaucracy and control had difficulty investigating the background of a Plenaxian. Once the surviving handful of Plenaxian refugees were released from generations of quarantine, they became homeless wanderers in the galaxy. It was fitting as well as pragmatic to use an alias from this true myth.

At the passenger entrance to the spaceport, he blended with the dozens of other pedestrians leaving their palanquins and luxury sleds to enter the first layer of security. His ident chip was accepted, his booking confirmed, and he joined the line to the last cordon before the relative safety of the departure area. A few of his fellow passengers were Byblian. Most were off-worlders, anxious to leave the arid climate and more oppressive air of control. An officer scanned and fingered all the belongings in his trunk while his partner swiped back and forth over a projected screen until the mustached man in the puffy silk uniform of the sultan's customs officers fixed him with a glare.

"There is no record of your arrival. How do you explain this?" The officer was about to alert scimitar wielding guards when a commotion broke out in the next line. Out of a departing traveler's grav container, the customs official produced a slim foil packet that promised the consumer the same dazzling delight of the colorful wrapping. Two giant guards lifted the owner of the luggage away, his sandals dropping off as he pedaled empty air beneath his billowing thawb.

"Dreamflower, authenticator?" Samar Burstead asked the customs agent. "A believer smuggling drugs? The Prime Designate makes clear our duty to travel amongst the unclean as righteous lights among the stars."

"I did not take you for a believer," the official said, making the gesture and Burstead returning it.

"I converted many, many years ago, authenticator. I hope to return in time for the pilgrimage."

During the distraction, the specs finished slicing the data stream feeding the agent's station.

The man looked down at the projection, perplexed. A record now existed where there had been none. It showed a history of many entries and exits by Samar Burstead, the most recent a few weeks ago. Further taken off guard by the reference to their holy book, the authenticator shook off his momentary confusion.

"Go with the Prime Designate." The man inspecting his open grav container waited for the senior's nod, the unit sealed, and he was through the last obstacle to leaving Byblos forever.

He took a seat in the lounge with a view of the flight line, the hemisphere of the command deck lit proudly to highlight the crossed scimitars and fronds above the name *Siderion Sultan*. Hidden behind the blast walls would be whip wielding taskmasters directing the stevedores in their last task, loading the human cargo. Humans were pliable and conformable, which is why slaves were always loaded last. If the slave pens were filled to capacity, the excess could be packed into spaces between crates.

He pictured the scene and the men he'd worked beside, glad he was no longer counted in their unseen number. Though of the underclass, they were some of the luckiest on Byblos. With a wage, regular meals, and some kind of roof over their heads, it would be the labor that killed them, not exposure nor starvation. He thought of the waif Aleyna and her suffering infant, then erased them like scrubbing a black mark off the polished floor of his first training barracks.

He'd see to it that Byblos's days as a haven for the slave trade would be coming to an end.

The luxury cabin was like all on ships this size. Cramped. But it had a real bed, a fresher, and a wall desk. Space enough in which to snap the bindings of the last vestiges of Wadih from his person for good. Dressed in simple garments, he settled in to slice the Hool's datapad when a sultry female voice chimed over the communicator.

"On behalf of the captain and crew, we'd like to welcome our first-class passengers. Once in jump space, the captain invites you to join him in the lounge. All beverages are available there and on request in your staterooms. Enjoy."

He'd prefer to seclude himself in the cabin, but social interaction with the other privileged elite leaving Byblos, their tongues loosened by the products of fermentation, might yield important information he could pass on to RI.

He'd make an appearance in the fashion of a high-class traveler, his thawb and sandals packed away, just like the veils of the flight attendants, whose caftans would also be discarded for filmy thin flights suits more seductive than bare skin. All would free themselves from the strictures they wore with pious devotion when on Byblos, the slaves chained in the holds below unable to do the same.

Relief would fill the recycled air. Ice would be clinking in real glasses and drowned in amber liquids. Laughter would come forth. The crackle of shock sticks and snaps of whips held by the Prime Designate's enforcers would be left behind in the sidereal universe as they traveled jump space.

Samar Burstead had been a real person who'd disappeared in the refugee camps, a second generation from the survivors of his planet to be born and die in the bowels of the barren moon where his kind had been quarantined. Adopting the guise of one who didn't wish to speak about his past was the easiest of roles. It would almost be as if, for once, he played his true self. Because even surrounded by his own kind, most things went unsaid. Their commonly held beliefs didn't require examination or reaffirmation through verbal discourse. The fealty to those truths was made manifest by deeds. From a lifetime spent in the black world, the single nod of recognition from a comrade was more meaningful than a brass band parade.

He missed the company of their comfortable silence.

He finished the message for his Nether case officer. He included the transcript of his interrogation of the Hool, and more of the evidence he'd collected about the Byblos slave trade, not the least of which was below him. Once they were on Xanan VII and he'd located the Hool lab, it would trigger the beginning of the end for not only the Hool, but for the slavers. The *Siderion Sultan* would be among the first to receive justice. On its first trip empty of all but crew, the Byblian ship would mysteriously disappear into the ether, never to emerge from jump drive.

He didn't know the nuts and bolts of how such a clandestine operation would be accomplished, but he could imagine. With operatives from diverse backgrounds, access to deadly technologies, and the authority to use them, Nether had the ability. He almost admired their organization. Within the ranks of Nether Ops were former Navy types. Like him, specialists in their own field. His devotions had been to the realm of things less scientific, though there was a science to what he knew how to do. Better than most anyone alive. Except maybe Rex himself.

But to its core, Nether was under the control of the House of Reason. The Legion? Not yet.

The duranium skeleton of the ship pulsed. They were moving out of orbit to make ready for jump space. Many was the time he wished he wasn't dependent on someone else's arcane mastery of the ways of piloting. He might share that common weakness with the rich travelers he would force himself to mingle with, but no other. Because for all their toys and riches, the privileged of the first-class ring of the ship were less evolved than a primitive chipping flint into a knife. They'd forgotten the most important lesson of their ancestors. He never had. It was the first rule.

The only safe place was in your mind.

Danger lurked in every shadow. It came with every unpredictable freeze. With the careless stumble that brought injury, sickness, then death. The citizens of the Republic—from the richest to the poorest—may differ from each other in the number of their comforts, but they were all alike in this way.

All of them traveled the stream of their lives floating on a myth.

The myth of safety. The myth of justice. The myth of fair treatment by the galaxy. Some myths were purposeful. His journey had taught him that. Some myths inspired. Captured the imagination. Gave purpose.

The Legion was a place of myths. The lure of its mystery once drew him into the fold, but it was the reality that made him stay. Until he couldn't. But what he'd sworn to do, he would. If there were a threat to his tribe, he wouldn't stop until he'd done everything to destroy it. He'd done it before. And for victory over those forces, they turned him out.

He thought better of it, and deleted the request to his case officer for tech resupply. He didn't want to be hampered by any delay in his travel. His implant still worked, allowing him subvocal control of his specs and the programs on his datapad. None of it was as good as Dark Ops armor or L-comm, but even a lone operator from his school had advantages above most anyone else in the galaxy. Weapons, he could always acquire, even on the most controlled world.

The second message was a copy of the first, but with additions. He'd easily cracked the encryption on the Hool's credit chip and sent the codes to the Society. The funds would join the other wealth amassed there, waiting to be used as needed. Nether Ops was his enabler, but it was to the Society of Primus Pilus that he held allegiance.

The third message was meant for the general alone.

At last, satisfaction. It had been a long time coming. Almost two years on the trail, nine months of it on Byblos. What brought him to this state room had been a journey of redemption that began the moment he left the Legion. He'd tried to adapt, tried to make a home, to find a new way. The old-fashioned books he'd collected for years at last sat on the shelves of a proper library, and he vowed to finally read them as he'd promised himself someday he would. But no matter how he tried, he couldn't finish more than the first few pages of any of them.

He'd tried interacting with his neighbors. Instinct told him their soft bodies and overly tanned skins meant there would be no deep connection to find, and they expended even less energy in extending a search for any commonality with him. In his cabin he drove his body to exhaustion to allow a few fitful hours of sleep each night. There'd been times that the habits of a lifetime served only to mock him, to remind him of who he once was, but he persevered. And when the Society finally called, he was not found wanting in preparedness. He was as ready as the day he left Dark Ops. The work began.

He read the messages one last time before the ship jumped and no traffic could be sent. He signed each with but a single letter.

H.

Adolphus Hartenstein—legionnaire, colonel, second and longest serving commander of Dark Ops—put away the devices and started his exercise. Despite the discipline of a mind he could focus like a laser, despite the plunge into the numbness of his exertions, the gaunt face and blank eyes of little Aleyna and the cat-like cry of the hungry mouth at her breast returned to him.

Later, he would drink. He could not fool himself he would forget.

Because of all the myths in the galaxy, the greatest truth concealed within the myriad legends of a thousand races was this.

There's no such thing as an ex-legionnaire.

02

Kel nudged Poul and jagged his head toward the situation room's exit. Their departure went unnoticed by the security director and staff, all locked on the overhead holo of the besieged outpost, the air thick with the tangle of conflicting reports. Poul held off until they were well down the corridor and out of earshot of the Catalinians before he started in.

"I already know what you've got planned, Kel. We don't have to be the ones to do this, you know?"

"If not us, then who?" Kel said.

Poul supplied the reflexive response. "If not now, then when? Is that it?"

They were so close that *brothers* didn't describe them. There wasn't a single word in Standard or any other language that sufficed. From before recorded time, philosophers and historians had tried to capture the essence of such a bond, and failed. Because not all the words of every language of every race could be wound into a rope as strong as the belief that tethered them together.

The belief that duty transcends any loyalty except to honor itself.

Poul wasn't trying to talk him out of the rescue. It was just their method, one as hallowed as the argumentative exercises that shaped the intellects of philosophers and clerics. But in their tribe, robes and burning incense were replaced by armor and the smell of blaster-singed ozone. Their sparring continued as they rode the speedlift down from the gargantuan heights of the central spire. It was a back and forth of a dissertation and defense, done on the fly and with an economy of words.

Kel ticked off a plan as they floated down the crysteel skyscraper. Poul refined the ad hoc plan, pointing out potential snags and giving alternatives. Just as it seemed they had a course of action, Poul waved a hand as if brushing it all away and laughed.

"You are one karking predictable piece of work, man. You always gotta be everyone's daddy. What would Bigg say?"

"That if you're the best, you gotta prove it every day."

"Hah! What a buncha sket. Bigg would say someone who shows off all the time is a spotlight leej. He's the last guy you want on a team. Means he's compensating for some secret failing he doesn't want anyone to discover. So, how about it, smart guy? Got some new existential crisis brewing I don't know about?"

Kel burst out laughing. "Takes one brooding teenager to know one."

Real comrades could say anything to each other without offense. Poul gave a snort. "Got me there."

Their decision to leave the Legion had been for reasons, some in common and some not. They both disliked that the Legion was changing and with it, so was Dark Ops. The flattery that Lanthanum Concepts heaped on Kel had been an enticement—not to mention the credits. But even those things hadn't been enough to make him seriously consider hanging up his bucket.

It was the crucible of Psydon that finally forged the different elements into the alloy that hardened both of their hearts to hold an edge tough enough to sever their anchor to the Legion. Lanthanum jumped at the chance to gobble up another Dark Ops legionnaire. The bonus Kel got for recruiting Poul was enough to finance the start for a home on Callie's World—a planet he'd only seen in holos and fantasies. Almost as surreal to him was the memory of Tara's words sealing his decision to leave Dark Ops.

If you don't come back to me, I'll just die.

The lift doors parted and they stepped onto a polished green stone veined with gold that led to streets similarly crafted from materials more exotic than duracrete, unmarred and pristine.

"Look at this place," Poul said, blowing through vibrating lips. "Pfft. I had an uncle who made models like this. His own little worlds, perfect in every way. He'd spend hours lost in them while my aunt would gamble away their fortune at the casinos."

The translucent towers cast only faint shadows over the city, rendering every space bright, clear, and perfect— the way the Catalinians saw themselves. Kel thought of them and their walls. They were zoo animals living in an artificial and dignified captivity of their own making.

"I don't like these guys much, Kel. But those kids don't have a chance without us. Let's do this. But we're not doing it *for* them. Agreed?"

Kel eyed his friend. The steam had been released. It was their way. "Agreed. They put some skin in this tile game, or they can stack 'em or pack 'em without us."

"Fair 'nuff," Poul said as Kel shifted the sled into drive and they took off for the short blocky buildings that abutted the perimeter wall along this section of Cataline City, away from the forests of translucent spires.

Their employers made it clear that when in the city they were to leave their aggressive and discordant appliances in their sequestered and out of the way compound. So, they kept their weapons and gear in those stubby buildings away from the inner city.

Poul was the first out of the sled. "It was getting dull here anyway. Let's jock up."

They checked gear. The RK-24 was no K-17. Thuringian blasters were luxury, top-of-the-line commercial weapons. A staple for the kind of blasters carried by bodyguards doing executive protection for the famous, for the palace guard of fabulously wealthy princes, and admired in the hands of those playing soldier in holo adventures beamed to the masses. The blended surfaces were the trademark of the arms maker, selling an allure of sleek sexiness along with deadly capability.

Not unlike the operators on the payroll of Lanthanum Concepts.

The RKs didn't hold up to the abuse a grunt routinely doled out but, they did say something about the person who wielded one—that money was no object. With extra care, though, the weapons were a close second-best to the K-17 they swore by.

The same went for their armor. It was a far cry from Dark Ops issue. It was weakly augmented for strength and nowhere near as highly rated as even regular Legion armor against so many levels of penetrating projectiles and energy weapons. It didn't have mimetic properties. Nor was it compatible with operations in the vacuum of space. But how often would needs like that come up in the employ of Lanthanum? They were no longer in the business of being the tip of the spear. They were problem solvers. Technical experts. In a way, salesmen, peddling the seductive promise they could give their clients whatever they lacked.

The HUD—while excellent—was also a far cry from the suite of bucket functionalities he once commanded with barely a thought. And comms? He tried not to remember how effortless it had been to communicate with a teammate halfway around a planet, or with a ship on station several orbits away, all in the unbreakable encryption of L-comm.

He'd once had the power to see all, know all, and survive all. At least, that's the feeling Dark Ops armor gave him. A confidence to be able to utilize every capability he'd cultivated in order to do the only thing that mattered—win. Though nowhere near as well outfitted, he consoled himself that they were still the best armored soldiers on Catalinia X.

Kel looked at the stack of letters collecting for Tara. There was a timing to when he switched from holos to letters. The first half of a job, he recorded daily holos and beamed them to collect as a packet in the nearest hypercomm relay until retrieved and delivered home by one of the three family ships. Closer to the end of a job, he switched to writing letters that he delivered to Tara personally—real letters, pressed to flimsi in his own hand with stylus.

She'd established her preference for the ritual after his first contract, explaining it this way. "It's silly to record a bunch of holos, only to deliver them yourself. There's just something about a letter. When you leave, I read them again and again, until it's time for a ship to bring me the holos from the current job you're on. Then I watch one every day and I imagine we're on hypercomm, talking to each other while you show me what you're doing on whatever world you're on. And about the time I'm through watching them all, you're almost home again. It's like I'm never without you."

I'll be bringing those soon enough, he said to himself when Poul brought him back to the present. "No such thing as an ex-legionnaire. Let's do it."

Poul was first to the light combat sled and hopped behind the controls. "When you're behind the stick, you recon by occupation too much. I don't care if you were on your way to getting a flight certification. This is no spaceship, mister junior jump pilot. It's a barely armored transport. Speed kills."

"You just don't like wearing a seat belt." If Poul hadn't taken the pulpit to spout his usual litany like some comedic religious practice, it might have worried him. Instead, it confirmed that despite all they'd been through, he was the same Poul he'd known since their first day together on Kill Team Three.

Poul snorted. "I like to get where I'm going in one piece, speed demon. You used to be the one holding everyone back, restraining all the young studs from taking too many risks. Without a team to be responsible for, you're back to being a wild man."

"Look who's talking. I wouldn't say you're exactly risk averse, either, team-daddy."

"Not as long as I'm running with you, captain laser brain. Besides, you're better than I am at running this weird ISR suite the Cats bought. You navigate. I drive."

They slowed at the entrance to the tunnel corridor and the guard post. Turreted auto-cannons ringed the perimeter wall, keeping the hostile world outside from reaching the shining crysteel towers and sky bridges of Cataline City. Their employers were scientists and technocrats. Wealthy. Insulated. Selfish. Maybe by necessity.

No different than for a mission in Dark Ops, Kel had studied Catalinia X in depth before their arrival four months ago. Know the history, the physical and human terrain, the geo- and stellar-politics of a planet—that told you everything.

Fifteen hundred years of the Savage Wars had served to disrupt and degrade humanity and its memory. The Catalinians escaped from a world of the same name. Where it had been, was lost to history. Their ancestors had no choice but to flee or be annihilated. There'd been no Legion then to save them from the wrath of the Savages.

In their flight from devastation, they found a planet suitable for their needs. One where they could start over. Where they could hide. With a single habitable continent sandwiched between dizzying ranges of jagged mountains separated by chasms deep enough to swallow gravity itself, it wasn't a planet of bounty. They named the lone oasis Superna. While not the paradise supreme of its namesake, with arable land, narrow waterways, and soil containing every mineral necessary for self-reliance, here they could hide until they chose the time to reenter the galaxy.

What must have started as a colony alike in people and purpose had at some point split. And the divide between them was greater than the fortress that separated the shining city from the chaos and brutality on the rest of the continent.

35

Kel had a way of reducing things. To him, what happened to diverge the paths of the two groups seemed simple—each embraced a different lesson from the Savages. One group learned that violence got them what they wanted. The other, that the galaxy held real terrors, and to hide from them.

It was barbarism versus civilization.

The security officer at the tunnel gate was on edge, nervously touching the blaster at his side as Poul glided to a halt. "Gentlemen, I can't open the gate for you. The city is sealed by order of the supreme command."

Poul whipped out the identichit. "We have full authority in the name of the supreme command."

The officer's eyebrows shot up. "I know who you are, gentlemen. You're the hired experts. But Cataline City is on level 5 alert. The Wendu hordes have overrun one of the outer garrisons and—"

Poul cut him off. "Not yet they haven't. But if they don't get relief from the siege, they will. Open up."

Locked in indecision like a bot running conflicting programs, the guard's head shook, mimicking the palsied tic of some degenerative disorder. "I have my orders."

Kel had already opened the direct channel to the supreme command and had the aide to the security director on holo.

"Mister K! Director Androlus is displeased that you departed during this crisis. You were hired for expertise..."

Kel was past trying to understand the roots of their sad predicament. Both ends of Catalinia X's cultural spectrum had taken the wrong lesson from the Savages. Liberty is freedom restricted by respect for the rights of others. To exercise that liberty, order must be established. Proven to Kel's satisfaction was the observation that throughout history, there were always those who required the threat of force to make them respect liberty.

And for a threat to be perceived as real, it had to be *used* when called for.

Auto-cannons weren't enough. And a wall will protect a pacifist for only as long as it takes someone on the other side to build a ladder.

"The quick reaction force is frozen in place," said Kel. "We're going to link up and lead them in for the relief of Boundary Station Two. Tell this officer to obey the authority of the supreme command and open the outer defense gate."

Androlus stepped into the picture. "You can do this?" His question made it clear he understood what Kel proposed.

"We will."

From either side of the director, the security committee broke into more arguments.

"If the garrison has been captured, then the moral authority for self-defense is over. It is a negotiation that must proceed."

"Yet we're here because the raiders have killed and destroyed essential equipment, despite tributes and ransoms."

The talk was more of the same futile platitudes and paralysis by analysis that had driven Kel and Poul to leave the situation room. When it boiled down to the bones of the problem, Kel saw it simply. The Cats couldn't bring themselves to violence. Not even to save their own people.

Kel had a momentary pang of doubt. Maybe Poul had been right. It wasn't their job to do this. He'd slipped into reading from an old script, wearing a role he shouldn't assume for people to whom he owed no allegiance. The heat that stoked in him to unleash the violence he could wield with precision, cooled. His allegiance lay elsewhere. Remembering that, he entertained a tiny glimmer of hope his plan would be shut down. The director raised a hand and the many voices in the situation room ceased as a single voice shouted the others down.

"A transmission. From *him*."

A burly, stubbled face filled the screen. He bared a snarl of missing teeth with lips that met imperfectly where a thick scar was. "I talk. You listen. These games you play with the Wendu have become tedious. It's time to return to a state of understanding. You're only safe behind your wall because it shields nothing we want. You aren't strong. We are. You owe us your tribute. That's all we want. To preserve our free way of life. It's the least you can do since you've always refused to offer us an equal place on this world."

The Wendu leader spoke with an intelligence that belied his derelict appearance.

Director Androlus scoffed. "It's an old argument, Fah-Kang. That you even claim such a right as a justification for your criminality is revealing of the stunted intellect that keeps your people living in barbarity. The law provides for arbitrations."

The rough man seemed to delight in being called barbarous. "Don't speak to me about law. We have guns. We both know there's no spine behind your words. My ancestors were disgusted by your ancestors' lack of will, as am I. We know how to beat your pathetic toys, and you're never, ever going to sully your own hands to bloody us. You're incapable."

"I have no interest in arguing your version of our history. What do you want?"

"I demand a normal year's tribute. Or when we finally crack the walls of this shell your contemptibly timid defenders hide in, I'm going to send you their tongues. Then you'll better hear the pleas of your people to return to honoring our strength and practicing the shame you should feel for your treatment of the Wendu. The choice is yours."

The screen closed.

Before the staff could erupt, the director raised hands to keep them silent.

"I have all the facts necessary to make my decision. There is no choice but to cross this Rubicon. The consultants have full authority to proceed. Mister K, I know you think us pitiful, provincial, and incapable. But we are not without our own sense of things. When I queried Lanthanum, they made oblique assurances about the skills and backgrounds of the men they would send. I contracted with another firm to research those inferences. I admit, the information intrigued me as much as repelled me. Mister K, proceed, but with restraint, yes? The Wendu are not the Savages, nor any other hostile race the Legion is known to have exterminated. They are our cousins. Their anger is not without basis. We hope someday they will embrace a different path to expiate it."

Poul's mouth dropped open. Kel placed a hand out to preempt him from voicing his astonishment. Despite the graphic and exigent threat the Wendu leader had made, the only violence that concerned the director was what he wanted to restrain him and Poul from using.

"We're going out there to save lives, Director. That's the priority."

Androlus cocked a brow, perceiving the ambiguity in Kel's answer. Restraint was a relative concept. So, before some guidance came to constrain how they might intervene, Kel headed the director off. "The longer we hesitate, the less likely it is there'll be anyone left alive to save. We have to go now."

The director was an administrator. Before being appointed to the position of security director, he'd been an organizational psychocoordinator specializing in resolving policy disputes between government departments. Logic had been some part of his discipline, and Androlus demonstrated it. "Whatever you may think of our sensibilities, Mister K, we admit, this is beyond us. We contracted with Lanthanum because of your firm's experience in resolving a wide range of difficulties. You may proceed."

The gate opened.

***

Time in jump drive was marked by an almost imperceptible vibration that lightly tickled the bones. Its absence woke him. A quick check of the chrono confirmed that the drinks which gave him his first deep and dreamless sleep in ages hadn't severed the connection to his innate sense of time. They were many hours short of their scheduled first stop. He dressed and headed for the lounge. A lone bartender was there to greet him.

"Back for more, Mister Burstead?"

"We dropped from jump. We can't be at the Delesian Palace yet."

"No, sir. It's just a routine cargo transfer. No cause for concern; we'll reach the Ancari system on time."

Hartenstein moved to the window. The view was limited to a swathe of nondescript space, but at a corner of the wide translucent section through the hull was a bright glow coming from the aft that hadn't been there before. It could only be caused by the albedo of a ship docked with theirs.

He raced back to the stateroom and hurriedly put on his specs, opening one holo screen after another to float above the desk. Sliced into the ship's viewers, he found the explanation. They were between systems with no planet in sight. A large ship was docked with theirs in the middle of nowhere.

He released the intrusion program to tap into the new ship's systems and let it work as he waved through the internal feeds to see what was happening below. The human cargo was being pushed from the pens, shoved from both sides to form a single file of bodies as shock sticks encouraged those who hesitated to follow the herd into the airlock. Finding the viewer in that particular lock was cumbersome, the feed to the holocams not ordered in any way he could conceive, until he finally arrived at the scene. A docking tunnel led from the open lock. It was all but impossible from the angle to see who waited at the other end. He watched as the last of the human cargo were shoved into the passage and after a pause, had his answer. A clawed appendage extended from the docking tunnel and made a chopping gesture to the Byblian crewman manning the lock, just enough for him to see the segmented arm it was attached to and the carapace it sprouted from. Ootari.

Either the Hool he'd interrogated hadn't been privy to the cargo's true destination, or by dispatching the Hool, his absence had triggered an alternate plan for their offloading. He waved the holos away to concentrate on the intrusion program's progress as the outer hatch sealed, indicating the transfer was complete and separation was imminent. Lines of undecipherable code filled the screen. Panic joined the buzz in his spine telling him they were in jump drive again.

The beginning of the end was ended before it could begin.

03

The city towers disappeared behind the wall and its automated cannons, their turrets plastered like scores of birds' nests on a cliff face. They floated in the direction of the beleaguered outpost, repulsors humming as they rushed past hectare after hectare of farms and rolling woodlands, not a person or agrobot to be seen.

"Some people don't have the guts for self-preservation," Poul said. "What these people need's a Gomarii to splice a mean gene into them. They want their steak, but won't butcher a rindar themselves. Maybe they deserve what they're getting."

Kel raised his brows. "Maybe they do. But they've reached the end of their rope, and they know it. And you don't think these kids deserve to hang from it any more than I do."

The capitulations had once been economical, paying tribute to their Wendu cousins to prevent disruptions to the productivity of the farms. Until the extortions and ransoms demands grew ever higher. The next strategy worked. For a while. Hardened bunkers were built to shelter workers and bots, and a network of drones warned when bands of raiders were detected heading for the farms.

For every tech was always another nullifying tech. It was no different here. The stasis containers that held the grains and fruits of the tribute to the Wendu were powered by crystal matrix cards. The Wendu were simple, not without technical ability. They repurposed the tech to broadcast an electromagnetic camouflage to foil the drones of the early warning systems. Raids resumed. Bots were destroyed, hostages taken, ransoms paid, and ever higher tributes demanded.

Enter the war bots, though, to call the Cats' armed and heavily armored guardians war bots was an insult to war bots. Their weak AI still needed human approval to act, making them little more than remote drones guarding the farms.

At first the raiders retreated, deterred at the sight of such imposing guardians. But curiosity led to the discovery that the war machines were mandated to always use less lethal bolts. Failing that, to intimidate by firing focused blasts by wide, missing margins. Warning shots. Only as last resort would a human-directed order intervene to direct the war bots' guns to fire on a person.

The Wendu's new method utilized a discipline not previously demonstrated. Squadrons of demons—utility sleds improvised into highly mobile guntrucks—required one element to sacrifice itself while other demons raced to surround and overwhelm a bot, whose dim AI was further retarded from action by the hesitation of their human controllers to touch the button that allowed the bot to use deadly force.

Farming technician became the highest risk occupation on Catalinia X. Like a drowning man, the Cats realized it was well past time they learned to swim. This was the situation Kel and Poul had been given to solve. To intervene in a dysfunctional process that had played out over generations, meeting problem after problem with half-hearted solutions.

They'd been building the Cats a real security force, teaching them how to use the drones and to run honest-to-Oba human patrols out of the garrisons sprinkled across the boundaries between the farms and the wildlands Kel and Poul had directed built. Frustratingly, the border troops only rarely conducted patrols, and those usually ranging no farther than sprinting distance from any of the garrisons. Mostly they hid in the safety of their bunkers to complete week-long tours at the outposts.

And now, one Boundary Station Two had been attacked, and with the greatest numbers the raiders had yet assembled. Surrounded, out of communication, and with a relief force stalled for reasons unclear.

"The QRF is held up at this grid, about five klicks this side of the outpost," Kel said. He'd been fighting with the friend/foe tracker the whole route. The blue triangle that was their identifier dropped off the screen every few kilometers, no matter how many times he reentered the code.

"We know why," Poul said as they floated into sight of the armored troop carrier, too large to be hidden behind even the stand of thick trees they chose as their station.

"The Cats would be better off hiring a company of mercs to clean up their mess for them. Cowardly is as cowards do. Pathetic."

Kel had been in communication with Cat command along the route, making sure the leader of the QRF understood that the advisers were now in the chain of command. Poul slowed them to a halt in front of the nose, effectively pinning the reluctant rescuers with nowhere to run. He wanted to dress down the officer in charge, but knew that would get him no good result. He recognized the youthful security forces lieutenant.

"Hello, Mister K. I've received orders to follow your command, but to use the minimum force necessary."

"There's nothing less minimal than what you've been doing, L-T," Poul said with undisguised exasperation. The lieutenant was not above umbrage.

"We engaged the attackers, Mister P! We sent warning blasts within close range, hoping to distract them so the autodefenses of the garrison could more effectively select targets, but the bots and the autocannons had already been knocked out. They swarmed us in their demons and we had to retreat to safety."

The QRF troop carriers were rescue vehicles, not the armored gun sleds they'd recommended be purchased. Still, it was unlikely the raiders could have disabled the massively armored vehicle with even their heavy mounted blasters, but Kel kept calm. "I don't have comms with the garrison. Has it been penetrated?"

"I don't know, Mister K. They haven't responded in some time."

"Then we have to move."

"But, if the Wendu have gotten inside, they'll have taken everyone hostage. We can negotiate their release. If we go rushing in there... they might kill them."

"We don't know what we don't know," Kel said, shutting the young officer down. He issued the lieutenant a brief op order, heartened to hear no objection at the conclusion. When they departed, the squat vehicle was floating behind their sled.

"Here's the grid, Poul." Kel released one of their sniffers to fly the route to the rally point and let the algorithm work. He fine-tuned a few areas of interest into higher resolution and risked an active bounce. Nothing from the scan indicated the presence of even a single raider guarding the wooded high ground within blaster distance of the garrison.

Poul tsked as he watched the feed in his bucket.

"Remember the hamsters? They were little furry Rexes compared to these kelhorns. What a planet. The Cats are cowards and the Wendu are incompetent," Poul said. "But at least they're motivated. We shoulda been helping the Wendu. I can teach competence to someone who's got aggression. I can't give anyone a backbone. Say we get our own eyeballs on the outpost and it looks like this is doable, will these kids put in the work?"

"I said we'd do it with them, not for them."

"I'm betting they turn tail any minute and run for the city."

"Then we take a leisurely ride home ourselves. That's the deal."

"I'm holding you to it, Kel."

At a suitable spot, they dismounted and moved to the rear hatch, waving at the driver through the viewport as they passed but receiving no greeting in return. Expecting the lieutenant to join them on the ground, when he didn't, Poul pounded on the rear hatch.

"Let's go. Time to earn your credits."

The thick door cracked open. Two squads of troops peered backed meekly through the slits of their helmets. Their armor was patchwork, but covered all the vital areas. "L-T and one squad, with us. The rest of you, stand by."

They led quickly through the woods, and put the squad in a perimeter to wait as he and Poul set off up the slope, dropping to creep on bellies to the feathered edges of the wood line. The right angles of the squat garrison stood out on a rolling plain of waist-high grasses that covered the terrain around the hilltop. The hills marking the wildlands climbed to the sawtooth horizon of sharp mountains that rendered all else on Cataline X untenable.

The garrison fortress was intact, but the gun turrets smoked and smoldered like wet wood thrown on a bonfire, the raiders and their multitude of demons haphazardly splayed around after the beach barbecue had ended.

Kel had brought big medicine with him. It was his personal rifle. A slug thrower, but in his hands, not inferior to any weapon he'd ever wielded short of a MK IV nuke. He activated the repulsor rest on the forearm, pushed the Braughton in front of him, and settled behind the optic.

Poul sighed. "If we had a Talon crew on call for CAS, we could mop that mess up in seconds."

"But we don't, so quit whining." Kel counted twenty demons, and three or four times as many raiders, grounded and strewn about in a haphazard manner that would give a sergeant major a conniption. The nearest raiders and their sleds were only five hundred meters away.

"The defenses are definitely shot to hell, but they haven't breached the garrison. The Wendu are planted like they're taking a breather while they figure out their next move."

Poul grunted agreement as the signal to reverse their crawl and slide back down the embankment. "I say we get on it while the Wendu are still on break-time. You anchor the flanks with Big-B, and me and troops will start in the center and work out."

"We take out all the demons, then I'll bounce to link up with the L-T and his squad in the truck. You keep any raiders pinned from up here while we move to contact."

Poul snorted. "A plan's just a list of stuff that isn't going to happen. We came all this way, though. What are we going to do, go home?"

They made it back down the slope to find the troops had contracted their perimeter to boot-touching distance. The L-T took a crouched walk to them and stayed hunkered, not raising to their height. Poul whispered gruffly, just loud enough to be heard. "Hey, what gives? I left you in a good perimeter."

"It's too thick for me to keep control. Too many trees and thick growth. I can't see all the men."

"It's as sparse as a botanical garden, L-T," Kel said. "And about as dangerous. Make your way back to the heavy and wait. We're taking this squad up to take out the demons." Kel projected the overhead from the sniffer bot onto the ground. "When I call you up, drive a route around this spur and post up here. Angle so you can use the firing ports and pour it on any demons and raiders you can engage until I move to you. Then when we're ready, we'll advance."

"On the garrison?" the lieutenant blurted.

Poul groaned as quietly as he could and still let it be known he was displeased. "No, to the officer's club for tea and crumpets. Of course, to the garrison. Move out."

While Poul hastily instructed the remaining squad, Kel set off by himself to a position overlooking the plains and the still smoldering citadel. Behind his rifle again the giddiness of anticipation at seeing the unaware raiders below made his hand shake as he hurried an adjustment to his optic. He was in the exact kind of location he searched high ground for with the dread of someone doing to him what he was about to do to them. This was a gift to the unbloodied Cats. From such a distance, a Repub army basic could pin down a squad by himself. Between him, Poul, and even the poorly prepared Cats, they should be able to make a slaughter. He laid two magazines close by, and started to pick the order of his targets.

Poul had been crawling back and forth, easing troops into position to Kel's left and right. His voice filled Kel's bucket. "We're up, but listen. All but one of these guys failed the rifle qualification. None of them have done much more since the basic course than doing the sim course and watching the holo on dismounted patrolling. Training isn't being conducted."

"With only two of us here, go figure. Oh well, learn by doing's always been my motto."

A raider stood and put his hand to his forehead like a visor and pointed in their direction.

Poul cursed. "We've been made. These kelhorns are no better than a kid on his first hunting trip. Light 'em up!" Poul fired a split second later.

The diamond space at the center between the crosshairs of Kel's optic paused on the housing containing the sled's enercell, and the rolling digits settled their count.

Had he not seen Kang earlier, this biggest of the raiders standing beside the demon would've been the one he'd pegged as the head honcho. The chieftain was mid-bark to the sluggish raiders around him when Kel pressed the trigger.

The power plant exploded in a mini supernova, everything in a ten-meter radius disappearing in a fireball of white fury. Modern charge cells were manufactured to not fail in such a way. But when the micro dose of neutronium housed within the core of the 8.6-mm rounds was released, the atoms within the power plant responded like the core of a trigger nuke. While not legal in civilian hands, Lanthanum had sources for the special rounds that didn't care about such technicalities. And Lanthanum trusted their operators to use such tools only in the direst of circumstances.

Kel could justify their use—if there were questions and a later during which his actions would be scrutinized.

In the space of a heartbeat, he shifted to the far edge of the loose herd of demons and hit another, then back to the opposite flank with the next pump of his heart. Silent pulses from Poul's rifle hammered raiders in the center of the herd, but no others joined his. Kel couldn't break from his work. It was Poul who did.

"Get to shooting! Now!"

Kel turned another two sleds into mini suns before the shock effect of their attack faded, and raiders regained their wits. Sleds powered up, gunners leaped to mount the flatbeds and man the heavy blasters on their decks, and riders on foot scurried like birds running to crusts of bread —the source of the bounty now located as from the hills. The pulse fire of multiple blasters rained in sporadic drizzles from Kel's left and right—over, under, near—but not on the enemy. The raiders continued to rally, the additional fire from their line having no effect.

"Only hits count," Poul yelled. "Slow down and aim."

Kel kept working the sleds.

Now that the demons were moving, the small targets that were the power plants were even harder to hit. But even a near miss with one of the special rounds still produced energetic effects on any part of a sled—or its occupants. The first real hit on their line from one of the demon's heavy blasters—accidental or not—struck far to Kel's right, followed by a scream. Kel seated his third and last mag of specials.

Poul had abandoned the troops to their own efforts in favor of adding to Kel's effective fire until all but a few demons were burning. A few of the gun sleds were making for the hills beyond, their drivers wisely abandoning the push to take the high ground, realizing their chieftain's punishment for cowardice would not be coming. Anticipating the path of a fleeing demon, Kel sent the last of the specials a sled-length in front of a demon's hazy mirage. He counted, not quite reaching three before the bullet arced down onto the rear of the sled, the sled's charge cell detonating just as the demon crested the top of the slope. Timing was everything. He seated a magazine of only marginally less lethal solids and reduced the magnification to its lowest to survey the battlefield.

The Wendu were grounded, but not through fighting. While the raiders weren't soldiers, they'd scattered as though they had the instinct. The one that said, *Get something between you and the guy trying to kill you.* Even if it didn't stop a blaster, something was better than nothing. Growth that appeared sparse could hide the largest man on his belly with a rifle. Ground perceived from a distance to be flat always hid tiny dips and depressions where a rifleman could take cover.

Scattered like grains of rice spilled on a thick carpet, raiders lay hidden from sight across the plain. If the Wendu were more capable of the rifleman's task than their own men, taking the ground between here and the garrison would be a bloody task for even a Legion squad, much less the Cats. Poul walked the line behind the prone troops as Wendu blaster fire shattered tree limbs above him. "Keep on it! Sights, trigger. Sights, trigger." He kicked the heels of a trooper whose weapon was silent. "Get to work! It's them or you."

Kel tapped the comm button. "L-T, the demons are out of play. There are dismounted troops everywhere between us and the garrison. Move to your new line of advance, engage, and hold from there. I'm on my way to meet you there. Don't let us down."

"Yes, Mister K. We're moving now." The lieutenant sounded less timid than Kel expected. Was it his admonition not to let them down or was it Kel's promise to meet them that had the right effect?

He glimpsed through the crystal ball that was Big-B one last time before abandoning the spot, catching the blur of a head dropping out of sight. He didn't have to wait long before the cranium's owner took another quick peek, giving away his position like a flag waving in the wind. The unnaturally circular black ring of a blaster nozzle poked out between light foliage. He drifted the reticle sightly rearward and pressed the trigger. The grasses concealing the shooter were suddenly painted in red mist.

The lumbering rescue vehicle appeared on the floor around the forested rise. Poul gave his approval. "You're nearly there, L-T. Another hundred meters to your right so the opening of that draw is at your six. Get those firing ports working every spot of cover between us and the garrison. I want your men sending suppressing blaster fire on every nook and stand of brush where a raider could be waiting."

Kel added, "I'm heading to you, L-T." He slung the Braughton on his back and picked his RK off the ground. "Okay, Poul, keep their heads down for me."

"How about you just stay deep in that draw and try not to draw any fire, how's that?"

"Okay, mom." Kel hurtled down the gulley in the controlled shuffle of a mountain runner to reach the bottom. He knew he was ignoring Poul's advice to stay low, but the thrill of speed coaxed him to be petulant. At the bottom of the draw, he took the hunkered posture Poul admonished him to use, and made a short dash across open ground for the rescue vehicle, its mass a wall as impregnable as a capital-class cruiser between him and the rest of the world.

As ordered, the firing ports were sprouting life like bulbs awakening in spring to sprout yellow blooms. It seemed that twenty centimeters of durasteel between them and danger did something to improve the aim of the squad inside compared to their buddies still on the ridgeline. Grass fires burned, blaster fire easily igniting the brown foliage, revealing crests of ever shrinking defilade and concealment. Whoever lay behind those features would be clawing fingernails off to dig themselves deeper.

A familiar, ugly passion filled him as Kel rapped on the rear hatch, syncopated with the syllables he yelled, "Troops, dis-mount." It was time to teach. And he was going to teach the Cats the most important lesson of all.

That when it comes to violence, there was no time like the present. The hatch opened.

"L-T, you and your squad with me."

Sensing doom, the lieutenant spluttered, "Mister K, what about the rescue vehicle?"

"You don't need it."

"But, Mister K, we can drive to the garrison and—"

"No."

Kel felt the eyes watching him from above more heavily than those of the gawking and dumbstruck men. An ethereal realm of spirit and memory flourished into an invisible jury that displaced the sky of Catalinia X. Faces blurry and faces distinct. Some human and others not. It was moments like this that he felt them the most. If anyone else had been able to sense what Kel did, he wouldn't explain who the ones watching in judgment were.

He wouldn't explain that on a nameless world, the donks had killed Tem, who watched. That in a jungle that still choked him with a heavy wetness, JP had died to save him, and that he was watching as well. That soldiers with none of the advantages of the Cats—just courage—trusted him as they risked it all for their cause, and that they watched.

There were fewer then, when they'd watched him drop a rock the size of a city block from the heavens down on an army, like a mythical and vengeful god. The longer he lived, the more had been added to their numbers. Friends that had been used like bots to be discarded at whim by the ones who wrongly thought of themselves as masters. Using not only him and his friends, but also his family, as a tool to control him. And for their arrogance, he'd destroyed them.

Along the way he'd lost people of many races, the best he would ever know—soldiers all.

And they watched him now.

They would be sickened and ashamed if Kel let these men risk nothing. If he let them hide inside an armored shell, making prayers of thanks that there were bots to do their violence for them. He made a silent offering to the ones above. *Not today.* Today the lieutenant and his men would tread the soil where the dignity of a soldier grew. And when he and Poul left this world behind, the Cats would know what that was. Or shrivel and die behind their walls. Or run to another world and start again. He didn't care which.

But today, they would do the work of a soldier.

"Get your men on line, Lieutenant, and spread them out." When no one moved, Kel yanked the nearest two men off the benches. He hefted each onto their feet by a single arm, coaching them as he did. "You can do this." He placed them where he wanted them and returned to find men trickling out to avoid his inevitable grasp, the lieutenant among them. "Now you, L-T. Don't make me do your job for you."

The lieutenant nodded and, in a high-pitched voice, repeated Kel's instructions as he guided the men into place. It was time.

"Poul, we're ready to move," he called.

"Got you, Kel." Fire from the ridgeline behind them intensified onto the plain.

"Bounding overwatch to contact. My squad. Three-second rushes. Ready, move!"

He had to kick, shove, and even drag them. Kel threw the last man to the ground and remained standing. A bolt narrowly missed him. The Wendu who'd fired it broke and ran from cover. He remembered a legionnaire barely older than he was at the time, but who'd already put into practice what Kel had only played at in training. He used the same words his first fire team leader had used that day.

"What are you waiting for? Kill 'em!" Kel shot the running Wendu between the shoulder blades, and the man somersaulted spectacularly, dead before he crumpled to the ground. The L-T was raised on elbows, head straining to see above the waves of grass. At the sight of another fleeing raider, the lieutenant rose to a knee and took careful aim. One bolt. Two. On the third attempt, he connected. He looked up at Kel, a shocked grin on his face.

Had he looked the same, once upon a time?

Poul's voice disturbed his reflection. "They're breaking, Kel. We'd do better to join you and bound from this side."

"Good copy, Poul. Holler when you're in place."

"You'll see us. I have a spot picked out. We'll push up in two or three bounds to a point just past you. Lay it down for us while we do."

"Squad, we're the base fire element. The other squad maneuvers. Keep it up."

The raiders knew there was no escape. And rather than throw up their hands, first one, then two, then a dozen fired. Kel was glad they did. He casually shot as many of the raiders as he could before Poul's squad had taken their ground and laid a base of fire.

"Our turn. Get ready to rush. Ready. Move!"

The lieutenant stuck himself like a leech to Kel's side.

"Watch and learn, young lieutenant."

They became the creeping and uneven ocean of a murderous, rising tide. First one squad, then the other.

With sparse words, he showed the L-T how to judge where the terrain allowed for longer bounds on the run before directing the squad prone to provide a new base of fire. Where the three-second rushes had to be used. And that the only fire that mattered was aimed fire.

The raiders were no match for the novice troops. Better armed. Better tactics. Better led.

It had been a paltry 500 meters to reach the slope of the outpost but, like crossing the finish line of a marathon, chests heaved to extract all the oxygen available from the dry air while others spewed the contents of empty stomachs. Their race held but a fraction of the steps in a marathon, but what they'd done was more taxing than a run twice its distance.

"Job's not done," Poul said firmly, but now with the understanding of a father teaching son. "Heads up, guns up, pull security." The men Kel had shamed, kicked, dragged, and threatened, acted like soldiers and forgot pain and fatigue in favor of duty. Men pushed past limits earned a nobility greater than any birthright. Soldiers in blaster-singed armor with the eyes of hunters granted each other membership in the only aristocracy that mattered, the peerage of warriors. Blood burning with acid and too tired to think, they might not know it in the moment, but tomorrow and every day after, they would.

They'd traveled the path of kings.

The L-T was beside him again, watching how Poul directed the troops up the slope and led the way to clearing around the outpost. "We told each other we'd never actually have to do the things you showed us, Mister K. Killing was too primitive, too base, too beneath us. But still I tried to imagine it. We believe murder is a sin against the universe, Mister K."

"It is," Kel said.

"Then this can't be murder, because I feel proud."

The young lieutenant had learned.

"Try to contact them again," Kel said.

The outpost hadn't been breached. Those who staggered into the light from the sanctuary of the outpost were met by angry men, and soon the rescued looked ready to retreat to the safety of the redoubt as their comrades shamed them. Aircraft brought more troops for the relief, and with them, Director Androlus.

"He's making a beeline straight for us," Poul said. The man was even paler in the bright sun, until his face flushed with outrage.

"This was completely unnecessary. The boundary station was intact and the men not harmed."

Before Kel could speak, the lieutenant was in their company.

"It would not have remained so, Director. After knocking out the defenses, the raiders were merely biding their time before they finished the task. With our resolve to discourage their irrational attacks on us, they have escalated in sophistication their methods to harm us. They were tunnelling to place plasma charges. Had we not intervened, most of these men would be dead. Bots manning autocannons are inadequate for this task. If we are to secure our lands from predation, we have no choice but to bring war to the raiders. We must do it not because we desire to punish the raiders, but to preserve the life of those we love. It is just and right to do so."

The director took a deep breath as if to vent the high pressure steam of a rebuke, but let it out with a gush. "There is much to consider. I expect a full report. Return with me, son. I must present you to your mother or face her wrath alone."

Poul's eyebrows raised with Kel's. *So the L-T is the director's son. Who knew?*

The L-T hesitated, looking to Kel for permission, then drew himself to attention. "No, Director, I must remain with my men. My responsibilities are not completed." He threw his father a salute, and departed without asking leave. The three watched the young man's back.

"Do you have children, gentlemen? No? Then I wish you the expectant joy that comes with the hope that one day your child will surpass you in all things."

The ride back was abnormally quiet. The last rays of sunlight flared on the edge of the horizon, casting a purple tint on Cataline City's towers. The top of the wall came into view, its harsh line chopping the beauty of the city like a guillotine, and with it, an end to their pensiveness.

"Maybe we had the Cats wrong, Kel. I was betting those kids would turn tail and run. Never in a million years did I think we'd be standing on that berm looking over a battlefield that those kids took one step at a time. And whod've thunk the L-T was the director's kid? You gotta admit, today goes down as one of the all-time great ones. I'm feeling like we did something more than just get a paycheck here, Kel. This was transformative."

"Maybe. Their brand of altruism is in for a real challenge."

"I haven't taken the deep dive into trying to understand them like you have, but you heard Androlus after junior dropped that logic bomb on him. He gets it now."

Kel humphed. "Their culture's small, and entrenched, and not everyone's in lockstep with how they're trying to deal with their problem. When word of this gets out, you wanna bet Androlus and the L-T don't have their heads on the chopping block? Get ready to pull out before our last month's up, Poul. Because no matter what our contract stipulates, I'm betting some Cat politician's going to try to see us charged with a crime."

"Whoa! Paranoid much or what? Where's the little lantern of smiling sunbeams that is Kel Turner? Where'd he go?"

The front of the sled erupted in a flash. A fusillade of blaster bolts came at them from the distance like snow crashing on a speeder windscreen. Poul jerked the stick to veer right.

"Holy sket!"

Kel's HUD filtered the bright eruptions from the impacts to make the flares only slightly less blinding, the concussions only slightly less deafening. From the first blast, Kel was on comms.

"Check fire, check fire! Friendlies, friendlies! Cataline City defense, do you copy?"

The repulsor revved to a high pitch as Poul made another evasive turn, and silenced in an abrupt death as a new volley hit them. The nose dipped on Kel's side and his stomach seized as the rear of the sled lifted.

"Hang on," Poul yelled as the sled rolled. The wild centrifuge spun several times before coming to a last crash on the passenger side. Poul's weight pinned Kel and he cursed him for refusing to wear a safety restraint. A tiny voice was in his bucket.

"Unknown vehicle, identify yourself."

"You lit us up, you frelling idiots!"

In the background of the open comm channel, Kel heard a distraught voice screech, "We authorized the bot to fire on the contractors!"

"It'd help if you'd get off me, man," Kel said, the door now taking the place of the floorboard. What was already a cramped cabin was even more so, turned on its side. With a push, he struggled to hands and knees, and something fell to rest beside him on the crumpled door. It was an armored leg.

Twisting around, he eased Poul down onto his back. Below Poul's left knee was nothing. Poul had been mute, his eyes fixed as Kel's were on the bloodless stump of the knee. Poul made the strange, bemused chortle of someone gifted an unexpected surprise.

"Wow. No blood."

His head flopped back.

"Kel, I'm think I'm in trouble."

04

The sculpture on the table distracted Hartenstein. It was all but impossible to ignore as the central focus of the suite, pinpoint accent lights further singling it out for attention. The confluence of so many finely intertwined spirals could only be produced in micro-G, the dazzling colors locked in glass sourced from sands unique to a small coastal region of Kashir. Among the other touches of extravagance—the synaptic sleep chamber, the aquatic lamps emanating light from a rare species of fluorescent marine life, the walls that shifted between reliefs of landscapes captured from the most beautiful worlds—the helical creation was yet one more mark of the orbital casino's exclusive atmosphere.

It was in this gilt cage that he must lock himself and report his failure.

Continuing to Xanan Seven was pointless. On arrival in the Ancari system, he took leave of the *Sultan*, wondering how long it would be until circumstances presented for Nether to whisk the ship to oblivion and the fate it deserved. With no reservation, it required most of his credits to secure a room, the only one available being the most exclusive suite in a place where excessive luxury was the standard. He paid the massive sum without hesitation. Credits were expendable, and expendables were to be expended, no different from a charge pack. Collected by the Society or counterfeited by Nether out of thin air, there would be more credits to replace the ones that secured this temporary base of operations.

The mega-rich and famous frequented orbital resorts like the Delesian Palace for the extreme levels of security provided by the Shang Syndicate. They advertised all forms of gambling at the many tables, spheres, and mazes, or on sporting events like the bloodsports fought in weightlessness in the grand dome. Rare delicacies were the common fare. The resort boasted a staff that catered to every whim. Unadvertised were the experience tanks, where guests who desired the ultimate escape entered a psycho-conscious projection through medically induced comas to play in worlds where they could be anything or anyone, do anything, anywhere. Others who preferred experiences in this reality but beyond the constraint of its judgments visited fleshpots stocked with tantalizingly forbidden human-esque aliens. Anonymity and privacy for their clients was guaranteed.

He made it clear he was here for none of those reasons. His only desire—isolation.

Being here was one of the few accidents of happenstance that fell in his favor. From the confines of the suite that normally bedded holodrama stars, the powerful, and other degenerates bored by their wealth, from here his encrypted hypercomm would reach all parts of the core without delay, nearly as securely as if surrounded by a legion of operators as he waited. But regardless of the general's reply, he'd already made his decision. He was through with playing the watcher.

I have taken this as far as I can alone, General. Action is required.

Acknowledgements to his reports returned almost immediately. Republic Intel ordered him to stand by for further instructions. The Society advised him to come in. But from the only authority who mattered—nothing. A week passed. Though the room had every amenity, it was a prison. It brought back challenges Hartenstein had felt in a similar place, surrounded by art collected from decades of travel in a galaxy filled with works seen by few human eyes, the anachronistic books, mementos and medals, and the inescapable noise of his mind.

He was certain the Gomarii lab would be on Xanan Seven. He was equally certain he would be rewarded by a summons to take action. That his beloved Dark Ops would lead the way to do what they did best, and that he would guide the kill teams who would do the job. He ached for the familiar feel of armor and the anticipation of a mission suited best to his talents. Had it been just a single lab and a handful of Gomarii and their Hool muscle, he'd have acted without hesitation and done the job himself. But it was much bigger than that. More than one of the Republic's enemies were engineering this. And he was just one man.

He checked the datapad a thousand times a day, making sure it was still functioning, yet it remained silent. Each day on Byblos had been the walk of a gauntlet lined by lashes tipped with despair. And every day he spent as the mute stevedore, he told himself it was just one more test of his endurance. From the day they forged him, the Legion instructors had engraved it into his soul. *Endure the unendurable. A legionnaire knows no other way.*

Men suffered more in their imaginations than in reality. He was right to prod the general for a call to action. But with the surety that he was right was also the dread that with the general's appearance, would also come the general's scorn for his failure. Because there was only ever that from the man. No one knew the general, not even Hartenstein's oldest confidant, his sergeant major, Nail, who'd been forced out of the Legion with him. Bigg was a friend for almost as long. Together they'd been inducted into Primus Pilus. It was a member named Hilbert who once shared his own ken about the man whose firm grip held the spear that led the Legion.

"The general can only have disdain for those around him. It's because they aren't—more. They aren't enough like him."

The reply finally came. It was not the answer to a prayer, but the opportunity to prove he could endure yet one more test. The order was so terse that by itself, it was a confirmation of the sender's authenticity, ensuring it more genuine than that of any billion-bit fractal code. It could only have come from one man.

Hold.

The single word carried more intent and direction than a thousand extraneous ones.

So, he waited.

He stoked his body in a molten fire like that which formed the glass masterpiece visible from all parts of his devilishly palatial and stifling room that was more prison cell than haven. But unlike the artist's product, the hammer he wielded to reforge the steel of his muscles would destroy the lesser work he stared at. As he lay in a pool of sweat, every muscle incapable of another contraction—for a brief and fleeting moment—the haze of so many conflicted thoughts and possibilities cleared.

Not because he'd finally pieced together the puzzle of the conspiracy he'd failed to expose, but because he'd come to a realization about the danger they faced. It was the sculpture on the table that inspired him. The many colors fused together, bubbles locked in the matrices of the curls and twists. It was that which focused him to awaken a tiny moment of clarity.

Like the molten material twisted by the artisan's hand, conspiracies are likewise works of art. And like all myriad creations contemplated for their innate qualities—whether to inspire a sense of serenity as he felt now, or to discomfort in ability to churn up tempestuous emotion—there is an artist for every work.

Some works are shaped in the studio of a single artist. Molded by talented hands and in strict secrecy, its evolving form witnessed only by select and loyal initiates, until the many materials metamorphosed into something of firm shape to be revealed, inspiring meditations on the masterful effort expended in its creation.

Senator VanderLoot's plot had been such. A marvel of sorts. And crushing the masterful but foul work was sweet. He'd been there to see the artist suffer in the knowing that his works would be forever lost. It had been the crowning achievement of his career. Not just because they'd brought some measure of justice to an unjust galaxy, but because the true measure of a warrior is demonstrated by the worthiness of his enemy.

VanderLoot had been a most worthy enemy. In a way, one more worthy than the Savages. They were an easy enemy. Not cloaked, not disguised, nor duplicitous. Which meant that in the span a thousand suns were birthed and died, it was only his tribe that could have brought to destruction such a terrible dynasty as what the politician had nearly established. Only Dark Ops could have ended it so efficiently, silently, and without leaving a trail.

Almost.

But the true pinnacle of his life's work had been producing the next generation of Dark Ops legionnaires. Turner and the rest had performed like legends. And he took pride that if he was not their chief creator, he was at least one of the artists to contribute to building such masterpieces. And whether exclamations of otherworldly perfection were made by the many, or only the select few, he'd been first among the select to see the proof.

It was the salve he applied to the burn of his dismissal as Dark Ops commander. To his forced retirement. The House of Reason may not have known the exact details of what he and Turner did, but their lackeys in Republic Intelligence surmised who it must have been to have done such a thing. Claiming no credit was likely that which identified Dark Ops as the architects and laborers behind the plan to dethrone the senator. Because no one but Dark Ops would have done so without using the move to extort more power for themselves.

Maybe that had been his only mistake.

It was no coincidence that he'd been cashiered and Dark Ops brought to heel. That appointed officers had been wedged into the previously impervious Legion.

The flowing glass sculpture glistened and teased, reflecting the twinkling light from above to reveal deeper veins of colors and textures locked within its frozen swells and twists, pathways like neurons and synapses awakening in his own cortex.

Unlike the sands that had been the protoplasm for the glassblower's creation as he floated in a weightless studio, the artistry of the conspiracy he contemplated was not wrought by the hand of a single author. Instead, it was something birthing itself. Like the stardust of a whirling nebula, or the strata of different sediments laid over eons to create the pallet of a painted landscape. Things formed by elements coming into contact with each other through inherent attractions, time and proximity coalescing the different constituents to form into a dreadful, almost inevitable and spontaneous creation.

This was the entity he had discovered. Where it would manifest, he didn't know. Only that time was running out to stop it.

The datapad on the nightstand glowed.

The face that greeted him was mature, but not old. Grizzled, but not ugly. It was nondescript. It was one that wouldn't stand out for any particular attribute. It was the face of an everyman. And while not ageless, it had not changed in the time he knew it. The voice was equally common. Yet, for one who knew to listen for it, there was the hint of many languages and accents, evident yet unidentifiable.

"Adolphus," was all he said by way of recognition. But to be recognized by this man, what more could a legionnaire hope to achieve?

"Are you in-system, General?"

The general never wasted words. "No. I'm as close as I have time to allow. You first. Go."

Hartenstein had prepared. "Turner's kill team only scratched the surface on Psydon. How this got ignored by

RI and the Legion, I still can't believe it. We know the Gomarii are just the mechanics. But the links with the doro, the Ootari, the Hool—there's sure to be others involved."

The general was silent, like a massive boulder poised to flatten anything smaller if given a push. Hartenstein leaned in to give it.

"General, when symptoms are deadly, a physician can't wait on a perfect diagnosis to begin treatment. Whether the disease is named or not, hesitation kills the patient. We're late in giving this the treatment it deserves. It's time to take real action."

The general's perpetual frown deepened, and Hartenstein regretted his flowery construction. Only this man could reduce him to feeling like a recruit who, no matter the question, had only wrong answers.

"I only mean..."

The scorn Hartenstein thought he earned didn't come. Instead, the words that came shocked, because they were rarer than the spark that turned primordial muck into life.

"I put you over Dark Ops for the same reason I gave you this task. Because... I know you. Because there's no legionnaire more fit for the mission."

The glow from the praise turned suddenly cold as the perfumed air dried his skin to goosebumps. For his part, he couldn't say he knew the general. Few could. Not even Nail or Bigg could admit to that. But since the time he'd become Primus Pilus, he'd simply come to learn that the general expected those entrusted with the soul of the Legion to act as if it were the Legion itself that held all the explanations. That words somehow interfered with correct action.

More than what it meant to be Dark Ops, that's what it meant to be Primus Pilus. To trust the Legion. When more explanation came from the general, it too shocked him.

"If I hadn't been distracted, I'd have prevented you from being cashiered. Perhaps none of this would've happened if I hadn't been gone."

It was as if a marble god had stepped down from his pedestal. First, a compliment. Now, regret. And like other flaws that made a human, the pause in the general's speech portended something he knew would be terrible.

"I came because I wanted you to hear it from me. They've already hit us."

The general explained, and fears Hartenstein never knew chilled him faster than the coldest vacuum found a crack in armor. It was incomprehensible. The rectitude he'd briefly felt at the general's words of confidence, the general's self-recrimination for what occurred in his absence, melted away, leaving only the weights of their combined failure.

They'd waited too long. And the price of their failure was a bill that couldn't be settled by all the destruction they could bring. Hartenstein found his voice. "If it's in the open now, then it can't be ignored. This means all-out war by the Republic."

The general sneered. "In the open? They've buried it. The machines of the Republic have made sure of it. There's a reason you haven't gotten instructions to proceed. You won't be getting any more help from Nether. RI's pulled them in, and you've been cut loose."

"How can that be? The whole Republic's at risk from this new weapon. It's as great a threat as the Savages."

The general dipped his head once in agreement. "Which means the time has come. It's total war."

Hartenstein frowned. "I thought you said..."

The general's eyes blazed.

"Not by the Republic. Just Primus Pilus. We're going to handle this."

"Alone?" Hartenstein had never disagreed with the general before. "VanderLoot's conspiracy was small. The Society stood behind my call to tear it down and bury it forever because it was so well contained that we could do it with complete deniability. But this?" He threw his arms wide. "The players are from more races and factions than we even know and spread across as many sectors. We need the whole Legion. And if Dark Ops is..." He couldn't bring himself to say it. Hartenstein's datapad blipped to indicate he'd received a packet and the general aimed a finger at it.

"I decrypted what you sliced from the Ootari ship before it jumped. They headed for the Cygnus arm."

If the first fortunate accident had been arriving in the Ancari system, then the Ootari fleeing to Cygnus was a piece of luck rarer than a win by the most novice gambler in the orbital casino he'd made his safe house.

"It all starts and ends there. Head there now. I've already got your team moving. They'll be waiting for you."

His team, the general said. "Aren't you headed to Cygnus, sir?"

"Not yet. Where this tech came from, the Gomarii can't have discovered alone. And what we need, I don't know if it exists or not. Turner's our best bet to find it. He's sat this out too long. I'm going to him."

The link closed.

Hartenstein was about to say, *Turner's gone*, but hanging over the datapad was empty space, and the sculpture beyond spoke to him.

For every work, there is an artist.

***

The view from the hospital window could've been used as an advertisement for Andalore tourism. Masses traveled on shaded greenways harmoniously weaving between buildings more like natural growths than skyscraper cityscapes, demonstrating a wealth second in the core only to Utopion. The perfection reminded Kel of a different paragon of civil planning, minus the feeling he was an observer to a social experiment gone wrong.

He tensed leg muscles alternately, unconsciously fighting the buoyancy of the floating chair, its massaging action, and the effect to silence familiar aches and pains. The doctor's pronouncement tore him from the placid outside view and back to his bedbound friend and the unavoidable and stark asymmetry caused by what was missing beneath the sheet.

Six months for a complete regen of Poul's leg. Two months stuck close to the hospital to monitor the template as it took hold. If it took hold. Only when they were sure the process was progressing correctly was Poul fine to return to Callie's World wearing a mobile unit until the process was finished.

When the last of the white coats left, Poul split his response between Kel and the other man in the room. "A cyber mod it is, then. We know lots of guys who've done well with a prosthesis. Some say it's even better than your own flesh and blood, and if it gets shot up—quick fix and I'm back in action. A couple of weeks with the new mod, I'll be up and running."

"Wouldn't let you back in with a cybernetic in the Legion," Kel said.

"Yeah well, the Legion isn't footing the bills anymore, either. I'll have to knock over a bank for the credits to pay for a regen."

Grant Odom said, "Nix on both. You're covered for all damages incurred on company time. It's your choice, but don't let cost or time off work be any part of your decision. You're Lanthanum. Your worth isn't measured in credits. Not those kind of numbers, anyway." He winked. "That amount isn't even a rounding error in the budget."

The Lanthanum executive never had been a legionnaire, but the path he'd traveled had taught him wisdom known to the kind of leaders Kel had always aspired to be like—that the man was as important as the mission. How the lesson had come to the corporate manger, Kel didn't know. But how he spoke reminded Kel of Bigg.

Kel tried another tack. "Karla'll wait for you, if that's what you're thinking about. She'll understand. Have you sent her a message yet?"

It'd been during breaks between Lanthanum missions that the bud of a romance between Poul and Karla Sullivan had started. She was right now crewing somewhere with her family on the *Callie's Promise*.

"I was holding off telling her until I got the whole story from the docs. The *Promise* could be anywhere. And if they're headed home, you might beat my message back." There wasn't a hypercomm array near the sector that contained Callie's World. Like everything else destined for the small colony, communications traveled there little differently than the goods and supplies brought home by each returning transport.

"Take the regen," Kel said. "Karla's a Sullivan. A spacer from a family of spacers. Separation's a way of life they're all used to. She'll wait. Dark Ops wives could learn a thing from them about patience."

Poul waved him off. "Don't get ahead of yourself, Kel. I'm not snagged yet. She and I haven't gotten that far."

"If she's decided you're the one, you won't even get a choice in the matter. Trust me, I know about these things."

"My job is to make sure you have what you need so you can be what you are—the best," Grant put in. "Just like you proved on Catalinia X. Whatever your choice, I'll take care of the details." Grant always spoke as though he worked for them rather than the other way around.

Poul saluted from the bed. "I'll let you know ASAP, Grant. Thanks."

Grant stood to leave. "If you choose regen, you won't just be lying around. You impressed the Catalines so much, they want an expanded package. It means years of steady work, and not just for the security section. They want an anthro-sociology development team, too. It's almost a billion credits. No one knows the needs for the Catline contract better. I'll put you on as a managing executive. It'd take a load off me. But don't let that be part of your decision. You two have bonuses coming. Big ones,

Lanthanum." He used the title as equivalent to *Legionnaire.*

Alone together, it reminded Kel of a similar silence as they walked down team room hall the last time, past the numbered doors in the pre-dawn hours of their final morning on Victrix.

Some may have considered the manner of their departure craven, even disrespectful. They ran out on people they thought of as more than family. But facing their friends had been too much. And in the same way Poul joined Kel to travel to Andalore and sign a Lanthanum contract, it seemed only natural to invite Poul to join him on Callie's World. Kel remembered how little Poul made of it, as though it were assumed they wouldn't be splitting up.

"I was already planning on inviting myself, but thanks for making it official. Don't want to go back to Greenhome and my sister's. It's time for a fresh start. New job, new life. Who knows, maybe I'll meet a ship captain's daughter who'll swoon over me, too? I'm twice as good looking as you. I'll have my pick."

Kel laughed. "The families are all about new blood, but if you treat Callie's World like any of your other hunting grounds, zero atmo combat quals won't matter when a family of angry relatives space you for disrespecting one of their womenfolk."

"Oba, Kel! I'm no hullbuster. I know how to act on leave, especially around your people."

Two of the three ships in the family fleet were there for Kel's first touchdown on a world he'd never set foot on but had already claimed as home, with as many of the Sullivans and Yomiuris as had been on the ground together at one time in ages. Poul was welcomed as a member of the family—that's how they were. It was the perfect time. Kel asked, Tara answered. With his closest friend at his side and surrounded by his new family, Tara's father performed the wedding ceremony.

The weeks that followed were a constant intoxication of electric excitement that made him forget that he'd ever felt troubled. And with Poul there, he had the confidence that he could do anything in this new life.

By day, the three of them worked together clearing the land Tara had picked out. Imagining what it would look like when the holos marking the borders and lay of plumb lines finally materialized into the stone and wood of a real home. The nights he spent locked with Tara, looking at the stars and planning.

With a small patch of ground cleared, their new life had barely started when it was time for the first Lanthanum assignment. Three months on Hythe, an unaligned world with an insurgency of radical collectivists trying to topple the elected government. There'd been assessments of the security forces, recommendations for training and equipment, and their proposals for how Lanthanum would assist. The mission may have been meant as a test of their abilities, but for them, it was routine. Dull. But, amazingly, for quadruple the pay of a legionnaire.

A short month at home. Just enough time to shed the disorientation of feeling like a visitor—and that he'd barely started to learn what it meant to be a husband—and a new assignment called. Lanthanum increased the difficulty setting for the next run.

Flanx had natural wealth. Mines of recently discovered Quillian crystals. And with it, predation by criminal gangs, well-armed and beyond the ability of the police and inadequate defense force to deal with. They'd gotten their hands dirty on that one. But the bonuses Lanthanum was paid to quickly resolve the matter generously trickled down to Kel and Poul.

There were more jobs. Missions frequently so similar to what he'd done in Dark Ops—some harder, some easier, all of them usually interesting—it was a wonder he'd never heard of most of the worlds and their problems while in the Legion. But it was because the Republic, no matter its ever-expanding reach, was small in comparison to the galaxy. And in a galaxy seeded with more conflicts than planets, Lanthanum thrived.

Being a Lanthanum contractor had perks not unlike being in Dark Ops. They were given tremendous latitude in how the work was conducted. The support was excellent, both in people and materials. Better yet—unlike being a foot soldier for the will of the House of Reason—Lanthanum had no internal bureaucracy to fight. No concealed motives behind what the company tasked them with doing.

And for the first time in Kel's life, there was money. And with it, pride. His skills and abilities were being recompensed in a way that recognized their rarity. And with each payday, he told himself he was one step closer to stopping.

Because Kel had a plan.

But his best friend losing a leg because of him wasn't part of that plan. And for the first time in a long time, Poul wasn't going to be there. Poul spoke and interrupted the reverie and drew Kel's attention away from what was missing beneath the sheet.

"Good news about the Cats. It wasn't for nothing, I guess. Maybe the eggheads in the sociopolitical section can help them sort out a better way to deal with the

Wendu." Poul blew out a long breath. "We had a good run, Kel."

He'd said it with a finality Kel wasn't prepared to accept. "Nothing's over, Poul. Not by a long shot. Look, this was my fault."

"Here we go." Poul rolled his eyes. "I told you before, knock it off with that sket. I only meant we had a good run without one of us getting shot to pieces. We beat the odds on that for longer than we had any right to expect."

Kel rubbed his temples, remembering the headaches when he was the one in the hospital bed. "I s'pose. If you don't count Psydon."

Poul became gruff. "I am counting Psydon, dummy. We've still come out ahead."

Psydon. There was never a day Kel couldn't close his eyes and smell the fetid jungle floor, breathe air so humid it was like drowning. He traced a hand over his stomach. He'd had the medics remove the tattoo, but the memory of its raised scars made his fingers feel it still. What they'd done halted the doros' break away from the Republic, but the House of Reason had ordered them to carry out a punishment as disproportionate as it was to spank a toddler with a hatchet.

And the price had been great. Kel left the jungle and returned to the sterile room and his friend.

"I did a search this morning. Found an SNN story from a few months ago. JP got the Order of the Centurion."

Poul pushed off the bed to shift hips before settling. "That took forever." His face said he was no more comfortable. It had been only a week since the Cats fired on them.

"The autotourniquet in those suits sucks," Poul complained. "My thigh hurts worse than where my leg got shot off. But it'll go away quicker if I'm back to my feet with a peg leg. It could be tomorrow if I say the word."

"Is that what you think JP would tell you to do?"

"Low blow," Poul groaned. "I know what JP would say. Same thing he kicked your ass about all the time. Remembering that there's a future. All right, I'll take the regen. Then we can get on with it. With everything. "

There was more to what had driven Kel to accept Lanthanum's offer than the lure of the credits. It was what he would be able to *do* with the money. And the strange juxtaposition that came with it. That from out of a life spent becoming one of the deadliest men in the galaxy, he could transmute a legionnaire's talents to make a better life for the people he cared about. To turn destruction into creation. A way to reap the flower of life from the harsh seeds he sowed in the galaxy.

And from the first, as glimpses of a plan came to him, he let Poul in on his vision.

It started back on the world of the insect-like Q when Kel had met an expert in adapting alien worlds to accommodate agricultures that could support human needs. When he thought about the time, the place, and who he'd been, it was with embarrassment. That was back before he learned how the galaxy really worked. Before he'd realized that control was an illusion.

But he'd come to terms with it. Because, wasn't his life proof that even if the galaxy laid more booby traps for him than on a Psydon jungle trail, it was still okay to believe in a million wonderful possibilities? It just required making a choice. Expect the landmines. Look for them. And carry on. Because as long as there was life, and people to love, there was hope.

And regen.

Poul laid his head back. "Did your former girlfriend get you set up?"

Kel snorted to show he was playing along. The civilian xenobiologist he'd tried dating on Q had been surprised by his comm, but after the shock wore off, she seemed happy to help in a detached sort of way.

"She was hardly my girlfriend. Tatiana was more repulsed by me being a legionnaire than if I was outed as a Savage cannibal. But, yeah, she helped me find the specialist we need. I haven't met him yet, but he sent me a contract. I just have to front his fee, and he's ready to travel."

Early in the settlement of Callie's World, the family had once done such an investigation. After a large investment in equipment and technicians that drained coffers with no result, they chalked it up as a bad idea not to be repeated. Though that had been a generation ago, they were once bitten, twice shy. Kel's attempt to convince the family that he'd witnessed just such a miracle was shot down as if by a tungsten rod from an OSP. Sullivan and Yomiuri stubbornness were encoded in their genes like the soil that resisted foreign seed.

Poul's forehead tilted. "Can't be cheap to have an overeducated farmer make a house call. I'm happy to split it with you. I told you, I'm all in. I'm making a home there, too."

Kel had him now. "Ha! So, you *are* thinking about putting down permanent roots with Karla."

"Don't evade, man. I'm as good at all the interrogation tricks as you are. The colony should be paying for this, not you all by your lonesome."

Kel waved away Poul's accounting. "I don't want to get people's hopes up. This expert won't know if it's even possible until he does the tests. Gene-modded crops customized for the planet like they did on Q—it's a massive undertaking. It'll let me give something back after all the trouble I brought to them. The expense doesn't matter. You know why."

Poul scrunched eyes tight. Had the pain returned in another wave, or was it something else? "That's some savior complex you got."

There were things unspoken between them. Some were professional. Part of keeping honest-to-goodness secrets. Some were personal. Things Kel thought were just understood. He flared. "It's how I want to do things, Poul. I don't need another reason. Let's leave it at that!"

"No, man. It's time to get this out in the open and done with, once and for all."

Kel knew what was coming, and dread filled him. It was the thing they swore never to speak about.

"The worst part of the Scarecrow conspiracy is it turned you into a martyr, just like the Cats. You aren't responsible for the Yomiuris' financial straits, or any of the other stuff that's happened. The Legion didn't get points because of you. Dark Ops didn't go white because of you. Stop punishing yourself. Had he known all about it, don't you think that's what JP would've said, too?"

But beneath the sheet seemed the proof that Kel, in fact, was responsible for bringing so much hurt to people he cared about. And like being out of ammunition, it made him angry.

"Kark you!"

"Kark you right back!"

Poul rubbed his thigh and grimaced in pain. "You used to be a medic. Is that how they taught you to cheer up your best friend when he's just got his leg shot off? By telling him to get karked?"

Kel's heart sank to the white antiseptic floor. "I didn't mean it."

"Gotcha!"

Poul burst into laughter.

Kel sat back. He never knew Poul had such an evil streak. Once his heart resumed beating, he joined Poul's laugh with a much weaker one. "That was messed up. A zhee dance of a thousand cuts would've been kinder."

"Sorry, not sorry. An opportunity like that only comes once in a lifetime."

"Let's make that the one and only kind of opportunity you get. No more getting shot to hell."

"To the extent we can control that kinda thing in our business, agreed."

Kel sighed as Poul rubbed his thigh again. "But the other stuff you said—I hear you, Poul. You're not wrong."

His friend pointed to the patch on his chest. "Forget what I said. It's the meds talking. The bright side is I guess I'll have an excuse for having no filter for a while. They say regen can be painful."

Grateful for a topic centered on Poul again, Kel said, "Joe Crane told me when they grew his arm back, it was just kind of an annoying buzz. He said he learned to ignore it."

"I'll drop him a comm and ask him about it. Maybe he'll get back to me, if he's not deep. Which he probably is."

Being in Dark Ops meant just that. Living a life submerged.

"I wonder how they're doing," Kel said wistfully.

"You mean, you wonder how they're possibly getting on without you. On top of your other problems, you're a narcissist, man." Poul winked. "S'okay, 'cause I am, too. At least, that's what the emotional support tech said this morning when she went over my profile. I told her that's a sket psychometric diagnosis, because the test can't differentiate between a guy who just thinks he's better than everyone else versus a guy like me for whom it's actually true."

"What'd she say to that?"

"She said it's called Legionnaire's disease." Only the truth was funny. They both laughed.

"Anyway, I told her she could tinker around in my kitchen if she wanted. Maybe it's the meds, maybe it's losing my leg, but I've had too much thinking time. I'm feeling like my brain housing group's low on coolant."

Kel could relate. "Besides diagnosing my personality flaws, what's boiling over on your stove, Poul? Care to tell me?"

The creases in his friend's face smoothed.

"I'm busting your balls because I feel a little guilty, too. I wonder how Team Three is able to get on without *me*. But I know they are. Whoever's running Three feels like we did—that they're the best. And that's how it's supposed to be. I'll always miss what I had. But the farther away I am from Dark Ops, the surer I am it was the right time to leave. The Legion goes on."

"And so will we," Kel said, committed.

"Damn straight. I'll hang around and get a new leg, and then we'll get back on track. But in the meantime, you gotta get home to Tara. I'll be along. And for my first meal back on Callie's World, I want nothing but stuff grown by your consultant, because for the creds your spending, it'll be the most expensivist meal ever."

"I'm reminded you know less about farming than you do women, Poul."

"Pfft. Look who's talking. You just got lucky, is all."

"Luck happens when opportunity and preparedness meet."

"Is that one from your super-original list of operator wisdom, hero?" Poul meant the list of pithy observations that had come to be known as Kel's Rules. Kel made the mistake of putting to datapad his observations about what he thought were the essential ethos and lessons for operators. The list had made its way around to the other kill teams, and he'd been both complimented and roasted endlessly.

Kel winced. "I'm never going to live that down, huh?"

"Not as long as I'm around. And that's gonna be for a long time, ya kelhorn."

05

As agreed, Kel waited at the vast arched entrance to Orion Station's main concourse. Businesses remained open all twenty-seven hours of the station day, and the thoroughfare at first div was the same bustling mix of races and classes he always pictured. The smells were as much a mélange as the people. Foods from vendor stalls, the sweat of laborers drowned by the perfume of a Cassari, the inorganic smells of chemicals from the many fabricating shops, all mixed in a way that excited him.

It meant he was one step closer to home.

He spotted his quarry first. He'd gotten little of a first impression from the still of the face next to the signature block but seeing him in person, searching uncertainly like a little boy lost, the xenobiologist struck Kel as fragile and soft in a way that stood in contrast to those of the profession he'd met on Q. Each had impressed him as hardy and energetic and seemed to thrive on laboring in the fields growing the work of their labs. This man looked— sickly.

Kel waved and received a nod. With a handshake limp as a noodle left in cold water overnight, the pasty man replied only, "Quint. Delaria. Just—Quint."

Kel had expected some sort of thanks or expression of enthusiasm regarding the job. When it didn't come, he shrugged it off.

"The *Supreme*'s in a docking hold, so it'll be a few hours until we can board. Let's grab some food and talk while we wait. Sound good?"

"Hmm. G-good. Idea," Quint said, straining syllables. Perhaps that's why Quint had avoided any live comm with him—Standard wasn't foremost in his wheelhouse of languages. There were human worlds where Standard wasn't the norm. But his intuition told him that wasn't the explanation. Tatiana had held back on him. She'd finished their comm with a recommendation tantamount to a waiter telling the diner to ignore the fly in his soup because it wouldn't eat much.

"Quint's brilliant and he's very competent. But, until you get to know him, he can seem awkward. He doesn't like to talk. He's got reasons. Anyway, there's virtually no one in the field who's not already happily employed by one of the big corps. You're not going to find anyone else."

During dinner with the scientist, the image of how she'd signed off with a smirk and a mock salute came back to haunt him. Quint avoided acknowledging Kel's pleasantries, instead locking himself to his screen over which he pushed around geometric shapes Kel supposed were genes or the compounds he used to manipulate them.

"Is that something you're working on for Callie's World?"

Quint ignored the question. Kel's limit had been reached. He couldn't begin to explain to the stranger how much he'd given of himself, the mistakes he'd made, the regrets he carried, all to earn the credits he'd transferred to the man's account, sight unseen. And if he were like Tatiana in other ways—like having an issue with him being Legion—then it was time to clear the air.

"Hey man, is there a problem? You don't have to entertain me like some kind of paid courtesan, but for the credits I laid out, I do expect some kind of respect. You may not like my background, but the people you're going to be around are my family. You get me? This isn't some corporate job. You need to tell me you understand what I'm saying about how you're going to act around us, or let's call this off right now."

Quint flushed and shook his head. "N-no. It's not that."

"Then what?"

"It's h-hard for me. I get n-nervous. She t-told me—"

He didn't let Quint didn't finish.

"Told you what?" he wanted to know.

"She s-said y-you were to be... t-trusted."

He'd made a bad assumption—irked by thinking Quint's manner sprouted from the same soil as Tatiana's prejudice about legionnaires. Why hadn't she just come out and told him that Quint stammered? Did she think he would judge the man unfit based on such a foible? Civilians.

He told himself it was just one more case where he had to go to war with the army he had, not the one he wished he had. Quint was the best he was going to get. But maybe it also meant that Kel was the best that Quint was going to get. There was a story he knew about a guy who chased windmills. It was time to make the best of it.

"Sorry if I came on strong just then. It's just, I have a lot riding on you, understand?"

Quint squirmed as if the cushion of the restaurant booth was broken glass instead of soft rindar leather. "I n-need to check on my equip-equip-equip..."

Kel saved him the trouble of finishing. "It's okay, Quint. When you're done, find me at the *Supreme*'s berth." He felt some of the same relief in Quint's face as the awkward man took his leave. Quint threaded his way through the crowd, nearly colliding with a tray-carrying server. He replayed Quint's words, without the stutter. *She said you were to be trusted.*

Kel laughed to himself. *Why is everything so damn difficult? Is there anyone in the civilian world who isn't a disaster?* When he got down to it, there were only two kinds of people. And he knew which one of those two he would always be.

He had Tara for the rest.

By standing double shifts to reacquaint himself with the ratings he'd earned but not practiced in months, the time in transit passed quickly on the *Supreme*. He was glad of it, for reasons more than just his desire to be reunited with Tara as soon as possible.

Cormac Sullivan was captain of the *Callie Supreme* and Tara's uncle on her mother's side. Their introduction had been unpleasant, made even more tense by the impending invasion of Psydon. Cormac Sullivan hadn't spared Kel any guilt for his part in Tara's grief, unfairly calling Kel out for the circumstances that made their separation necessary. Cormac's iciness hadn't melted away with the yellow sunlight that bathed their wedding day.

Unlike the other members of the family who were disarmingly friendly and familiar—even when Kel forgot their names—the captain's continued gruffness made him walk on eggshells around him. His first shift on the bridge, the fiery Sullivan hair and skin that turned nearly as red when flustered was on full display.

"Reporting for watch, Captain."

Cormac pushed back from his console and grunted. "Touch nothing. Observe and report to First Officer Kandit if there's any issue." He pointed to the first officer, then was out the door before Kel could speak.

"Don't take it personally, Kel," Chelly Kandit said. He was a big man with a big smile. His cheerfulness was omnipresent. "Once he gets to know you better, he's a pushover. Didn't Eric give you the same kind of treatment when you first met him?"

Tara's dad had treated him with a similar stereotypical revulsion of a ship's captain for a dirtsider, like someone waiting for a pet forced on their hospitality to soil the carpet when their owner's back was turned. But would it take Kel having to save Cormac's life to melt him, too?

"Like Cormac said, holler at me if anything comes up. Meet you in the hold after your watch?" Chelly was a weightlifter, specializing in moving the greatest possible masses in all-out red-faced, eye-bulging efforts, howling at the top of a movement in a way to make a rabid doober take notice. Chelly didn't make it far through their first session together, eager to try to best Kel. Chelly fatigued after the first round of the routine and dropped to a few repetitions of each subsequent exercise before falling behind and then quitting altogether, wheezing like an old accordion.

"This time we do *my* workout."

"Whatever you say, Chell," Kel said.

"You should be worried. I'm going to crush you."

Kel rolled his eyes. "I give you high marks for optimism. I've made men sweat breast milk, cry blood, and leak hot mud down their legs all at the same time. I'll humble you if you make me, Chell."

Chelly's sour face meant he'd conjured up the images to justly accompany Kel's descriptions of supreme human suffering, emasculating the man's gale force bluster down to a weak breeze tickling a limp airfield wind sock. "You can't smoke someone so badly in PT those things happen? Can you?"

"I speak the truth. Because it's happened to me."

Chelly made another squish-face. "Are all legionnaires as crude as you?"

"Crude? I'm the least vulgar leej you'll ever meet, Chell."

"And Poul?"

"He's been on best behavior around the family. When he's back, tell him you're going to crush him in a workout and see what he says, then what he does."

"I get it. How about we just work out, how's that?"

"Wise man, Chelly." Kel liked Chelly, but there was a friendly lesson coming to him later.

Don't threaten a legionnaire with a good time.

***

The first day home was always a busy one. Two armfuls of a squealing Tara followed by hugs and pounds on the back from everyone else was a reunion clipped short. The colony had a presence that ebbed and flowed with family rotated home by need or choice. Pregnancies, radiation exposure limits beyond what a DNA repair booster could do, projects like the power grid that needed a senior engineer, or just the human need to breathe more than a few days of fresh air under skies somewhere other than a spaceport—the roster of who was on Callie's World changed regularly.

They started the work—tradition and proper necessity— and it served to remind him why he was first drawn to these people. The whole community joined to unload, organize, and store the delivered goods with the unity of purpose of a company of recruits drilling for graduation week on Tiberius.

As the last stasis locker sealed, Cormac Sullivan grumbled like a man with a lot on his mind. "We're back to a year's surplus. Without more units, we can't store more if we had it, not that we can afford more storage, much less items to fill it." Everyone knew the family pushed a boulder up an incline to which there was no peak, but Cormac's gloom was an unnecessary reminder—and a wet blanket on the mood building for the celebration feast to come.

A silver-haired woman groaned and turned on her heels to leave the communal storehouse. Selva Sullivan hadn't shipped with her husband on this last cruise. Tara's covert whisper was as expert as if she had an implant herself. "Three months apart hasn't helped them."

With Tara nestled beside him at the long table, he couldn't help but take notice of Cormac at its head, his wife many seats away. Tara caught him off guard. "I know what you're thinking."

"Bet not. I was thinking I understand why they're on the outs. Cormac's a pill."

"No you weren't. You were thinking about how to help them."

Had she read his mind? Because he'd just been thinking that if Quint could solve the problem of a self-sustaining world, it would be so monumental in its grace that it might even be a stitch in mending the tear of a distressed marriage.

"Poul chewed me out for having a hero complex. I guess it's a lesson lost, not learned. How'd you know that's what I was thinking about?"

She pulled him closer with one arm while pinching the air with the other. "I'm *this* close to my psych-sōsh degree," she said, meaning psycho-social therapy. "You're an archetype right out of the book. You're going to be my first client."

"I thought you were going for your first grade medico licensure. You never said a word!"

She winked. "Surprise! You're responsible. You're the one who got me interested in a med rating all those years ago. A rating as a counselor seemed like a natural fit, and we don't have one in the family right now. I'm writing my next case study on you."

"You're not!"

"I'm not, but I should." Her grin was a copy of Poul's when he'd floored Kel with his ultimate gotcha.

His eyebrows shot up. "I never guessed you were so evil."

She poked him in the ribs. "I have all kinds of secrets. I learned from the best."

Family duty fulfilled and with stomachs too full, they

finally took their leave for the walk hand in hand to the site of their sprouting home, no longer just a blueprint projection. The footings and foundation were sealed in river stone. The roof, exterior walls, and flooring were in place. Stacked around the clearing were a portion of the goods they'd unloaded that day. Solar panels for the roof, the household water purifier, and the kitchen appliances. He would start installing them all this week.

"The windows and climate system could arrive on the *Dream*'s next run. Then we can move out of my parents' house for good. Come on. I'm anxious for you to read to me." She led him to the firepit and spread out a blanket. Rather than mess with a fire, he set a heating unit near them and touched it to life. She patted the ground beside her as she held out the first flimsi from the stack, ready to start their ritual.

He accepted the letter but before he began, tried an old persuasion. Many times, he'd urged her to space with her family while he worked to build their fortune greater.

"Maybe this next contract you space with the *Dream*. I know your family misses you. The homestead's almost done."

"I know what you're on about, but it's not the case now and it won't be then. I'm busy when you're gone. I help the children every day with their studies, and someone's always dropping by to help with the house, and there's my course work. I'll ship again when you're done with Lanthanum and we can do it together."

Then she said what she always did when he retreaded the subject. "Duty now, for the future."

And each time she trumped his objections—her dictum about duty, an oath as sacred to her as any he learned in the Legion—he marveled. And each time she renewed it to him, he made his own silent promise. The future wasn't a goal. It was a destination. And he would lead them there, soon.

She laid her head on his chest and closed her eyes. "Quit stalling. Read your first letter to me from Catalinia X."

He relented and unfolded the stiff pages. "Dearest Tara. I miss you daily, but you know that."

"That's always a good start to a letter. Even if I know it, you're still supposed to say it. Every time."

"Yes, ma'am. Where was I? It's going to be a clear day, which is good because the security forces don't like rain. They're a hassle, like just about everything on Catalinia X, but the work's easy and it's a close second to Callie's World for nice weather. You've seen the holos. The city's pretty amazing, but I'd never want to see the like sprout up out of our settlement, not in a thousand years. I hope our world stays simple, tiny, and ignored by the rest of the galaxy."

As had become their habit, while he narrated his own letters, she commented after every sentence until he finished that day's missive. "The holos of the city were amazing. But something like that here? My great-grandfather didn't claim this planet so we could make it like Liberinthine or any of those other duracrete cesspools. Poor Poul," she jumped ahead to current events. "What will you do without him?"

"I've already told Lanthanum I'm not going anywhere until he's ready."

She squeezed him like the tourniquet that saved Poul's life. "Six months. I still can't believe it."

"Which? That he got shot, or that I'm not going anywhere for a good long while?"

"Both. I'm so sorry he got hurt, but if it means we get to

be together for so long, then I won't feel so bad about it, if you know what I mean."

"I do. And he'd understand how you meant it, too. I wonder if Karla knows yet?"

"I'm sure she does by now. The *Promise* was heading into bright star territory to pick up freelance freight work." Bright star space was what spacers working the edge called the densities where stars and people flourished in the core. "Coming out of their first long jump, they'll have checked the data stream. Who knows? When it's time for him to come home, they might even end up near enough to Andalore for Karla to bring Poul home herself. Wouldn't that be something?"

"You think she's settled on him?"

"I know she has. And Poul?"

"He won't admit it to me in those terms, but yeah." Kel shivered. "I'm not used to the night air blowing in off the mountains just yet. Are you ready to go back to your folks' place?"

"Almost. Let's stay right here a little longer. Is that the converter?"

In one of the containers was the waste converter that would recycle the products of their bodies into organics. When mixed with enzymes and the local soil, it would enable them to grow a little food in the tiny garden they planned. Not with all the converters of all the homes together would there be enough nutrients to build a sustainable agriculture. But Quint would soon start to work on that part of his grand plan for Callie's World.

"Not joining us for the banquet was a bit of an insult. You smoothed it over with the family by saying—what's his name? Quint?—saying that he was exhausted from the trip. It didn't help to make anyone less skeptical about you wasting credits to bring him here."

"He's a bit—insular, I'd say." The awkward scientist insisted on putting up his own shelter near the edge of the settlement area. Maybe it was for the best.

"How'd he do with Uncle Cormac during the trip?"

"Quint stayed in his cabin, so we didn't have to find out, thank Oba."

"The clouds are coming in. It may rain."

"Then we should get back to your parents' before it does."

"No. Come see." She led him by hand up the rough sawed planks to the covered porch and into the front room. At her touch, a heater glowed to life, revealing her surprise. On the floor, a bed with pillows and thick blankets. The nest was topped by the quilt Auntie Meiko had given them for a wedding present, patterned with nebulas and galaxies of all shapes, with hearts and the *Callie's Dream* at its center, the cream cloth of the spaces in between the swatches signed by all the family.

"It's well past time we made this a real home, Kel."

As he lay with her body against his, he had only one thought.

When the time comes, how will I ever find the strength to leave again?

***

"That's him, Chap-Chap," Doc said. "The big boy. Gotta be. Head for him."

"You are a master of the obvious, Doc."

"Still makes me a master, ya kelhorn. More'n I can say about you."

In his usual manner, Rex's message said only to retrieve the passenger and be prepared to follow his orders as if they came from him. General Airani's message was equally lacking detail, but the assets he'd assigned them were tantamount to a blank check for something big.

Chappy eased the sled in the direction of the tail ramp. The lone man not in work coveralls out-massed any two of the spacers directing the loader bots. "Wolfhound Six wouldn't have assigned us an Excalibur and all the works if this was just an escort job."

"Fact. Check. Him. He's got leej written all over him. But he looks kinda old to be an operator."

"He might look older than Rex, but that don't mean nothin'. *That's* a killer."

The two had been together since Legion basic and the only two of their class to be posted to the Cygnus arm. It had been the first of bonds that only grew firmer during their years together in the Wolfhounds.

The Wolfhound Regiment was a secluded monolith in a Legion that was itself an island. It was the last regiment like the Legion of old. And it was that which made a Wolfhound think of himself as better than any other legionnaire, even if measured against those in the fabled world of Dark Ops.

The Wolfhounds persisted in the purest and most original form of the early Legion regiments, relying on nothing and no one. There were no basics or hullbusters or space-swabbies in the Cygnus sector. It was the domain of legionnaires. It was a Wolfhound holding the stick of the Talon that brought death from above, a Wolfhound who commanded the might of a Magnus grav tank, and a Wolfhound in every fast-attack sled, mech, artillery piece, or flying murder machine.

Years spent fighting in the farthest reaches of the remote sectors of the Cygnus arm had made the two friends stand out in a regiment of standouts. Doc and Chappy had started in an assault company—the backbone of the Wolfhounds. With pride they'd both been selected to become mech operators, commanding the walking death dealers more mobile and nearly as heavily armed as their tanks. The Wolfhounds were the last in the entirety of the Legion to still use the giant combat machines, persisting in the same way the Wolfhounds persisted, untouched by the changes that molded the rest of the Legion.

And it was together that the two were pulled by General Airani himself to make the move to Zeta, the small section that operated directly beneath the Wolfhound commander.

There was only one Dark Ops, and it was under the control of Legion Command, doing things no one knew, things leejes whispered to each other about with a reverence due such an assignment. Dark Ops was rumored to be a unit that lived a holo-action drama about spies and assassins, believable but for its improbability. But if the pair had once been like other Wolfhounds in believing that Dark Ops was a myth, Doc and Chappy had come to know that Dark Ops was real.

If for no other reason than the list of indispensable lessons on Zeta's team room wall that had come from somewhere, from someone who knew.

General Airani hung the commandments known as Kel's Rules there himself, having recently received them from an old teammate on Victrix. "Bigg sent this to me.

Thought it might be of interest." Who Bigg was, he never elaborated.

Before coming to the Wolfhounds, Airani had commanded a kill team in the nonexistent unit. And it was the young Captain Airani that built the same capability for the Wolfhounds with Zeta. Now, he commanded the Wolfhounds.

Zeta had been passed to only one other's care. Captain Malik was a leej as comfortable behind the stick of a Talon as he was behind an N-22 sniper rifle. And he refused promotion every time—assuring his men he always would —saying that Zeta was where he'd die.

As far as Doc, Chappy, and the other Zetas knew, Dark Ops were wannabes. What Zeta did was the stuff of real legend—not rumor. Like working with Tyrus Rex. *The* Tyrus Rex. Trusted to know that the general and the bounty hunter Rechs were one in the same. And if the man they were sent to retrieve had been sent by Rex, then whatever came next would be as legendary as anything they'd come to expect.

Chappy slowed to a stop near the ramp.

Doc whistled. "Guy's even bigger up close." Before they could dismount, the weathered giant dropped his gear in the bed and vaulted into the rear seat.

"Let's roll, leejes. That our bird?" Devoid of markings but unmistakable for anything but a ship of war, the Excalibur-class ship sat alone on the edge of the field.

"Yes, sir," Doc said, introducing himself and Chappy by full rank and name.

"Knock off with the sir, Sergeants. Is the support package in that?" The man was definitely a leej.

"Yes, s..." Chappy caught himself. "Ready and waiting. General Airani sent us with everything including the kitchen sink."

"Good."

Doc gave Chappy a glance and they both put on buckets. "He remind you of someone, Chappy?"

"He's got Rex's word deficiency, if that's what you mean."

"He didn't send us some intel weenie to babysit. He a Dark Ops leej? Sent from the core? How come?"

"Knock it off, you two," their passenger said. The hair on the backs of their necks stood up beneath their armor. "Wait till I'm on L-comm and I'll read you in."

Both gave a thumbs-up.

Hartenstein grunted. "I was in a bucket before you two were so much as glimmers in your daddy's eyes."

06

The first week was days of satisfying labor and the nights, only her. Quint busied himself and shook off all offers of help. Kel was paying the man a fortune. That Quint immediately threw himself into the work was a relieving validation to Tatiana's recommendation.

It was the second week he noticed it.

It was a low-grade irritability that ground his mind like gravel beneath his feet. It manifested in a kind of contempt whenever someone wielded a sealing applicator or lifted a solar panel in a way he wouldn't have. It caused him to politely chase off any family who turned out to see if they could lend a hand. Instead, he worked alone the mornings Tara was away teaching the children, laboring as though his first squad leader was standing over him, ready to criticize every act as careless or slow.

He knew his irritability for what it was. The hyperalertness. The compulsion to find a danger that wasn't there. Professional paranoia. It was something he'd always been able to control. To turn the volume down on when he was home. But wordless music in his head presaged he should tense for a fight he couldn't yet see.

Without Poul, there was no one here he could really rely on.

He stood on the roof, the last panel in place, and looked around. The sun was at midday, which meant Tara would be home soon. At the edge of the horizon beyond the far rise was the landing field, a flat plain wide enough to accommodate two of the family's three massive cargo ships at the same time. He could just make out the mirage rising from the sharp irregularities that betrayed the superstructure of the *Callie Supreme*, grounded, empty, and penurious.

Between his vantage and the huge ship was the valley of their settlement. Thick trees that would look at home on any human world separated and partially concealed dozens of other homesteads and the village center. The fields growing the lush but otherwise useless flora encroached on all sides.

He'd taken to wearing a blaster, though there wasn't a single threat, human or animal, anywhere on Callie's World. His mind buzzed with a premonition. If a band of zhee raiders dropped from out of a spotless sky, he was totally alone.

Suddenly, he felt a fool. It was the worst kind of trap he'd fallen into. The folly of someone blind to the realities of the galaxy—not him. It was a mistake to believe that here lay an ideal of safety, an oasis like the Pthalo of his youth. Even there, placidity was artificial. The hurricanes that once wrecked the coasts had been banished by the weather control satellites. But everywhere else in the existence he'd experienced, maelstroms whipped into a frenzy when least expected.

It would happen here.

He should burn those fields and doze away the trees to make a clear kill zone around the settlement. He should have used the money to buy heavy blasters off the black market and place them in a perimeter of defendable bunkers. Kel had wasted the last two years on pipe dreams. And it would never be more apparent than when Quint would inevitably tell him it couldn't be done.

Tara waved as she appeared from the forested path to break him from his dark thoughts. "Is that the last one?" she yelled up to him.

"Yup."

"You've been working too hard. You've gotten most everything installed all by yourself. You don't have to treat building our home like it's a military objective," she chided.

"I thought you'd be pleased."

"Of course I am. Let's take the afternoon off. It's play day. The kids all want to see you. It'll be fun."

"I'm coming down."

When they were together, his anxieties diminished. He thought he'd concealed his worries, but he'd heard it in her voice. Concern. She knew he was having a hard time. He'd told her about it. Life was always two things for him instead of one. Out there, he was here. Here, he was out there. But for as long as he could remember, he'd felt that way, even before he met her. With each rung of the ladder down, he promised to leave what had intruded into his peace up on the roof to burn away in the heat of the solar collectors.

After a kiss and a hug, she took his face in her hands. "Are you alright?"

"I am. I'm just—" What had he been fretting over? Looking into her eyes, he couldn't remember. "I just don't want this to ever end."

But as they walked back along the path, he knew it would.

Kel played their games, wrestled them in hordes, threw balls and flying discs, trying but failing to remember the silly games he wished he could teach them from his own playground days. Surprised at the dizziness he felt after playing pilot in the game the children called "topsy-turvy reentry," he shrugged off indefatigable children as gently as he could while staggering to Tara as they persisted in pulling him back, begging him to play one more game.

"C'mon, Uncle Kel. Hide and seek, hide and seek."

Tara clapped her hands in command as Kel plopped beside her on the shaded bench. "He's sitting this one out, kids. We'll watch."

Squeezing lids tightly until he thought his eyes might burst like dropped eggs, Kel's vertigo settled. "I've been tested to 10-G centrifugal force without so much as a tiny wobble afterward. They spun me around so fast with that blindfold on, I nearly lost my lunch."

Tara laughed. "They cheer loudest when someone hurls."

"They're all pilots in the making."

Hide and seek was the same everywhere. One of older boys was the seeker, leaning against a tree, counting aloud with eyes shielded in the crook of an elbow as the rest scattered.

"Look at little Telly." Tara pointed to a cute towhead.

"He's a natural sniper if I ever saw one." Unlike the other children who hid behind tree trunks, the tiny man had found a small depression between wild shrubs, deeply shaded by the grove of trees. He pulled fallen branches heavy with green leaves around him, and flattened under their cover into the shallow nest he'd made himself. Before he disappeared from view, he gave Kel and Tara the grin. The one only a child could produce. Behind it was the barely containable anticipation of the thrill to come. He knew he'd already outsmarted the seeker.

One by one, the seeker found them. They raced from his grasp, only to be run down and tagged by the older boy. Shrieks of playful excitement and curses of defeat turned to laughter for the children, and for the two observers.

A feminine voice called unseen from the classroom building. "Break time. Everyone, come in for a snack."

The children dashed away. And from the hiding place where Telly had gone undiscovered, nothing. Kel watched the spot, expecting the boy to rise and answer the call with the rest of his playmates.

"Do you think he didn't hear Calista?" Tara asked, watching the same spot.

"Telly!" Kel called. "C'mon out, buddy, go get your snack."

Just when Kel was about to move, half-thinking maybe there was something wrong, the foliage erupted. "Suwpwize!" the little man announced with arms raised high. "I won! I won! You nevuh could find me!"

Telly looked around. The smile vanished. The tears came.

"They lef' me. They lef' me behind." He burst into sobs.

"Poor baby," Tara clucked as she opened arms to catch him at full run, tears streaming down his face.

"They didn't find me. I wanted them to be find me. I wanted to be found."

The sobbing boy clung to her legs as Tara stroked his back. With the compassion and empathy Kel thought only a woman knew how to give, she consoled him.

"Shh. It's alright. I know, baby. It's a joy to be hidden, but a disaster not to be found."

First came the lump in his throat, then the tear. He brushed it away as he sniffed back another, thinking he'd avoided attention. But Tara saw. Keeping the tiny boy pulled close, she placed an arm around Kel's waist and squeezed him to her.

"You're not hidden. Not any longer. I found you."

Even he didn't know why he'd been struck the way he had.

How was it that she did?

"I know. I'm so lucky. I love you, Tara."

"I love you, Kel."

That night he woke with her at his side. It had been a dream, but not a dream. It was as real as any memory. He was proud. And strong. So sure of himself. Bigg was there, and so was Tem. It was just the three of them on the hill. Armored, perfect, invincible. Between them and the setting sun was the perfect, uncontestable domain where they were kings. Where wasn't important. It could have been anywhere. What was important was the feeling that lingered with him in those the first few lucid, twilight moments afterward. A wholeness he'd forgotten. A time of no doubts, no regrets, no fears. Only the anticipation of the next mission.

Awake and unable to return to that place of his dreams, the feeling faded. The Kel in the dream wasn't him.

Because that Kel lived one life. This Kel lived neither one life, nor two. This Kel was living half here, half out there.

Two halves did not make a whole.

***

By the third week, he'd made the adjustment. Why his transition was so severe and prolonged, he could only conclude that Poul's absence was the differing factor. He thought he was beyond being subject to the same powers that controlled regular humans, the need for routines, the familiar, the predicable. And that's what it was to have Poul at his side. A comfortable dependence. He forgave himself that weakness. Because if it was that, reliance on Poul was no shame. He only knew that his disorientation was over. Just as the children's game had challenged his balance and disrupted his equilibrium, the distress had thankfully dissipated and he was returned to ease.

He was happy.

The house was as finished as he could make it. He spent the mornings in pleasurable exercise before helping with communal chores. It was no effort to work joyfully with the others and Tara agreed that if there were any in the family who still believed Kel had brought the family ruin, the resentment had been erased. Midday he'd meet Tara at the school and play with the children before they took the shaded trail home.

He liked who he was here.

If this was to be the routine for the remainder of the six months home, he couldn't imagine a better one. What waited was so far away, he could still pretend it didn't exist. This morning, the image of an inverted Quint surprised him mid-exercise. Kel righted out of the handstand, and let his widest grin loose on the introvert.

"Hey man! How's it going?"

Quint stared uncomfortably at Kel's feet. Reading him was as difficult as trying to guess what a reptasaurian was thinking. "I need." He took a breath. "Need to test f-farther out."

"Where do you want to go?"

Quint pointed to the base of the mountains. "The biome ch-changes there. F-foothills."

It was the first time Quint had asked for help. "No sweat. I can borrow a hover and have us there easily in an hour. Can we do what you need in a day or do we have to stay out?"

"N-no. J-just today."

"I'll meet you at the garage."

The ride was a quiet one, and Kel didn't force conversation, instead letting the rush of the treetops he skimmed over occupy him. It wasn't the same thrill as with legs dangling out of a SLIC, but what was?

He followed Quint's hand gestures and made gentle racetracks over the differing landscapes near the rising slopes. The trees became sparse and shorter. Rivulets trickled down shallow channels. Like contours on a map, patches of subtly different vegetation marked the varying elevations. Finally, Quint spoke.

"Land there," he said without the usual stammer, indicating a gentle spot free of gravel washed down from the mountain runoff. Quint waved off help to unload his equipment. "I'll be..." He circled an arm around.

"Can I borrow your spare shovel?" Kel asked. "I saw some flowering shrubs I thought I might try around the house for Tara."

In his first overtly recognizable human expression, Quint raised eyebrows, showing interest in the prospect. "Good. Idea."

Kel tapped the pistol at his side to get the man's attention before they parted. "I might do a little target practice, so don't be alarmed if you hear me shooting." Quint made another welcome indication he could communicate like a member of the human race, giving an over the shoulder wave and vigorous nod that he understood and wasn't concerned.

Kel found a stand of the shrubs he'd seen from above. They were even more interesting up close, bearing tiny purple, green, and yellow flowers blossoming from a single plant. He chose several small ones, careful to dig wide and deep around each. With ample soil clinging around the roots, he carried them back to the hover. The leaves were somewhat brittle, and Kel wondered if the soil around the house was too moist for the plants. With luck, maybe it also meant they wouldn't need much watering in their new home. Quint must've thought it was at least possible the plants would survive the transplant, otherwise, wouldn't the expert have frowned instead of indicating the possibility was intriguing?

He knew Tara'd appreciate the thoughtfulness, regardless if they took hold or not.

He deposited the harvest in the hover and checked on Quint's location. He was a hundred meters away, digging on his knees with a hand spade to fill containers from each elevation of his excavations. After a short walk, Kel came to the draw that had caught his aerial eye as suitable for the purpose. Where soil had washed down the tapered head of the slope, protrusions of white shale poked out of the ground, leaving a multitude of natural targets for his practice.

He drew the pistol from his side. It was an anachronism. A slug thrower. By any title appropriate to an alien race—genius or master or wizard—the doro craftsman who'd gifted it to him had called it a soul-forger.

He unloaded the eight heavy shells from the capstan, taking a moment to appreciate the swirling colors locked in the metal of the receiver's surface. The wood grain warmed to his grip as he sighted on one of the rocks and the world around him assumed unimportance. He let the actuator drop without allowing the sight picture to waver an atom's breadth, then repeated the sequence several times before reloading the weapon.

The first target was fifty meters. Free of any distraction from the task, he fired. The pistol's sights lifted, and the fist-sized rock splintered. The next was farther up the slope, the one after that even farther, until he selected one two hundred meters from him. This was the test. Either he was returned to equanimity, or he wasn't.

At this distance, each and any element—breath, pulse, the sway caused by the slightest wind—moved the sights. The antiquated weapon was made for this. It was a tool for self-discipline. This was the magic of the soul-forger. Only by mastery of himself could he hit the target. And he and the target were connected. He was the target; the target was him.

The sights aligned and he pressed the trigger.

A loud boom came from overhead.

He searched the sky until the dot of the craft making the sonic boom appeared below a cloud bank. It wasn't the unattractive rectangular mass of the *Promise* or the *Dream*, neither of which were due home for months. It was also small, and its profile seemed tailored for speed in an atmosphere. The ship assumed a shallow attitude for descent. It calmed him slightly. A steep screaming dive of a gun run would've filled him with a worse dread than he felt to have relegated earlier premonitions to the bottom shelf in his cellar of concerns. His wrist link buzzed.

"Attention in the settlement." It was Toran Flannagan, one of the *Supreme*'s crew, on duty in the town operations center. "We have no communication with the ship dropping out of orbit, but it's on a vector for us. Captain Sullivan's the ranking family member, and is calling all flight officers, bosuns, and deckhands with security ratings to meet him in the common hall for instructions."

Cormac Sullivan's voice came over the link. "The pilot's just identified himself to me. He's the owner and sole crew. It's a private vessel, and he's asked permission to ground. Sounds like he's made a navigation error and needs assistance. It's unlikely there's anything to be alarmed about. But like Toran said, report as instructed. It's only one man. Everyone else can continue with your normal routines. I'll report as soon as I've met the pilot and know more. Out."

Kel was already on the run. "Quint, let's move! On the double. We're heading back. Now!"

The scientist was on a dead run and no sooner landed a foot into the hover than Kel revved the repulsors to lift and pivoted to point the reverse course home. Maximum altitude for the hover was only a dozen meters above the height he'd run it earlier while amusing himself with reminiscences about flying over the jungles of Psydon. A hover's repulsors were configured to lift large loads just above the ground it pushed against. They could fly if lightly laden, but no matter the tricks he knew, he couldn't turn this one into a Talon by any secret magic.

Tara didn't answer her wristlink.

"W-what's w-wrong?" Quint finally asked.

He poured his thoughts out like an upended bucket. "Sullivan's wrong. No one could be here by accident. And even if it is one man, if he's the wrong sort, he could cut through everybody in the settlement like a laser saw. I'm an idiot for leaving my RK home. If I had a spare blaster to give you, could you even use it?" It was an accusation, not a question. He let his thoughts out of their bottle. "Tara must be at school and busy with the children. She's not like the rest of her family. She's busy taking charge and getting the kids and the women somewhere defendable. That's why she's not answering."

He had an image of Tara, firmly telling Calista and the other teachers that the captain's weak posture toward the visitor was a mistake, and they needed to act of their own accord. Above all, the children had to be protected.

He'd lost track of the lustrous, curved ship. He tried the wrist link again and this time, she answered. "Kel, where are you?"

"On my way. Where are you?"

"I'm running home. I was busy getting the children to the stores complex. It took some doing for me to convince Calista it's the safest place. I'm on my way to get my blaster before I head back."

"You did right. Get your blaster, but I want you home. Understand?" He was about to explain more. That he loved her for being a protector. That it made his chest swell with pride. But that she had to be safe—for him.

He didn't get the chance.

"Kel, there's a man on our porch. He's waving to me. Kel! It must be alright! He looks like—you. He's a legionnaire."

"Tara! Run!"

She didn't reply.

"Captain Sullivan, this is Turner. Get everyone to my house, now! Tara's by herself and the visitor's *there*. He's armed. Hurry!"

***

The indicator no longer flashed hot red, warning engine criticality on the way to meltdown. Only because Tara had assured him everything was okay had he throttled back from 110% to the mere 100% he pushed the power plant.

The clearing in front of his house held a gathering. He cut lift and the crowd spread like insects fleeing the sole of a boot. He flared repulsors to max, showering loose soil on those who realized too late the coming touchdown wouldn't resemble a dropping feather.

"Where is she?"

Cormac Sullivan was there to answer. "She's inside. I wouldn't have left her alone if she hadn't said it was one of your friends in there with her." The captain's face turned the bright pink of a Sullivan heating to anger. "You need to let your old Legion pal know what's an acceptable hail procedure. He may have a ship, but he's no pilot. He completely ignored my directions to land on the beacons. And you aren't much better. You could've hurt one of us if you'd blown that approach."

Agreements from the assembled joined the captain's.

Men like the captain, with responsibilities and the authority that came with them, thought of themselves as rough men and wanted others to see them the same way. Kel flicked the retaining strap off his holstered pistol, killing whatever further derision waited on Uncle Cormac's lips.

"Move aside, Captain, but don't go anywhere. Be ready for violence. If I don't come out—kill him before he can reach the women and children."

A sea of wide, white eyes parted for him. The stunners they carried hung limply at their sides, supernumerary and useless as dull-edged dress swords. For all the callouses on hands and scars from plasma burns, whatever they thought themselves, these were not rough men.

At his shoulder was the one he least expected. The scientist didn't share the stunned looks of the spacers. Maybe Quint didn't understand what was happening.

"No, Quint. Stay with them." The man nodded, sparing Kel the wasted seconds of a stuttered reply.

The front door was open. He ascended the stairs to see into the kitchen threshold where Tara sat with her back to him. At the other end of the long table was a man too big to be screened by her narrow shoulders. Beside the ice-filled glass sweating onto the polished wood sat a bucket.

The face staring at him was that of a stranger. The eyes he didn't concern himself with. It was hands that mattered most. The stranger was communicating by the silent language of Kel's tribe, arms pressed to the table with fingers spread wide. It only meant that to reach the out of sight blaster he would have to be fast, not that there was no harm in him.

"Your friend Marks is here," Tara said with a smile, holding a glass of her own. "I've been telling him about the settlement and—" She stopped midsentence. Kel's focus remained on the visitor at their table.

Kel moved to place a protective hip in front of Tara's shoulder. "I don't know you."

The stranger peeled fingers up to show open palms. Running in Kel's mental processor was the conditional logic the programmer of an artificial intellect only wished he could duplicate. *If* the intruder made a threatening gesture, *then* at the speed of thought, the action of the simultaneous draw and fire would come.

"I know you, Turner. And you know me."

Kel prepared to draw. "Don't call me a liar in my own house."

Tara pulled away from the table to stand behind him. The intruder's voice softened, but the harshness didn't leave, as though he was incapable of disguise.

"No need for that. We *do* know each other. I can prove it."

The stranger's armor was an ideal of form. He'd never seen the like. The warlock to conjure this armor must have abandoned his trade. Attempts to surpass this ultimate achievement would have been pointless.

Could he be another Lev Schuck? The legionnaire-turned–Nether Ops, modded so heavily that Kel nearly ended the man's life because he no longer knew his face. But Nether had no accoutrements for their minions as sublime as what sheathed this man in deadly perfection.

"Enough sket. Who are you?"

The man leaned back, confident, cocky, and invulnerable to menace. The chair creaked under the weight of his armor. Kel couldn't have been less prepared for how a single word could make him question his own sanity.

"Rex."

07

Only a decrepit wisp in a hover chair could rightly make claim to be General Tyrus Rex. The man who'd fought the Savages to extinction. Who'd personally formed Dark Ops. The absent head of the Primus Pilus Society, for whom the seat in the hall on Tiberius was reserved, empty, but emanating the eternal watchfulness of the legionnaires' legionnaire.

This man was too young. But it was the air of factual conceit with which he'd made the claim that held Kel's instinct in check. A blow was always answered with blow. And the incredibility of the man's claim was a gauntleted fist to his chin. But instinct served, it didn't decide. It was an unfettered mind that controlled words the same way it commanded the finger to lightly caress the flat face of the trigger and wait, before the choice to take a life was made. The next thing the man said would decide if he called the man out for his lie, or moved the finger off the trigger to rest against the metal receiver of his intent.

"You're Captain Kelkavan Turner. Born on Pthalo, son of a legionnaire. Your parents died in an accident when you were in Legion basic. You chose to stay and finish. It was a mark of the legionnaire you'd become. But it was on Antione where you got made. The youngest leej ever selected for Dark Ops. It wasn't your fault the House of Reason took notice of you. You were too competent. To their way of thinking, it made you dangerous to be left alone."

The stranger rocked forward and said one thing more.

"Hartenstein sends his regards."

His repudiation, *You're not Rex,* buried itself where primordial thoughts gave birth to words. He took eyes from the visitor and found hers. "Tara. Tell your uncle and the rest they can leave. Go with them and help Calista with the kids. Please."

It hurt to see her turmoil. She looked back to the seated man, who read her thoughts. "I haven't come here to harm your husband, Mrs. Turner."

Her face held no reassurance. "Because you say so, Kel," Tara said, and left. Watching her go was a relief and a remorse, reminding him that life had returned to being more than one thing at the same time. The men outside received her with the curiosity that awaited an oracle descending from her temple to make proclamation.

He faced the man who, for now, could be Tyrus Rex.

"Do you believe I am who I say I am?"

Who else could know what he did about Kel? And he'd sealed it all with Hartenstein's name. He could've asked him. Was he the Rex he'd been taught to revere? The one who led the Legion to destroy the last of the Savages. Who by acquaintance had elevated Hartenstein, Nail, and Bigg to the esteem of cohorts to a god. Or was he a different

Rex? A descendant, christened with the same name and burdened to live up to the legacy that came with it? Or was it something else?

There were things in the galaxy he knew to be more incredible than what he now accepted.

"Yes."

"Good. Because I came to discuss more important things. What Hartenstein's been doing, for instance."

Kel took Tara's seat and gulped the last of the icy liquid from her glass. It was rain puddled on the duracrete of a spacefield pad, turned to hissing steam beneath the heat of a blast nozzle. It did nothing to quench his fever.

"When they cashiered Hartenstein, when they brought Dark Ops to heel, allowed points to be placed—it was all part of their plan to weaken the Legion. I've been away. And there was only so much the Society could do to squash it. They've preserved the Legion as best they can, eyes on the things they can see. What they missed, what got buried... Turner, what was in that jungle lab on Psydon, it didn't start there, and it didn't die there."

The Hool had released a nano weapon on them. It instantly and mercilessly killed their Rafeer brothers. They'd radiated the secret complex with a weapon so restricted the House of Reason had to approve its use. Then the doro hordes overran their position, and were turned to atoms by the air strikes, JP along with them. What became of the Hool prisoner carried to safety by the autonomous combat multiplier—the AI called Bertie—they never learned. For whatever information Republic Intel extracted from the prisoner, Kill Team Three had paid the price of its freight by their blood.

But it was more than the wounds to their bodies that he and Poul carried with them off Psydon.

"I came to tell you. Turner, a weapon was released on Victrix. It was a nanoplague. Like the one on Psydon. One designed to kill *us* and only us. Dark Ops is gone. They're all dead."

Kel stammered like Quint. "W-what? H-How?"

"The incident's been covered up. Washed away. It never happened."

"You mean Victrix has become the next Plenax? That's impossible! Everyone knows the Plenaxians couldn't contain the nano weapon they deployed on their own people. The Republic must be tearing itself apart over this!"

"There's not a soul with a mussed hair over it. No one knows."

"Someone knows!"

"Listen, Turner, what's important is this. The Hool figured it out. How to make a nano weapon perfectly selective for the traits that mark whatever target they choose. We don't know how, only that it happened. The rest of the planet's oblivious and the galaxy's carrying on in ignorance. For all anyone knows, Victrix just pulled up stakes overnight and abandoned the base. From Mount Fronius to the team rooms, it's a ghost town. Sealed by Repub Army."

The Dark Ops compound was contained in a natural valley. The small spacefield sat between the cantonment area of a few nondescript buildings and the mountain that had once housed a planetary defense system with which to fight off Savages. Beneath Mount Fronius was the underground complex where they planned and launched the most secret missions in the Legion.

"But how could it have been done without *anyone* knowing? All of DO couldn't have been there when it happened. Operators and whole teams would've been out on missions. There was support staff, civilians, families."

The warm sunlight that spilled into the home faded behind heavy clouds. "Missing. But there weren't many there anyway. The change was already coming before you and Radd left. It wasn't long until Legion Commander Barrow cut DO to half the number of kill teams. As old blood was moved out, no new blood was allowed to replace it. DO was getting smaller and weaker all the time, locked on Victrix to do... nothing."

Kel would never have imagined Dark Ops relegated to unimportance by the Legion. "Then why attack it at all if DO was already on its way to extinction?"

"Maybe the enemy didn't know that."

"But they knew where to hit us!"

"You know how that happened."

In Kel's time, Dark Ops had gone from a covert entity to one casually spoken about—by name—even by those outside the Legion.

Kel analyzed out loud. "The Legion being weakened wouldn't be enough. Dark Ops would have to be removed. But a nano targeted for just Dark Ops? We're all just legionnaires. There's nothing different about an operator from any other leej. Is there?"

Rex's lip curled. "Dark Ops would need to be eliminated to make whatever else they have planned easier. We don't know how they did it. But Victrix was the perfect place to test run their weapon. And it sent a message."

Terror's goal was to terrorize. This was the definition of terrorism.

"The only message they'd send is to call down their own annihilation."

Rex scoffed. "The House of Reason's thrown up walls. Legion Command's running down bureaucratic mazes meant to neutralize them from action. It's the same strategy the politicians have always used, because it always works. Deny. Delay. Obfuscate. Because if humans are distracted for long enough, they always lose interest. And forget."

"Why would the House of Reason do that?"

"As if you need to ask, Turner. You of all people. The politicians hate the Legion as much as any of our enemies. They just don't have the guts declare it openly like an honorable foe. Their day's coming. Article 19 exists for a reason. But we need to root out this enemy first. The Society's chosen to act. We go to war."

When first inducted, he reserved a suspicion that the Society of Primus Pilus was little more than a lodge. Some kind of fraternal order for exemplary legionnaires. Meeting in secret to reward themselves with the exclusivity that came with membership. But he'd learned.

They were the first spears of the Legion.

He'd been made privy to the origins of the shadowy organization, almost as old as the Legion itself. Its purpose was to preserve the Legion, at any cost and against all enemies. And when he saw how the Society helped him destroy the conspiracy the Scarecrow extorted him to participate in, any reservation about the Society being nothing more than a boys' club was silenced with VanderLoot's last gasp.

"General," Kel chose the address, unsure. "You are General Rex, yes?"

"Call me Rex."

Kel's red light had extinguished. The fire in him where the Legion once burned was dimmed by the calming amber of the wood home, the warm glow the wavelength of Tara herself.

"Why are you telling me all this, Rex?"

Though Kel hadn't said it, Rex heard it. Kel saying he was done. That he had a new life. That it was one that didn't include Rex or the Legion. Rex's lips curled in disgust and a mushroom cloud paling the one Team Three had unleashed on a Crude base engulfed the room.

"You think you can hide here? That just because you got a little fatigued, you aren't Primus Pilus anymore? You don't get to say you've done enough. Because you aren't. Your share isn't done."

This wasn't Bigg telling him he'd support him whatever he decided for the course of his life.

"You owe. For this—" Rex flung his hands up, "—for everything you are. You owe your share. And a legionnaire's share doesn't end. Not until every one of our enemies lives every day looking over their shoulder. Not until they all lie down. Not until diving into a black hole is their only escape. Not until then will you have done your share."

This wasn't Papa Bear igniting in him the rare self-worth that came to only one in a trillion souls when he told him he belonged with the best. Rex wasn't giving him the chance to join anything.

"With or without you, this will happen."

He was being threatened with exile.

"And if you aren't already on your feet, ready to get back in the fight, it means I was wrong to say I knew you."

Rex wasn't wrong. It was Kel who'd been wrong.

For Kel, the definition of legionnaire had always lived in the cast of his mentors. The ones who taught him, watched over him, accepted him as an equal. This wasn't Hartenstein. Or Bigg. Or Nail. Or Braley Yost.

Every one of them, the men who'd made Kel, were a shadow of this leej.

Rex's eyes pierced him. They churned in opposing energies. Pain and compassion, cruelty and duty, malevolence and grace. And within those furies were all the living and the dead Kel had taken the oath with. Like Rex, they judged him. And in their eyes, he saw his own reflection.

And he didn't like what he saw.

If this was the soul of the Legion, then Kel could be no less. But Rex's accusation of weakness didn't stir him to anger. Instead, Kel burst into laughter. An unaffected deep and hearty laugh.

"You *do* know me."

Rex's cocked eyebrow meant he was just as surprised as Kel was by his laugh.

"Here's what I think. If the man sitting in my kitchen is *the* Tyrus Rex, it's proof of what some us have thought all along. You've been at this a long time. Longer than anyone could believe possible. No one ever talks about it or wants to admit it, but here you are. And because I've seen some things, too, I know almost anything is possible."

Rex said nothing.

"Which means you've seen it all and done it all. Over and over and over. But yet, by your own admission—you were gone. Your eyes weren't on the things that mattered most. Which means, you're human. And whatever it was you were off doing, it wasn't enough to keep you from dropping it to come back. Because no matter what else, you always have to return to being who you are. You say you don't know me? Hell, Rex, I *am* you, you bastard."

The miniscule smile Rex gave quenched the last of the flames in the room.

"You're not the first man to ever try for something else, Turner. So, I take it that you're ready to work?"

"Yes I am."

If Rex was capable of forgiveness, it came in the only word that mattered.

"Okay, then, Legionnaire."

***

Rex pulled a credit chit out of his gauntlet and tossed it to Cormac Sullivan. Spacers treated everything material with suspicion. The captain caught the translucent card and raised it between thumb and forefinger to the sun, as if examining a bolt for the invisible crack of an impending shear. The etched hologram reflected six zeros behind the first digit.

Kel's eyebrows arched, but not the captain's.

"Is this meant to bowl me over? I'm poor. Not stupid. This only means there's more to this than the *Supreme* being a yacht for my niece's husband. Whatever the hell he's doing, if this is what you're offering, it stinks of something I shouldn't expose us to."

Though Kel had known him only a short time, he intuited Rex had no gentle touch with which to smooth

Cormac's ruffled feathers. His prediction came true with Rex's growl.

"First time you'll ever be paid for a run *from* your backwater. If a million won't cover it, give it back. I'll take a detour, drop Turner off myself, and he can charter a ship from a captain who needs the creds more than you do." Rex held out an open hand.

Kel cleared his throat. "Cormac, if anything comes up to make you even a little uncomfortable, I'll cut you loose. But there won't be. I'm hiring you out because it's the fastest way to get me on my way. Plus, you're free to take on any haul that works with my destinations. This is going to be a profitable and comfortable job for the *Supreme*."

Cormac still held the chip. "Comfortable? I'm not comfortable about anything to do with you, Kel. I want to know what you're up to."

Until now, Tara'd been a silent member of the confab on her porch. "Uncle Cormac! That's enough! It's only your prejudice toward Kel that's making you second-guess a windfall contract like this. The whole family's told you time and again how my husband's put himself between us and danger. What he does, he does for all of us. Why you refuse to believe it, I don't know, but that's on you!"

Cormac made an exasperated cough. "As if I'm without cause! After all he's exposed this family to! My sister's always been the favorite and just because you are, too, my little niece, that's no reason for everyone to wipe the slate clean about the man you chose. He's brought nothing but trouble. And right here's more of the proof." He thumbed at Rex, who raised an eyebrow, perhaps mildly impressed.

Tara glowered. "I'm glad it's out in the open then, Uncle. My turn. I'm a full member of the syndicate. If you turn this contract down, I'll canvass votes for a board meeting to discuss our confidence in your captaincy. A million credits! On top of Kel bringing a xenobiologist here on my household's financial back! I've had about enough of you running my husband down."

Cormac fondled the chip as he avoided Tara's eyes. "I haven't said no." He pocketed the chip and puffed up, trying but failing at a scorn equal to Rex's. "It's no secret we're barely making it. But I need to understand the potential exposure to my ship and crew, same as for any contract. A million creds isn't so much."

Tara smirked. "It's triple what we get for a good haul, and you know it. That plus Kel's assurance this'll be no riskier than any other job should be enough to convince you to accept. If not, then me crewing with you should lock it as a guarantee. Or do I need to call for that vote?"

It was Kel's turn to make a guttural noise. "We didn't discuss you going."

Rex groaned. "Family squabbles are for family." He marched off the porch, giving every indication that was all the goodbye he needed to give.

"More to come," Kel said to them both as he set off to catch Rex.

Rex's ship fit the clearing with only millimeters to spare between dense tree boughs port and starboard. It was a slick piece of work to put a ship of this size down without additional crew to help the pilot spot. How a legionnaire of any stripe had become such a masterful pilot, Kel wondered. Rex touched his gauntlet to command the ramp.

"I went along with this in order to move things along. You've got your ride until you're ready to ditch them. Your family's gotten some welfare courtesy the Society, and I've given you enough creds for anything else that might come up. When you drop from jump, there'll be a hypercomm packet with the clearances waiting. Along with your recommission. Major."

Kel snorted. "Which means you already knew I'd accept. So, it's safe?"

"Clean. The attack was contained to the Dark Ops cantonment. It's all been sterilized and locked down. Get what you need. By the time you're done there, the Society will have something for you, maybe even the location of 'the Section.' We have her image and biometrics. It will lead to the lab."

Sarah. She'd been sent with them to the Savage moon to retrieve a weapon. Under duress, the scientist told an incredulous Team Three that the black lab called the Section held secrets from across the galaxy, many of them attributed to pre-human races possessing knowledge and techs unimaginable. They'd barely escaped annihilation by the very thing they'd been sent to retrieve.

The Scarecrow had insidiously manipulated himself into control of the Section, severing its connection to anyone but him. For her part in the Scarecrow's maneuvering to use Team Three in his quest for ultimate power, Kel forgave her. He came to see Sarah as sincere, ethical, and brave. In her way, she was like space divers and other thrill seekers. She lived for the juice she got from being in the Section, making whatever government entity she and her fellow scientists worked for unimportant, unspoken, and unquestioned.

Being black was sometimes like that.

Kel hadn't given it much thought over the years. With the end of the Scarecrow, he assumed the Section had either been brought into the light or died in the dark.

"Rex, even if I find her, I don't know if what you think's there... is even there."

"There's something useful there, and whatever it is has been hidden long enough. We want it."

"And if I can't find it?"

"Stop dragging this out. I have places to be." Rex stepped onto the ramp, hefting his bucket over his head as he walked into the ship. Kel recognized this as his last chance.

"Wait. There's something I need to know."

"You've got what you need. What is it?"

Kel vomited his secret doubt like sour bile he could no longer swallow. "Am I responsible? Did the House of Reason gut Dark Ops and undermine the Legion because of me?"

His bucket seated, Rex's voice came through the speaker as stern as chemicals concentrated into acid.

"No fail, Turner."

The ramp raised but before the finality of the vacuum seal of the perfectly mated duranium hatch, Rex mumbled something as if musing to himself. It came out of him in a guttural language Kel did not recognize. Kel parroted the words, failing in comprehension no matter how many times he repeated them, but Rex had nodded as he said them, as if approving.

"You're damn right you're responsible."

***

Kel reached home when the second boom of the morning echoed over the valley. He looked up to see Rex's ship vanish into a cloud bank. The hover was gone from the front yard. He called her name as he climbed the stairs but Tara was also gone, her kit bag with her. Tossing what he needed into his own grav trunk, he saw the trail of dried mud flaked from his boots, and removed them as he cursed. Locked with the clay caked into the soles of his boots were the crushed petals of red, yellow, and purple.

He used the hike to the settlement center to rehearse. He'd send Tara home with all the tender care his mother used to pick up a spiny oyster and tease it open for its green pearl.

A hover intercepted his course, Chelly behind the controls. "Hop in. Got us a big one, huh?" Kel settled next to his cousin-in-law—a mock relationship he used to describe his connection to virtually everyone in the family —and they coasted for the *Supreme*.

Chelly's accusation was lightly disguised by his grin. "All that stuff about protecting the women and children. Seems like you got us worked up over nothing if it was just a friend wanting to hire us out." Chelly had been among the group in his yard. He still failed to understand the encounter could have spelled bloodshed instead of profit.

"Chell, next time a ship drops from out of nowhere carrying a stranger in armor who could kill everyone without breaking a sweat, I'll let you run the show, how's that?" He added a wink to soften the blow.

"Fair 'nuff."

The ship was in sight and Kel sighed. Maybe the silver lining to being in tight spaces with the prickly Cormac would bring an opportunity. He'd use today's event the way he had for his in-law's crew when faced with similar evidence their idealism had consequences as grave as flying into an ion storm—he'd educate them.

"How soon do we lift?"

"ASAP. When I asked him what the job was, Cormac just said, 'Ask our client, he's running this family,' and headed for his stateroom. I let it lie. Cap's always a rainy day until we're on the flight deck and earning creds. But with a payday like this already in hand, I can't figure out why he's even more cloudy than usual. I watched him and Tara ride in together and, brother, was she ever giving him an earful. Fill me in."

"I'm the bad weather ruining Cormac's flight plan."

"Forget about it. Cormac's moody and the trouble between him and Selva isn't helping. But he's the best captain I've ever jumped with. Where we headed?"

"Arinox." Victrix was *their* name for the planet and more specifically the base for Dark Ops. One they used to help confuse attention away from the otherwise unassuming world that was the home to their operations. Had been. Trying not to picture team rooms turned into tombs, the bodies of brothers contorted in rigor on their floors—it only made him picture the scene in even more unwanted detail.

"Arinox? Never heard of it."

"No reason you should have, Chell. Quiet place. We won't be there long. I just need to take on a small amount of personal cargo there before our next hop. Could be to a little place called Tiberius. I don't know yet. Our flight plan may change."

"Tiberius? That I've heard of. That's what's got Cormac out of sorts. This isn't some milk run. This is some kind of secret legionnaire thing."

A few seconds of Kel's silence brought a guffaw from Chelly. "Ha! Knew it. We're all supposed to pretend like you aren't what everyone says you are. Well, I say, awesome!

Finally, we get a shot at some of the excitement the *Dream*'s had. This oughta be good."

Like a puppy with a new bone, Kel let him enjoy his chew.

Sheila Kandit was purser on the *Supreme*. She met them at the head of the gangway with her green Sullivan eyes and a smile, and gave her husband a playful slap on his passing rump. "Captain says we lift in two hours. He didn't answer when I asked if I was to list you as passenger or crew, Kel."

"I can stand watches and fill in anywhere I'm needed, Sheila, but only on the first leg of the jump. I have work of my own to do from there. I'll let you know if that changes."

"No one's worried about you pulling your weight. Securing a payday's as good as loading the hold yourself, Kel. You're in a married stateroom on the same ring as ours. Tara's getting it set for you two right now."

"She's not lifting with us."

Sheila smirked. "You taking bets on that? She's second engineer, backup navigator, and primary medic on this cruise, buddy. You want us to lift without her, you're going to have to scour the roles of family here on refit to find replacement rates for hers. How good a juggler are you? Because that's the skill you need to do my job. Think you can replace Tara's billets in the next two hours before Cap gives the order to lift?"

Tara and Sheila were cousins, but may as well have been sisters—the kind who told each other everything. It'd been less than an hour since he'd chased after Rex. "It didn't take long for you to backstop Tara's plan to sabotage me leaving her behind. I'm impressed. It was that easy?"

Sheila winked. "That impressed you? I didn't strain a muscle locking that load down, much less a synapse." She tapped her temple. "Give me a real challenge sometime. Welcome aboard the *Supreme*."

He threaded his way through family in the narrow halls, greeted with grins and light fists on shoulders as they passed. He struggled with a few names and who was Sullivan or Yomiuri—birth, marriage, or adoption into the syndicate family indeterminable. He found the berth. A cleansing breath, and he pressed the panel. Tara stood with hands on hips, blocking his way like a sentry.

"Can I come in?"

"Depends, spacer. Family position falls second to rank on a cruise. If you can't stay in line, then you may be berthing with the teens in a deckhand hammock until you learn to respect senior crew."

"Understood, engineer's mate."

She let him pass and closed the door before hugging him. "You've been pushing me to space again for the longest. Do you not want me to go because... you fibbed to Cormac? Is what we're doing risky?"

"How can you even ask me that, Tara?"

"Then it's as I suspected. It's not risky for *us*, but it will be for *you*. That's why you don't want me along. When are you going to leave us and go your own way?"

How did she know?

Tara checked her chrono. "I have to go, Kel. But after shift, I deserve a full explanation."

"Okay." Where would he start? The living ghost of the legendary Tyrus Rex? Murdered Dark Ops comrades? Nano weapons and a galaxy wide threat to human existence? A mission to find ancient alien tech Rex thought they needed from the Section?

Rex had told him the time for secrets was over, but how much of it could she hear without being driven as crazy as it made him? His thoughts were interrupted by a chime from Sheila.

"Kel, your friend's down here asking permission to lift with us."

Kel frowned. "Quint? I'll be right there."

Quint was on the gangway with nothing but a small case and a datapad in hand. It seemed another blow to the fragile building blocks of Kel's long laid plan. He exploded. "Are you quitting me, Quint? What I paid you I earned in blood, and I want it back! Go get all your gear. We'll wait. I don't want to come home to find a single trace of you left behind, dammit."

Quint denied everything with a head shake so violent, Kel thought his scrawny neck would snap. "No! I found s-something. I think I can f-fix what's wrong, but I can't f-finish without access to the s-stream, and maybe some other s-stuff."

Cormac suddenly appeared. "What's this?"

Sheila answered for the tongue-tied Quint. "Captain, our guest wants to berth with us on this trip. Says he needs to retrieve something so he can finish what Kel brought him here to do."

The scientist's denial doused Kel's anger as quickly as liquid nitrogen cooled red metal, and relief welled out like steam. "Quint—that's great! What'd you find?"

Quint sucked a deep breath as though recycling Kel's expelled energy for himself, spewing sulfur words like a volcano.

"What'd I find? Proof. Everything the Republic says is a lie and everything they have is stolen! That's what I found!"

He'd not stuttered.

Cormac narrowed eyes to slits, then harrumphed. "Sheila, find this man a berth."

08

Doc and Chappy waited as the Legion pilot with the name tag *Slabside* presented a pad for the stranger's palm. "I have a confirmation set from General Airani. If you don't mind?" A moment later, the pad dropped and the pilot snapped to attention. "Your mission command's confirmed, Colonel Hartenstein. Orders?"

Chappy and Doc likewise snapped to stiff attention. Doc made an impressed whistle. "*Colonel*. Told you."

"Shh. He's telepathic."

As if he were, a glance from the newly identified colonel froze them. "At ease, everyone."

The co-pilot's name tag read Drizzy. The crew chief's, Romper. His order went unobeyed and like Doc and Chappy, the three aviators remained braced. It was time to set the tone he wanted for their working relationship.

"I mean it. Relax. My rank is supernumerary on this operation. Slabside, lift as soon as you're ready and put us into jump for the Quanta system. Any of you leejes been to Ozydna?"

The pilot relaxed a little. "Yes, sir. The Wolfhounds are why it's still the Free and Benevolent Protectorate of." He smirked as he used the title with irony. There was only one Ozydna.

"So I'm aware," Hartenstein said. "What can you tell me?"

The co-pilot, Drizzy, continued. "It's been a few years back." He looked at Doc and Chappy. "Were you guys on that one?"

"We didn't get much of the action, Chief," Chappy said. "The first assault company smoked the Azali corvette at the spaceport and had the raiders cleared out before our company could get any."

"I flew second seat in this very bird," Slabside said, patting the bulkhead.

Doc shrugged. "It was a slaughter, alright. We ran mech patrols for a few weeks—show of force to reestablish stability and all that. Gotta represent the Republic." The Wolfhounds were a presence in the Cygnus arm since the Savage Wars, policing the sector with a blanket of protection for Republic interests.

The crew chief, Romper, shook his head. "They hate us until they need us, then it's all Republic flag waving, flowers, and hugs and kisses. Until we leave, that is."

Doc chuckled. "Every race you ever heard of and some you haven't are there making bank. Even their donks stay behaved because they got it so good on Ozydna. As much money as the protectorate gets from what they let go on there, you'd think they could afford to have their own army. Is it time for us to save their butts again, sir?"

They'd all confirmed Ozydna was the kind of place Hartenstein surmised. "Mission brief in flight. You two. Take me to the MSC."

The air crew saluted and he returned it. It would take either electrical shock torture or time to get them to relax around him. He didn't have a stunner baton, so time would have to do it.

"Lead on, Sergeants."

Doc keyed the mission support container to open wide, revealing racks of suits and component parts. He could practically hear the gears mesh in the colonel's head as the huge hands touched the items within. "Me and Chappy got the MSC together, sir," Doc said gingerly, not sure if his narration was wanted or not. "Good thing Rex's message had your seven-dash-one in it, because your size isn't normally in one of our pre-loaded packages."

Chappy squinted in discomfort. "Nothing we got said you were a colonel, sir."

Hartenstein barely heard him as he took a moment to appreciate the racks of Mark Fives. The return to deadly functional armor would clothe his symbolic rebirth. It would once and for all sever him from the many masquerades he'd lived under. He thought about his books and their many poetic analogies and philosophic aphorisms. He'd looked to them to find meaning to cope with his exile from the Legion. None held words that rang true or suggested the author had once walked in his shoes. But there was one proverb that came to mind, and it unconsciously passed his lips by the power of its appropriateness.

"No man crosses the same river twice. Because it's not the same river, and he's not the same man."

Doc and Chappy shared a glance as if saying, *Is this guy frelled in the head?*

Hartenstein chuckled at their reaction. This was indeed a different river he crossed. "No more with the sirs, I said. And no *colonel*, either, got me? Call me Howler. Let's get started."

"Howler, sir?" Doc asked, only to be taunted by Chappy.

"Didn't he just say to lose the 'sir'?"

Hartenstein picked up a bucket. "It's a call sign I haven't used in a very long time."

It had been the first handle he'd ever earned, the moniker bestowed after his first drop. It felt right. Howler was who he'd been at the beginning of his Legion career, and it was a fitting link to the present and the opportunity Rex had given him to bring his story to a close with honor instead of the ignominy with which it had been ended. "Let's get to work, boys."

The pair stripped from their own armor to ease the task. It was two hours into the fitment when Chappy and Doc stepped back to admire their work. "That's as fast as even a Wolfhound tech's ever gotten someone into a new suit," Chappy said.

Doc wiped permagrease from his hands. "Pretty obvious Howler's an armorer himself, Chap." *Howler* came out in an unnatural and strained way, but Hartenstein accepted it as a good start and moved to a clear space in the bay. Doc and Chappy held back, knowing what was about to occur. He crouched low, sprang, kicked, punched the air, and rolled forward to rise into a fighting stance with the power of a mountain. Seemingly satisfied, he said only, "Buckets."

All of them buttoned up, he motioned Doc and Chappy to join him around the work bench like a briefing room table. It was time to fulfill his promise to read them in.

"I've been under for a while. Rex got me up to speed, but I have as many questions for you as you have for me. I don't want to make any assumptions, but Rex said you two had his full confidence. Does that mean you know who he is, beyond what you were told when you became Primus Pilus?"

Chappy shrugged. "Yes, sir. And, no, sir."

Doc stroked the chin of his bucket with the considered seriousness of a judge. "Wolfhound Six told us how it is. What we know is good enough and what we don't know doesn't matter. We're not just Wolfhounds. We're not just Zeta."

Chappy picked up. "See, sir, it was after our first time working for Rex when General Airani nominated us to the Society."

"That was a hairy one," Doc said, adding vague color to the story as if it helped clarify Chappy's muddy and awkward answer to Hartenstein's question.

Chappy picked up the tale again. "Rex said it wasn't necessary to go to Tiberius for the ceremony. Said we were added to the roles, and it was done."

"It was a special day for us, sir," Doc said with a gulp.

Chappy broke the solemnity of Doc's heartfelt admission. "We're detached to the general when he's in Cygnus. We get what he asks for. We do the groundwork."

Doc picked up for Chappy as Chappy often did for Doc, proving to Hartenstein that the two had been together a very long time. "Sometimes we go with him on one of his jobs. Sometimes they're hot, sometimes they're little more than errands. But we don't get read in to much. And we wouldn't expect different. We've always assumed it's the same when he's doing whatever it is he does outside Cygnus, that he has someone like us assigned to him from Dark Ops. But you're saying that's not so, sir?"

"He hasn't done similar with Dark Ops, no."

In their difficulty to relate what they thought they understood about Rex, Hartenstein understood intimately how it was a thing nearly impossible to put into language. It was like talking about a firefight after the fact. At the time, it made sense. But later, as you walked through it with the guy who'd been right next to you, his remembrance made you question your own. Everyone's fight was as different as it was the same. There was a truth you'd both witnessed, though it was unknowable through words, because words failed. Just as how the three of them were joined in the unknowability of Rex, but nonetheless knew the truth of him.

Hartenstein admitted his own truth concerning what he thought he knew about Rex. "I don't know what Rex has been doing. He hasn't been around in a very long time, not since he turned Dark Ops over to me. That's been twenty-five years. And since then, he's been in contact with the Society only rarely."

But even for the blind alley it was, trying to illuminate the mystery of Rex, it felt like relief. It was medicine for an ache he hadn't allowed himself to feel. Though he was with men he'd just met, they were his people as sure as if he'd known them as long as Bigg or Nail.

Cures are sometimes discovered in the interactions of previously untested combinations. He wasn't alone anymore. "Rex told me the time for secrets was over, but it seems he didn't mean as it applied to him."

Their common ignorance was accepted by solemn nods, sealing their new bond. Doc pushed this common starting point forward and in a new direction. "You commanded Dark Ops, sir?"

The question made Hartenstein grin, though they couldn't see it. "I did. But I started as a baby in the Guards. Then 131st. Recon company. Went O. Then 187th."

Doc asked it. "Savage action?"

Hartenstein nodded.

"Were you ever a Wolfhound?" Chappy asked.

"No. But I was there when Rex went around Legion Command to get the Wolfhounds their own Dark Ops. He's who made Zeta happen."

Doc perked up. "You knew General Airani when he was a captain in Dark Ops?"

"Topper was as fine a kill team leader as we ever had. Rex was Dark Ops first commander. And from the beginning, he planned a Dark Ops for every sector command. But he got shot down, time and again. Finally, he did what he could where he could, and sent Topper to the Wolfhounds so Cygnus got its own Dark Ops capability. The Wolfhounds are so far from the flagpole, it was how he could fly under Legion Command's sensors. Thank Oba he did."

He wasn't yet ready to tell them that due to Rex's wisdom, Zeta was the only surviving Dark Ops.

Chappy shook his head. "Funny how the Legion resisted something so obviously necessary. Why didn't they listen to Rex?"

Doc grunted knowingly. "You know why. What's right with the Legion, the other branches are clueless about. What's wrong with the Legion, ain't different. Brass don't like elites. Thinks it makes the rest of the Legion less elite, instead of treating covert ops as just a different mission set. Thinks it's un-Legion-like and somehow dirty. Leejes with long hair, mimetic armor, different weapon packages and all. They're happy to leave the black world to Republic Intel, even though they can't do what we do. But they ignored rule 17, and Rex was all-like rule 18 to make it happen. In the best interests of the Legion, ya know?"

Wrinkles creased Hartenstein's forehead. Doc's continued reference to some set of rules as if they came from a testament he'd never heard of irritated him to the point he couldn't ignore it any longer. Before he could ask, Chappy groaned and lit into his friend.

"Oba, Doc. I wish that list had never been posted on the team room wall. You may be my best friend, but worshipping this Kel guy like he's some kinda priest of all-things-operator—it's just too much sometimes. Knock it the frell off."

Was Doc referring to Kel's rules? Again, before he could speak, Chappy was there to deflect attention from his friend's exasperating habit. "You must've had the best job in the Legion, Colonel. Running covert ops with the whole galaxy your area of operations. The entire Legion to draw from for operators. Reporting only to the Legion commander—and him only to the House of Reason. Amazing, sir."

Doc was oblivious as to how Chappy had saved him, and followed the false trail as surely as a hopper to bread crumbs in the snow and the snare that waited. "I can't imagine all the missions you ran in those years, Colonel," Doc said.

Hartenstein sighed. The moment was gone. And it was being called colonel no less than three times in thirty seconds that had done it. He was, and he wasn't. Rex had

Primus Pilus reactivate him and his rank—at least as far as anyone in the Cygnus arm and under General Airani's command knew. But he'd never hold a colonel's command in the Legion again. That wasn't his or Rex's purpose for him.

He was an operator again. No more, no less.

And once the three of them started in earnest, they'd learn to accept him as that. As Howler.

"Which brings us to why we're here."

***

Doc and Chappy were silent at first when he told them, then cursed at the revelations as Hartenstein had done when Rex told him about the craven attack on Dark Ops. It focused the three like lasers aimed at the same target. In just a day of planning and preparing together, Hartenstein found he'd fallen into a level of comfort and trust with the pair he'd long missed.

Doc worked the slice as they dropped into the system outer belt.

"The ship we want *was* in Ozydna's main spaceport," Doc reported.

Hartenstein smacked fist into palm. The chance was coming to correct his mistake. "I've been kicking myself for screwing up and letting those people get waylaid without me being able to follow."

"That's sket, sir," Chappy said, quickly correcting himself by adding, "Howler."

Doc pushed back from the station where he'd worked the data stream like a jeweler cutting a rough gem into perfection. "Boss, to have done anything different than what you did all by your lonesome—impossible. It was fast work to slice what you could before the Ootari ship jumped. How Rex busted their code, well, he's got slicing skills even I don't."

Chappy humphed. "You're sure it was the same ship? Everything the bugs build is just like them—duplicates off the same factory line."

"100% it's our ship. It's gone now, but I got the flight plan they filed. Could be genuine, you never know."

Hartenstein waved the question away. "Holding them accountable is a problem for another time. I want to hear options."

Chappy was ready. "Ozydna's a safe haven for a fee. The protectorate doesn't have a military or much of a police. They can't offer much of a defense against raiders, but they do have one hell of a customs system and a damn good orbital monitoring net. They always get their pound of flesh and they do it by making sure everything goes through the capital port in Truexx. The only way to draw the attention of their customs enforcement service is to try to land anywhere but there."

Doc said, "The protectorate only cares about collecting their taxes. How their visitors earn the creds to pay 'em, they don't concern themselves with."

Chappy continued to build. "If we knew even roughly where the lab was, risking a stealth entry to do the recon and call in the standby assault force would make sense. But since we don't—" He let it hang for Doc to pick up.

"I can't get much more from this far out in the system without boosting the signal and giving ourselves away."

Chappy kept the furious mental pace going. "I'm not saying the pilots can't get us dirtside without the protectorate detecting us, I'm saying there may be a better way."

Doc tagged back in. "To get into their internal system, I need to be close to hide the slice. But once I do, I'll find something in the customs and port operations systems that'll tell us where the Ootari's cargo went. To transport 150 people from the spaceport to wherever they're at now, there'll be a trail. It won't be as easy as a cargo manifest listed as 'slave transport,' but I'll find something that'll give them away."

"Doc'll find it," Chappy said with confidence.

"Roger that," Doc said. "Moving that much human cargo overland takes a fleet of cargo carriers. And if the lab where they're doing their experiments is nowhere near Truexx, it'll be even more obvious, since they'll have had to use atmosphere haulers. And that's a lot of people to move."

The pair were continuing to rise higher in Hartenstein's estimation. "What I hear you two saying is our best bet's forgetting a stealth insertion."

Doc winked. "We hide in the open, boss. That port's higher trafficked than Orion Station. We get this done with the least hassle by being one fish in a school of fishes. We're just leejes dropping in for a shopping trip."

Chappy capped his vision for the op. "When we do find them, boss, we recon the objective, then lead the assault force in for the rescue and to nab the crew. And that'll bust this thing wide open so we can bring the war to 'em wherever else they are."

They'd convinced him. "A plain jane landing it is."

"What about the Ozydna Protectorate, Howler?" Doc asked. "What happens to them?"

Thinking about things on a scale beyond the tactical was the mark of someone seasoned in covert operations. Rex had truly chosen well. "If we get evidence Ozydna's turning a blind eye to slave traffic, Republic Intelligence and the Ex-Planetary people will be forced to investigate. There'll be House of Reasons delegates screaming for the protectorate to be held accountable."

"Invasion? Regime change?" Doc asked.

Chappy blew a raspberry. "Pfft. That'd kill the golden goose. The diplomats'll threaten to flood the place with troops to police them for violating the universal ban on slavery unless they promise reforms. It'll end up with the protectorate paying a buncha fines and allowing the Republic to get a bigger footprint here to monitor things."

Doc shook his head. "Reckon so. Then it's back to business for Ozydna, but with the Republic fingers in the local pie."

"I see you gentleman have a good understanding of how things work in our Republic. Which is why we keep the Republic station on Ozydna out of the loop until after the fact."

"Unbelievable, sometimes, who we work for," Doc said.

"Don't fool yourself, Doc," Chappy said. "It's all too believable."

***

The sky above the Truexx spaceport swarmed with craft in all stages of landing and departure. The port agent had the universal air of bureaucrats everywhere, clothed by the righteous cloak of the government regulations he enforced, leaving him unintimidated by men armed and armored who arrived in a deadly war machine.

"Will you be honoring the landing and access fees to the protectorate by credits or by apportionment of value from goods imported?" A thousand years on Ozydna had marked the descendants of the first humans its peculiar radiation resulting in a mutation that pigmented their skin bluish. He'd seen similar on other red sun worlds, but not as marked as it was on Ozydna.

"This is an official Republic vessel; we don't pay fees."

"Do you have diplomatic purpose and documentation?"

Hartenstein hadn't prepared for that. "No. Our purpose is not diplomatic."

"I'm sorry for your misunderstanding." He didn't look sorry at all. "Republic governmental vessels have favored status on Ozydna and the agreement assures the applicable discount, but only visits under diplomatic banner provide full fee exemption."

The agent produced a pad. "Representatives from many system governments come to Ozydna for reasons other than diplomacy. Official vessel, but here for purposes of—tourism," the agent synthesized their visit into a convenient category as he entered it on his pad. "Cargo?"

"None. We're here to acquire some."

Hartenstein and the crew chief accompanied the agent as he made a cursory inspection of the hold to ensure there was no cargo he could assess for tax. They waited patiently as the official calculated and presented the itemization. Ship tonnage fee. Landing area volume fee. Ozone and heat impact tax. Oxygen consumption fee for six humanoids. Cultural accommodation fee. If there was a discount, Hartenstein intuited the agent had discretion to assess other fees to offset any reduction the treaty was meant to provide.

The agent reacted to Hartenstein's shock as he read the number by throwing him a conciliatory bone. "Protectorate customs levies only a minor fee on departure. You will certainly do well by purchasing goods on our world."

A covert insertion would have been worth the risk. It was easier to pay the landing fee than fight it. The wide smile of the victor revealed even his teeth had a blue tint.

"Welcome to the Free and Benevolent Protectorate of Ozydna."

"Got it," Doc said with Chappy supervising over his shoulder. "Ten freight carriers. The trucking firm has tracers on their vehicles. Their destination." A topographic holo appeared and Doc turned from the console to direct icons onto the representation.

"That's only a hundred klicks from here," Chappy said. "Just outside the suburbs of one of the Truexx capital satellite cities."

"This looks solid. Good work. I'm sending Wolfhound Six the warning to release the assault package to move for the system. You two get us suitable transpo."

"Moving," Chappy and Doc said as one.

Hartenstein paced the duracrete wondering what was taking so long. This was a commercial spaceport. It should require minutes to either rent, or failing that, surreptitiously steal suitable transport. Unless of course, he'd been wrong about Doc and Chappy's skills. He hadn't grilled them about specific talents—Rex obviously thought highly of them—and they assured him Zeta's train-up cell was patterned after Dark Ops. He'd been content to leave an accounting of skills unexamined any further.

Patience thin, he was about to comm when something caught his eye. A ship exited a distant hanger, black fumes pouring from its exhausts, and assumed a tilting course toward this side of the port. It was aerodynamic as a brick. Transatmospheric cargo craft were universally blocky and not built for maneuverability. Trailing the rectangular body were long tail booms protruding stabilizer fins like some aquatic creature—the only feature streamlined on the entire craft. The tone of its repulsors pitched high and low as it lurched ahead, then as suddenly reversed, crossing between traffic of sleeker agile craft on the taxi lanes like a drunken jaywalker crossing a speeder racetrack.

The ship crossed the last of the lanes and made an unexpected course change and increased speed. It was headed straight for him. Hartenstein anticipated becoming a bug against the blunt nose and looked for an escape route. The ship swerved to circling the parking deck around the Excalibur, coming so close that its output field vibrated Hartenstein's teeth.

Excalibur's crew chief appeared next to him from thin air. He blew past Hartenstein at full speed, waving arms overhead, bellowing at Legion drill instructor volume, "Fifty meters! Fifty meters! Get the hell away from my aircraft."

The right seat of the transatmo's cockpit was empty. In the left, a wide white grin broke on the blue-skinned Ozydna pilot, who touched his brow with a single finger to acknowledge the protests of the furious crew chief. The ship lowered and his fears were confirmed. In the rear of the cockpit, crowded like foil-wrapped meat sticks packed tightly in a ration, were Doc and Chappy.

Hartenstein groaned as he clicked teeth to open L-comm.

"What the hell, you two? This couldn't have been simpler! I said suitable transport! That's a transatmo. It's only a hundred klicks to the site we want to check! We need a hover or a roller. How're we low viz in that thing?"

Chappy and Doc were front and center from the transpo before he could proceed to the next phase of his planned tirade to itemize the deficiencies defining how they'd failed the simple job delegated them.

"It's better than you think, sir," Doc said, abandoning Hartenstein's preferred moniker, no matter what had been agreed upon. It was a reasonable default when being ass-chewed by a colonel.

Chappy was quick to help. "Sir, it's our best option. These blue-boys are as civil and servile as a Vanu butler, but they're stubborn as a bull rindar about their rules."

The furious crew chief, Romper, wielded a knifehand at the pilot descending from the transatmo, grinning and bowing in supplication rather than with the prideful arrogance of the typical captain.

"Hey! You don't taxi within fifty meters of a grounded craft. That's law everywhere in the damn galaxy! Especially around a Republic military craft. That goes karking *double* when it's *my bird* we're talking about. Do you have some medical condition I should know about before I kick your ass?"

"So sorry, *tulok*," said the otherwise human man, skin as deeply blue as a child's candy-coated tongue. He continued his bobbing bows, his Standard broken and spoken in singsong fashion. He made a single deep bend as he turned open palms towards Doc and Chappy. "I was following direction of the *tulok-suu*. I am very best safe pilot."

The blue pilot's eyes led him cautiously up from his bow as he examined the crew chief cautiously, halting his gaze at the Legion crest on his name tag.

"You Legion, too, tulok?"

Romper squinted. "Damn right I'm a legionnaire. So?"

The blue man returned to making clipped bobbing bows. "Because legionnaire best deadly killer. They protect us. Crush our enemies. Scare whole galaxy. Feel no fear. Contain no remorse."

A corner of Romper's mouth lifted. "Hey, look, I already told you I was a legionnaire. You ain't gotta sell it to me. But, you still got an ass-chewing coming. Listen up."

Hartenstein tuned out the crew chief's salty tutorial to the blue pilot as Doc tagged back in to take some of the beating.

"Sir, no guests can operate any craft bigger than a skitter in Truexx. It's a union thing. We get close in the transatmo, we got us some skitter bikes in the back we can use to travel where we need. And if it turns out the packages aren't there and we gotta cover big distance fast to follow any intel we get, then we already have this local ride that won't draw the attention taking the Excalibur would. Rule 62, ya know, a backup for everything, gear or contingencies."

There it was again. Kel's rules. Hartenstein once more sidelined his amusement at setting Doc right about the origin and the originator of the rules he seemed to revere.

"All right, gentlemen, say we do need to go transatmospheric. The Excalibur can't spare a pilot to fly *that* thing. They have to be ready on standby if we call. And we sure as hell can't let that guy fly."

Chappy looked to Doc then back at the colonel, confusion broadcast in a way that not even a bucket could hide. "What do you mean, sir? I'll fly us." He'd said it as if it was the most natural conclusion in the world.

Hartenstein's surprise couldn't have been greater if he'd been told an unknown relative died and willed him a petting zoo. "Huh?"

"He sure will, Howler," Doc said with pride. "Chap's good. Zeta splits phase two operator training between slicers and flyers. I went data stream exploitation while Chap got three months of stick time."

Hartenstein's visor rested on Chappy in a way that caused him to cross his arms defensively. "None of us are the sky jockeys a Wolfhound aviator is, but we do okay, sir. I can't do raw nav calcs or deep grav-well piloting, but I can program jumps between close systems if they're stable. And atmospheric flight ain't much harder than piloting a mech, once you get used to it."

Hartenstein's incredulity wasn't completely resolved. "Zeta operators learn to fly?"

Doc's voice lilted. "You mean, *you* don't fly, Howler? I thought Dark Ops—" He didn't make the full statement, but Hartenstein heard it nonetheless.

I thought Dark Ops was the best.

Hartenstein ignored it. "Kudos. You can fly. What do we do about *him*?" He thumbed to indicate the groveling Ozydnan, still bobbing and smiling as the crew chief burned the blue-skinned pilot in place with more of his safety lecture.

Chappy snorted. "Far as he knows, he's flying us. Till he ain't. No sweat, boss."

Doc thrust an extended index finger and pinky, and jiggled his wrist like a spanner wrench. "That twarg-eater will cog on the realsō when I sup him." Chappy returned the gesture enthusiastically.

Hartenstein sighed. The two had adapted to the constraints of the local environment with flexibility, versatility, and logic. Better than he'd given them credit.

"Apologies. I should've trusted your judgment. It's going to take me a while to get up to speed with your methods. But, one thing—speak Standard I can understand. I don't know what realsbō or any of that other babble means," he said.

Chappy coughed into his fist. "Realsō. But, sure thing, sir."

"Howler," Hartenstein corrected, offering his call sign as yet more apology for his ire thinking their procurement ill conceived.

"Howler," Doc allowed, and picked up a share of the gear at Hartenstein's feet. The crew chief was no longer yelling but clearly hadn't abandoned his urge to do grievous bodily harm to the pilot, who patted the skin of his ship as if simultaneously blaming and excusing it for causing the incident.

"Ship is no harm meaning, tulok. I are giving best piloting. Safe always, like mother with child in buggy." Which of those the blue-skinned pilot was in the relationship wasn't clear.

Chappy picked up the last of the equipment. "I want to right seat this thing some on the trip out so if I do have to fly it, I won't be cold on the stick." The pilot was grasping for the crew chief's hand, who snatched it away from the blue man's puckering lips.

"Then it's absolutely time to go," Doc said. "Because blue-boy's about to get body slammed."

09

"I am master twenty years," the pilot said to Chappy after powering down. "You are sure-sure on stick, tulok. Someday, you come work-fly Ozydna, haha!"

"Thanks, Captain Palkifor," Chappy said, twisting his mass out of the narrow right seat to stand.

"I wait here for cargo?"

"Yeah, you wait here," Chappy said, backing down the aisle to extricate from the cockpit.

"After take on load, more new place go-go? You not say yet."

"I'll let you know."

Captain Palkifor patted the control panel gently. "No matter. We yours one week." It was the shortest time period for which they could contract the ship, made clear that if they were done sooner, there would be no refund for the unused time.

"Captain, you might as well get some shut-eye. May be awhile before we're back."

The pilot reclined his seat and grinned. "Ah, tulok-Chappy! You know respect. Not like many guest. Most nice of you. Late the hour. Make flight checklist after rest. Ready-ready again lift when you say, tulok." He folded arms, closed eyes, and almost immediately his nostrils made two-tone flute music, sharp whistles in, flat ones back out.

"Wow. You go lights-out as fast as a leej. I wish you dreams of blue women, ya goofball."

The three leejes drew no attention on the streets and after only a few detours, Doc found the location he wanted. The roof was sharp and unsuitable as an observation post, but as the tallest building in the dense urban quarter, if they could find a suitable spot high enough, they should be able to get eyes on their target.

Doc let a drone lead them cautiously on a route through the mainly vacant building to the top floor and an empty suite holding dusty crates and broken furniture. A single narrow window faced the plain, allowing only two of them to crowd for a view of the distant landscape. There was nothing but open ground for klicks around the target, a single spur road leading to the strange complex from a distant highway.

Doc checked the distance in his HUD. "Five klicks and some change as the drone flies." He released the sentinel drone and stepped back to allow the colonel his place at the window. All kept thoughts to themselves as they watched in their HUDs. It was easy to be overwhelmed by so much information, both visual and technical. To the experienced eye, the dazzling colors of the feed, richer than daylight, meant it was dark night the drone flew through. "I'll concentrate on the EM if you keep on the gross viz," Doc asked his partner.

"Rog," Chap replied softly.

The main structure of the compound lay in a bowl excavated to leave high berms as a barrier to ground observation. In the bowl was a high walled quadrangle with a tower at each of the corners. The single road channeled through the earthen walls ended in an entrance glowing with the signature of a high energy barrier.

"That just screams 'prison,' don't it?" Chappy commented.

"It doesn't exist as far as the local records show," Doc said. "Hmm. There's a detection grid running." The drone hung stationary a kilometer from the target and continued gathering data. "The bands they're running won't see the sentinel. I'm going to ease in for a closer look."

What had been glowing gray blobs indicating the presence of multiple persons within the towers now resolved into distinct shapes and took on a purple hue. Few species had such a signature in the thermal spectra, none of them human. The image further refined and magnified. The peaked carapaces of their thoraxes and clawed terminal appendages left no ambiguity as to the identity of the species.

"I count eight Ootari. Warrior-caste," Chappy said. "And they got pulse-cooled heavy blasters. Those towers have faceted energy shielding. That'll defeat just about anything short of the main gun on a Magnus grav tank. They're serious about what they're guarding. We got our jackpot, Howler."

Hartenstein stayed silent as he let the two talk it out.

"Creeping on them ourselves is right out," Doc said matter-of-factly. "Even if they had no detection grid running. Ootari see multi-spectral. Mimetic camo signals bad intentions—worse than if we just strolled up, waving at 'em like lost tourists."

"Not many people know that about Ootari," Hartenstein said.

Chappy clucked. "We know bugs. They didn't build that compound. Everything they build's always a dead giveaway from all the crazy angles they use—some kinda insect thing. Means they're renters here and the layout will be typical human-centric."

"Unless they dug the substructure themselves," Doc added. "They do love to tunnel mazes. Frelling bugs."

The two voiced Hartenstein's exact thoughts as they formed, and it was further antidote for the toxin of his prior crisis of confidence in the pair. Like a queasy stomach making you regret eating from a street vendor stall, his had been warning the two might just make him sick from more screwups. Now, his gut was back to a concrete-solid intuition that Doc and Chappy were pros.

"Ootari and Hool think we're loose and they're tight," Doc said. "Well, I got something'll tighten them all the way down to their waste ejection ports. I'm launching micros."

"Can we risk an active feed to watch live, or should you let 'em collect autonomously and bring it back?" Chappy asked.

Doc considered. "Clock's running and that'll take too long. They can't detect L-comm band transmission—and they won't see the micros, especially if I E-X-E the decision program as they search. I'm risking it. Now, quiet and lemme work, Chap."

The micro drones dropped from the much larger sentinel, hovering on station and monitoring the entirety of the compound from above. New windows opened in their HUDs. The micro drones—the designation boastful as they were closer to small insects in size—dropped into the central courtyard. Doc enlarged the view from one paused at a door on the inner wall of the courtyard. It traced a rectangular path around the durasteel seam. "No EM output, no external mechanicals. There's nothing I can slice into. That portal's manually controlled from the interior. I'll keep looking."

Chappy grunted. "I know all I need to know, Howler. It'll take the assault group a couple of hours to hit orbit. I say you call 'em down. By that time, Doc'll have the layout sussed down to the last centimeter. It'll be plunk for the boys."

Hartenstein didn't ask for a translation. "Agreed. It's enough to get the ball rolling." He clicked and sent the prepared L-comm burst. He waited only a few seconds before receiving one back. *Tango-Two*, appeared in script. "The task force'll hit the orbital hold point and wait for our release." When they green-lit the assault, it would be mere minutes until the compound was swarmed by assault craft and dropping Wolfhounds by the score.

Chappy's return to proper verbiage seemed a sign of anxiety. "The grid on the target's solid, and the lead Talons'll have our pathfinder beacon as a backup. Zero worries about a no-lag drop direct on the site. It's relying on the sentinel that worries me, Howler. When we let it light those towers with targeting beams, their detection grid can't help but alert to it. They knock that drone out, we got no backup. And you know what that means."

Hartenstein did. "If we lose a precise paint on those towers, the Talons may end up flattening the place."

For a simple assault, such imprecision wouldn't matter. But this was a hostage rescue. From their current observation point, they weren't close enough to mark the targets with the extreme precision the Talons would need to avoid collateral damage.

Hartenstein humphed. "Then we have to get close enough to mark those targets for the Talons."

Chappy voiced the other alternative. "Or, we take them out ourselves."

"The timing's the problem," Hartenstein said.

"I got us inside," Doc exclaimed. Where he'd found access, Hartenstein had missed during his and Chappy's discussion.

With rapt attention, they watched as Doc managed the micro drone's path through the interior, pausing to expand several holo displays around him.

"Chap, work the sniffer for me."

Hartenstein didn't have this level of expertise so he didn't offer help. The micro drones traveled at ceiling level where they would avoid the most attention, slowing only when an Ootari appeared. A holo developed above them and in a few minutes, the first level of corridors and rooms was a complete map. The anticipation that prison cells packed with humans and labs full of icy glowing Hool would appear went unfulfilled.

Chappy blurted, "Doc! Sniffer's got fresh human DNA—lots of it. And Hool! I got trace on one, no, two pincushions!"

"Payday coming, Howler," Doc said coolly without breaking his trance on the multiple drone feeds. "Moving to sub-levels."

"Doc, I need you to check this," Chappy said. "The sniffer's giving me strange readings. Strong DNA degradation, it says."

"Wait one, Chap," Doc said as he opened a new holo in a position of superseding the others floating in front of him.

"There!" Hartenstein blurted. One of the feeds went dark, then brightened as the drone creeped from whatever access it had traveled to reach the new space. Humans packed cruelly tight to each other like stim sticks in a carton. Ootari claws pushed crackling stun batons against human flesh, causing victims to collapse in tetanus, forcing others to trample the victims or suffer the same pain themselves. Cramming the last into the space too restrictive for life, a door sealed as the guards pulled back, a faint millimeter of space returning with their exit.

"The drone came out in a cell," Doc said. "Oh no! Just look at them!" Sunken, lifeless eyes focused on nothing. Patches of bare scalp stood out like blight on a lawn. Naked bodies wept sickly exudates from open sores.

The view flared white, then failed to return.

Horrified, Chappy said, "That's what the sniffer was reading—disintegrated DNA! They fried them! It's a death chamber!" His words chilled Hartenstein through his armor.

Doc worked furiously. "Here it is." A new window showed the exterior of the horror show they'd just witnessed panning slowly in all directions. Ootari herded and dragged scraggly humans by ones and twos up and down hallways, past subjects lashed to tables or floating in cylinders of viscous fluid, strange devices glowing from the walls. A Hool sat at a slab, manipulating a holo above a human. Laser scalpels dissected the subject—alive— jerking and twitching with each slice.

Hartenstein recoiled from the holo. "We go! Now!"

***

Quint followed the script he'd read from for his first passage on the *Supreme.* He appeared in the wardroom at off hours to collect one of the prepared trays meant for crew on irregular shifts, retreating to his cabin for a reclusive meal with the haste of a mouse scurrying for his hole with stolen table scraps.

Until Kel witnessed one significant anomaly in Quint's pattern. Remarkable because it brought the recluse in contact with the only other person on the ship competing for the title of least gregarious.

Kel was sliding into the wardroom to grab a sandwich to wolf on the fly. He had five minutes after a shift monitoring the jump drive before he was due to help out in environmental—scrubbers needed constant maintenance and tuning—and caught himself mid-step into the hatch. Cormac and Quint were huddled backs to him at one of the tiny corner tables in close conversation, like conspirators settling on a story before the cops came.

Before either saw him, he reversed direction. He munched the protein bar that always rode in his cargo pocket as a contingency, wondering what it was that personalities as oil and water as those two had found in common. He mentioned the incident to Tara that evening. Her response caught him off guard.

"Let's have Quint here for kaff."

"That's how you want to spend our first free shift together?" Tonight's third shift was their first together that wasn't a sleep cycle for one or both. Since lifting they'd had little time for more than a quick kiss as they brushed, one coming while the other was going. He suspected

Sheila'd scheduled things to keep them apart as much as possible, but his initial anxiety about Tara lifting with them was forgotten, as was hers.

Rex had said no more secrets.

Rex's permission for him to share with Tara what he chose was stunning. The few hours of waking time together Kel had dedicated to spilling everything about what he was doing, and why. Rather than cause Tara grief, it brought her peace.

"Secret weapons, secret enemies, secret societies... I don't need to hear any more," she said. "You'll do what it is you do, and I'll help if I can, even it's just staying well out of the way."

She was truly one in a billion.

Tara explained why she wanted Quint to be third wheel on their date night. "I want to know what Quint meant. Aren't you curious? Everyone else is." The air still buzzed with talk about how Quint's anti-Republic outburst had won Cormac over. Eventually, Kel was going to corner Quint and pry it from him. This was maybe not the time of his choosing, but it was for Tara.

"I am curious. But even if you can coax that rodent out of his hole, I doubt he'll talk that much, but, okay. Give him a try."

She struck a provocative pose and blew him a kiss. "I'm irresistible."

Kel smirked. "I seem to remember holding up against your powers of persuasion that very first time you knocked on my cabin door." His improbable and serendipitous collision with the Yomiuri family had been highlighted by a late-night visit from a teenage Tara. Her unexpected appearance had ignited two contrary but thrilling mental images, the stronger being that of her father pushing Kel out of an airlock to suck the freeze of deep space.

"I was sixteen." She winked. "I've learned a lot since then."

"No argument. I've never asked, but what the hell did you think was going to happen if I let you into my cabin that night?"

Her face scrunched in dread of something awful on the way, like watching a recruit with carbon solvent on his hands use the bathroom before washing.

"What?" he coaxed.

She relented. "I s'pose it's time I told you. It was my mother's idea to go to you that night."

Kel's jaw dropped. "Impossible! Maureen *wanted* you to, to... what if, you know... the worst had happened?"

"If we'd gotten to know each other, and I decided that's what I wanted, a baby would've been wonderful."

Kel's perception of the event put him in a flat spin beneath a malfunctioning parachute canopy. She smiled with condescension. "My big Dark Ops legionnaire who's been everywhere and done everything, haven't you ever noticed how much diversity there is in our children? Especially when almost all of us are either Sullivan or Yomiuri?"

"Well, sure, but..." He had to pause as he considered. He'd rarely seen both parents and children together at the same time to look for resemblances between offspring and mother or father. Every child needed some time with dirt between their toes, and that meant one or both parents often had to be absent in a merchant shipping clan.

Tara became very matter-of-fact. "There are practicalities to being part of a colony like ours. Genetic monogamy's a dead-end for a gene pool as limited as ours. If a potential father with new alleles is good stock, well, it's always the woman's choice—and one everyone supports, even encourages. Children are a gift, and genes don't determine who's loved and wanted. Even most married couples choose donor gametes after a natural conception or two."

Kel put a hand to forehead, expecting a fever to match his boiling thoughts. "You're blowing my mind right now. You're saying your mom saw me as good breeding material, and sent you to get knocked up just to bring new blood into the family gene pool? That you'd have raised a child I fathered... without me?"

She laughed. "Well, it wasn't strictly like that, but it was a special opportunity. I've wanted children ever since I can remember. And I wanted your children from almost the first moment I got to know you."

"Oba, Tara! You were a little girl!"

"Hardly, Kel. I was already a woman, no matter how you thought of me then."

He tried to unravel what seemed a contradiction. "Wait a minute, then why haven't you let the medcomp reverse your fertility freeze already?"

"Because, that night when you sent me away, it only made me more convinced you were the partner I wanted forever. When I told my mom what happened and what I thought it meant, she supported me taking a chance at making a traditional family with you—the same as they gave me and my brother."

"Your dad was in on it, too?"

"Oh, not *that* night! But Mom let him in on it, later."

How many secrets were there in the galaxy? Was he really so naïve? "I can't believe I'm just learning that all this was going on behind the scenes."

She reached out to him. "We have something some others in this family don't have—a choice. When we're finished with the separations, we're going to have babies. Lots of them. We can have natural children *and* raise them together. Your genes mean we don't have to worry. And as long as our progeny are careful in their choices, they can partner within the colony and have natural genetic children. And if they choose to bring in more outside genes, even better."

Kel was still shocked. "I'm going to have a talk with your mom someday. Anything else I don't know about the family I married into?"

"Just that you're expected to knock up as many women in the colony as you can."

He gulped.

She burst out laughing. "Gotcha!"

That was twice his heart had been stopped by someone he trusted like no other—first Poul, now Tara. "Cruel, Tara, cruel. Poul's rubbed off on you."

10

Hartenstein crashed out of the room, disregarding the stairs to leap landing by landing down to the street. Doc and Chappy were chasing after Hartenstein on their own skitter bikes, mere seconds behind after recovering gear before following.

"I'm going to need your deadnet, Chap. You have to fly."

"It's in my day pack, Doc. You'll need the specials off my bandolier for a blind cave scrum."

"What's that?" Hartenstein asked from the lead, leaning hard to miss a drunken pedestrian on an uneven course across the pitch-black street. The rush of the bike spun him like a dancer's pirouette, its wake barely cleared when two more bullets whizzed at him from the dark, splitting to either side, completing the challenge to the man's weakened equilibrium, his lopsided centrifugal movement collapsing like a top at the end of its spin.

"He'll remember to look both ways next time," Chappy muttered. They broke from the dense urban sector to arrive at the small loading field and the waiting transatmo.

Hartenstein gave full reverse thrust to make the bike stand on its front repulsor dish. "I asked you what a blind cave scrum is," he said midair, using the momentum to propel his leap, landing alongside the ship. He dashed to the pax access and punched the access panel. His question went unanswered as the two kept up their discussion, their bikes whining to a smooth and distinctly different halt than he'd chosen.

"I'll take the heat off for your arrival, Chap," Doc said, as he blasted past Hartenstein and into the ship, disappearing aft for the cargo bay.

"What am I, a doorman? One of you answer me."

Captain Palkifor appeared from the cockpit, brushing sleep from eyes bloodshot on blue. "Hulla-bullah? Time to go?"

"Time for you to go, buddy." Chappy reached up through the portal to grab handfuls of flight suit and snatched the captain from the ship.

"Aiyeee!" the pilot screamed. "My bad-bad I teach you stick! Hijack! Crime! Assault on me!"

Doc sprang from the fuselage with armfuls held to his chest. The ground shook with the weight of a man in full armor carrying heavy ordnance, causing the pilot to shriek and then yell in all directions.

"Helpa! Helpa! Hijack me. Aiyeee!"

Chappy put a single finger to the man's nose, silencing him. "When I woke up this morning, I promised myself I wasn't going to kill anyone who absolutely didn't need it. Are you feeling needy?"

The captain turtled his neck between his shoulders and made meek. "I no should teach you stick. Not nice-nice steal my ship."

"Just shut up. You'll get it back."

Doc was on the nearest bike and speeding away. "I'll holler when I'm ready, Chap. Get airborne and hold."

"Roger, Doc. Good luck."

Hartenstein surrendered to ignorance and followed Chappy into the ship. As he lowered the hatch, the pilot thrust his head through, risking decapitation if the sensors failed. No such luck. The descending hatch halted.

"Guests no operate, only union, you no guests! You pirates! We call Republic. They kill you for this!"

Hartenstein put a palm on the blue face, and shoved. "I am the Republic." The hatch finished sealing. "What the Republic's supposed to be, anyway."

In the cockpit he bent to rest an elbow on the back of the left seat. "Hold on," Chappy warned as the ship rose and rotated, smoothly and without the turbulence his warning had promised.

Hartenstein said, "Can you do anything fancier than taxi around?"

"Late, late, and too late for that question, boss. Doc, where you at?"

"Almost there. Another couple minutes I'll be through the city. When you're set, I'll be lined up and ready to go for it."

"What's he doing, Chap?" Hartenstein asked, still not clear on what the two had planned. "It's past time I know. What's this blind cave thing?"

They set off and Chappy aimed them for a dense collection of skyscrapers. "Sorry, Howler. Light speed op tempo's kinda our thing. Doc's draped himself and his bike with both our sniper deadnets. It should stealth him from their detection grid. Should. Their bug eyes'll see him, but he's gonna come at 'em so fast, they'll have to shoot before they can think. He's just got to get about four hundred meters from those walls to bloop in as many specials from his launcher as he can. Then, we're up."

Specials described many kinds of ordnance, all especially nasty, everything from thermobarics to nukes. "What specials?"

"Dazzlers. But these also have rod burners."

Hartenstein's eyes widened. Dazzlers sent out an EMP that fried any equipment not heavily shielded, but rod burners? They were—illegal. "Rod burners are banned!"

"That's why we make 'em ourselves. Blinding weapons are universally outlawed by every convention. So's slavery and human experimentation. If anyone's left alive, they can file a complaint with the House of Reason. We gotta be alive to care."

Chappy sucked wet air through clenched teeth. An apartment building popped out behind a much taller structure as the bulky ship suffered through a long arcing bank. Windows glowed opaque through drapes, parting to reveal sleepy residents resurrecting to life to see what storm approached. Hartenstein clenched every muscle, but the sounds and forces of the certain crash disappeared down the path of possibilities unrealized. He was sure when the time came, he'd find there would be a paint scrape down the right tail boom from a rub with one of the patio decks.

Chappy clucked to himself, "Not even close. I got you solid on my plot now, Doc. I still got a screen of buildings between us and the compound. When you kick it off, I'll give it up to make our own run straight at them. That'll buy you some time."

"Rog. See you on the inside, Chap."

Chappy punched a panel, it flashed orange, and he hit the override to the tailgate lock. "Back of the bird's open, Howler. Get yourself set. Hope you didn't forget how to run a hypervel launcher. We might luck out and Doc's shots blind all of them, but there could still be a lot of heavy blaster coming our way. Don't fall out when I pitch her ass-end around."

"Sket!" Hartenstein said, cursing in more ways he'd forgotten as he spun on his heels to rush aft. Repulsors revved and the burst of acceleration was a giant hand at his back pushing him along like an encouraging friend.

The Longbow hypervelocity launcher was in its case. Lighter than a Stone blaster but more awkward for its length, its five rounds of rail-accelerated warheads were medicine for most anything less dense than the cold star mined for the neutronium that tipped the micro missiles. He slapped the locks off and grabbed the balance point of the tube just behind the control unit.

The weapon was as long as he was tall. He cradled it with one arm and started for the open tailgate, just when the deck took a sharp roll.

"Hang on, Howler," Chappy yelled. "They know we're coming now! That blast was close. Doc's gotta launch soon or we're cooked. He just launched. Get ready!"

He leaned back to stop from toppling off the last deck plate and down the lowered tailgate, grabbing onto the last spar to keep from becoming a part of the blurry landscape rushing below. He braced. The reverse thrust would be coming any second.

The launcher's command menu and reticle appeared in the central vision of his HUD. He keyed the charge cell to power the rail coils. It would overheat and seize to uselessness if he didn't discharge a missile in the next two minutes. By that time, he'd have launched the first of the Longbow's warheads, or he'd have timed things badly. A wasted missile would be the last of his concerns.

"They can't take it out of your pay if you're dead—that's a rule." He heard the words in the Spilursan drawl of his first fire team leader. He was very far from the "then" that was practically a dream now. But in all the years since, he'd realized that no matter how much he learned, all he ever really needed to know, he'd learned in the Legion kindergarten that was his first squad.

Chappy's warning to brace came with their deceleration. He pushed rearward through the soles of his boots, leaned back, and tightened his handhold, picturing the bar fracturing like bones he snapped as easily as dry twigs when his younger grip was challenged. If the handhold did crush to his grip, he'd topple out into the dark wind, his pride at past physical prowess the consolation prize for being an idiot.

"Ass-end coming around, Howler. Nail 'em."

The compound rotated into view a few hundred meters away and the deck leveled. Even with the shielding of his HUD, he squinted from the intensity of the searing light. Doc had placed the specials with perfection. Radiating from three distinct spreads in the courtyard, suns burned, dimming, but not dimmed. The gunners manning the heavy blasters in all four towers were blind. He knew, because beams of dense plasma shot out wildly in random directions, none yet aimed at him.

Standing center of the open cargo bay, he was the lone spectator to a grand performance, the stage lit for his entertainment alone. The destruction coming by his hand filled him with joyful anticipation.

Both hands full of launcher, he settled the reticle on a tower. Before he could get a lock, the ship lurched and Chappy's curses assaulted his ear. The nose rose, the twin booms behind the cargo compartment dipped low, and the deck became an inflatable raft riding atop a wave, rushing for shore to crash into the rocky beach of the nearing compound.

The booms pitched up, and he raised the launcher. It was now or never. The reticle bounced erratically and as it moved to cross the nearest tower, he fired, hoping for the best. The hypervel missile reached the target as instantaneously as thought, the explosion blinding like another rod burner. His HUD went totally black.

The deck rose and he just knew this time he would be tossed into emptiness for a very short freefall, his HUD coming back on line just in time to see the ground meet him face-first. He fell solidly sideways onto the deck. As if the smack of his bucket against hard durasteel had something to do with it, his vision returned. With a tilted view of the world, he oriented for a brief second.

One tower was gone. He was on a knee, raising the Longbow for a second shot, when the tower he aimed at exploded in spectacular yellow fire. A red streak leading from the burning tower stolen from him burned an afterimage in his retina. It meant that Doc was alive and bringing the fight with his Stone.

Bolts from the remaining towers continued to pierce the night sky in all directions. He shifted to another as a lucky blast found the horizontal stabilizer between the twin booms, and a shower of sparks and shrapnel knocked him onto his back. He flipped prone to see the smoke pole resting at the forward bulkhead and scrambled for it on all fours like an animal.

A forgotten voice came to his ear.

"Coming on station, clear the airspace." It was the Excalibur pilot, Slabside.

Out the open bay, a tail boom wagged like an animal's tail through a screen of raining sparks. A purple flash came from above, the Excalibur's main gun, the path of the blast nearly vertical, and a third tower came down on itself like an imploding silo.

The co-pilot's voice came in. "Chappy, clear the airspace or we can't get a shot on that last tower."

Slabside's voice was calm and analytic. "I know a frozen stick when I see one. Bank us right, Drizzy, I'll take the shot." The last remaining tower held a motivated—but blind—Ootari, firing in random directions like the epicenter of a lightning storm.

"Whoa. Whoa. WHOA!" Chappy hollered. Gone was the grace under fire they'd heard from the angels above them.

Hartenstein was thrown against the fuselage, landing against a porthole and sticking to it like a magnet, pinned by gravity. The ship slid over the compound wall, hurtling broadside at the last tower. The individual blocks grew distinct at an alarming rate. Mimicking one of the pill bugs that fascinated him as a boy, he curled into a tight ball. This was going to hurt.

Crash!

Like a marble in a drum rolled down a hill, he bounced around the cabin. The air crushed from his lungs with the last great collision, and he went black. He came to with the realization that if the tumultuous movement was done, they must be on the ground. Why they hadn't yet exploded, puzzled him. Every part of his body screamed from being stretched worse than a bout of groundwork wrestling with Nail.

Hands pulled him upright. "Get up, Howler." Chappy pushed a K-17 into his hands. "We gotta bounce; this thing's on fire."

"I'm good," Hartenstein said reflexively, but he wasn't. He shook off his fog as he followed Chappy through the wreckage and into an open sky. The reticle in his HUD flashed, indicating his K-17 was linked and hot.

"Ground team, we're inbound to assist recovery," Slabside said on the all-channels.

"Negative, Excalibur." It was Doc. "I have eyes on the team. They're clear of the crash. Remain on station. Keep anyone coming this way off us, how copy?"

"Copy. Wilco," came the reply. The Excalibur circled tightly above.

There'd been some missing time, but Hartenstein was clear now. They'd crashed outside just beyond the berm surrounding the compound. Where towers had rained blaster fire were neither the towers nor the blasts—only flames. Doc stood in the light of their flickering, shouldering the Stone. The main gate exploded in white and purple plasma fury.

Hartenstein turned his face to shield him from another fuzz-out in his HUD. Glancing rearward, he paused to marvel. Using the ship like a battering ram against the last tower had definitely voided its warranty. The mountain of burning trash behind him bore no resemblance to the transatmo it had recently been. Had he come from inside that mess?

He turned back to see Chappy at Doc's side, heading together into the burning maw of the main gate. He set off for them, fighting the viscous sludge in his suit. The cushion melted and relinquished the fight against his motion with a few more steps. He'd been a young sergeant the last time shock foam had deployed to keep him from being turned into canned tomato paste.

Byblos suddenly seemed like a pleasant vacation.

Chappy and Doc were firing into the courtyard. He dashed to Chappy's shoulder and brought his K-17 to bear. Across the rubble strewn and burning courtyard, Ootari lay piled where they fell defending the main entrance to the inner ring.

"You good, Howler?" Doc asked.

"Never better. Let's do work."

They glided through the wrecked gates and weaved through the smoldering obstacle course in the courtyard, headed for the welcome mat of dead Ootari. Stepping around and over dead bugs, the three entered as one. Hartenstein pushed to clear the left corner. A down but not out Ootari was rising at his feet. Efficiency drove his actions. He raised a foot and slammed it down onto the back of its carapace, pushing the bug down onto its peaked chest. With explosive force, he thrust down a second time, punching his foot through the shell as if crushing a child's toy. He withdrew his foot, dripping thick green ichor and yellow organs.

Doc gestured down a passage with his rifle. "That way's blocked by a dropped tower."

Chappy likewise thrust his rifle barrel in front of him. "We go this way."

The passage dropped to a ramp. Doc halted. "Howler, pull those two smokers off my back and toss 'em."

Hartenstein grabbed the globes and, one after the other, tossed them ahead with an underhanded lob. The pair of smooth orbs bounced once, split in midair along their equators to protrude a ridge and stuck unnaturally to the ground on landing. They stayed frozen for an instant before coming awake to race away by their central wheel, billowing trails of smoke.

"Will the sleeper affect anyone but the humans?" Hartenstein asked.

Chappy's back was to them, watching the rear. "Nah. That's the beauty. It'll get any human out of our way so anyone left standing is clear to grease."

Doc stared into space, following the progress of the feed in his HUD. "And the smokers are pumping out a snowstorm, too. Not even a bug can see through that. Another minute and it'll be a blindman's bluff for anyone but us. Hmm. Drones show map complete."

Hartenstein diverted attention to focus on the window in his HUD. Cell after cell, room after room, the nano-drones had mapped and marked. Humans were tiny green dots. Non-humans, red triangles.

"It's just the one sub-level. Let's roll," Chappy said. They all stepped off as one.

Hallways, intersections, corners—like all terrain, they serve the one who best knows how to use them to advantage.

The first Ootari stood alone, several humans dropped unconscious below his barbed legs and backward bending knees. It swiveled from side to side, extending claws to find what it could no longer see from the end of its faceted eye stalks. Its massive thorax invited blaster fire.

They bypassed more humans rendered unconscious, lying in death-like repose from the sleep gas. It was an indignity little different from the others forced upon these unfortunate souls. And they were the ones guilty for it—doing harm to the very people they came to save. Right now, some might be drawing their last suffocating breaths. It had been a split-second decision and the best of only bad options and still, the consequences of their choice to sleep the prisoners had to be ignored.

Until the killing was done.

Stunners, low velocity bounce rounds, and their surging momentum—a weapon they wielded like no other force in the galaxy—overwhelmed opponents accustomed only to dominating helpless creatures.

"Grand central ahead," Chappy said. It was the end of the main corridor and the cul-de-sac housing all the grisly scenes that had unhesitatingly driven them to unleash their violence without hesitation.

Doc pointed his muzzle at a portal. "Two fish—in *that* room." What they saw was a reconstruction of the environment they'd rendered blind to any eye—but not to their HUDs. Outlines defined the shapes, and colors filled them by their heat and radiations. Hartenstein blinked hard three times to return to an unaugmented view and waved a hand to part the thinning cloud of silvery particles and smoke. The air on the other side of the observation window was clear.

Chappy snapped his blaster level. "Hool!"

A spiny agnathian stared back at them. The Hool twitched. As though pulled taut in all directions by invisible tethers, it stretched its limbs wide, then dropped them like a marionette with cut strings. Hartenstein watched its spasms diminish before becoming still—a familiar sight but not a welcome one. Partially concealed behind the base of a clear cylinder where a dissected human specimen floated, another Hool lay in the telltale rigor of self-envenomation.

"They got off easy," Chappy said. "I hate Hool."

Hartenstein wanted in there. "Do we have a micro inside that lab?"

"No," Doc said. "They're looking outside-in, same as us. Sucker must be sealed tight."

"Breach it?" Chappy asked.

Hartenstein considered. It felt wrong not to enter. "So we have no sniffer in there to tell us if..."

Doc shook his head. "No. But if there's stuff in there like what they unleashed on Victrix, I don't know if the sniffers could detect it. That team on Psydon that found the first lab must've had very, very specialized detectors. We got nothing like that till the task force gets here."

Chappy blew out a disgusted breath. "There could be something in the air around us right now."

Hartenstein checked the mission chrono, and in disbelief checked it again. A scant thirty-two minutes had elapsed since they'd preempted the Wolfhound assault with their own. And what had occurred in that time was the longest year of his life. "We can't help what we can't help. We leave the lab for the techs, then."

Doc let his K-17 snap to his chest. "Until they do, we got work. Some of these people may be smothering. Howler, the sleep agent's gonna have 'em all down for Oba only knows how long. We need medics down here with the first wave."

Hartenstein clicked teeth to comm the Excalibur. "Slabside, target's secure. Run deconfliction with the task force and prioritize us a med response for the prisoners. "

"Roger, sir. We've been monitoring. We're solid outside. We've menaced away a ground party responding from the city—but there's a med wagon with them. Should we let them in to assist?"

"Negative. Anyone not sealed tight needs to stay back."

"Understood."

They raced to pull bodies from cells holding avalanches of unconscious flesh, carrying as many as they each could out of the dungeon to deposit them on whatever ground in the courtyard held spaces not burning.

Chappy carried three bodies in his arms like cordwood, holding them until Doc had taken the last and straightened from folding a child-like woman onto her side and into the recovery position. She reminded Hartenstein of another.

"It's a miracle they're all breathing," Doc said.

"That's the last," Chappy said. "I'll make another sweep to be sure."

"Most of these look pretty healthy, Howler. I mean, better than the ones we saw—you know. I guess these folks hadn't gotten the worst of what was waiting for them. Yet."

Hartenstein sighed. "I count 119 we brought out." The tally begged him to do the math, subtracting that from the number they should have saved. He ignored the arithmetic. Instead he checked his chrono and worked a different problem while looking to the sky. "Shouldn't be long."

Chappy reappeared. "No one left down there." He made tiny nods as though approving the destruction around them. "Not bad."

Hartenstein choked. "Are you messing with me, Chappy?"

Chappy stiffened. "Whatcha mean, Howler? It wasn't perfect, but look what we pulled off. The three of us!"

"Why d'you let us get so damn close to the target? And crashing into that tower? I thought you said you could fly? We should be dead, Sergeant."

Hartenstein realized he'd unconsciously revived the colonel-to-sergeant relationship, but Chappy was neither defensive nor subordinate. "Well, Howler, it's like I said. I'm no Talon pilot. And that sure as sket wasn't no Talon. Dang thing can't hold a hover, the repulsor thrust lags something terrible, but I made do, even after a brush or two by those heavy blasters. And I hit that tower juuuust right. Not bad in the moment, if I do say so myself. "

Hartenstein did a double take. "Wait a minute—you make it sound like you crashed us into that tower on purpose instead of on accident."

Chappy took an extra second before answering. "Which would impress you more?"

Being tongue-tied was a first for Hartenstein. Chappy carried on.

"We got a saying in Zeta—it's results that count. In fact, when we get home, I'm adding that one to that list Doc loves so much."

"By the way, Howler," Doc said. "I never heard you howl once. I got a better handle for you. Bug Stomper!"

"Stomper," Chappy said with finality. Hartenstein watched the pair as they shared the strange hand gesture with each other. He'd gotten what he wanted. Chappy and Doc were completely comfortable treating him like a teammate—no more, no less.

"What's that thing you're doing?"

Doc made the gesture again, rotating his wrist rapidly to make his thumb and pinky trace back and forth horizontally. "It's a Z. For Zeta. Get it?"

Layer on layer of L-comm traffic was followed by an airspace equally layered with Talons and landers, turning the sky into a Pthalo party cove jammed with yachts.

"Look alive!" Doc said. Marching toward them was a spread of Zeta commandos and at their center, a pair of leejes who did not appear as though they needed any kind of protective cordon. Armor matched physiques, and both were imposing, even among those surrounding them.

"I knew Captain Malik would be bringing the crew," Chappy said. "But I didn't figure General Airani was coming."

The ring halted to put them at center with the two leaders. The five legionnaires faced each other and mutually snapped to attention. General Airani held his salute in front of Hartenstein. "Sir, it's an honor to see you."

Hartenstein dropped his salute first, as though he were the senior. "General, the honor's entirely mine." The two braced shoulders. "Good to see you, Topper."

"Let's talk, Howler."

Captain Malik coughed. "C'mon, you two. No more goldbricking. Show us where the work is." As they stepped off together, the captain tapped the ear of his bucket for Doc and Chappy to join him on the private channel.

"What's the story, boys? Is that *the* Hartenstein? That's gotta be the biggest damn leej I've ever seen! Wolfhound Six called him *sir!*"

Doc cast a glance back. Howler and the general were alone. Howler's thumb jabbed over his shoulder in their direction.

"Sket! Chappy! Howler's talking to the general about us."

Captain Malik laughed. "Someday you two will run out of ass to chew. What'd you do now?"

The prospect made Chappy chuckle. "Ah, you know, sir. Just solved problems."

Hartenstein and General Airani continued speaking as a containment dome raised around the compound like a stasis field over a bakery cake. "How'd those two do, Howler?"

Hartenstein felt a deep ache, spreading from his joints into his spine, rising to his head as it throbbed in the slow beats of a bass drum. He checked the med tracker in his HUD. In the last few hours he'd popped twice the max allowable number of boost tabs.

"Topper, I'm going to say something I've never said to anyone in my life. Take me to the nearest medcomp. Truth is, I'm too old for this." He thumbed over his shoulder at his new teammates.

"Those two broke me."

11

Still reeling from Tara's revelation—doubtful she could pull the recluse Quint from his cave—Kel made the brew while thinking about Quint's righteousness declaring the Republic both thief and liar—as if he'd been the first person to ever come to such a conclusion about the House of Reason. Whatever sparked his rage, it couldn't be worse than anything Kel already knew about the political class and what they did to maintain power.

The door opened to the Quint he was accustomed to seeing: timid and unsure, resisting Tara's hand on his elbow—just for an instant—to check that it was in fact just Kel and that it was in fact just a stateroom, before succumbing to her invitation. At some level, he was still untrusting of them and the environment. No matter Tara had a naturally gentle touch to which she'd added a lot of training, he thought she was in for disappointment about getting the odd scientist to speak his mind to them.

They sat together, Quint awkwardly erect and holding his cup stiffly as if he were a shape-shifting alien copying human etiquette he'd learned while studying a holo. He brought the cup to his lips in a ninety-degree course and sipped. The corners of his mouth curled pleasantly, and the tension released from his torso as though an eighty-kilo rucksack had slid off his shoulders. It was the power of kaff.

It was at this moment Tara struck with all the subtlety of a tungsten rod from an orbital support platform.

"Quint, what did you mean about the Republic being thieves and liars? Are you one of those Mid-Core radicals I see on the news?"

Quint choked and splurted. Kel relieved him of his cup before more kaff slopped out on their rug. "Subtle," he teased Tara as she dabbed a dark spot on the sofa.

Quint took a heaving breath, coughed into his fist, then sputtered out, "I'm n-not one of those Mid-Core militants. But what I s-said, I s-stand by."

Kel handed the cup back. "You said you had proof of something. What'd you find on Callie's World that made you so hot?"

Quint took the cup and the refill and collected himself before resuming. "Y-you might not be r-ready to hear it. In m-my experience, not many are."

Tara touched Quint across the table. "I've learned things to be true that I never dreamed possible before I met Kel. I'm ready to try to believe anything you have to say."

Quint didn't pull away from her touch the way he had whenever Kel had tried for such rapport. He even smiled. Quint wanted this. His stammer diminished, as though the topic lent him confidence. "What do you know about t-the Corps of Exploration?"

"Nothing," Kel said.

Quint nodded as if it was the answer he expected. "N-not many do. You'd be surprised h-how little is known about the early history of expansion into the galaxy."

Not me, Kel thought, but instead said, "Sure. The diaspora from the mother world is kind of fuzzy. And of course, the Savages didn't do much to preserve things for future generations to study."

As if gears out of sync had been the cause of his stammer, they suddenly meshed into smooth travel as Quint perked up in agreement. "Exactly. I was in advanced studies on New Byzantium when I discovered references about the Corps in the archives. See, from the beginning— long before the Republic—it was private factions racing to find and claim habitable worlds. Eventually, mainly because of the Savages, those efforts were corralled under one banner. The UPA."

"And from the United Worlds we eventually got our Republic," Tara proceeded.

Quint nodded. Records about the early galactic explorers are sketchy. "We know those different groups searching the galaxy decided to cooperate, and the Corps of Exploration came from that. It's that period that's important to what I'm explaining. Because records or no, there's evidence of things that occurred in that period that are better than written records. The genetic evidence being one."

Kel stayed quiet. This was the most and the clearest Quint had ever spoken.

"I had a professor. Dr. Nicholas Avila. He had a theory he shared with me—in secret. See, he'd been ostracized and nearly driven out of the academy because of it. He believed the Corps of Exploration encountered not only the first alien races like the zhee and wobanki, but evidence of ancient, extinct races. And technologies that disappeared with them. But it was all just conspiracy talk. No solid proof. Discussing the possibilities was a fun exercise in 'what if,' but not much more.

"I kind of forgot about our discussions. Until I got out into the field. And found things. Things my co-workers weren't interested in hearing. Things that couldn't be explained—except by his theory."

"What theory?" Tara asked, intrigued.

"The Corps found a way to tamper with the genomes of entire biospheres. Which is what I found on Callie's World. The common genome of all life on your world isn't naturally resistant to hybridization or mods. It was tampered with."

"Why?" Tara asked.

Quint fired back. "For control, that's why!"

Kel wanted to say that was too fantastic, but knew it wasn't.

"Why do you think that?" Tara asked.

"Bear with me, and I'll try to explain. You have some medical training, yes?"

Tara and Kel both nodded.

"Good. It'll make it easier if you already understand something about genes and DNA. How it adapts and changes over huge spans of time. It's an immutability of all life in the universe. Always. Cosmic radiation causing mutations in the DNA is the mechanism. And it's detectable in the genetic history of all life everywhere. We map it. We know how to work backwards to formulate what a gene once expressed, and sometimes how it will next mutate to express new changes."

"Evolutionary adaptations occur over huge time spans, though. Millions of years," Kel said.

"It does. Changes do occur over shorter periods, over thousands of years, but those changes are minute—too miniscule to cause ostensibly detectable differences in any organism's appearance or function. But the drifts and shifts are always there, even on worlds with minimal ionizing radiation. Nothing remains unchanged over time. Except on Callie's World. And *that* is unnatural in the universe."

"I don't follow," Tara said.

Quint explained with understanding. "The planet's genome is frozen. Not only completely resistant to mutation but unadaptable by the usual means we use to alter any biome's organisms to produce proteins and sugars we can process. Worse, I suspect Callie's World was once closely compatible with human needs. And what changed the genome there occurred suddenly. It's as if someone rewrote your world's genetic code. I need help to work it out, but near as I can estimate, somewhere about 1500 years ago, that's what happened. In the heyday of when I think the Corps was out doing just that."

"Doing what?" Tara said.

"Establishing control. Think about it. If you have the ability to make a world's flora sterile to human crops, you control everything! You control which planets are occupied and by whom. You can make a planet *undesirable* because of the massive expense required to inhabit such a world. You understand that better than most anyone. You can choose to leave it sterile, and make the residents of such a world your customers in perpetuity, turn them into captive clients. You can use such a tool to discourage any power blocks you don't want from settling that world. And when you decide to—*poof*—reverse the process and settle your people to increase the wealth and reach of your power block. But the Savage Wars interfered with the Corps' plan, just about the time it started this process around the galaxy."

"And Callie's World?"

"I bet it was one of the first where they perfected their technique."

"You've found the same condition as Callie's World elsewhere?" Kel asked.

Quint nodded. "I've found evidence of that kind of manipulation on other worlds, but never with a penetrance as strong and complete as what I found on your world. Like I said, it's not natural in the universe. It can only be the result of some severe manipulation."

"There's no tech that could do what you're talking about."

Quint took a sip. The kaff brought no trace of pleasure to his face. "No kind of tech we know about."

He'd seen at least one incredible device that was the result of exploration into the deep black of the vast galaxy. Savages or no, the people stranded on the hostile moon had once been human. A great purpose drove them to remain isolated, a whole society dedicated to harnessing the alien tech they'd discovered, building the giant mountain that controlled entropy itself. It had nearly killed him and his friends.

Kel said it plainly. "Your professor thought the Corps of Exploration found some incredible kind of alien tech, then harnessed it in order to control the settlement of the galaxy."

Quint took a deep breath. "Dr. Avila had a student like me once, one who made it his mission to prove that's exactly what happened. He succeeded. Dr. Avila cautioned him to keep quiet. Instead of going public, he used what he'd learned to advance science, integrating ancient tech into his developments. It made him rich. But he became unhinged. And when he started talking to the wrong people about what he knew, he disappeared. You've probably heard of him. His name was Xenon Boothe."

Kel gulped. Quint was providing veracity in ways he could not imagine Kel understood.

Quint focused on Tara. "You asked me if I was a radical, like those people in the mid-core spouting off about breaking away from the Republic. I grew up on Hashford," he said as if it was sufficient explanation.

Tara shook her head. "I've never heard of it."

"We're an old world. Small. Always been independent. The Savages may have overlooked our world, but what they missed, the Republic's capitalized on. They've dominated our economy and meddled in our politics forever. Invading us and making us slaves would have been a kinder than how they've kept us under their thumb. Forcing trade deals on us, taxing us in every way they can, all while asking us to be grateful for a connection to them.

"The Republic's the only government in the galaxy so obsessed with control. And their roots are in the people who masterminded the Corps of Exploration. There's a path leading backward to the Corps and forward to the Republic. My professor's theory about the Corps is correct, and Callie's World serves as the best piece of evidence yet to support it." He met Kel's eyes.

"You were a lifeline to me, Kel. Dr. Avila warned me. His theory nearly ruined him. When I ignored him to share my revelations with my own colleagues, I got labeled a whacko. No one would hire me. Tatiana was the only one who didn't turn her back on me. I swear, this is the last thing I ever expected or wanted to find. What I found on Callie's World—there's no other explanation."

Quint, collapsed back into the cushions, spent and resigned, finished pleading his case to the highest court and ready for final judgment. "I'm speaking the truth."

Kel folded his arms and nodded.

"I know you are, Quint."

Quint was stunned as the starving thief caught with the family silverware, then voluntarily handed the contents of the owner's cabinet and told, "you need it worse than I do."

"You believe me?"

Kel did. "Because I've seen the proof for myself that an ancient alien influence is being wielded in the galaxy for terrible purpose."

And he'd be face-to-face with it again soon.

Victrix awaited.

***

Hartenstein forgot his aches. "I thought you said they were all healthy!"

The surgeon removed his bucket. Major William Eversoll was a leej, but he was still a doctor. And some things had to be communicated without a filter. Bad news was supposed to be expressed with eyes as much as voice.

"And now, they aren't. One by one they flatlined in a daisy chain like breaching charges in series, and nearly as fast. From the first to the last, it was just minutes."

"Doc Eversoll, you make it sound like this was out of the blue," General Airani said.

"It was, sir. The first was a young adult female. My medics were trying to resuscitate her when I arrived. She was frail as all of them, but a cardiac dysrhythmia would still be unusual in such a young person. A severe electrolyte imbalance would be the expected cause, so we moved her to the medcomp for a mitochondrial reset. That's when it happened.

"Everywhere, the victims all started arresting, like tiles on end, tipping over one after another."

Hartenstein pictured the cascade.

"But the cardiac arrests were secondary, not the primary event. We watched, helpless, as the woman in the medcomp turned gray, then black. She lost cohesion. Just... melted. Cardiac arrest was the first event, but what initiated it was a result of a cellular degradation effecting every physiologic process all at once. Not all of the victims progressed to such a state of decomposition." He shook away the image. "But some of them did."

"I know you and your team did your best, Major," General Airani said.

Hartenstein pointed to the bucket in the doctor's hand. "You unbuttoned, so I take it we're in no danger."

The surgeon shifted the lid to his waist catch. "We've scanned and rescanned every square micron of air. It's clean. No pathogens of any variety—natural or otherwise—just the typical scattered viruses and bacteria found in the atmosphere around any population. The lab has a level-five seal—the highest. It means they were prepared to contain infective particles down to small proteins like prions and cetellian dust—stuff smaller than the smallest nano particle. Whatever's inserting a killer code into DNA, there's zero trace to tell us what it is. Just because it was nanos they found on Psydon, doesn't mean it's the same weapon they used here. Anyway, I ordered an additional quantum seclusion barrier around the lab as a precaution."

Hartenstein spoke incredulously to himself. "We saved a hundred and nineteen people. Except, we didn't." He put it aside. "This isn't the center of their conspiracy and these weren't the leaders. We need intel now so we can maintain our momentum and keep moving up the chain. Every minute we delay works for them and against us. The only data storage is in that lab. Time for you and your people to get in there and figure this out, doctor."

The Wolfhound surgeon let him down easy. "Sorry, sir, I'm just a leej with a medical degree, not a scientist. Whoever goes in there—it might be a death sentence. Maybe we unleash whatever it is that's in there. What killed these people is like nothing I've ever seen. There was a sudden, irreversible drive that sent every cellular process to equilibrium, then reversed. Any genetic weapon I know of doesn't work like that. It's difficult to make any weapon target even a small loci of critical genes in a way that has an immediate effect on the host. What this thing does is the result of an attack on thousands of genes all at once. And it did it to them all. The people they bought on Byblos? They may have all looked similar, but that was just because of their terrible state. I checked; they were as genetically diverse as a Legion recruit company. Ancestry from just about every variety with about every human trait known."

General Airani said, "You're trying to make a point, doctor, but I don't have the background to understand where you're leading."

The surgeon looked worried. "Gentlemen, I have a lot of concerns. I'm explaining why I'm not the leej for the job, nor is anyone in the Wolfhounds. Ever since the colonel briefed us about Psydon and Victrix, I've been racking my brain to make sense of it. Especially what happened on Victrix. The intelligence you got presumes the Hool used a nano weapon like what they had on Psydon, but that it can kill discriminately for traits selective to Dark Ops leejes. That's not possible."

Hartenstein hadn't said *where* the information came from, and both he and Airani were about to protest when the doctor discharged their enercells.

"Bear with me, gentlemen. I need to give you a crash refresher in basic genetics.

"The genotype of an individual is their genetic code— their unique sequence of DNA. In turn, it's those genes that determine the traits a person expresses—what color hair they have, for example. The environment can alter some of those traits, but they aren't coded backwards into a person's genes and those acquired traits can't be passed on.

"It goes against all known science that a trait can be acquired and, in turn, become coded into your DNA— despite the euphemisms we use like saying 'things are trained until they're hardwired into our DNA.' You can't learn mathematics and pass that to your offspring with your genes. You can't become a galaxy-class athlete and pass your acquired ability to lift the most mass on to your children. Dye your hair blond a million times, you don't change your DNA to eventually make that unnecessary.

And whatever makes a Dark Ops operator an operator, unless it's something he's already born with, there's no genetic marker to identify him as different from any other leej.

"So, unless you tell me that the big secret of Dark Ops is they're selected by whatever that marker is, and no else has it, then what the analysis says happened—didn't. Or, there's something the Hool know that no one else does."

Airani looked at Hartenstein. "How about it, Howler? Some secret genetic selection for Dark Ops neither of us knows about?" Hartenstein shook his head.

"Here's where I'm going with this, gentlemen. Let's propose what happened on Victrix is evidence the Hool actually figured out something no one else has, and that's how they did what they did to selectively murder Dark Ops on Victrix without killing every other human on the planet as well. To develop their weapon, they'd have needed subjects for experimentation. Any missing Dark Ops leejes?"

Hartenstein thought. "Maybe." He knew of at least one operator who was lost and never recovered.

"Assuming this much, then what we shut down here—as terrible as it is—it's the least sophisticated of what they're doing. Based on the subjects they were experimenting on, I think they were mapping the full spectrum of human traits they could individually target. If they can already do the other thing, identify and target acquired traits they want to select for, this was child's play research for them. Simple housekeeping. And that makes me wonder. Are the Hool snatching bankers and engineers and pilots and other sorts of unique people and taking them apart to find out what makes them the way they are?"

The doctor's conjecture was worse than Hartenstein had considered. The major continued.

"That's why we need the big guns to pick through this."

The Wolfhound commander folded his arms and sighed. "I understand, Major Eversoll. Sorry, Adolphus, doc's right. The Wolfhounds are the most versatile legion in the Legion. But we don't have the expertise we need for this. We have to bring Republic Intelligence in and whatever other experts from the academies on Utopion to investigate. It's going to take time to unravel this. We have to accept we're in a holding pattern for a while."

Hartenstein wasn't so sure. "Doctor, it's no coincidence it was right after we rescued them that all these people died at once. How do you suppose that happened?"

"I have no idea."

"I do. I think I've seen something like this before." He clicked to L-comm to find Doc and Chappy. "Where are you two right now?"

Doc's sleepy reply told him. Most likely they were where any real leej would be in their boots—flaked out in some shady spot. "Chap, wake up—it's the boss."

"KTF," Chappy blurted awake. "Wuz up, Stomper?"

Leejes were leejes.

"I need you two to bounce to the cyber cell and comb the EM trace for anything unusual."

"Like what, Stomper?" Doc asked with a yawn.

"A pulse transmission, a micro burst—something meant to be blown off as inconsequential if a security scan picked it up." He checked his chrono. "It could've swept across this location anytime from when we first attacked the prison until a few minutes ago. All the prisoners we liberated are dead. I once watched a subject known to be nano-enhanced be killed remotely by his nanos. Afterward our slicer searched the trace and found an EM burst that hit us at the same time our guy got melted by his bugs."

Dread filled Doc's groan. "Oh, no! Those poor people."

Chappy made a grunting sound as if he was pulling Doc to his feet. "Never mind, Doc. We're on it, Stomper. We'll get back to you ASAP, sir."

General Airani had been listening. "If there was a signal sent…"

Hartenstein moved his K-17 from his back to his chest. "Someone sent it. There's still game to be hunted on Ozydna."

***

Cormac and Tara waited with him by the lock as the navy shuttle docked with the *Supreme*. Cormac offered to land, but Kel insisted they remain in orbit. He'd not shared with anyone but Tara his reason. Rex said Victrix was clean. But perhaps better than anyone alive, he'd seen what a bioweapon could do. It was the memory of watching his Rafeer friends mysteriously die right beside him outside the underground lab on Psydon that made him want his family separated from Victrix by clouds and satellites.

Tara wiped a tear as the green light indicated the exterior seal was solid. Cormac grimaced.

"There's something you're not telling me, Turner, and I don't like it. But I can't see how this puts my ship in any danger. We'll be waiting for your comm."

"Sorry," Tara whispered into Kel's ear as she hugged him. "I can't help but worry. I'm no legionnaire."

"Thank Oba for that," Kel teased her. The inner lock opened and a pair of basics faced them. The officer picked Cormac as the ship's master. "Permission to board, sir?"

"Granted. Welcome aboard the *Callie Supreme*, gentlemen."

Both carried sidearms. Their uniform was a splotchy drab gray camouflage. It was one Kel hadn't seen before, but he wasn't surprised. New uniform patterns blew onto basics as regularly as if brought on by the changing wind of seasons. Each new iteration of their uniform rarely seemed adapted to give any real improvement over the last. What kept the basics in perpetual stages of molting was the whim of some good idea fairy in charge of such things in their army. The captain sized Kel up with poorly disguised incredulity. "Major Turner?"

"Thanks for the escort, Captain. Let's be off."

The boatswain's mate guided Kel to a seat by a window, and the two basics crowded behind, blocking him in. The orbital skiff was small, but Kel's intuition tingled there might be more to it than putting the ranking guest in position for the best view.

Arinox was a beautiful world, but it was the tiniest part of it, Victrix, that occupied him as they descended. Mount Fronius once held the planetary defenses for the hemisphere. The noon sun glinted off one of the targeting dishes marking the position of a battery site. It was the gravestone of a silent guardian that stood atop a wall, watching for a Savage attack that never came. His eye was drawn to the faint shimmering translucence caused by the containment fields covering the adjacent cantonment area like so many clear plastic bowls upended after washing to dry near the kitchen sink. They aimed for the landing field, now a featureless gray bull's-eye, barren of aircraft and the human activity to support them.

Three black dots contrasted against the duracrete, tracing the path of the road along the perimeter fence of the main compound. In a bucket, he could have zoomed in at will to identify the vehicles, but they were surely combat sleds operated by the basic MPs. To the south were the many training sites. If there were an afterlife paradise, it would look like that, a playground of shoot houses, ranges, and fields where he and his comrades would spend eternity practicing.

They touched down and bright light pierced the cabin through the hatch. Kel fell in behind the captain to exit, the sergeant a pace behind. He knew what was coming. He had no ill criticism—he'd have set it up the same. As his feet touched duracrete, he was surrounded by a dozen basics with blasters aimed at him. His trickle of admiration evaporated. Fingers rested on triggers with safeties disengaged. Worse, their muzzles pointed as much at each other as they did him. They wore poorly sized armor plates in ill-fitting carriers, leaving critical anatomy exposed, as if chosen for comfort rather than protection. A major stepped forward, a grinning MP beside him, presenting ener-chains as the gift that came with his surprise party.

"You're coming with us, 'Major.'" Quotation marks bracketed the way he'd called Kel a major. "Your authorization's bogus, and you are, too. The Army's only too happy to oblige Legion Command's request to arrest you."

12

Kel hadn't come armed nor worn his Thuringian armor. He wasn't here to fight a bunch of basics and offered no resistance as ener-chains went around his waist and arms. He was genuinely sympathetic, after a fashion. It wasn't their fault they sucked, nor that they were arresting him. He apologized for any misunderstanding about his credentials as they took him into custody. Putting them at ease was the only way to get an advantage.

Their base of operations was a cluster of fab units occupying the fork in the road that led to the cantonment area gate. They put him in a room bare save for a chair and a corporal.

"I've seen my share of legionnaires, but you'd have to be the sorriest bucket head of them all," the corporal said. "Everyone knows their sergeant majors skin and eat guys for having hair as long as yours. You're a terrible spy.

How'd you think you'd fool anyone with that haircut, dirtbag?"

The young MP took Kel's silence as a challenge.

"Nothing to say, mop top?"

There was only so much he'd take.

"As you were, Corporal," he snarled. The basic braced. "Speaking to a detainee when you're not authorized corrupts the reliability of any interrogation. Your post's outside. I suggest you get there."

The trooper made juvenile mumbles, but turned to leave. "Not because you said."

They had his datapad, but missed the specs tucked inside the thick jacket lapel. It was just this kind of complacency he'd hoped to create by acting the polite but aggrieved party. There was nothing to do but wait patiently for an opportunity. They chained him to the chair which prevented him from conducting his peripatetic process when he thought. He had no chrono, but the throbbing of dependent swelling from hands at his side for so long confirmed hours had passed. Finally, the door flew open.

"There's been a mix-up, Major Turner," the MP officer said as he entered the code to release Kel's chains. "I just got the comm confirming your ident. I don't know what the problem was, but I apologize for the misunderstanding. This site's classed Cosmic Three and it's got everyone erring on the side of caution, you understand."

Kel rubbed his wrists. "I do, Major."

"There's a Legion provost for the sector on the way. My orders are to keep you here until your man arrives to confirm your authorization access for himself. This situation," the major looped a finger in the air, "I'm sorry about what happened to your fellow legionnaires. We've

201

been assured we're in no danger from the trace theta radiation left over by the accident, but sealed or not, everyone's tense. Especially given who this base was used by."

That this was the secret home of Dark Ops hadn't remained much of a secret since Kel left. An accident involving a malfunctioning theta bomb was the cover used to explain the reason for the lockdown quarantine of the site.

"Looks like I'm your guest for a while. Can you point me to the head and the mess, because it's been awhile for either. My datapad?"

The major grimaced slightly. "Sorry. We have to hold on to that until your auth is confirmed. Then we'll clear you through with whatever you need to conduct your investigation. I assume the provost has the codes to pass through the field? Because, we don't."

"It'll all be settled," was Kel's oblique reply.

Alone in the fresher, he tore apart the loose seam and retrieved the specs. Rex said the orders were forgeries—just like his promotion to major—but would stand up to any scrutiny. What else was Rex wrong about? Was the bioweapon that killed his tribe still alive beneath the containment field, waiting to do the same to him?

His specs paired to the pad. So far, his intuition about the MPs was proving correct. Wherever his datapad was, it wasn't in a containment cage. His datapad and its programs might as well still be riding in his cargo pocket. First he'd have that meal, then he'd take the offer of a bunk.

Off duty troops milled about the center of the fab village, some playing boost ball in the pleasant Arinox night air before hitting bunks or readying for their shift on patrol. Basics weren't lazy or incompetent. He'd served proudly with many. But vigilance required a discipline that was enforced by all levels of leadership. What he'd seen of the troops guarding the site didn't inspire him that way. Even for MPs, this was the dullest of duties, riding around a sealed and empty installation while ground sensors did the actual task of watching the perimeter in full spectra like an unblinking eye.

Alone in the bunk room, he went to work.

Lanthanum's slicing programs were good, as good as those of Dark Ops—maybe better in some respects. Next to Poul, Sims had been the best slicer he'd ever had on a team, and thought even he would've been impressed how effortlessly he sliced into the basic's weakly encrypted comms. Another minute for the stealth package to finish its intrusion and he'd be ready. The sensor suite would technically see him, but the subtraction program would scrub his presence from the output feed. It was the next best thing to EM camouflage and required no suit. As long as he wasn't seen by one of the roving patrols, his entry into the Victrix compound was virtually guaranteed.

What he'd do then, he'd have to rely on some luck.

The icon blinked green. This was his only opportunity before the Legion provost arrived to confirm he was here without authorization—of anyone but Primus Pilus and its founder, that is. He returned outside and leaned against the fab with nonchalant ease and pretended to watch the game for a bit, then made for the common fresher, slipping past it and into the woods. He didn't need a map to direct his course perfectly for the Victrix main entrance.

Abutting the landscaped entrance and gatehouse, the wall was only five meters high. He'd scaled it before with the team, a frequent exercise to test security around the base. To anyone making the drive down the hill only to be turned away at the gate house, it allowed a narrow glimpse between the tree lined road of the boringly plain collection of nondescript buildings in the distance, layered in such a way to block visual access to any pedestrians in the compound. The entrance was normally heavily monitored by the contracted security providing protection and access to Victrix, but was now as much a ghost town as the rest of the base.

The comm traffic between the patrols and the operations center ran through his implant. He lay in the brush, his entry point in sight. Kel watched through the foliage until a sled operated under night vision slowly hummed past in the dark.

"Checkpoint alpha, clear."

"Roger, Patrol. Fifty more laps like that and your shift'll be over."

A chuckle. "Copy that, Sarge. Still on for that pick-up game after some shut-eye?"

"You know it, Hanks. You got lucky today with that corner shot from outside."

"We'll see, Sergeant," the MP promised.

"You do it again and I'll take your shift behind the wheel and you can stay in the ops center sipping kaff."

"It's a bet, Sarge."

The sled disappeared and he checked the tracker positions of the other vehicles a final time in his specs before standing. As long as the ops center crew depended on the sensor program instead of reading the inputs raw, he'd be in. After weeks of guarding what was essentially a graveyard, their complacency would be his ally.

Monomolecular razor wire was the first obstacle, and a familiar one, strung and stacked to make a wall in a pyramid of three coils running the open space between the wood line and the perimeter road. They'd taken his gloves with his other pocket effects, but what escaped their attention was that his clothing was duralon. Knife- and puncture-proof. With sleeves pulled down to cover his palms and fingers as best he could, he broke into a sprint and launched for the razors. In a practiced combination resembling an amalgam of bear crawls and worm wriggles, he reached the peak, rolling over the last sharp coils and onto the ground beyond. The subtraction program killed whatever motion the sensors in the wire picked up, and the comm traffic remained the stuff of bored soldiers engaged in boring tasks.

It would be minutes until the next sled roved by, but he dashed, feeling exposed in the open space. The gatehouse entrance was dark, the gate sealed, but the stunner was active. There were concealed autocannons, but his specs read them as dead, just as there were no emissions from any other source ahead. The faint glow of the containment fields rose eerily in the distance. He built momentum as he raced to the wall.

He sprang, the toes of one tacky sole aimed at a crevice between blocks, stretched fingertips finding a millimeter of purchase. Another alternating climb of brief contacts before a last explosive spring upward, and the finger pads of one hand curved onto the top lip of the wall. With a one-arm swing, he made himself a pendulum until his other fingers could reach, then pulled himself up and over in one motion, correcting course at the last moment to drop between the sharp-spiked vegetation meant to skewer anyone trying to do what he'd just done. A few thorns snapped off against his shoulders, and he winced as one brushed sharply against the back of a hand as he threaded his way through the last of the green barrier.

Another sled passed the gate checkpoint, making the same dull report, then he sprinted off. He took a circuitous path through patches of greenspace in the direction of the glow. It would only serve to conceal him from the simplest unaided observation, but a race down the kilometer-long boulevard was unthinkable, even if it was likely without consequence.

Some habits died hard.

The nearer he got, the more the shield took on a static appearance until, standing before it, the tingle of flowing electrons made his hair stand on end. He keyed the program with a hard blink to his specs, and the static slowed its frequency over the huge surface everywhere. Would the change in the pattern be visible from a distance? It flared wherever a bird or one of the winged reptiles collided with the field. Perhaps it would appear similar if anyone was looking. The static slowed yet more, then halted. The icon in his vision flashed. He took a deep breath and threw himself forward. An ice-water plunge seized him and the next thing he knew, he was coming to with a headache and a mouthful of grass.

The barrier behind him was back to the high velocity of racing static waterfalls. Just ahead was the quadrangle bound by the buildings that housed Dark Ops and its support. That was the good news. The bad news—he was now cut off from his datapad. He removed his now useless specs.

He'd played this out many times. Where to first? He came for what was stored in the sustainment cell—his armor, the only comrade he could resurrect to life. Then, he'd find a way into the armory. Finally, he'd take a ride through the underground tunnel to the isolation facility inside Mount Fronius and filch everything he could from the munitions depot—everything he could pile onto a flatbed. From there? There were concealed exits on the far side of the facility meant for emergency egress. He'd make his escape to the civilian port, and either call for the *Supreme* or charter a lift to orbit.

That's what he'd do.

So when his feet steered him to the teamroom building, it was as if he were the boy who'd been told not to touch the stove, but extended a finger for the fiery heating element anyway. He had to see for himself. Beneath the jungles of Psydon had been a flame, and if it consumed his brothers, he had to see. The outer door recognized his palm print, sliding silently aside to admit him. As if he'd never left. As if he belonged. As if it honored his presence as the last member of the tribe to return home.

His footfalls awoke lighting in the stairway and he found himself in the long corridor, door after numbered door like milestones marking the highway of his life. He stopped in front of the swirling five-arm galaxy bearing the skull and knife, the red number 12 at its center. He took a deep breath and placed his palm on the panel. A strobing light filled the corridor, blinding him, and a loud voice boomed from the other end.

"HALT! You are in a restricted area. The use of deadly force is authorized. Present your empty hands in clear sight and do not move."

He complied, raising his hands high, and froze. The voice held deadly intent, but though stern and commanding, spoke Standard with traces of an accent that hinted a strange joviality no matter the stern commands. A more lyrical voice spoke.

"Here now, Phillip, hold on. What's all this, then? Captain Turner? Is that you?"

The dazzling pulses of light penetrating his tightly shut lids dimmed, and he cautiously peeled open an eye for a test. Two massive bots trotted at him on stick legs, blocky heads suspended at the tip of outstretched necks leading them to his point of capture.

"Bertie? Phillip?"

"It is!" Bertie said. "Captain Turner, as I live and breathe. Look 'ere, Phillip, it *is* Captain Turner. Or is it major? We've been keeping tabs on things outside the quarantine field with a bit o' quantum tunneling 'ere and there. Most entertainment we've 'ad in a bit. We lost track of you for a while there. It was that alone made us think it might actually be you, sneaky Pete that you are."

Kel lowered his hands. "I never expected to see you two again. I've missed you guys a thousand times."

The blaster on Phillip's back jerked upward in two short, precise lifts before aiming at his chest again. "Get them grubbies back in the air, Mister Turner, sir," Phillip said.

Bertie sighed, "Phillip's right. You shouldn't be here. We're mates, but you're proper nicked now, chum."

***

"What happened here, boys?" Kel said with hands high. The AIs spoke like it was old times, but the blasters aimed at him from atop their backs were the darkening cloudburst on their reunion picnic.

"It was a right mess, sir," Bertie said. "Tragic. We wuz dead in storage but as you know, we're ever awake and listening. It was bloody awful, sir. We couldn't do a thing.

We were released remotely and set to a recce. Haven't seen the like since, well, you know, Psydon."

"Shush, Bertie," Phillip said. "We've no auth to speak to 'im about it. I'm alerting the gray goons we've got an intruder."

"Hold up, Phillip," Kel said.

The AI shook his head. "All due respect, sir, you of all people wouldn't want us to ignore our duty. Plus, you're in no position to give orders 'ere, it pains me to say."

"Errr," Bertie disagreed. "I mean, we're not keyed to 'is command *currently*, but he does hold command authorization in our programs, that is, if'n he still knows 'em."

" 'ang on, Bertie! You can't be squawking about such!"

Kel searched his memory. "Quasar three seven two five, cycle twelve." He'd chosen the code carefully. Quasar was a command call sign from one of his most dangerous missions. The numeric was a date awful and special, the day his parents had died. Cycle twelve represented his evolution to command a kill team. All so long ago, all unforgettable.

The blaster from Phillip's back raised muzzle to the ceiling, and the eight-legged bot rotated in place, his bulk filling the hallway wall to wall. "Please present for biosig." A pad appeared from the bulky frame. It glowed at his touch.

"Command authorization accepted, Major Turner. Orders, sir?"

"There's nothing to see in there, sir," Bertie said. "Phillip and I, we did the recovery. Gathered them all, said the words over each of them, and sent them to join their brothers by the fire, sir."

"From the dust of stars you come, and as dust you shall return," Phillip recited. "So says the good book. We did best's we could, sir, to do them honor."

How the two AIs could be so human still amazed Kel as he swallowed the lump. "Who was here? I mean, any of my..."

Bertie projected a list of names. "Most from your era were gone, sir. But there were a few."

Kel scanned the names. The list was alphabetical. It didn't take long to find the first.

Matthew Biggetti.

"Bigg," Kel said painfully.

Phillip's blocky head bobbed sympathetically. "Yes, sir. The sergeant major stayed on, even though they gutted this place. He did all he could to keep everyone's spirits high, to let them all know they were doing great things, and they had to be ready for the call again. It was a travesty, how the Legion did these men, sir."

Bertie grumbled, "Bloody well painted a target on their backs, they did. Whoever did this, they wuz practically handed an invitation and pointed at the door."

His eyes searched the list. Gabriel Harding. "Hardball," Kel gulped out.

"He took Team Twelve, sir. Did an 'elluva job as team sergeant, he did," Phillip said. Kel recognized too many more names, like Joe Crane. But none hit as hard as Bigg and Hardball. Maybe there were more who were safe, alive, and elsewhere in the ranks of the Legion.

"That's all of them, sir," Bertie said as the list ceased climbing and extinguished. "Only even number teams remained staffed, and most of them only a few operators serving as little more than place holders. Everyone else had done left, or been pushed out."

Rex said the roles of Dark Ops had shrunk dramatically. Maybe it was a good thing.

"Let me in," Kel said. His order was obeyed without comment from either AI.

It was the same team room. Honoring their history, mementos and images of the team from his time were still on the wall, with very little new apparently added, as though it were a shrine to better times, a promise that what once was, could be again.

He was drawn to the central image amidst a collection adorning the wall beside the team sergeant's desk. It was the day he'd led Twelve and the airborne troops of the Scarlet division to take the field, Gabe in the pilot seat of the mech, teeth stained green with stimleaf, as they all crowded around the captured mech for the photo he felt guilty for taking. He peeled it off and put it in his pocket.

He opened the drawer, not sure what if anything he might find there. He recognized the notebook, bound in Dreex leather, worn at the corners from the many miles traveled in the owner's cargo pocket. Pages and pages written in Gabe's hand, words and whole lines crossed out, scribbles in the margins. He thumbed through it, stopping at a section written meticulously and with none of the edits. Stanzas from previous pages were copied in perfection, topped by titles difficult to read because of the curly flourishes used to mark them. He snapped the book closed.

"We may not have much time. The Legion provost for the sector's on 'is way."

"If it's as you say and this job's off the books, then we'd best be off, sir. Shopping days are busy ones when the stores have so much to offer."

They led him to the sustainment wing and a storeroom where a container popped open to break stasis, revealing armor as pristine as the day he'd meticulously cleaned it, hung it on the rack in his cage, and saluted it before leaving a last time. He put it on. "Find Radd's armor and get it into a grav container. Is there an MSC in the depot?"

"Several, sir. Loaded and ready."

"How about an OSP?"

"Not in years, sir. All mothballed in the sector depot."

The armory opened to Bertie's command. A rifle was a rifle. It didn't matter if it had been one he'd once held. He grabbed the first K-17 in the rack, checked it, and slung it. The bots grabbed more weapons and soon they were heading for the lift. In all his years, he'd never had cause to use the access tunnel beneath the spacefield. It was used by the support section to move materials between the sustainment complex and the insect warren that made Mount Fronius nearly hollow.

The bots deposited their baggage into the flatbed hover waiting by the lift, then set off in the lead into the long tunnel, its vanishing point obscured by the darkness ahead. "What all do we recover in the depot besides an MSC, sir?"

"Whatever we can grab, Bertie. Enough to outfit a kill team for sustained, unsupported ops."

"Jolly good, sir! You have a kill team assembled! Is Mister Radd with them? I look forward to laying his kit at his feet, sir. A proper V'ictry Day morning celebration's what it'll be like, sir, presents for all followed by an enormous breakfast with the whole family."

Kel checked up to avoid rear-ending Phillip, slowed suddenly and neck stretched ahead like he sniffed the air ahead. "Bertie, shush. Listen."

Kel concentrated, but heard nothing.

"The air exchanger's talking nonsense," Phillip said. "You talk to him, Bertie, I never can understand him like you."

"Huh?" Kel exclaimed.

Bertie understood. "Machine language, boss. They all talk. Damned uninteresting and self-centered most of it is, sir. Housekeeping bots complaining about messes. Kitchen appliances feeling unappreciated. This one's babbling on about the work the anti-intrusion system's going to cause him."

"Here now! What's he bitching about? Having to process all the ozone the lasers'll make?"

A menacing red grid of criss-crossing lasers appeared behind high-energy fences marching at them in advancing succession.

"Run!" Phillip yelled. Kel floored the tram after them.

"Turn it off!" Kel yelled.

"I'm talking to the bloody thing now, sir," Phillip said. "He's refusing to stop! Now you listen 'ere, mate," the AI said in stern tones as they fled.

"Shite!" Bertie said, slamming to a halt as a grid materialized, blocking the way. Kel locked knees and elbows as he braked. He pictured the coming rear end collision that would launch his friends into the thresher— their heads already tucked back to avoid the ruby-red mesh, chests millimeters from the humming beams.

The flatbed hover bounced off the bots' rear quarters with no more effect to the pair than if he was a cripple crashing his hover chair head-on into a durasteel wall.

"Rude bastard!" Phillip spurt. "Not you, sir! I mean that bloody twit and his cheese graters."

Bertie's head pivoted fully to the rear in the way that always made Kel picture his own neck bones cracking and splintering. "Blocked fore and aft, sir. You see 'ere now—" the AI began a stern lecture to the unseen entity, when Kel's stomach went into freefall. The floor dropped, walls rushed up, and they came to a sudden stop. A red grid sealed the top of their box like a lid.

Phillip cursed. "Now who's gone and gotten nicked? Insult to injury!"

Bertie joined. "Foul and unnecessary, what that!"

"Dammit, boys! You had to know there was an anti-intrusion system running. I figured you'd dealt with it."

Phillip apologized. "Bloody thing baited us! Laid up all quiet like he was plumb dead, sir!"

"What now? Can you shut it off?"

Bertie said, "I'm trying, sir. Damned unreasonable, he is. Say, what's this?" The grid vanished from above. The floor elevated gently and soon rejoined the tunnel. The way ahead was clear.

"Good job, boys."

"Twern't us, sir," Philip said. "That anti-intrusion bugger's sulking about someone ordering him off his screw-about. Won't tell us who."

Behind them, the laser fences remained aflame and impenetrable, one after another, all the way back to the lift area. It was the choice of no choice. "Seems obvious. Probably every MP they've got's waiting for us at the end of the line." He swore. "Karking hell. We're busted. Nothing to do but get on with it."

"Drat!" Bertie said as they started forward again. "We've ever so sorry, sir."

"We'll get free of this yet, sir," Philip said. "Somehow." He didn't sound confident.

"Shush, boys, and let me think. See if you can get a read on what's waiting for us in the depot."

"Yes, sir," the two answered as one.

It was a silent ride to the end of the access tunnel and the waiting lift. In that time, Kel had come to only one conclusion. "You should stay behind, guys."

"I speak for Phillip when I say, we're with you, sir," Bertie said. "They'll just shut us down again. We'd rather surrender on our feet, next to you."

Philip sighed. "We'd a good run, mates. More's the pity we couldn't see it through, but it was good to be in the scrum again while it lasted."

Kel resigned himself. "Nothing to do about it. Let's go then, boys." They rode the speedlift up.

Phillip's snake-thin neck snapped stiff. "Sir! There's just one bloke in the warehouse bay, waiting like the headmaster to dress us down and expel us. Shouldn't be much of a task to get past 'im. Permission to use stunners, sir?"

Before Kel could reply, the lift doors parted to reveal a single legionnaire in the vast and empty bay, hands on his hips, the brow of his bucket tilted forward in disapproval.

"Don't you three take the prize."

Kel knew the voice as well as his own. "Braley!"

"Lucky for you, Kel Turner, I'm the sector provost. Come out of there and let's figure our next move."

Kel made a running tackle, hefting his armored friend off his feet in a bear hug, and cheered. "Braley Yost! Oba, watch over me!"

"Lieutenant colonel now, no less," Philip said behind them.

"I'd have expected no less. Good for you, sir," Bertie said.

Kel released his first kill team leader. "How'd you know I was here, Braley?"

"The Society's on the move, Kel," Braley said, on his feet again and holding Kel at arm's length. "I'm going with you."

"That's the best thing to happen to me in a while, brother, but I don't even know where that is yet."

Bertie coughed. "Say, Mister Turner, sir, if'n it's not too much bother, mind telling us what it is we're about?"

13

"They messed up, big time, Stomper," Doc said, thuds of dead run footfalls punctuating his speech. "They used a harmonic tunneling frequency. Mimicked a burst of cosmic radiation filtered through an atmosphere. A millionth of a second's worth. Damn near undetectable. With a time parameter to screen for of when the prisoners got murdered, it stood out like a kelhorned big red flashing arrow. Just before I lost the transmitting source, it was on the move. Wanna bet they're beating feet for the capital to make orbit ASAP?"

Chappy's voice vibrated like Doc's. "We're on the bounce for the Excalibur, Stomper. Meet us there. Wolfhound Six, we're asking approval for all assets so we can make who killed these people pay."

Doc said, "I need TARU, sir. I need them to get us a fix."

"The word's given," General Airani said. "I'm spinning up the Wolfhounds. Go, Howler. We'll take our cues from your team."

Hartenstein barreled out of the wreck of the prison, inspired to make more of Ozydna look the same. "Make a hole," he yelled to leejes manning the tunnel access through the containment field. The detail didn't waste time checking the ident of the bulldozer headed straight for them. Leejes knew the sight of one of their own moving to purposeful homicide as well as they could read the signs of a blaster's impeller chain overheating. The screen to the portal gate dropped so he never broke pace. The Excalibur's tail pointed at him like a freeway off ramp with Doc and Chappy waving him ahead from the summit like coaches at the finish line.

"Are you limping, Stomper?" Chappy asked.

"No," he said, limping up the last of the ramp.

The crew chief, Romper, was on the deck. "Howler's on board, Slabside. Let's fly."

The Excalibur lifted and turned, providing his first daylight view of the site. Doc and Chappy said lightning operations was the Wolfhound's thing. There was a timeless phrase that described combat operations as a "fog of war."

It had never seemed more appropriate.

A pulse fence provided an expansive perimeter around the prison, extending all the way to the main road. A pair of Talons circled overhead. Of the many vehicles halted outside the control point, a luxury sedan stood out. Stepping out of it was a member of the Republic diplomatic mission, marked by his purple suit. Beneath the cluster of tents, the Wolfhound JAG and the regiment's executive officer would be busy putting out fires with both the Protectorate and the embassy.

Pride and envy competed for his attention as the ramp sealed, signaling the end of this act of the play. Pride in the Wolfhounds and what was carried on out of sight. Envy at its commander. Topper had been his junior in Dark Ops. He'd become the head of a machine with a thousand living parts. It was the career that could have been. Then, a moment of relief came to him.

For a brief time, he was reliving how his life was when he was a sergeant. An operator, again. Topper could have the headache.

"What've you got, Doc?"

Doc held up a finger. "Just a sec. I got TARU." Doc faced away as he spread holos only he could see, carrying out a conversation only he could hear, the silent pantomime only another leej understood, and he did.

"Aw'ite, you give it to me, Chappy."

"We don't depend on secondhand castoffs and filtered reports from Republic Intel or anyone else. TARU's our technical assistance response unit. They've been in the capital, doing their job sneakin' around and collecting—any and everything. They go everywhere the Wolfhounds go, updating our target folders on people and places so's Zeta and the Wolfhounds are as current as possible when we get the next call. Doc's putting the TARU boys on the trace he pulled. There's a residue from what generated it, but it's too weak to read by any gear except what TARU's running. I tell you, they can track a ghost from his haunt back to his grave. What they can do, Howler, it's freaky, I tell you."

Hartenstein hailed the pilot. "Slabside. ETA to the Truexx spaceport?"

"We can have skids on the deck there in ten minutes, Howler."

Doc was back. "Howler, TARU's telling me they've got a ping on what generated the signal. I'm bringing them into the conference. I've got Wolfhound Six and Zeta-Six linked in, too."

The holo of a cloaked figure materialized in the bay. The hood pulled back to reveal a blue-skinned Ozydna male.

"Go ahead, Snack-Pack, this is the mission commander, Howler."

"Pleased to meet you, sir," the blue man said with all military propriety. Hartenstein bet Snack-Pack also had the local singsong dialect down so even their one-way trip atmo pilot would feel at ease telling him any secrets he knew. "What Doc sliced got us a pattern that in turn let us locate the signature of what had to have generated it. We've followed it to a mixed residential and business block of the city, but lost it before we could get close enough for a point fix. My best guess is our target was near the prison, sent the signal, waited around long enough to make sure it was effective, then hovered like a madman to get back to Truexx. This area must have a mission support site he returned to in order to gather up his goods before making his exfil off-planet. Likely we lost the trace because the transmitter went into a shielded container. It'll be something sizeable. Probably a grav trunk—something big enough to house a neutron dampener. I've got the team surveilling the block." The blue legionnaire's report was succinct, dense with information, and clear. Hartenstein wished Doc and Chappy would learn from Snack-Pack's example.

General Airani took over. "What's your recommendation, Legionnaire?"

Snack-Pack was prepared. "We can seal this area with a company of Wolfhounds, but if we're wrong on the location and spook him, we may lose him for good. We're only going to get one shot at this and we don't have a positive ID yet. But Doc's correct—the highest likelihood is he's heading off-world. Let's give the rat a place to run. Our best bet is to keep eyes and ears out, and when my team has him pegged, we grab him, either in transit or at the port. It'll depend on the operational environment he's in when we find him."

Captain Malik spoke. "I have a team in low-profile, already spreading a net inside the spaceport terminal."

"Can we seal the spaceport?" Hartenstein asked.

General Airani took the question. "Not per se. I don't have the legal authority to apprehend one of their citizens without their assistance, and I don't have authority to indefinitely ground the ship traffic of a sovereign state to keep our target from escaping. I'll do it, but it won't be long before the House of Reason has me digging foxholes on an arctic moon for the rest of my life."

Snack-Pack was speaking to someone out of the holo. "Gentlemen, my team says we have a strong candidate. A comm originated from the area we're surveilling, an alphanumeric message in Standard to proceed to the spaceport. It was received by three communicators, all at the same location closer to the spaceport. High likelihood it's our target and he's revealed at least three accomplices. All four potentials are on the move as we speak."

Captain Malik said, "They're heading for a ship. Best option is to permit all opposition elements to achieve unity of location. We only broadcast intention at the time of action. Point ambush at the spaceport. Render incapable.

Seize, board, search, and exfil with alacrity. We leave the Protectorate dumb before they have time to holler."

Wolfhound Six's decision came with a wry grin. "Do it."

He stood in the hangar next to Doc and Chappy, stationed in hiding with teams of other Zeta operators. Loaded on fast-attack sleds and ready to assault, they resembled the possessions of fleeing refugee families, hung off the sides of vehicles wherever space permitted.

Quantum entanglement was a phenomenon Hartenstein had studied in his university days. The theory that there was an interplay of connection between everything in the universe from the smallest particle to the largest. The mind-boggling proof was that substituents of matter—things as immeasurably tiny as electrons—could be separated across even astronomically measured distances, yet, somehow, be connected. The way dancers in a ballet made individual movements, yet one joined another in concert of position and direction as though by invisible strings between them.

It never made sense to him. But it served as an allegory for the faster-than-light speed interplay that joined and directed the many disparate Wolfhound elements as they prepared. TARU's efforts morphed the operation to change, evolve, and adapt. It played out for Hartenstein in real time on the command, control, and intelligence feed running in his bucket. He was not the entanglement's architect nor director. That time was past for him. Still, he was a part of it, and it felt good.

Snack-Pack spoke over the command net. "Target-One just entered a taxi, headed for the spaceport. He's tagged T-One on the C-two-I feed. He's pulling a grav trunk with a neutron dampener. He's wearing one of those long cloaks the locals prefer, with the hood pulled over his head. But he's not a local."

"How can you tell he's not indig to Ozydna?" Captain Malik asked from where he was hidden with another team, likewise waiting to assault across the airfield.

"Can't tell what species he is, but he's wearing some kind of atmosphere helmet under that cloak. That's all the physical description we have for you. A drone has T-Two through Four nearing the port. They're also in local garb. But their kinematics give them away. Highest probability they aren't locals either."

"The protectorate's laws don't shield off-worlders," Chappy narrated on their private three-man channel. "Means they're all fair game."

"The first three rodents are headed for the cheese," Doc said as they all watched.

The three accomplices had moved on their own to the spacefield. T-Two through Four rode the hover from the terminal, heading for the many grounded yachts. The sled eased down next to a silver-skinned, deep jump beauty, removing any doubt as to which was the escape ship. It was as Snack-Pack had observed. Dressed in the same local robes, their gaits gave away their alien nature. He anticipated unwrapping them like presents to reveal which species they represented in the conspiracy.

"T-One just arrived. He's in the terminal."

Hartenstein sorted through the many feeds running in his bucket. It was like watching a huge aquarium. He was aware of the many smaller fish swimming in all directions, while concentrating on the big one with the most interesting colors and largest dorsal fin. Second nature, no matter how long he'd been out of a bucket.

A Zeta team in civilian garb staked out the departure area. When they apprehended T-One, a simultaneous assault would launch to take the transport holding the other conspirators. Prisoners in custody, the Wolfhounds would be back to their expeditionary base at the seized prison in minutes. Followed by Wolfhound Six submersing in a task worse than burning all the human waste collected in all the field freshers of a dozen regiments— managing the aftermath of the operation. The Protectorate would howl and the diplomats in the Republic embassy would stroke. Both would want his head.

But that was a problem for later.

The team leader poised to snatch T-One alerted. "Zeta-Six, we have T-One in sight. Ready to move as soon as he clears customs."

Captain Malik responded. "You have a go."

Wolfhound Six was on all channels. "All elements. I have control. Stand by."

"This is it," Chappy whispered. Hartenstein joined Doc and Chappy on the running boards of the last fast-attack vehicle. So far to the rear, he'd get no trigger time today. If the emergency assault on the prison had been his final act as the tip of the blade, it was a good one to go out on. At least, he'd be as close as possible to the action to witness the sharp edge of the Wolfhounds make their cut.

"Launch, launch, launch."

The lead FAV shot out the hanger doors and Hartenstein prepared his grip. As he'd anticipated, their ride went from zero to breakneck in a heartbeat. Their element was not the closest to the silver-skinned yacht, confirming again for him that their FAV would deliver them as redundant bodies, little more than spectators to the assault.

"WHAT THE HELL," came over the Zeta net. "All elements—T-One... he vanished into thin air when we made our move. It's not mimetics—he's gone! I can't explain it."

Hartenstein searched the feed. The icon marking T-One was missing.

Chaos erupted and he closed everything in his bucket but the command and team channels. Had he just bragged he could filter through a hundred voices to track as many activities will? Sometimes you had to pull the plug on the aquarium and let all the little fishes flush down the drain, leaving just the big lunkers. The team and command channel were all that mattered as he focused ahead on the silver yacht.

An excited voice hit his ear. "There he is—popped out of nowhere right beside the ship. He's boarding."

Hartenstein was on the wrong side of the ship to see for himself, but the icon for T-One reappeared in the feed just where the observer described, at the foot of the gangway, and now moving into the ship.

"Hold at the phase line, don't crowd the mechs," Captain Malik reminded them all.

Their sled separated from the others to make the spread surrounding the yacht from a generous distance. It was covered on all sides—save up. That, too, was in the process of being denied.

"I never get tired of that scene," Doc said.

"Miss it sometimes," Chappy agreed.

Hartenstein looked with them skyward. It had been decades since he'd last seen a Stingray drop mechs. A trio of the delta-winged carriers converged overhead. Beneath the belly and each wing, Mark 7 mechanized combat walkers hung suspended by the shoulders. As one, the bat-winged craft sank like the repulsors were cut, then froze midair to hover over the yacht. Pylon clamps opened, dropping the mechs the last dozen meters onto the airfield.

An all-hail warning rang out. "Heave to and power down. Heave to and power down." Yet the yacht started to rise.

Chappy tsked. "That's a bad idea."

The anthropoid machines hit the ground running, and like a game of bash ball, the silver ship became the player in possession. The first mech to make contact was piloted by a leej with a shark-tooth grin painted on his bucket. The Mark 7 leaped, graspers finding purchase on a stubby lift wing. More mechs leaped, clawing the yacht with metal fingers. Some slid off, raking silver skin away as they did. Some found purchase on landing sponsons, wings, and tail.

Yet the craft rose.

"Never say die, I guess," Chappy mused.

"Never seen a pilot disregard his ship like that," Doc said. "Must have good insurance."

Another Stingray blotted the sun as it dropped a single mech down onto the hovering ship. In one claw it held a monomolecular slicer the length of a leej. The pilot drew the sawtooth blade over the fuselage like a knife through warm butter, then leaped away. Hartenstein had a premonition of disaster. The ship started a slow motion descent, titling into a broadside swoop as it sank.

FAVs and dismounted leejes scattered.

Masses and velocities produced momentums. Mech pilots released grips and dove their metal avatars to abandon the craft. Their own ride reversed at full repulsor thrust, nearly heaving him off the running board. Where they had been a split second before, the tail of the grounded yacht skidded mere meters in front of their retreating path.

The fate of those in the path of destruction was obscured by the silver ship, ground to a halt.

Hartenstein was off the running board and bounding for the bird.

"Assault, assault, assault."

The yacht was on its belly. Mechs landed around the ship, cushioned on rear bending knees flexing low. He lost sight as he dipped below the tail to reach the aft access hatch, breached partially open from fuselage deformation. He reached two hands into the gap and tore the portal away.

He was in.

Doc and Chappy trailed as close as the space allowed to join his juggernaut drive into the belly of the beast. Sparks rained from conduits and plasma swam along the roof, not yet ablaze. A bulkhead separated the tail from the passenger cabin. "Coming through!" Chappy pushed ahead. He'd carried a breaching ram from the FAV. With both arms he swung the tool rearward, then drove from hips to plow the tool's broad face onto the hatch. On contact, a concussion field materialized to augment his mechanical force. The hatch dimpled and folded in like foil, falling onto the deck.

Hartenstein barreled through, K-17 ready.

The four-point harness fell away from a robed figure. At contact range, he stunned the passenger in the chest, the body slumping back from whence it had risen. Two other figures remained belted in cushions, unarmed, and unmoving. He bypassed them to rush the front of the cabin where another robed figure rose.

Its hood fell back as it stood erect, revealing a clear spherical helmet. Through the green vapor filling the helmet, abundant folds of loose yellow skin piled a squat face. Above a wide snout, a pair of beady white eyes pierced the mist to meet him. Squat arms fumbled to reach inside the robes for a device belted around the rotund abdomen.

A rapid hammer of two stun bursts from his K-17 and the alien dropped. He tore the device off by the belt and dropped it. A coil of ener-chains came off his waist, aimed for the center of the round alien's body. They struck, stuck, and uncoiled to snake and wrap in dependable fashion around the dense torso and limbs.

"Fish face," Chappy yelled.

Hartenstein snapped around. A passenger he'd left for his teammates past was out of its cushion and safety restraints. A Hool cast its robes aside to reveal every spine erect, the tips slick with slimy poison. Chappy let his weapon snap to his chest.

"Play pincushion with me, will ya? Ain't even gonna scratch my armor." To prove the point, Chappy sprang, grasping the Hool in a bear hug, hefting the agnathian. Before the Hool could choose to suicide, Doc was jamming a hypo into a neck crease bare of spines.

"Not this time, you don't, fish face," Doc said.

Chappy held the Hool out like an infant while ener-chains completed their wrap. "Night, night, sleep tight. Don't let the fish poison bite." He lowered the limp Hool back into the acceleration cushion.

Hartenstein was blocked from seeing more than glimpses of Doc and Chappy's process to work backward and secure the first one he'd stunned on entry and the other he'd bypassed, seemingly unconscious or paralyzed in fear in its acceleration couch.

A loud voice was in his bucket. "Blue coming in. Fire in the hole."

Hartenstein spun to see a plasma charge flash, burning a neat leej-sized rectangular portal in the bulkhead at the fore of the cabin. Leejes birthed through the breach, until the entry team halted its drive, there being no space left to pile in to.

The fire suppression system had been flooding gas into the cabin, most of it escaping through the many rents and tears in the ship, but visibility decreased by the moment, indicating the system was catching up.

"Get these prisoners out before they suffocate," Doc was yelling. "Daisy chain—LET'S GO!"

Hands accepted the ener-chained bodies as they passed them forward and out of the wrecked yacht. On his way, Hartenstein spotted the belt and device he'd torn off the helmeted alien, and dropped it in his dump pouch. Doc was last out onto the permacrete, debris scattered in all directions like the aftermath of a Xalatan nega-cyclone running into a farmhouse. Hartenstein scanned the chaotic scene. A pair of mechs worked together to upright an FAV from its side, while another pushed debris to clear a path. He marveled that no leejes lay anywhere. The Zeta assaulters had been scattered like game pieces swept off a board.

"Head for the RP," Chappy said. A rally point was marked in his HUD, and Hartenstein joined his teammates to move upstream, passing leejes headed back to the yacht. Lights flashed and dull sirens screeched from rescue vehicles attending the wreck. Armored leejes intermingled with blue rescuers in yellow fire suits, both sorting through the wreckage. At the rally point, a cluster of leejes parted and General Airani stepped out, spreading arms to encompass the landscape.

"Adolphus! Bloody hell! First spear or no, it's not meant to be literal."

Hartenstein shrugged. "Right place, right time, I s'pose, Topper."

Chappy took in the scene as well. "Not textbook, but pretty impressive,"

Doc nudged him. "Two crashed birds in a day."

"That one ain't on me," Chappy reminded him.

Hartenstein ignored them. "What's our casualties, General?"

"Amazingly, zero. Let's go and see… just a second, Howler." The general dropped into another convo. "Understood. No additional detainees picked up. Commence exfil. Buccaneer Company takes security and trail."

The company commander affirmed the order with his unit's motto. "Buccaneer, by Oba."

Hartenstein had spoken many such mottos in his life. Death from above. Swift, silent, deadly. To the edge and beyond. When you said it, it said everything about you and the unit you represented. Whatever Topper had wanted him to join in seeing, the general would be engaged with his combat staff a little longer. He found Chappy and Doc mid-conversation with another Zeta, distinct by the splotchy gray pattern selected for the urban op.

Doc snorted. "What kind of maniac thinks he could power his ship out of a mech platoon dogpile?"

The new man said, "The pilot was a blue-boy. He didn't seem too badly injured when we peeled him out of the cockpit, but we had to turn him over to the Ozydna rescue crew. Doubtful we'll ever get to ask him what the hell he was thinking."

"Stupid laws," Chappy grumbled. "Anyway, it came out alright, Jelly. Don't sweat it."

The new man shrugged the consolation away. "Easy for you to say. You guys snagged the gold ring. Again."

Jelly assumed a stiff attention aimed at Hartenstein as he arrived. "We weren't introduced earlier, sir. I'm Lieutenant Jelenik."

Hartenstein extended a hand. "Howler, Lieutenant. Good to meet you."

"Jelly's one of our team leaders, Howler," Chappy said. "And a good one. Wait, did I say that out loud? Disregard."

Ignoring him, Hartenstein asked, "Are your people alright?"

Jelly grunted. "Yes, sir, amazingly. I barely missed getting toppled myself. Only a couple of guys took a bad bounce. A few dents, but no internal damage. We got too close, too soon on our perimeter before the mech drop. We'll be hot-washing this fiasco with the whole crew soon as we hit the FOB. Never seen Captain Malik so perturbed. Zeta made a poor showing and damn near let the mission fail. And in front of you, too."

It was a compliment that his opinion counted to the Zetas. "Nonsense, Lieutenant. Too many bones in the air at the same time, and any one of them can come up double skull when they stop rolling. It's the nature of what we do."

A shrill commotion reached their attention.

"That is them! I am certain."

Restrained by a cordon of Wolfhounds, a small blue man jumped up and down as he screamed.

"Very bad men. Very bad. They to blame for everything. Why you no shoot them?"

"I see your little buddy made it back," Doc said.

General Airani approached their gathering. "Fan of yours, gentlemen?"

Chappy snapped stiff. "Yes sir."

The general made a coughing chuckle. "Let's go. I want to see these detainees myself."

Doc and Chappy trailed Hartenstein and the general to where the dustoff Talon sat. The Wolfhound surgeon Major Eversoll met them on the ramp.

"Sir, our detainees are three-S's: stable, stripped, and secured. A medic's monitoring and guarding each. It's an interesting collection. Do you care to inspect, sir?"

"Lead on, Doctor."

A leej monitored the readouts over each slab where a medcomp held the four detainees in induced comas. The Hool was obvious. Stripped bare, its spines lay flat and dry, bathed in the red light of the surrounding chamber. The next was easily identifiable by the spikes protruding from the shoulders—a Kimbrin. The simian humanoid with short brown hair over its body was a moktaar.

The last slab held the alien that had pulled the vanishing act. It was naked save the fishbowl helmet sealed at the fat neck, the ample folds of its loose yellow skin piled beneath the rim of the helmet like frosting melted around the base of a cake left too long in the sun.

Chappy blurted what Hartenstein thought. "What the hell's that?"

The surgeon was there. "We don't know."

Doc had pushed next to the tending medic to check the monitor himself. "What's with the atmo-helmet?"

Major Eversoll blew out an exasperated sigh. "I had no choice but to leave its enviro-helmet on. It's a mix of 13% each chlorine and methane; the rest is the usual inerts with only a trace of oxygen. The physio-scan says it metabolizes the methane as a source for cellular carbon."

Doc's voice raised higher. "The methane it breathes is its energy source? It doesn't eat?"

"Maybe, Doc." Even the surgeon called him that. "What its metabolism does with the chlorine, we're still trying to figure out. There's not a humanoid world in the records with that atmosphere."

Another leej marched into the Talon med bay to halt in front of the general.

"I've prepared the writ, sir. To the necessary level of certainty, I've certified all four are non-Republic entities and meet the definition for security detainee. If I can get your signature, I'll copy the legal team at the embassy mission and we'll have cleared the first hurdle to holding them indefinitely."

The general gave a cursory scan of the holo document before attaching his biosig. "Fusion cell's going to have their hands full."

Hartenstein pulled the belted device from his dump pouch to add to the items in the clear bin next to the helmeted alien's slab. "This's what he was going for when I stunned him. It's some kind of dematerializing tech. But there's no such thing." His brain raced. "What are these four doing together?"

Wolfhound Six was grave. "We will soon discover."

The private channel in Howler's bucket opened. "Ugh." It was Chappy. "Briscoe and his fur-snake are up."

Doc cackled. "You're just jealous Trixie didn't take to you first."

Hartenstein didn't so much as groan. He was learning that rather than asking the pair to explain, sometimes it was just easier to wait and see. But he could tell their banter meant interesting things were coming. Some unique Wolfhound means to peel back the next layer of the veil.

Besides.

He was too tired to ask.

14

Bertie and Phillip loaded the collection recovered from Victrix into the hold of the *Supreme*. Kel ordered the AIs to play dumb until he gave the go-ahead to reveal themselves, and the crew directed the pair as if they were typical loader bots. Useful, but dumb.

"Over here with that, bot," a pimpled deckhand ordered sternly, making Kel think it was the first time someone lower in the pecking order was under the youth's direction. He made a mental note to find time for some early mentoring.

Phillip bobbed his head subserviently, as if he were the dull bot he played. Neither of the affable AIs would mind the charade or the abuse they were taking. In fact, he regretted not being privy to the entertaining chatter certain to be going on between Phil and Bertie right now, bantering like teenage boys buzzed on their first ale. After their long internment, the thrill of new surroundings and new people would be as close to an intoxicant as the AIs probably had. They were people. Better than many flesh and blood ones he'd known.

While Kel and Braley watched the bots work, Chelly in turn watched *them*. He was trying to be low-key, but failed, his twitchy glances to the armor on his left and right undermining his normally assured air. Kel was about to discuss their next move when Cormac appeared from the hold. The captain squinted from the bright sun that always baked the Victrix airfield, put on a pair of dark shades and with their comfort, held for a moment to appraise the scene on the ground before striding down, puffing up as he did. Kel made the introductions.

"Captain Cormac Sullivan, this is Lieutenant Colonel Braley Yost, one of the new passengers we're taking on."

Braley's armored hand thrust out. "Thank you, Captain Sullivan. I appreciate the hospitality of the *Supreme* and her crew."

Cormac briefly accepted the hand, then grunted like a salesman challenging a credit rating. "Can I speak to you alone for a moment, Turner." It was not a request.

Faced off with Kel, Cormac made a show of giving his armor a disapproving once-over, prompting Kel to take a deep, cleansing breath in anticipation of the abuse to come. "I see you're up to old tricks. There's enough ordnance for a war being loaded on my ship. I'm about ready to kick you, your new tin-can buddy, and all your hardware to the curb if you don't tell me what's going on."

Chelly interrupted loudly. "Inbound." All eyes snapped up as a boom broke over the airfield.

Kel didn't address Cormac's threat. "We can lift as soon as we take on these passengers, Captain."

Undeterred, Cormac held.

"I didn't want to be your private yacht because I knew there'd be some kind of hijinks like this. That armor tells me all I need to know." Cormac reddened as his accusations built. "You're using this family like a disposable tool for whatever games you're playing for the Republic again. And when we snap in two, you'll toss us in the trash heap. The proof is *there*. That isolation field—I know what that means. You promised you wouldn't place us in any danger."

Kel's game plan to win the long fight with the captain had been to bob, weave, and parry. To do anything but hit back. "And I'm keeping my word, Uncle Cormac. There's no danger. The reason for that containment field and what's under there, I can't go into it, but it's more important than—"

"Here we go," Cormac mocked. "More lies on the way."

Cormac was like the nuisance tree limb that swayed against his house whenever the wind blew. He'd trimmed it, but still it wasn't enough. Cormac was like that tree. It was time to fell him for good. "Captain or no, you don't talk that way to me again. *Your* family is *my* family. Got it?"

Cormac blinked, but Kel wasn't about to stop until he'd splintered the trunk.

"I owe you not one more reason to convince you of that. So instead, let's settle things between us in an easier way. You bought the ticket. Now—you ride the ride."

Cormac inspected his boots, embarrassed by the truth. The captain had taken his money. Before Kel could topple him and his pride, the flare of landing repulsors deafened and stole the last swings of his axe.

It would wait. He spun away to join Braley's side as the ship came to rest. Braley clucked, "Those two had fits when I left them in orbit. But I wanted them in reserve in case we both needed rescuing."

Steam bathed the shuttle. Without waiting for the descent of a ladder, two leejes hopped onto the duracrete. Grav trunks obediently followed like war hounds as they marched through the dense exhaust, warrior-angels parting the clouds of a mountain fortress from where they watched the mortal world. The first to break from the mist was just as large as the mythical archangels of war he'd compared them to. There was only one leej he'd ever served with who came close to the size of his former Dark Ops commander, and it brought a grin to Kel's face.

Meadows.

Curt was a force of nature. A giant among giants, in more ways than size. Kel had been around the galaxy with Meadows. He chose him over Poul to be Kill Team 12's team sergeant. And Meadows had never left him wanting. Yes, Meadows was taciturn. He was often a bully. Occasionally and at the most surprising of times, he metered out a compassion tinged with remorse, as if apologizing for his nature as a single-minded, concentrated, well of hate. Kel held him as one of the many models for what an operator should be.

With some exceptions.

It was only next to a Meadows that the other leej making his epic entrance could appear small. Jon Simons was more the kind of operator Kel held as the model for a common mold from which to cast a kill team. Quick to laugh, quick to level death, quick to put himself at risk for others, Sims was also as extraordinary a slicer as he was everything else.

Like Philip and Bertie, it was Kel's turn for heady intoxication at a reunion with his own kind.

Hammer fists to chests went around until Sims hefted Kel in a bear hug. "Good to see you, Kel, even though circumstances suck."

Meadows had a second go at Kel, slamming a fist into his chest so hard, it rocked him back on his feet. "That's for missing your promotion. Your ident says major."

"It's fake," Kel said.

"So, Captain, then?"

"Just Kel, Top."

Sims said, "I don't want to ruin it, but when can we talk about..." He indicated the shimmering domes over Victrix.

"Later. Pop your lids and let me introduce you to the captain and co-pilot."

It was a rule for self-preservation learned early by those who worked around moving machines that the surefire way to get crushed to paste was to get between them. Cormac and Chelly had stood back from the metal melee. Now Kel gave the all clear and waved them close. Kel was about to make the introductions, when Meadows touched an ear to indicate his implant. "Colonel Yost, the skipper wants to confirm you're releasing the *Acheron*."

"Tell them we've got our next transport. Pass on my thanks, Sergeant Major," Braley said.

Kel whistled. "The *Acheron*'s a cruiser!"

Braley's eyebrows bounced. "I'm a big shot, now. Sector provosts have all kinds of weight."

Before he could resume introductions, Tara was at Kel's side, reaching as much of a tiny arm as she could around his waist.

"Most importantly, brothers, it's time you met Tara, my wife."

In brilliant contrast to the men's continued distance, Tara showed disregard as she giggled, "I feel like I already know each of you. Braley," she said as she threw arms around him. "Sims," she did the same. Both returned her embrace her as if she was made of porcelain. Their grins remained beyond her release.

"And I know this must be Curt." The other leejes joined Kel to chuckle as Meadows stiffened, arms awkwardly held wide as if unsure he had the control necessary to avoid crushing the tiny doll in a return embrace. He was saved from making whatever reply he percolated by the glide of a combat sled coming to rest. An MP sergeant leaped from the back to land in a wide stance, hands on hips, confidently booming authority.

"Listen up, Legion. You don't run the show around here. There's no authorization for you to remove any evidence from the scene. Stand fast until the major arrives and we inspect whatever it is I witnessed you load on to this civilian craft."

Braley stepped forward, but his path was cut off by the mountain of Meadows and the thunderous steps that ground the surface like a rockslide rolling to crush the MP. Any sane person would have softened their posture. Or shown military courtesy by assuming parade rest. Diffused the situation by affecting even a tiny smile, no matter how forced.

Anything but what the MP did.

With arms at sides and fists balled, the MP expanded his chest and lats like an adolescent posing in a mirror after a few pushups.

Sims spluttered. "Pfft. FPS. Fake physique syndrome. Him and everything he knows is about to get nuked."

Whether his badge made him stupidly courageous, stupidly confident, or just plain stupid, it was fatally bad judgment.

Meadows's knife hand stopped at the sergeant's nose.

"Check that attitude, Sergeant. You don't talk to my colonel like that, much less a sergeant major. You're a sorry pissant of an NCO." Meadows placed a palm against the basic's chest and, before the surprised MP could react, shoved. The sergeant flew backward into the open compartment. Meat collided with steel to make the universal sound that brought a tiny flinch in the abdomen of any listener, no matter how accustomed to primal violence.

Sims cringed. "Oof. Too much, too soon."

The driver gawked in wide-eyed paralysis.

Meadows was stern, but calm. "The sergeant's military bearing was unacceptable. I corrected it. Tell your major what happened."

The driver snapped stiff in his seat. "Yes, Sergeant Major!"

"And tell him this ground was paid for with Legion blood. Take off."

The relieved driver sped away.

Kel snorted. "Is it just me, or is Meadows more Meadows than ever? Let's finish this reunion in orbit."

Cormac bristled. "What kind of trouble are you getting me into, Turner?"

Chelly's smile was electric. If he'd wanted excitement, he was getting it. "We need to get airborne, Cap."

Cormac groused, "Might as well. An empty hold's a bankrupt hold. Even if we had a destination, there's no paying haul off this rock." He moved to joined his first officer to head back into the ship. "I'll put us near a jump point until you have a destination for us, Turner." For now, it seemed Kel's choice to fight back had succeeded.

"I heard what you said to Cormac, Kel," Tara said. "You were right."

Meadows shrugged. "Who wouldn't be thrilled to have *us* around. Weird. I'll get us loaded, Colonel." Curt keyed his grav trunk and moved to take a step for the ship, but checked himself. He paused to look down at Tara, and spoke softly. "I'm glad to finally meet you, ma'am." He found Kel's eyes. "I know why you left. Hardball had it." As if he'd explained all he could, he marched away.

"And with that," Sims said. "We'd best scoot."

Tara pivoted to take a last look around, resting on Mount Fronius before closing eyes and sucking a deep breath. It was a thing Kel had seen the spacers do. From whatever green hills and sweet air they found themselves leaving, they took a tiny taste, as if it would sustain them until they again breathed the sweeter air of their own green home. Exhaling, she said, "It's a beautiful world. I wish there was time for you to show it to me."

Sims took a longing look toward Victrix.

"It was the center of our universe, once."

That the subtle jump drive hum wasn't penetrating the air of the hold was a conspicuous admission they had no destination yet. The leejes drew crates in a circle, bringing the ire of the kid who'd ordered the bots around.

"Hey! Keep that space clear!"

The loadmaster was a woman named Syraph. Crew had been sporadically dropping in to peek at the new passengers through her office window. She heard the young deckhand's testiness and leaned out her door to intervene, saving Kel from having to.

"C'mere, Curt. Leave Cousin Kel and his friends alone."

Hearing his name, Meadows looked at the source, only to realize the bosun was speaking to the youth.

"You got a namesake," Sims said.

Before obeying, the frowning boy's displeasure came a last time, though a little more politely. "Please put things back in order when you're done. I'll check the tie-downs later."

Meadows gave the kid a look of mild admiration as he marched off. "Kid's got guts."

"So'd that MP," Sims said.

"You know better than to confuse a death wish with guts," Meadows pronounced.

Another crewman slid into the hold, the visit to the loadmaster's office an excuse to sneak a glance at the new passengers through the office window.

"Buckets," is all Kel said. Bertie and Phillip lowered themselves on all fours to lie eye-level with their comrades. "Probably best if I start." He gave them the entire story, starting with the reason for his return home alone from Catalinia-X, the revelatory appearance on Callie's World by General Tyrus Rex, ending with Victrix and their reunion.

Silence. He knew they were picturing what the team rooms had looked like before he arrived to find them empty.

"If you don't, then I've got questions," Kel said. He looked at Sims and Meadows. "What happened to push you both out of Dark Ops?"

"Oh, I've got plenty of questions," Sims said. "It's just a bit much to take in all at once. But I'll go. The unit was getting weird. It was Bigg who nudged me to take the job at ASC. These two were already on Tiberius, so it wasn't like a total exile from Dark Ops."

Tiberius was a center of Legion training, from basic to everything else. The Advanced Skills Course took senior legionnaires to new levels of deadly proficiency. "Instructing was better than sitting around doing nothing, which is what we were doing. And it wasn't a total waste of time, either. I picked up some of the latest slicing tricks I'd gotten a little behind on while I taught the intel course. Bigg said that whatever transition Dark Ops was going through, I'd be back when it settled out. Not even Bigg could've seen this, though."

They waited for Meadows to take his turn. Sensing he was required to speak, but always one for few words, he said only, "Bigg. And Colonel Yost." He said it without the hint of the same silver-lining Sims used to paint the portrait of his recent career.

Braley filled in. "Bigg reached out. He insisted that a provost needs a hatchet man. It came with a bump."

"Congratulations, Sergeant Major," Kel said.

Meadows deflected. "It's had its moments." There was neither satisfaction nor pride in his voice.

Sims took up again. "I kept in touch with the guys. Some returned to their old regiments. A few followed you and Poul's lead and decided if it wasn't Dark Ops, they might as well retire or leave the Legion altogether. The writing was on the wall, but some stayed. Like Hardball. And Bigg."

"And now they're dead." It was a typical Meadows segue, saying what no one else would with the callousness of a robot.

Sims was less abrupt. "And that leaves us. Sir, can you finally tell us what it is we're doing?"

Braley sighed. "Things are in flux. Primus Pilus is working. There are things happening on several fronts. The first step was this."

Meadows shook his head disdainfully. "I'm ready to KTF, but... this thing with your secret boy's club. Again."

"What about Primus Pilus?" Kel asked.

Meadows mumbled. "It's just... I don't want to say more."

Sims flustered. "Oba, Curt. What is it you think you can't say to us? You've seen all the crazy stuff we have. You were with us every step of the way to take down the Scarecrow. You were on Psydon to see what the Hool were up to. Maybe you weren't with us to see for yourself the frelled up things those Savages were doing on Proteus Four, but you know it was all real. And it ended with the Republic ordering up a planet buster to erase what was there. There's secrets, and then there's *secrets*. You've been part the biggest. What about Primus Pilus has you tongue tied?"

Meadows stayed mum.

Braley took over. "My fault. I should have made it clear as soon as I told you and Sims what happened on Victrix. Neither of you hesitated to come with me, even knowing we were heading into a deep, dark abyss, more or less by ourselves again."

"Of course I did," Sims said. "Nothing matters except this fight. I'm ready to bring it. Especially if the rest of the machine is doing the opposite."

"Same-same," Meadows said. "Wrong's wrong. Right's right. Consequences don't matter."

Braley said, "I never doubted. And what I should have made clear immediately is that between us, there's no barrier, no privilege by rank, nothing to prevent anyone from speaking their mind. We're a kill team again. Pure and simple. Whatever you're thinking, Curt, lay it all out."

Meadows considered. "All right, Braley. I'm not a card-carrying member of your cult, but I saw what they can do. They helped us whack a frelling senator. And I've kept my opinions to myself ever since. But, I've always wondered. Isn't that what killed Dark Ops? Someone figured it out, and gutted us so we don't do it again. And not just Dark Ops. The Legion got points! Because of what we did. I dare you or Kel to tell me I got it wrong."

Kel couldn't. Because Meadows was right.

"So what happens if we do this thing?" Meadows continued. "Will they destroy the whole Legion when someone figures out a handful of rogue operators did something this big again?"

Braley was there to answer. "The Society answered the call to take down the Scarecrow in order to *save* Dark Ops from becoming a tool to be misused in more conspiracies. And to save the Legion. And the Republic. It's no different now."

"Fact," Kel said. "Except, it's much, much worse. Don't you see that, Curt?"

"It doesn't matter," Sims said. "If Legion Command's keeping this shut down, if the House of Reason is back to being nothing but a bunch of power-mad lunatics, then we're all there is. We do this for our Dark Ops brothers. For all humanity. Because we're the *real* Legion."

Meadows rolled his eyes. "Of course we are. It ain't that."

"Then what?" Sims was near boiling. Meadows snorted.

"It's up to me to be the practical one? You know I got no problem with killing anyone who needs it. But how the hell are just the four of us going to bring all the pain? Because Braley already said not even Primus Pilus knows who did this yet, and that everyone's against us finding out."

Kel had the first dose of medicine for Curt's ailment. "It's like Braley said, getting us together was just the start. Rex is working on the rest."

Meadows glowered. "And *that*. Some twarg eater says he's Rex. *The* Rex. And you buy it?" He scowled his accusation.

"I do," Braley said.

Kel tagged on. "I know he is. He founded Primus Pilus for just this reason."

Meadows slapped his forehead. "So we're back to your frat house boys. Not filling me with confidence, gents."

Kel had the next dose. "We have a concrete objective. Rex wants to wipe out this conspiracy, but he's not organizing the attack on just that front. He thinks there's a way to nullify this nano weapon. He's confident the opposition developed this weapon from tech no one could possibly have developed on their own. He said he knows for a fact there's an ancient alien influence in the galaxy, and it's been the factor in so many of the odd things we've been a part of. He came to me because he thinks I have the best chance at finding the way to shut this thing down. He thinks what we need is in the Section. And Sarah's the key to finding it. We start by locating her."

Meadows's confusion was honest. "Huh?"

"He doesn't know the whole tale, Kel," Braley said.

Kel ran Meadows through what happened on the Proteus Four mission. How VanderLoot manipulated Dark Ops into what had nearly been a one-way mission to steal a paradigm-shifting tech that manipulated the essence of energy—another tool for VanderLoot's pursuit of power. Removed from the influence of her minder, the brilliant scientist placed with their team admitted who she was and her purpose. She worked for an entity that

247

collected and researched technologies ancient and even extra-galactic. The Section.

And it had all been under the exclusive control of the Scarecrow.

Sims was somewhere far away. "It was my first mission with Three when we snatched that trillionaire tech guru, Xenon Boothe. He cried and pleaded with us not to take him in. Said they were going to kill him because he knew too much. Said all our greatest advances weren't really ours, that all of our tech had been stolen from some ancient alien race. When we found Patrick in that hellish prison, hung like a specimen and stripped down to his nerves, as if that wasn't bad enough, then we found Boothe's name on their roster. When I think about it, I still feel sick."

Meadows had none of Sims's weary regret. He seemed relieved. "Easy enough, then. We have a hard target to hit. *That's* what we do. No big deal."

But Kel didn't have the last dose for the cure. "No one knows where it is. All we've got is Sarah's face." Kel tapped his temple.

Meadows's head fell back. "I shoulda known. Got it. All we gotta do is find one person out of a galaxy of a trillion people."

Sims smirked. "Suddenly, I find myself with Curt. We had a lot more to go on when we tracked down the Scarecrow's minions. And a lot more help. That isn't much to go on."

Braley said, "We know the Section exists."

"You're making Meadows's point for him," Sims said. "We don't know *where* that is. So, what's the plan? Kidnap some top level RI or Nether ops goons and choke it out of them? I doubt VanderLoot let them in on it. I'm betting it's the only real secret in the galaxy."

The AIs had lain silent as disciplined pets. "Err," Bertie said in his comically lilting voice. "That's not exactly true, now, is it?"

Kel didn't expect this. "What?"

"Well, sir, Phillip and I've had a lot of time on our hands since then."

"Bertie's right, Mister Turner. It were kind of a puzzle we amused ourselves with while we was shelved. Like where does Oba live, where in the body is the soul housed exactly, what's the meaning of existence, and how does the subspark routine fit in? That sort o' thing."

Bertie countered his friend's comparison. "Well, hardly like that, Phillip, old boy. It weren't the same kind of supernatural musing at all. It was rather a concrete bit of analysis and detective work, eliminating..."

Meadows's hand shot for Bertie's spindly neck like a viper striking. He pulled the rectangular head to his face. "OUT WITH IT, BLOCKHEAD."

Released as suddenly, Bertie recoiled back. With perfect diction and little trace of his usual accent, he obeyed.

"With a probability of 98.739 percent, the Section is located in the ternary star system of Qualatus, on the artificial world of Imprimus. It exists solely to maintain the Imprimis Academy of Research, an independent center for study of cosmology and the physical sciences. The system contains the binary black holes of Galiata and Fornus, coinciding with the most frequently appearing wormholes ever discovered in the galaxy." The AI's head sank onto his body. Kel could've sworn he shivered.

Phillip scooted alongside Bertie on all fours and placed his head against his friend's. Kel had never seen them act... scared.

Meadows groaned. "Was that so hard?" Seeing the pair cower like beaten dogs, regret filled his eyes. He made his contrition. "I'm sorry, for..." He twirled a hand around as if indicating he apologized for the very air around him. "I just reach a limit sometimes. Won't happen again."

The bots relaxed back into normal posture. "We apologize as well," Philip said. "Whatever you may think, gentlemen, it's been difficult for us."

Bertie was somber. "We hurt, too."

"We know," Kel said.

"Thanks for sending our brothers off well," Sims said.

"All right, all right," Meadows said gruffly. "Let's get on with this. Where's this system?"

A holo of the five arms of the galaxy projected in their midst. Two icons flashed, one their current location, the other at nearly the opposite side of the galactic center. Kel was inspired.

"We have a destination. Time to get Cormac and Chelly up to speed. Because I have a stop to make along the way. We're going to pick up Poul."

"To do what?" Meadows shrugged. "You said he's gimped."

Sims shook his head.

Kel laughed. "You never disappoint, Curt. Good to know we're officially back to kill team norms. Poul's going with us, because a kill team is five. And because he deserves to be with us to see this thing done. And we need him."

"Yeah, yeah," Meadows said. "I guess it won't matter if he's hobbled. This isn't much of a manhunt. It'll be locating and surveilling a target who's not on the run and doesn't know she's being hunted. Dull. Right up Radd's alley. You too, Sims. Massaging data streams instead of doing real work."

Sims rolled his eyes. "I seem to remember you being glued to our intel cloud matrices back on Nemanjic."

"And I'll be making sure you don't botch the job. Maybe this island in space for misfit electron pushers is the perfect hiding place for this Section, or maybe it's a citadel guarded by wobanki mercs. If it's housing all the secrets that let the Scarecrow secretly run things, there'll be someone there who needs the KTF, and I'll be bringing it."

Braley said, "I've always said you're a man for all seasons, Sergeant Major."

Kel's body vibrated in anticipation. "Now we can work. What do we know about Imprimis?"

15

The navy carrier that was Wolfhound Six's HQ remained in-system, but far enough from Ozydna to give them the shield supplied by a distance that made it inconvenient for visitors. The intrusive Republic representatives were currently engaged in dealing with the aftermath of what the Wolfhounds had sprung on their otherwise placid diplomatic mission. Republic Intelligence was involved, and their station chief and a host of diplomats swarmed the prison, still under guard by the Wolfhounds. The experts Major Eversoll had recommended were supposedly on their way.

After a pass through the Navy medcomp, some sleep, and a few of the largest steaks in the navy's stores, Hartenstein was back to status quo—an aging operator. He was with Doc and Chappy in the Wolfhound fusion cell, ready to unravel the mystery of the identities of the four disparately alien detainees.

To the notice of all the Wolfhound fusion cell staff, a new leej stepped in. He wore utility silks rather than armor. Wrapped around the leej's neck like an ener-chain collar was the pet they'd told Hartenstein to expect. It was covered with stringy red fur. If it had a head, it remained hidden, buried beneath the bushy tail. He'd seen more bizarre animals than he had years in the Legion. Scaly lizards with stalked eyes and a dank odor, too ugly to be thought cuddly by any but the odd leej who took pride in how his pet disgusted the rest of them. He'd seen fur balls who rolled to locomote themselves. Animals with scaly bodies who propelled by odd numbers of legs in ways only Oba thought well adapted for their evolution. Leejes collected pets from around the galaxy like children sought souvenirs from vacations.

This one reminded him of none of them.

"Ain't he the prima donna," Chappy said. "Strutting around with his girlfriend like he owns the place. That thing's a security risk, I tell you."

"Why does Briscoe's pet creep you out?" Doc asked.

Chappy shivered. "I bet he lets that thing *massage* him in all kinds of sick ways. I'm putting my bucket back on."

The leej with the mink stole grinned.

"I heard that. Don't be a kelhorn, Chap. You'll hurt Trixie's feelings. You're going to be apologizing again when she busts these subjects wide open like your mom."

Chappy made a hand gesture. "This is for you, Brissy."

The interrogator returned the gesture. "I heart you too, Chap."

Hartenstein was skeptical about the strange talent the animal supposedly possessed. "That animal's actually a telepath? Where'd it come from?"

Doc explained. "We found it on Tulinax Seven. Briscoe was on our team. We'd just finished a job and were checking out an outdoor market before we left. One of the Tullies pulled us into his stall, trying to interest us in raw Panthellian diamonds. They were fakes, of course, but in a cage in the back, was *that.*"

Chappy hadn't put his bucket on, despite his threat. "Anyone could see it was miserable, poor thing."

Doc teased. "See, Howler? Deep down, Chap's all heart. Where was I? So we're in this Tully's tent when we see this strange animal in a cage. Brissy gets closer. The guy tells him to be careful, she bites, and he's been warned. Brissy starts cooing at it like it was a baby. This red fur ball stretches out, perks right up, and before the guy can say anything, Brissy has it out of the cage and it's like the two were long-lost buddies. The merchant's stunned. Says the little thing's only ever snarled and tried to bite him or anyone who got close. He got her in a trade, no idea where she came from, and he's only too glad to part with her. For a price. Anyway, Brissy's got a new pet, and the two are inseparable. Pretty soon, she's with him in the team room, on missions, everywhere. He can't wait to pop his lid so he and Trixie can snuggle.

"Then one night, we're hanging loose and playing head-game."

Chappy snorted. "Head-frell, you mean."

It was more lingo Hartenstein didn't know. "That you have to explain."

"Never played? It's the latest thing. Better than Galacta-Box. You control the holo characters and everything in the games by neural link. Instantaneous, no delay like when you use a controller. It's like it's really you in the game.

Totally speeds up the action. You can change the characters, create worlds, it's pretty spiff."

Chappy shook his head in disgust. "Oughta be banned. It's a frelling security risk too, just like Trixie. The Nemanjic make 'em, so you know it's suspicious tech. Gotta be loaded with slicing codes to pull your credit codes right outta your brain and read the swipe patterns off your datapads. What else would you expect from the Nems? Buncha criminals."

Doc blew him off. "Yeah, yeah. Anyway, a bunch of us were playing mind-game, and there's a break in the action. Briscoe's there with Trixie, wrapped around his neck like usual. He and Chappy were talking about... well, you tell him, Chap."

Chappy's face twisted. "We were, uh, reminiscing about a visit to a, uh, Tennar palace."

Hartenstein cocked an eyebrow. Chappy chose his words with care.

"Anyway, all of a sudden, the holo changes. It's a point of view sorta thing from Briscoe's perspective of a very, very sharp Tennar girl in his lap."

Hartenstein got the picture.

"We couldn't believe it," Doc said. "Long and short of it, it turns out Trixie's telepathic. Trixie was reading Biscoe's mind and projecting it *right into the holo emitter of the head-game console.* Crazy, right?"

Chappy carried on with the story. "We hauled ass for Doc Eversoll's office to show him. Captain Malik gets involved, then the general. Next thing, Briscoe's off Zeta and in the fusion cell."

Doc explained. "Trixie can read anybody. Even aliens. What they put together for interrogation is more sophisticated than a head-game console, of course, but same-same. When there's a tough nut, they bring in Briscoe and Trixie. She loves the big guy so much, she'll do anything for him. He asks the question, she probes the subject's mind, and it all plays out like a show."

Chappy pointed at Briscoe, who was in conference with a major from the fusion cell. "I'm not saying the two of them aren't useful. I'm just saying that for an operator like Brissy to leave Zeta in favor of a full-time love affair with a space weasel, it's twisted."

Briscoe and his pet stepped in front of an interview room, the captured Hool restrained in a chair on the other side of the glass.

"This I have to see." Hartenstein moved nearer to Topper and the fusion cell commander. Briscoe stroked the fur around his neck, frowning at what he saw through the window.

"Sir, you know Trixie has to touch her subject. Neutralized or not, none of us would lay bare hands on a fish face."

"Fair enough, Sergeant Briscoe. We'd never ask you to put Trixie at risk," the major said. "She's too valuable an asset."

For the first time, Trixie uncoiled and lifted from around her partner's neck to reveal her face. Floppy ears perked and a pair of black eyes shined. A button nose sat on a short snout. She pushed up on pairs of short paws and extended her nose. She purred loudly and the corners of her lips lifted in what had to be a smile. The major offered a bare hand to allow a pink tongue to lap it.

"Trixie appreciates that, sir," Briscoe said.

"Ugh," Chappy said. "Wanna bet Briscoe lets her—"

"Shh," Hartenstein cut him off.

General Airani took his turn to be rewarded with a lick from Trixie. "What about our unknown alien, Brissy? Doc Eversoll says it doesn't pose any tactile danger. We think that one's holding on to the treasure."

They moved to stand in front of another interview room. Like the other restrained detainees, the yellow alien behind the glass was dressed in a prisoner's white paper gown. Atop the mountain of loose skin sat the helmeted head and the thin green mist it breathed. Its small white eyes were fixed on the one-way glass, aware that it was being viewed.

"How about it, Trixie? Do you want to work? Can you show daddy what's in the bad man's mind?"

The purring grew louder as Trixie wagged her bushy tail, then yelped the same two syllables several times.

Hartenstein's eyes bulged wide. "It sounded like she said... *bad man*? Can Trixie talk?"

"Just for Briscoe," Doc said.

Of everything he'd seen of the Wolfhounds, from their version of Dark Ops to their aviators and mech platoons, it was this that forced him to admit the Wolfhounds were a regiment unlike any in the rest of the Legion.

"This may take a while, Howler," Doc said. "We can come back later to see the finished product. Maybe you want to get off your feet for a spell?"

"Not a chance," he said, mesmerized. "And I'm ready to run circles around you pups."

"Wasn't saying you couldn't, Stomper," Chappy said gingerly.

In the room was the holo apparatus and a pair of leejes. Briscoe entered. "Hey Terry, hey Stacks. Ready to work?"

"Go for it, Brissy."

Trixie's body was long and flexible, and Hartenstein counted eight pairs of short legs as she uncoiled like a spring stretching long as she scurried into Briscoe's hands. "All right, daddy's best girl, the bad man's hiding things, things we want to know. Can you show us what it is? That's my good girl."

Trixie took a cautious sniff, then put her front pair of legs on the alien's chest and stretched her snout to touch the helmet and look in its eyes. As though the clear helmet that separated it from the curious Trixie was adequate protection, the alien stayed still—until Trixie coursed around the squat neck. It shifted side to side to shed the red vine circling its neck, viscous rolls of loose skin earthquake failing to shake off the visitor. Undeterred, Trixie wrapped herself below the helmet, wriggling into the folds of flesh before coming to rest, satisfied with her nestling place. The alien strained to see what lay beneath its line of sight, but sensing no further movement or constriction, surrendered.

Briscoe chuckled lightly and teased the alien. "Comfy, yes? Don't get attached, buddy. I'll share her, but she's my pal."

The major had a list of questions he passed to Briscoe. "Let's start with the basics, Sergeant."

Briscoe asked the first, adding his own syrupy enticement. "Okay, pretty girl, concentrate now. Where are you from?"

Doc whispered, "They haven't found anyone who can shut his mind to her, not even a Gomarii. Doc Eversoll says it's a universal that sentients form mental image pictures as part of the thought process. Trixie sees it and transmits it. Crazy, huh?"

A holo formed. Through the perspective of the alien's beady white eyes, a planet covered in the green mist appeared, the yellow surface making Hartenstein think perhaps it was actually red beneath the thick atmosphere.

Doc was enthralled. "They always picture whatever it is they're questioned, even if it's only for a second. It's like, 'don't think of a pink doober.' An image of one pops into your head, even if you tell yourself not to. The first thing they show is the truth."

One of the techs spoke. "Got it, Major."

The holo changed to a more mundane world.

Doc snorted. "See? Gas head's trying to evade, but it won't work. They'll keep working this line of questioning to get him to betray what'll let them locate his home."

"What's the night sky look like?" Briscoe asked, adding praises and promises of rewards to Trixie.

"Really, Howler, this is going to go on for some time," Chappy said. "I've seen a bunch of these. They'll bounce to an entirely different topic to unbalance him, then on to something else, then back to the beginning. Eventually, they put together complete answers."

Hartenstein had been so intent on the scene, he didn't notice the new spectator joining.

"It's something, isn't it, Colonel?"

The Zeta team leader Captain Malik had appeared silently to watch the interrogation.

"I'm..." He searched for the right word. "Impressed."

"Speaking of impressive, sir. What you did at the spaceport, not to mention the prison—I haven't had opportunity to say so—but both were some piece of work. Guess I shouldn't be surprised. Rex picked you to run Dark Ops. Do you have a minute, sir?" The captain with a touch of gray at his temples stepped back, inviting a private conversation. Hartenstein knew the Zeta team leader had refused promotion in favor of remaining in charge of the covert unit.

He grunted. "Call me Howler, Captain. What's on your mind?"

"Zeta didn't make a good showing on this op. We've become too insular. I'd like an outside perspective. Wolfhound Six's on board, and to tell the truth, the team's pestered me since the moment we left Ozydna. We want to pick your brain. Would you consider spending some time with Zeta?"

Chappy whistled. "What the frell's that?"

Hartenstein and Malik stepped back in view of the interrogation cell. A new image hovered above the emitter. A dome enclosed a huge city on a barren rock floating in space. The light of three dim and distant suns reflected off the massive cap and the buildings within. Elsewhere on the lone celestial body, patches of smaller habitations surrounded by dishes and antenna-like projections pointed in the same direction. What they aimed toward was obvious. As unusual as the three stars in the system, a pair of tiny swirling orange clouds floated in a central patch of emptiness. At the center of each, a darkness blacker than any black sucked in the light of everything around them.

Next to Briscoe, the fusion cell major's excitement was registered in the expression of the two techs running the equipment. "Jackpot on the first try."

The image disappeared, and Trixie raised her head from beneath the bushy tail to find Briscoe, panting with a tiny pink tongue. The sergeant praised her.

"You're doing great, Trixie. Daddy's so proud of you. Let's try some more, okay?"

Duly praised, the slender animal yipped in joy and wagged her puffy hind end, before burying herself again in the wattles of the neck folds to earn more accolades. The major pointed over the sergeant's shoulder to the list. "Hit him with this, Brissy."

"Special places mean special reasons for being there, my friend. What's your special reason and who do you meet there?"

An image briefly flashed, then disappeared to be replaced by a nonsensical flurry of mundane scenes.

"D'ya see that?" Chappy said. "That was a human. Fart breather immediately tried to scrub its first reaction by thinking of a buncha garbage. Is that what it eats?" The current image was a POV of a bowl of soupy brown liquid.

Hartenstein pushed to the window and hit the speaker switch. "Bring that first scene back, please."

The technicians complied, and the split second view they'd had of the alien's first thought returned to hang next to the scene of the isolated planetoid. A human female, her blonde hair pulled back in a ponytail, held an object in her extended hands. Behind her, benches and shelves were covered with unrecognizable items, each housed in its own stasis field like a grocer's store.

Hartenstein recognized the plain woman as if he'd seen her just yesterday.

"I know who the woman is."

It was Sarah.

Like everything about the clandestine mission Dark Ops had been ordered to carry out on Proteus Four, the scientist and her handler's purpose had been concealed from him. He was a young sergeant when he'd witnessed the Savage civilization and their fearful technology on the eerie moon. He'd been ordered to forget it, though he could not. And it nearly remained a ghost from his past until he was ordered to send Kill Team Three to investigate the moon. They'd nearly perished, and the moon had been destroyed to hide what lived there, all at the behest of the Scarecrow.

But what survived was the knowledge that somewhere existed a collection of powerful and ancient relics.

He inspected the images again. Like a lone cactus in a vast desert of three weak stars, the remote station was the sole life to bear witness to two twirling black holes that ate everything around them. And seen through a haze of green mist by beady white eyes, was Sarah, amidst a collection of enigmatic objects, one of which she gave to the alien.

The alien who'd commanded the death of the helpless people Hartenstein had failed to save.

And mixed in it all had to be the answer to who'd murdered the leejes of Dark Ops.

Doc had several holos open. "Nowhere like it anywhere. The Qualatus system. Imprimis is a research community. They like their privacy. High security. Visitation's tightly controlled."

"Who is she, Howler?" General Airani asked.

"Topper, I've got a story to tell. Then, I'm sure you'll agree, Rex would want my next stop to be there." He pointed to the holo of the domed city.

"Imprimis is my destination."

They worked quickly. The *Seraphim* sat in the cavernous bay of the navy destroyer. Similar to the craft Dark Ops once had for their most clandestine missions, it was a sleek civilian transport without any connection to the Legion or the Republic. Navy and legionnaire crewmen swarmed over the craft to ready it. Topper agreed the aircrew Hartenstein knew would remain with him, as would Doc and Chappy. Hartenstein spoke with the general as the loading continued.

"Slabside says we'll be in jump a full week to get there, Topper. We'll have adequate time to figure the rest out on the way."

The general had approved the mission without hesitation, as Hartenstein predicted, though the specifics were lacking. Rex had thought the Section held the cause and solution to the looming threat.

Wolfhound Six frowned. "I'm not concerned there, Howler. It's just that, as sector commander, I've had control over what we've been doing in Cygnus. But there's no help coming if you get into trouble on this. And it can't come back on the Legion or the Republic. Howler, you're on your own on this."

Hartenstein smirked. "Qualatus is well outside Republic or any other territory. There's no one to fluster. But don't worry. I have no plan to go in there guns blazing. No one's going to know we were ever there."

"Find what's there and get back. I expect by the time you do, the fusion cell will have squeezed a complete picture out of these prisoners. And when we have it, whether it's one planet or a dozen, the Wolfhounds are going to hit them all at the same time, and end this thing once and for all. Any word from Rex?"

Hartenstein shook his head. "Nothing. I don't even know if he's received my messages."

Topper frowned. "He's only ever spoken with me a few times over the years. The last time, he was even harder to read than what I'd call normal, for all I can say about the general. It was like he was only partially present. Like he's... lost, or something."

Howler had noticed it as well. The vagueness Rex used was his brand. Almost as if he himself didn't know why he did what he did. "None of us knows how old he actually is. Could it be he's... senile?"

"What about those two?" Topper asked. Doc and Chappy were loading containers onto the ship. The *Seraphim* was as unassuming and nondescript as a Talon or Excalibur were threatening. "They probably have spent more time with the general than anyone. When they return from one of their jaunts with him, I ask them. I know they're being honest when they say they don't know what Rex is up to, but have they said anything different to you?"

Hartenstein chuckled. "I need a translation when I ask those two about the weather. For the most complex subject in existence like Rex? We have a barrier to communication about everything except KTF."

Topper joined him to laugh. "It's a new generation in the Legion."

"Let's hope there's many more to come."

16

The hold of the *Supreme* had become not only their operations center, but the center of life on the *Supreme*. Since Kel released Bertie and Philip to be at ease among the family, word of the pair's wit and simpatico had turned a trickle of curious off-duty crew into a veritable flood of visitors, transforming the normally graveyard quiet hold into a festival.

"It's not exactly a QSZ, is it, Kel?" asked Poul.

Quantum Stasis Zones were the most secure rooms in existence, guaranteeing complete exclusion from the devices of enemy espionage or transfer of any information reviewed within to pass through its walls by any means other than what was stored between a visitor's ears. What was said in a QSZ, what was read in a QSZ, what was planned in a QSZ, stayed there.

"Nope, though it kinda reminds me of the old Three team room."

Chelly tested Sims in exercise and feats of strength, only to lose every one of his own challenges. Meadows and his young namesake had formed a bond when the older Curt offered to show the younger how to service a K-17. Even the retiring Quint had taken to the cloud of activity that filled the hold. He remained absorbed in his own projects, tied to the crate that was his makeshift workstation. But if he wasn't seeking to engage, neither did he retreat from the community around him.

In his own way, he was belonging.

The captain had become less irritable since departing Andalore. He'd groused about the trip to retrieve Poul, but with stasis units stuffed to capacity with perishables, he'd become almost cheerful. "Finally, a paying haul. And a damn good one at that. Just don't ask me to get within a light year of those anomalies. Not gonna happen. Don't care who's paying the bills, Turner. Black holes are a deal-breaker."

Cormac currently dominated Phil and Bertie's attention, reviewing navigation and jump plots, conferring with the AIs to ensure they did just that—to the chagrin of the children waiting to ride the bots like ponies around the hold. Who enjoyed it more, the kids or the AIs, Kel wasn't sure.

Poul pushed back from the table and the many holos. His leg was cased within the device, a sort of single-piece armor protecting the growing limb from the outside world as it worked its magic. If he was still experiencing pain after the blue-on-blue foul-up, it was disguised by the omnipresent grin he wore. Kel felt the same well-being, Poul completing the scene as they watched their teammates and the circus around them. It was a family reunion of bizarre circumstances. Virtually everyone he cared about was in one place.

Meadows was allowing young Curt to examine his vibro-blade. The teenage crewman was appropriately cautious not to touch the lightly glowing edge as with a guiding hand, Meadows corrected his slicing movements into the thrusts, jabs, and ice-pick motions that let the blade slide through most anything short of armor to bloodlessly bury into flesh.

Braley mused aloud. "A family at work and play together, like another tight-knit profession I could name. It's quite a life you've built for yourselves."

"It's not all games and picnics, Braley," Poul said, patting the regen unit. "Lanthanum keeps Kel and I busy, which is fortunate, because it takes a lot to keep all this going. You might not know it, but we're always just one step ahead of disaster. But, yeah, there are a lot of perks in between."

In his friend's description of their life, Kel heard the same ownership he took toward the future of the Callie's World colony. Though Poul had only hinted there were new reasons for the committed way he spoke, he'd take an end-run around him by asking Tara what she'd heard. While on Andalore, they'd been close enough to her family elsewhere in bright star space to allow a live hypercomm with the *Callie's Promise*. If Karla Sullivan and Poul were closer to a permanent commitment, Tara would know. They'd both been so busy since commencing the long jump to Imprimis, they'd had little chance to discuss it.

"Who's that again?" Braley asked, indicating Quint, still locked to his own holo models of complex molecules, testing interactions between them in rapid combinations.

Kel explained the xenobiologist's role.

"So Imprimis ends up becoming a serendipitous destination for another reason," Braley correctly observed. "Can we use him as cover for entry into the central city?"

Imprimis welcomed few visitors. The station was a center for the study of cosmology, but many intellectual disciplines were represented among the minds of Imprimis. Only those of academic accomplishment met their strict criteria for entry into the cloistered inner community reserved for researchers, where the repositories of centuries of study were housed in their many libraries. The Imprimis academy of sciences, its labs and research centers, and the infrastructure that supported it, was an independent country on a planetoid not part of any system government.

A small section of the dome was available for tourists and visiting spacers, and even then, the controls for entry and exit were nearly as oppressive as for those visiting a prison. Belongings allowed in were limited to necessities and screened thoroughly, and basic personal effects like specs and datapads were scanned on entry and exit without exception.

Those studying the mysteries of the universe from the remote outpost guarded their research jealously. There was little internal security, or need for it, among the intellectuals residing there, and the technocrats had turned the functions over to a robot police force. It reminded Kel and Poul of another community of intellectuals and their attitudes about the tools used to maintain the civility of their society.

Imprimis kept an open contract to attract freelance spacers who would make the trip to the remote outpost, high rates enticing and ensuring a regular supply of the perishables needed to sustain an artificial colony—not so unlike Callie's World in that regard. A cargo of foodstuffs was a perfect cover for their purpose, and one that placated Cormac by the number of credits it promised. But as far as how they would penetrate the inner city to search for Sarah, it was a plan in the making.

Like Braley, Kel had considered using Quint's doctorate and research interest as cover for an overtly plausible way into the city. "Quint's already sent a request for an entry visa, but that will limit him to the area reserved for visiting researchers. I have a better solution. There's a job listing for a counselor, and we just happen to have one with the genuine credentials to match."

"Tara?" Poul asked.

"A hire with a critical specialty can emigrate with their spouse. They can't have many applicants. It should at least be enough to get her and I through the security zone and into the heart of the city. We'll doctor our manifest to list us as passengers, with our port of embarkation Andalore, bound for Imprimis as tourists investigating employment."

Poul said, "Eggheads prolly need more counseling than the average Joe, all that angst and pressure trying to figure out how Oba made the universe, afraid to admit to themselves they can't do it." Poul rarely talked about it, but he came from a world settled by a fundamentally religious people. "It's a good cover, Kel. Beats having to sneak in. From there?"

"I'll turn loose every micro-drone we have to scan the place, and with all of you plus Philip and Bertie running the feed and slicing the Imprimis internal systems, if she's here, we'll find her."

Braley gave an approving nod. "And if our former teammate isn't there?"

"Even if she isn't, the boys are certain the Section's here. They'll find it. And when they do, then we do what we do. With Sarah's help or without, we don't leave Imprimis without what we came for. If it means filling this hold with every bit of alien crap, so be it."

"And the locals?" Poul asked the obvious. They both looked to Braley as the senior they'd always known for the word of approval. Braley shrugged.

"Who's going to stop us?"

***

There was one other ship on hold around the Imprimis planetoid, unable to dock in the small port until the *Supreme* cleared her hold and retreated to orbit. It was a small carrier and like the *Supreme*, was delivering perishables and visiting scholars.

Kel and Tara joined Chelly and Sheila at the Imprimis customs station. The official was pleasant, if not somewhat obsequious, a rare attitude among those whose function was collecting taxes and fees. "Your visit is timely, and such a large shipment is welcome." She transferred payment to Sheila, who accepted the sum into her slate.

"It worked out well for us. Perhaps there's someone with whom we can discuss making this a regular destination for our cooperative? Surely, it would be more cost effective and reliable to have a supplier on long-term contract?"

The woman turned dismissive. "Such has not been the case." She placed the crew and passenger manifest for all to see. "You're welcome to disembark crew for respite. We permit no more than twelve visitors at a time into the Atrius Anterum. Visitation of the public library and the gardens of the Anterum offers many vistas of the suns and the unique singularities of Galiata and Fornus. There's always the rare chance one may witness the appearance of a wormhole. Do you desire reservations for all your crew?"

"We do," Chelly said. "We'd like to remain long enough to allow the entire ship's complement the opportunity."

"A wise decision. Imprimis is unique in the galaxy." The official hummed. "And I note you have two passengers requesting emigration review."

Tara played her part. "I'm Tara Turner, and this is my husband, Kel. I've come to investigate an open position as a counselor."

The official opened the form and attached credentials, and brightened as she read. "Excellent! Will your husband be accompanying you? It will require a full security review and then a physical screening before you're permitted to pass into the sanctuary, but with that completed, I can arrange an interview immediately. Imprimis welcomes quality professionals. Life on Imprimis can be a hardship for the families of some of our citizens, especially those not here for their own scientific pursuits. Our last counselor departed for that reason."

"May I ask," Kel said. "Why is there such high security associated with the academy?"

The official paused to compose her answer. "The academy supports advanced research into many of the physical sciences. The products of their advances have many clients in the galaxy and maintaining the integrity of those is critical to our reputation and the demand for our research. May I ask, are you also seeking employment based on academic qualification or professional expertise, or would you be a dependent here on Imprimis? I ask, because couples seeking to emigrate who each have employable skills are those that tend to do best in our small community."

"I'm a security specialist." Kel had included his resume, an honest but not detailed one, including his Legion service and verifiable employment as a consultant with Lanthanum Concepts. The official smirked.

"Our security and information containment department is fully staffed at this time." She clearly froze at the single line noting his Legion experience. "Our *physical* security needs are virtually nonexistent and are provided by semiautonomous police bots that use nonlethal means of restraint and apprehension to intervene in personal disputes. But they're more of a deterrence and rarely utilized in our community. It's another reason for our strict entrance requirements. We find excluding non-academic professionals from our population largely eliminates societal elements with such traits."

The next she said as a thinly veiled insult. "We need no unskilled labor. Yet, the opportunity to take advantage of the educational opportunities on Imprimis are encouraged."

Through Kel's implant, a number of voices spoke.

"Pretty clear what she thinks of your skills, you big knuckle-dragger," Poul said. "The drones you released in the free-zone are feeding us now."

Bertie was quick to follow. "I've kept the drones in the section reserved for filthy visitors. If we push them into their inner sanctuary where the hoity-toity do their ego-stroking, it may be noticed."

Phillip joined. "The nano-drones could pass their screen into the sanctuary, but they'll only feed to a receiver on the same side of the field. If you want us to monitor, it needs to be micro drones. Cold and dead, they should make it through on your person without detection. The L-comm band won't ping on their scans."

"Thanks for explaining the diff between nanos and micros, kelhorns," Meadows said. "I thought we'd established how critical and timely information should be communicated." When no reply came, Meadows finished. "That's what I like to hear."

Kel gave a "hmm," as sufficient acknowledgment to everyone who could hear him. Thinking her synthesis of Kel's skills properly received, the official gave a conciliatory smile.

"But I'll pass your resume along to the administrative offices. It shouldn't take long for your clearances to be processed." She returned attention to the *Supreme*'s officers. "You may leave your first group of visitors when you move your ship out of the receiving dock and I'll transmit a schedule for you to shuttle subsequent groups."

An attendant escorted Tara and Kel out of the port and into their first glimpse of Imprimis.

The dome that was the Atrius Anterum was a small city itself, a diorama preserved under glass. Trellises of thick leafy vegetation grew along the periphery, giving the impression of a tall garden wall, and more climbed against the brown stone architecture reminiscent of academic centers seen on many core worlds, antiquated and providing an air of tradition.

The promenade wrapped around the central library that accommodated visiting researchers, and the guide pointed out the hotel and other amenities nearby.

"We have infrequent visitors, as secluded as Imprimis is, but it's common for some to remain for many months. Many doctoral dissertations are footnoted from sources attributed to the Imprimis visiting library. It's the finest in the galaxy."

"I can only imagine what the inner sanctuary has to offer," Tara said.

The guide exuded pride. "If your application for emigration is successful, you'll undoubtedly find it impossible to leave once you experience it for yourself."

Around the library were many unoccupied galleries. Through the peak of the dome, the three system stars hovered in close proximity to each other. The massive dome of the sanctuary obscured much of the view below, but just off to the side of its large radius, undistorted through the curvature of the smaller dome they walked through, sat the twin yellow swirls with the emptiness at their centers like a pair of distant eyes.

"The views are even more remarkable inside the sanctuary."

Tara placed a palm to her heart. "Their power is so immense, and intimidating. But it's also inspiring, as though the singularities are watching your every move."

Sims grunted in Kel's ear. "They ain't gonna see this coming, I can tell him that."

The guide smiled. "I think you'll find true fulfillment here. Come, this won't take long." They were led to a side thoroughfare that ended where the smaller dome met the much larger containing the true city of Imprimis. A pair of police bots sat on either side of a portal, and a gray uniformed official stood from behind a table to greet them.

"I have the authorizations here, Parellis," he addressed their guide. "Please approach one at a time for a second retina and biometric scan." The gate guard handed them each a placard. "Please wear this at all times, displayed on the outside of the visitor cloaks. You'll have to leave your specs and any data devices."

Kel bristled. "I was told basic personal devices were allowed."

"No. Only residents are allowed to pass with their data devices. Not to worry, they'll be secured here for your retrieval when you exit." They deposited their devices in a tray. "And a final personal scan will complete the screen, if you don't mind." Tara stepped in front of the scanner, and a green bar passed over her from head to toe. The guard motioned to Kel. As the beam traveled over him, he stole a glance at the nearest bot. It was nothing special. Programmed to intervene by spraying freeze foam or using low power stunners, it used a weak AI to detect physical confrontations between participants. It was only after the fact that a human arbitrated the events and determined who was the instigator of any violence. They were advertised as being able to contain riots of a hundred people with a single bot.

"Not to worry, Mister Turner, sir," Bertie said. "We're sliced into their systems. Even if the scan picks up the drones, we'll silence the alert."

"And as for as those dull bobbies," Philip added, "we can turn them off at will."

"Getting better at it, boys," Meadows said. "But still, redundant."

The pair had already assured him that was the case, and that's the only reason he'd forgone putting the small cylinder with the drones in a very uncomfortable place instead of wearing it tucked beneath his belt. The guard nodded and Kel relaxed.

The guide held out a pair of saffron-colored cloaks and made a clipped bow. "The placards will direct you to your destination. Good luck, Mrs. Turner."

Moving walks carried gliding residents through more of the same green framed thoroughfares, the touches of the architecture academics everywhere seemed to prefer providing a grounding effect against the dark sky, ternary suns, and black holes that formed the ceiling of their reclusive world.

Kel waited outside while Tara had her interview. Alone, he found a stone bench between a pair of short flowering trees, one of the many spots for quiet contemplation the academics esteemed as vital, and retrieved the cylinder from his waistband. He pulled the two halves apart like an egg, let the drones drop onto the trim grass at his feet, and subvocalized through his implant.

"Give 'em marching orders, guys."

Only because he knew they were there did he detect the movement of the tiny machines as they traced paths through the grassy blades, climbed the trunks, then disappeared to fly invisibly away.

"Eighty drones live, Kel," Poul said.

"I can bring more tomorrow," he mumbled. "Tara will at least get a second interview out of this."

"Pfft," Braley said. "Your missus is a charmer. She'll get a job offer after the first five minutes. Then you can look for apartments and that sort of thing while we work."

"We're hoping it's not going to take that long," Sims said.

"It's a big place. At least five thousand residents and a lot of territory," Poul said.

"We only have to see her once," Meadows said.

"Yeah, then we have to guide Kel to her," Sims stated the obvious. "It's another level of added difficulty without specs."

Kel cleared his throat. An older man approached and took the other end of the bench. Noting Kel's yellow cloak, he engaged Kel in pleasantries, and he explained his presence and received well wishes.

"What do you do on Imprimis, if I may ask?"

"I'm a cosmologist. I've been on Imprimis forty years, studying what can only be studied here. The external observatories are where I spend my time, but it's good to get a bit of green beneath my feet once in a while." He removed his sandals and spread his toes wide in the grassy blades in a way that made Kel like him.

"Forty years must make you one of the most senior professors here, sir."

"It does that."

"I'm interested, what's the history behind the founding of Imprimis? I've searched, but found next to nothing to describe its origins. An achievement so massive and perfect must have taken generations and trillions of credits to establish. Yet, until recently, I'd never heard of the academy."

The older man sniffed. "It's true. We keep to ourselves and the history of the Imprimis academy is ancient." He winked. "It's because it was built by visitors from other galaxies who found their way into ours by the wormholes."

Kel raised his eyebrows.

The man smiled. "That's the rumor, but I've found no evidence for that. Still, it lends to some of the charm of this place for those like us who investigate the secrets of the universe."

"Then who was it that had the resources to build an artificial habitation in such a remote part of the galaxy?"

"You've an interest in early galactic history? Imprimis is dense with scientists, but few acolytes of the liberal arts have interest in this place. Is that your purpose, you're a historian?"

Kel chuckled. It was a far more courteous reception that he'd gotten earlier. "No, sir. As I said, my wife is being interviewed for a position. I'm just curious."

"Curiosity is the soil of all learning, young man. It's what keeps me young here." He pointed to his temple. "But to answer your question, I don't know. The academy is over a thousand years old. We're an institution that is self-perpetuating, like the hydrogen fusion of a star. And like such, our light is essential to those it touches."

The elder man checked the time, wished Kel good luck, and departed.

"Thought he'd never leave," Meadows said. "The ship's getting ready to pull out. I've got a package of more drones together and I'm staying with the first tourist group. I'll either make a dead drop or pass it off to you directly, Turner. Out."

Not long after that, Tara appeared.

"I have a second interview tomorrow. We're invited to stay in the Atrius Anterum guest lodging." On the rolling walkway and headed for the outskirts again, Tara gazed upward the entire ride, the heavenly oddities a mural to everything.

"It would be something to live here. Maybe not forever, but they made it clear I could pursue almost any other field through a doctorate as part of the employment package. It would be a change of pace from having to eke out a living on the edge, don't you think?"

"Is that something you'd consider?"

"No. It's just fun to think about possibilities."

They collected their data devices and walked the main concourse toward the library and the hotel. In the square were crew from the *Supreme*. At a table sat Meadows and his young pupil. Kel plopped next to them as Tara went to join another group. Meadows eyed his robe.

"Color looks like a damn Navy safety vest. Makes you stand out like a recruit marching out of step."

The younger Curt was captured by the view above. "Cousin Kel, is this the kind of place you go when you're a legionnaire?"

"You've spaced since you were a baby, Curt. This can't be so exotic."

The youngster scoffed. "Pfft. You see one spacefield, you've seen them all, Cousin Kel."

Meadows gave a gruff snort. "This is the kind of place you go *through* in the Legion. You only stay if someone there needs their ass kicked. Then it's exactly the kind of place the Legion visits. Give us some space, huh, kid? I'll take you through how we do a target analysis for an assault on a dome hab like this, show you all the weak points."

The youth perked up. "Sure thing, Curt. Thanks."

Kel cocked an eyebrow. "What's that all about?"

Meadows shrugged. "Leej in the making. Hey, he asked! I'm just doing my part as tour guide to how we see the world." Meadows passed him another of the small cylinders under the table.

Kel clicked to a window in his specs and Poul's face. "Anything?"

"That'd be too easy. No, you'd have heard from us right off. But the boys have the drones turfed out in a high yield pattern—some stationary, some roving. You know how this goes. If we need to draw this out, will the captain fake a problem with the jump drive to buy us more time?"

"I think so. What about locating the Section?"

Bertie answered, "We're on that, too, Mister Turner. Phil and I are running every bit of stream we've sliced into, and we're into it all, guv."

Phillip chimed in. "Detective work's our spesh-ial-ity, sir. Bit o' time, it'll be Bob's your uncle and Fannie's your aunt."

"Keep me in the loop. I'm taking my wife out for dinner and what I hope will be luxury accommodations for our first hotel experience together. Toodle-oo, leejes."

"That's how you keep romance alive, Bertie. Next time you run into one of those cute autonomous war birds, you take a page from Mister Turner's book and do something similar."

"'Ere now, Phillip. Only if she's got a friend for you."

Meadows groaned. "For Oba's sake, blockheads, do we have to have another counseling session?"

It was the middle of the night when Sims's voice woke him. "Jackpot, Kel. Get some specs on."

He pulled them off the nightstand and sat up. A window ran in one eye showing the operations center and Sims at a station of holos. In the other eye, a window opened showing a thin, plain young woman riding one of the walks. The view enlarged on the face.

It was Sarah.

"I take back what I said about you two," Meadows said, joining the conversation.

"No discrepancy in the biometrics whatsoever, Mister Turner," Bertie said. "It's her."

Kel checked the time. "Tara's meeting is four hours from now and they gave us both entry visas. She's going to her interview while I recon Sarah's movement pattern in the terrain. Then Tara and I are going for a prolonged walking tour of the area until she appears. You'll guide us in, and I'll make contact."

"And if she balks?" Braley asked. "Even if she's pleased to see her old life coach Kel, when you try to walk her towards the tail ramp of her life, we don't know if she'll jump with us."

Kel winked. "Then be ready for the reunion party."

17

Kel studied routes through the city as he'd have to leave his glasses behind in the sanctuary. His specs played the views collected by the drones and he memorized the overhead map and ground level views until it was time. At the administrative office, Kel begged off the escort's invitation to accompany them.

"Thanks, but I thought I'd use the time to get a sense of the sanctuary. I have a feeling it might come in handy soon." He gave the man playful wink.

Sims was in his ear. "You're having too much fun."

Meadows snorted. "Turner loves an audience. If we weren't listening in, he wouldn't be pulling that guy's chain with his smarmy acting."

The escort beamed at Kel's enthusiasm. "I think you may be right, Mister Turner. The head of our medical staff's meeting Tara this morning, and I think there may be good news when you return."

Kel gave Tara a peck. "While you impress your future boss, I'll go find us another adventure."

"I know you will." Tara returned a confident smile. She was enjoying playing secret agent. He pulled the hood of the cloak up and hopped a walkway to carry him deeper into the sanctuary.

It was still early, the time when any city surged like a morning on-shore breeze bringing waves to announce the day. He tuned his Oba-given Mark-one, Mod-zero eyeballs to manhunt mode. The required yellow cloak of a visitor to inner Imprimis was a convenient burden, working equally well to disguise his gaze with its deep hood.

Few women on the streets sparked his intuition with even a suggestion of Sarah. Ages shifted toward the older scale, paralleling his expectations about a society of high-level academics. The drones had Sarah's physical characteristics and motion patterns, and searched at a rate approaching light speed among the masses below. It was unlikely his old-fashioned groundwork could beat the surveillance and detection programs, but if he saw her first, it would prove the adage once again—chance favored the prepared.

Technology worked in synergy with an operator's acumen, not in place of it.

The numbers of travelers on the streets diminished, and as he surreptitiously searched for Sarah, he practiced the words he would use, imagining her reactions, picturing shelves of strange devices with unworldly powers.

The slice into the Imprimis data stream showed the ID of the Sarah Wittawat he knew. The same thin face, her hair pulled back so tight, it narrowed her almond eyes—

mysterious reservoirs of the secrets he'd come to ladle dry.

It was with a fearful honesty that Sarah had revealed who she was and why she'd been sent along with them to the Savage moon. He remembered how large those eyes had grown at the sight of the mountain that was the Savage entropy machine. The Imprimis ident file confirmed the many doctorates in physics and engineering she'd claimed to the team, only after Kel crippled her handler—the pitiable Patrick—with a severe case of Trexellian food poisoning. And their threats to put her out an airlock.

There was guilt, having to threaten her so. Sometimes, shame came with duty. But always later, the remorse. Even Meadows had it, a regret that visited regularly. What had Hardball once quoted to the team?

Duty's as heavy as a mountain; death, light as a feather.

In the end, only duty mattered. That's what survived beyond your name, not your regrets.

"You're on it, Kel," Poul said. "That red stone building's where she disappeared to last night, and she hasn't come out."

Bertie spoke up. "It's listed as offices of the Antiquities Research Section. A great bloody number of sub-levels it has, too. There's a helluva meshwork of tunnels and chambers beneath this whole rock, dating back to the original excavations needed to support the construct of the hab. But the labyrinth beneath that spot—none of 'em connect to any of the rest."

Phillip broke in excitedly. "Mister Turner! The drones hit on alpha and beta particles coming from down there. 'S too deep for cosmic radiation. It's generated artificially, it is. I'm putting highest probs *that's* our Section, sir."

"Kel," Braley said. "We've gotten permission to bring the *Supreme* back into the terminal for a maintenance issue. The other ship's pulling out to accommodate us. It may be a few hours yet but once we're in, Captain Sullivan's promised to keep us there. Meadows's posted up in the Anterum, and Sims and I are suited heavy for a QRF. If you need the go-to-hell plan, we'll be ready."

It was less than ideal, but perfect existed only in manuals. "I'm heading back for Tara, then we'll take our tourist stroll. As long as Sarah decides to get some fresh air in the next few hours, there's a good shot at making contact today."

Tara waited on a bench, perking up at the sight of him. He sang his question loudly for the passersby's benefit. "D'you get the job, sweetheart?"

Her eyebrows shot high, mocking his question. "Was there any doubt?"

"Of course not." He hugged her and whispered into her raised hood. "Ready?"

She pulled back and gave him a knowing nod. "I told them I'd have to discuss it with you, and they suggested we take the day to wander the sanctuary while we consider."

"I found some prospects for suitable digs. Let's go."

There was no suitable place to loiter where Sarah was last seen, so they played the part of wanderers curiously exploring the sanctuary. They walked grids and cloverleafs, the epicenter of their journeys passing through the intersections nearest the unmarked building the bots were certain contained the entrance to the storehouse of secrets beneath the planetoid.

The dual suns and black holes were navigation points as constant as distant mountains. Tara joined her hood to

Kel's. "Is there a chance I'm going to be in for another show of you doing those things you do?" He'd once had to repel a boarding party bent on seizing her family's ship, culminating in a one-man assault on the pirate vessel, all in micro-G. Kel squeezed her hand in reassurance.

"Hardly. She'll be surprised, but with you there, she'll be even more ease. We play this as a friendly encounter with an old friend. Then, we go somewhere quiet and talk this out."

"Hmm. And I thought operators only slayed donks and broke bad people's expensive things. Turns out, your job's more like mine—reading people. How disappointing." She gave him a playful nudge.

"You're having a good time, aren't you?"

"You're the one who taught me that fun's something you have right now, not something you save for later."

"She's a natural, Kel," Poul said in his ear. "She's juiced."

"Well, here's another saying," Kel said gently. "You control the juice, the juice doesn't control you."

Meadows mocked. "That one on your stupid list?"

"Yes, Kel," Tara replied, admonished.

"If Sarah's the person I think she is," Kel said, "once she hears what I have to tell her, she'll jump to help. What she's shown me about herself, those kind of things don't change about a person."

It was a defining moment on the Proteus mission when Sarah voiced a reality Team Three had yet to admit: that there was no way to escape the Savage weapon they fled. She'd been first to say the Talon crew coming to their rescue had to be waved off, then bravely waited to meet her death with Team Three, like a real leej.

Fortunately, it had turned out differently.

They were on another casual loop of their circuit when Poul's voice blurted, "Got her! She's in an Imprimis Academy blue cloak, head uncovered, carrying a bag over her left shoulder. She's moved onto a side street, opposite direction of her residence. Take the central boulevard mover, head toward the chancellor towers, and I'll talk you in."

Trotting, the moving walkway doubling their velocity as they weaved past annoyed travelers blocking the passing lane. It was cumbersome, not having a HUD to follow, and after numerous sharp redirects and jogs to intersect with Sarah's path, he spotted her.

A touch of gray streaked the tight bun of straw hair. She stood alone, inspecting the window of a clothier display, a holo of a young couple swinging a joyful toddler between them as they walked a beach. She seemed wistful, and Kel wondered what regrets she carried. Scant pedestrians glided by on the moving path. Atop a traffic island, balanced on the point of its inverted cone body, was a police bot. Its four arms hung stiffly at its side, the cyclops red eye circling its squat head like a search light. Kel pulled his hood back just enough to expose his mouth, and used his most musical affect.

"Sarah! Is that you? How wonderful to run into you."

She turned to find the speaker, craning and squinting to see the face that owned the voice hidden deep in the hood. Kel withdrew his hood enough to show his face to just her. Recognition sparkled in her eyes and the curl of a smile began. As quickly, she recoiled a step back and flustered a startled recognition.

"Kel! How?"

The red eye of the chrome police bot ceased its rotation. Sarah's mouth was opening wide. Tara moved.

Her disarming smile led a light touch on the alarmed woman's arm. "I've heard so much about you. I'm Tara, Kel's wife. I'm so happy to finally meet you. I'm taking a position here on Imprimis. And we thought we wouldn't know anyone here!"

Tara had clipped the wire of the bomb about to explode.

Sarah's posture eased, and she moved closer in cautious curiosity. Hers was not the fearful nor timid voice he'd remembered. It was with the conviction of a scientist meeting a charge of fraud that she frowned and said, "This is no coincidence, is it?"

Kel smiled sadly. "No. Is there somewhere we can talk?"

"You can't be here," Sarah seethed in a whisper. She glanced sideways to the silvered watcher, its crimson eye sweeping left, right, and back in a narrow arc covering their group. Sarah beamed a wide smile. She placed a hand gently over Tara's, but her voice menaced.

"If I yell, the bot will foam us all. Are you really Kel's wife?"

Tara grinned. "I truly am."

She cocked an eye. "Are you really taking a position here?"

Tara spoke truthfully. "I've been offered a spot in the health department as a counselor."

Sarah relaxed ever so slightly. It was time for Kel to go for it.

"But, you're right to suspect us. Something worse than what we found on Proteus is being unleashed. I need your help. Can we *please* go somewhere and talk about this?"

She stood her ground. With feet planted wide she folded arms, resistant as a wobanki to following a path to the river. "Why?"

"Because if what's needed to counter this weapon isn't in the Section, the galaxy's in trouble."

She squinted with skepticism. "What weapon?" She was not convincing easily.

"It's a genetic weapon, probably nano based."

Sarah scrunched a corner of her mouth dismissively. "Like Plenax? Rapid printing immunos and releasing self-replicating counter nanos is the cure. Well within the emergency response tech developed because of Plenax."

Kel fought to stay relaxed. The police bot's crimson sensor made another sweeping rotation, then returned to pause again on their assembly, scanning for the telltales that preceded any human disharmony, preparing for unrest. Kel exaggerated a polite chuckle and bobbed his head in agreement to comfort the bot's algorithms.

The bot's burning orb resumed a roving orbit.

He cast off the actor's mask, the urgency and gravity of his message impossible to conceal any longer.

"Remember Victrix? You're one of the few outsiders ever allowed there. Remember Team Three? Remember all those legionnaires like us, all of them ready to give their lives to protect the innocent? Well, they're all dead."

Sarah gasped. "How?"

"We only know what happened shouldn't be possible. It was done with a weapon targeted for *just* Dark Ops. No weapon exists in the known galaxy that could select a target based on their inner thoughts, or oaths, or whatever acquired characteristics it uses to find its victims. Which is why our best intelligence suggests the Section is the most likely place to have the answer and what we need to fight it."

Her eyes widened. "Sims? Bigg? Braley? Radd? Are they—did they..." She recited their names as if she'd seen them yesterday.

So, she did remember the people who'd done their all to protect her.

"Bigg was there, and many, many more. All poisoned by something that *chose* them out of an entire planet of people."

Her hand found her face as if to hide her reaction. "It... could be possible."

She was coming around.

It was time for Kel to make the last crucial connection to reawaken a past and join it to their present. "You once insisted we needed you or we'd all die. And you were right. We need you again so that *everyone* doesn't die."

Tara clasped her hands as though praying. "Kel told me how brave you were that day. How selfless you were. That it was *you* who made the difference when it really mattered."

Sarah went somewhere just then, only for moment, traveled to the memory of a place impossible to forget. She made the invitation loudly.

"This is the nicest of surprises! Let's go to my place and catch up."

Kel bathed in relief.

"About time," Poul said in Kel's head.

They fell into step, following Sarah onto the walkway and rode in silence, until Sarah's mumbles became a thin stiletto piercing his ears. "I can figure this out. I have to." She said it over and over until he nudged her to awareness of her chanting. "Ugh," she broke from her anxious soliloquy. "A *kill team* on Imprimis! Tell me you're not here to destroy the place, Kel!"

"Once we have your help, we want to be gone as quietly as we arrived, with no trace we were ever here." Kel no sooner stated his desire to be invisible than his attention landed on a hooded man in a blue cloak on the intersecting walkway.

It was sometimes the small things. The tiniest telegraph of a taut posture, a strained facial expression, or the intent impossible to disguise behind eyes calculating the timing with which to pounce. Things not even an artificial intelligence could compute. The stranger drifted back a step, shielding himself behind another pedestrian to escape Kel's gaze.

The eye sees what the mind knows. And Kel knew danger.

"Sarah, don't look around. Do you have a security detail assigned to watch you?"

As instructed, she didn't turn. "Never. Why?"

The team remained silent in his skull, but it was time to invite the voices back into his head.

"We've got a tail. There's an unusually stout male checking us out, bearing toward us about twenty meters off my three. He's trying to be inconspicuous, but he's not good at it. Blue cloak. Slight beard. Wearing specs."

"That's a thug if ever were I seen one," Bertie said.

"Spot on, mate. Big brute's what he is," Phillip said. "Blue cloak or no, he's no stargazer."

Sims spoke. "Good spotting, Kel. I got him tagged in the drone feed now."

Closing from the other direction on their same walkway, Kel spotted a second similarly solid man. The hood was up, but through the specs underneath its peak, eyes snapped away from where they'd burned Kel a split second before.

"I've got another, heading straight at us."

"We see him, Kel," Poul said hurriedly.

Sims was calm. "Could just be peepers and not hitters."

Kel agreed. "Help me watch them." His intuition was decisive. He shifted left, urging Tara and Sarah farther away from the advance of the man gliding their way. Kel tensed, ready, but the man drew his hood higher, stepped to the outside edge of his own conveyor, and looked away as they passed. Kel checked their three.

"Where'd the big guy go?"

Poul answered immediately. "He took a hop off the walk and made for a side street at a hustle."

Sims reversed his opinion. "It's a leapfrog team, Kel, and they're setting up to come at you."

Kel calculated. "Maybe. Keep feeding me their moves. They know I spotted them. If they're just watchers, they'll let us go and someone else on their team will pick us up later. Best we just let them."

Poul was there. "The goon who passed you just reversed course and hopped on to your walkway, a hundred meters behind you. Not moving to close distance —yet."

Kel took Sarah by one elbow, Tara beside her. "We're getting off ahead." The next traffic island neared, its signpost the police bot posted on its peak. Pedestrians entered and exited the walk from an open square filled with cafes and tables, benches and gardens, crowded with citizens oblivious to the thrumming surge of violence building in Kel's chest.

He nudged them toward the slowing lane to exit onto the square, the momentum of the walk powering their hasty beeline for the pedestrian overpass to the walkway exchange. "Tara, whatever happens, stick with Sarah, like we talked about."

"Yes, Kel."

Poul spurted out, "WAIT ONE. Kel, big boy's back. He broke into a dead run, headed for the exchange. But check this, he's fuzzed, wearing a dead net or something similar, but it's not fooling our drones."

"Sket," Kel cursed. "But they're good enough to know our moves, know we've got eyes in the sky. Who's the opposition? Organic or outside players?"

Braley was there. "We watched the ship that came in after the *Supreme*. They didn't leave anyone behind, and the most recent visitors to Imprimis before us were here six weeks ago. This must be organic Imprimis security."

Poul said, "Whoever they are, Sims is right—it's a leapfrog team, moving to hit them front and back."

Kel hurried them. "Sarah, take us to the Section. It's closer than your apartment."

"I can't take you there!"

Meadows was flustered. "Enough of this. I'm ready to call Quasar. The blockhead twins are sliced in and'll cut the cord to those robocops on our order. I'm already moving to blow through this piddly gate guard and be there ASAP to back up your exfil. QRF, get ready to bounce."

"Hold that," Kel said. "I'll call Quasar if necessary. Just stand by."

"Bah," Meadows spat. "Bad idea, Kel."

It happened quickly. Like a grav tank silently gliding from out of a cloud bank to kick off the first salvo of the battle, he appeared from the crowd. He was smooth and efficient, the hand with the stunner part of the unceasing momentum of his drive straight at Kel.

The tip of the baton lit purple an inch from Kel's chest when he caught the thick wrist. Block and strike were never two acts. They had to be one. His knife hand was already jabbing for the softness behind the specs, the glasses peeling up like a garage door to admit his probing fingers. The big man's chin lifted, exposing the short central column between the pillars of corded neck muscles. It was all Kel needed. His knife hand returned in a fist to snap a stiff punch at the knobby Adam's apple. Cartilage cracked beneath his knuckles. He pulled the specs off the wide face and tossed them as the brute toppled backward with a spasmed wheeze as he fell. The dropped stunner was kicked away by pedestrians rushing to break away from what would surely come next.

Kel grabbed the shoulders of both women, forcing them beneath his sprawl. "DOWN."

Streams of freeze foam shot above them like firehoses. Shouts of dread and shrieks of panic filled the air. The chaos prevented even those immediately cognizant of what was coming from escaping, and thick foam coated them all.

And as abruptly, ceased.

Expecting stunners or more foam, when it failed to appear, Kel raised up.

The bot remained balanced on its pedestal, four arms extended, foam drizzled slower and slower from the terminal nozzles until even the tiniest blobs ceased their dribble. The red sensor on the squat spherical head faded and died like a candle run out of wick.

"C'mon." Kel bent to lift the women crushed beneath his body slam, when something smashed into the space between his shoulder blades like a speeder with no safety governor. Barreling forward from the collision, Kel smashed face-first into a trio of pedestrians, locked in place by the foam coating. His face-first impact with the rock-hard shell brought a grunt from him and shrieks from the human sculptures, helpless to avoid the crash, wailing in relief when realizing it had no effect on them.

From split lips, he spat hateful blood and spun.

The thug who'd rear-ended him straddled Sarah, bending to snatch her upright. At their feet, Tara contracted into a ball, then exploded, her foot planting a perfect kick into the side of the assailant's knee. The man's clothing stiffened at her blow.

He wore the same reactive garments as Kel.

Tara's blow failed to send the knee in a direction it was not meant to bend. But it forced the assailant to stagger, his grasp on Sarah broken. She'd bought Kel the split second he needed.

He sprang like a dancer expecting to be caught by a partner's sure arms. His first foot landed on a thigh, grasped the man's shoulders as a counter, and thrust his knee like a spear into the man's face. The specs split in two and dark blood sprayed from the crushed nose. He rode the man down and drove all his weight on to the chest with his drop. The material stiffened beneath his knees, but wind gushed from the man just the same, caught between the anvil of the ground and the hammer of Kel.

The women were on their feet and moving as he joined their escape.

"Run for the Anterum."

Crowds surged, thinning and thickening in their way as Kel pushed them through the shifting masses, some of them victims of the control foam, insects caught in amber.

He spotted the main mover. It stood still, as did the other walkways around the interchange.

"Good move shutting down all the systems, especially those kelhorned bots. We're heading out of here." He threw off his cloak.

"Er, uh," Philip stammered. "*We* didn't. I mean to say, it weren't us who shut everything down."

As predictably as night followed day, Bertie continued. "We wuz about to, when it all went dead."

Kel'd had enough. "Quasar, quasar, quasar."

Braley's voice was smooth as chilled ethanol. "Moving."

"Frell Quasar," Meadows blurted. "I'm already through the gate, headed your way."

Kel stole a glance back as they ran. The biggest thug struggled to help the other up, in little better shape himself after Kel's battering. "Boys, can you ghost into one of those police bots and use it to foam our pursuit?"

"Negative, boss," Phillip said. "We've been trying all along. We're completely shut out."

Poul spoke. "Kel, the real cops are locked in their stations. Comm traffic's a mess, but they're as confused by the situation as we are. The opposition's *not* Imprimis internal security. We've got real bogeys."

Kel had already abandoned covert subvocalizing. "No kidding." He let it go as they ran down the frozen boulevard until a narrow side street appeared and he guided the women around the corner and pulled them to a halt. "Keep running. Meadows and the QRF are making to intersect with you. I'm staying to keep these two busy. Go."

Tara took Sarah's hand. "Do as Kel says. Tell me where to go."

He watched the women disappear around the next corner, Sarah step for step with Tara. She must've kept up the physical regime he'd taught her. "Make pick up on the women, I'm on pursuit deterrence."

"QRF, make for the women," Meadows said at a pounding dead run. "I'm on route to Turner."

Kel regretted there weren't two armored leejes making for him, too. But if he could hold the attackers off long enough for Meadows to reach him, it would be as good as a Mk 4 nuke come to save the day.

"Oppositions closing behind you at a run," Poul said. "Slowing, getting ready to pop the corner. Run for it, Kel."

Instead, Kel sprinted to the corner building. *Ambush me?* He spit thickening blood away from his lips. *See how you like it.* He tore open the seam of his lapel and fished out the monomolecular blade. It was a composite of highly compressed organic fibers, thin as a card, and had again proven undetectable to scan. Had they patted him down, it would've been discovered. Now, he was glad he'd risked it.

He'd bleed them, bad. Wherever skin showed. He rotated the thin trefoil into a reverse grip in his fist.

The pair appeared wide of the corner, sliding wide to see what lay ahead. Rather than rush, they began a steady angled stalk to close on him, their first pro move. The thinner one blew bloody snot out of a busted nose in a bullish snort. "I'm after the target. You got this twarg-eater?"

The bigger man replied hoarsely with a single syllable strained through the gravel of his injured voice box. "Go."

Their second pro move he noticed mid-spring as he leaped to block the path of the thinner man. Both held weapons as he did, blades held along forearms in reversed and concealed grips. Both effortlessly twirled their blades point forward.

In Kel's experience, there was no such thing as a knife fight. Knives were weapons for assassination. For murder. A last-ditch tool for self-defense. Wherever his own garments covered skin, he was safe. But his assailants had the same shields. His choice was made.

Blood would flow.

He closed, landed, launched in one beat, aiming his cross-step side kick at the man with the smashed nose. His lightning-fast attack had caught the sinewy thinner thug mid-turn, about to start his run after receiving his partner's release. They'd both misjudged Kel's ability to cover distance and reach the runner. The thuds of the larger man pouncing from behind him would leave him little one-on-one time with the runner.

Kel's foot brushed the man's shoulder. The thin man saved himself from catching Kel's kick square, and was spinning to slip the impact. The thin man continued his spin, finishing his rotation to bring a slash at Kel's head. Kel recovered into balance, his forearm rising with circular power to draw an arc, blending with the attack to deflect the arm up, the blade brushing Kel's hair. He flowed in with his own knife hand to a return in a downward arc, hooking the edge of his blade over a wrist holding a black blade longer than Kel's. With open palm, he pressed against the man's extended arm, and with two opposing motions, expanded.

The scream of a deep cut told him all as he broke contact and spun to find the larger attacker, too late. Kel was turning when the knife edge sliced for his face. He dove backward, throwing himself over the collapsed ball of the man he'd successfully crippled.

Distance was the friend he needed. He rolled up into a dead run and blasted away. Shrill words from the man holding the half-severed wrist chased him.

"KILL HIM, CHAP! KILL THAT BASTARD!"

Where was Meadows? Kel didn't know where he was running to, just—away from the bull charging behind him. He wiped at the stream of blood gushing over his eye, wincing as he accidentally spread the gash on his temple wider.

A thunderous presence was gaining. Had he grown slower since the Legion, or was his pursuer one of those men whose size worked to deceive his speed? It was a choice of no choice. Turn and meet his executioner or become a meal for the dreex about to land on his back? He was pivoting as the massive man launched for a tackle. Grasping the shoulder, Kel swung around, blended, and turned to become the predator and not the prey. His blade tip was headed for the protuberance at the base of the square neck to drop this grav tank like a bolt of lightning from an OSP.

A stumble or a counter, the effect was the same. The point struck between the shoulder blades and snapped against nanotubules hardening on contact. The man he intended to impale vanished in a rolling collapse and Kel was thrown forward, tucking head to chest to take the street down his rolling spine. He toppled over, desperate to find his feet and turn to meet the juggernaut recovered from the near piercing of his spine.

The attacks he fended off from this one man were more like the poundings of a dozen laborers wielding sledgehammers and pickaxes, determined not to stop until the boulder they worked was rendered to gravel. Fists, palms, knees, and a knife pounded and poked in unending arcs and angles for every part of his body. Kel's forearms shielded his head as he slipped the blows. Half blind, crowded and shut down from returning in like, he was surviving by feel alone.

He disengaged with a short bounce back to create kicking distance when a snap cut flicked up from under his line of sight, missing his good eye by a micron. Kel followed in with the returning knife and chopped down on the retreating knife wrist, exposing the centerline a narrow breadth. He exploded with a dozen fists to drive the brute to take his own disengaging hop backward. Landing weight forward on the balls of feet, he brought the knife forward and spat at Kel's feet.

"Whoever you are, I'm taking your head, working against humanity, you murderin' savage." The human tank launched.

Too tall to be from a high-G world like Paladon, Kel's subconscious touched a familiarity to their battle. It was like his many sparring sessions with JP. But JP had taught him.

With a little help from gravity, even steel would crush under its own weight.

He shot deep and low onto a knee, leading with a fist to the groin, the material stiffening against his knuckles. The man's bulk nonetheless rose. Kel's shoulder was now deep between the thighs, his other hand grasping material soft from a contact blended not sharp. Kel pressed into the brute's trunk with chest, shoulder, neck, and face to make two bodies into one. He lifted, spun, and turned in the same effort. The massive weight glued to him, he drove hips up and rotated, the top of his circle continuing over and down, intention set to drive his attacker through the pavement and into the caverns somewhere below.

The smash of the skull against the ground conducted into his own body. He released his grip from the heap and raised up. The long black blade was on the ground. Now in his grasp, he turned in a crouch.

No more running.

The second thug burst on the scene dangling a bloody hand, a blade in the other. Seeing his partner piled on the ground, he hesitated only long enough to growl a promise. "You'll pay, twarg eater."

Kel was already in the air, knife forward and aimed to bury in the throat still growling with a wasted threat. A thunderous voice bounced off the walls like overpressure from a door charge.

A wall of dark armor blindsided him. Steel arms as thick as tree trunks engulfed him.

A bucket speaker boomed in his ears. "Turner, stop."

Poul's voice was in his head. "Kel, stand down."

The vision in his remaining eye surged and throbbed like the waterfall of blood pumping down his blinded eye. With feet dangling off the ground and arms pinned at his side, he raged to free himself, the sharp drag of a knife surely on its way to sever his neck. But the constricting bands crushed him till his breath became a whisp, his struggle futile as flapping arms beneath a torn parachute canopy.

Everyone, everywhere was telling him to cease.

It was the voice commanding him from the bucket that finally reached him. A soft baritone resonated in his chest, the authority of a descended angel proclaiming forgiveness instead of promising destruction.

"It's over, Kel. Let it go."

It seized his power and his rage vanished.

"I'm setting you down, son. Relax."

Feet on the ground, the vice released him. Kel staggered back, nearly tripping over the unconscious man piled up behind him. Behind the giant leej the other thug was on knees, gritting teeth and for the first time, Kel noticed the constriction of the autotourniquet creasing the top of the bicep. Meadows crashed beside him to a halt.

Kel heard but didn't comprehend the dulcet words Meadows used as though he calmed a ferocious dog. "Hartenstein. That's Hartenstein. Those two goons you destroyed, they're leejes."

Kel allowed Meadows to twist the black knife from his grasp. He took a deep, controlled breath.

"How?"

The bucket came off. Looking down at him was a grizzled face with blue eyes and silver temples. Kel's amazement spilled out.

"Colonel Hartenstein?"

The colonel had grown older but was no less imposing, the weathered statue of a mythic hero.

"And those two are—legionnaires?"

Poul was in his ear. "Colonel says they're Wolfhounds. They're here for Sarah, just like us."

Meadows gave a mocking, evil cackle. "Wolfhounds? Pah. They show me nothing."

18

Bertie and Phillip had released the infrastructure back into function—minus the police bots. An ambulance had them all at the health center in minutes. Braley and Sims were outside the treatment bay, managing the damage of their Imprimis-wide disruption. The rest of the scrum were crowded in the trauma bay with Poul listening in from the *Supreme*.

A medic cleaned Kel's scalp wound, struggling against the bleeding renewed by his probing. Tara gently pushed the medic aside. "No offense. Let me." She pinched the laceration lightly at the peak near his hairline. Kel silently bore down, refusing the nociblock so to be clear and ready for what was unfolding. A tisseal wand in her other hand, she advanced the glowing tip down the cut, smoothly knitting the deep slice until reaching the eyebrow.

"There. You can apply the bandage."

The medic made an appreciative assessment of the neat closure, then picked a nano dressing applicator off the tray. The gel smeared in a blob. Tara saw more evidence of the inexpert hand. "Works better if you dab. I'll show you," she said and placed her own hand over his to correct the motion.

Fully sealed, Kel released his clench. The acid burn in his abs meant he didn't need to work them for another day, maybe two. It was not a workout to recommend.

The medic's appreciation was sincere. "It's different from the simulations. Thanks," he said, and cleared away the field of instruments. "We've never had this many in our trauma bay."

The two leejes he'd tangled with were on their own slabs. The one called Chappy lay inclined but with his eyes closed, the medcomp massaging his head in a panoramic of shifting colored lights, his many gashes and abrasions sealed in nano gel.

In the next bay, the physician worked the medcomp's robotic arms over an armboard lit by a sterile field and a wrist not nearly as amputated as Kel had tried for. The one called Doc observed the repair work with detachment, purple bruises around both eyes but nose straight, maybe even straighter than when Kel had rearranged it with his knee.

Noticing Kel watching, Doc shot Kel death beams his way through the narrow apertures of swelled lids. Mistaken identity to blame for this leej and his partner trying to kill him as hard as he did them. In as contrite a way as he could muster, given he half expected at any moment to be fighting the two in the medbay, Kel offered a truce.

"You alright, leej?"

"No thanks to you," Doc snarled back.

Kel was ready to finish it.

Meadows scoffed. "Sheesh. Turner didn't kill you two, though he could've. Consider yourselves lucky." He chuckled viciously. "Lucky I wasn't there before Hartenstein saved your butts."

Doc ignored the abuse like only a leej could, returning with vigor to scowl not at Meadows, but instead at Kel. "Who the hell are you?"

"Name's Turner. Kel Turner."

Doc's feisty resilience faded and paled. Bruised lids strained against swelling to spread wide.

Meadows laughed. "I've seen that look. That's the kisser of a leej who just heard that unmistakable click after stepping on a mine. He just realized he's around to wonder why he ain't dead. You look like you need a stim stick, leej. Guess you got a rep even in Cygnus, Turner."

Colonel Hartenstein groaned. "How about we settle down, Curt?"

Meadows ignored him to praise Kel. "Saw the whole thing while I was on the hustle. Your time goofing off with Lanthanum didn't turn you soft. Still, maybe better you'd killed them, Turner, 'cause the next time they jock up for work, the memory of this beatdown's gonna twist their guts. But I reckon it's no shame to be aced by you."

Failing to reign Meadows in, Hartenstein readied anew. "Sergeant Major..."

Meadows cut him off roughly.

"That I am, *Colonel*. And I work for the sector provost. *You* got cashiered and retired. So I'm betting that you're a colonel the way Turner's a major, I got that right?"

Hartenstein admitted it. "I retired from the Legion, that's right."

Meadows huffed. "Thought so. I smell the stink of your secret boys' club. When Colonel Yost's through putting these Imprimis turds on notice that the Legion holds this rock, we're going to clear some things up about how this op's being run."

Kel waved Meadows down. "All right, all right. We'll get things cleared up soon enough, Curt."

The physician pushed back from the medcomp monitor and loudly proclaimed, "I'd say you're *all* lucky." His assistants were finishing the procedure on Doc and applied a regen sleeve to the wrist. The doctor marched over to inspect Kel's head.

"Medcomp says you're otherwise without injury. The sleeve'll regen that lacerated wrist in a few days. The one with the head injury's going to have a headache, but no lasting damage. I came here to get away from such idiocy." He humphed a last disapproval and departed.

Doctors were the same everywhere.

The medics had finished cleaning up around the two slabbed leejes, and stood mumbling and casting furtive glances at the collection of rough men in their medbay. With a knife hand, Meadows menaced them.

"If you're done, clear this space. Scoot!" He pushed them out of the room and sealed the door. "Now! Time we get some things straight. I want to hear it, *Colonel* Hartenstein. How'd you and your two buddies end up targeting Turner for a dirt nap?"

Hartenstein looked weary. "Fair enough." He pulled up a stool as though it was no short explanation coming. "You know what happened on Victrix?"

Kel answered him. "We've just come from there. I saw."

Hartenstein sighed. "I can only imagine." Everyone allowed the silence until Hartenstein continued.

"I've been working this for almost three years. Been tracking the Hool as they gathered human slaves from the Gomarii for test subjects. After I learned what happened on Victrix, it was obvious we were too late heading this off. I went to Cygnus to get help from the Wolfhounds. They're the only regiment not under Utopion's cloud of disinformation. On Ozydna, we found a lab like the one you discovered on Psydon. It was there we got the lead that brought us here."

Meadows spat. "If that's the case, you shoulda showed up here with more ass. Clown-show's what's this's been. We shoulda been coming at this thing full-on with a whole regiment, right from the start."

"We are, Sergeant Major," Hartenstein answered calmly. "We have the Wolfhounds with us."

Meadows was unmoved. "If these two kelhorns are the best they have to send, you're not filling me with the warm fuzzies, Colonel."

Hartenstein showed heat for the first time.

"Doc and Chappy are the equal of anyone in Dark Ops. Maybe better. We were prepping to bring down the Wolfhound assault on the Ozydna prison lab when the Ootari guards began exterminating the test subjects. By ourselves, we assaulted the prison to stop it."

Gesturing, he swept his words aside. "But it ended up being for nothing."

"What happened?" Kel prompted.

"You've seen it. Remember how young VanderBlanc's nanos killed him? Same. Only this time, they triggered in a hundred fifty people. I knew what happened. It let us locate the ones who threw the kill switch on all those poor people. We grabbed four non-humans trying to escape the planet. A Hool, a Kimbrin, a moktaar, and another alien of a race we haven't encountered before. Breathes poison gas. That's the one we have getting the goods directly from the Section."

Kel looked around. "Where's Sarah?"

"Outside with Colonel Yost and Sims," Hartenstein said. "She's cooperating to get the dust settled, but I'd be happier if she were in chains."

Kel puzzled. "Why's that?"

Hartenstein glowered. "Turner, she *gave* the enemy whatever it is that let them make the weapon that targeted Dark Ops. Something from out of her collection. We have it direct from a psych scan of the unidentified alien. As clear as a 3-D holo. She put a device right into his hands—a prime member of their cabal."

Kel frowned. "No chance there's more to the story?"

"Not when we have it like we do. I'll show you all later," Hartenstein said. "I'm here to find out what it was she gave our enemies. Then she's going to give us the counter Rex says is there and we finish this. For good."

Meadows was boiling. "Roll that back. *Who* says there's some gizmo gonna do this?"

Hartenstein returned the glower. "Tyrus Rex."

"Fer Oba's sake." Meadows rolled his eyes. "I've thrown in with you all before. Because it was *right*. We *had* to. For Dark Ops, and the Legion. But this cult of yours is too much for me. Okay, let's forget this sket about General Rex for a minute. Explain why your boys tried their best to cashier Turner."

Hartenstein was contrite. "Bad luck. We had no idea the *Supreme* was anything but a merchant ship. We picked up a haul the same way you did to get us access, but we had no cover to get us inside the sanctuary. So when we got our berth and the *Seraphim* was being unloaded, Doc, Chappy, and me infilled through the sublevels of the port beneath the sanctuary."

Kel nodded. "We considered that ourselves. But I went for something potentially less kinetic."

Hartenstein continued. "It was the best we had to work with. We found a good mission site in the substructure, and got drones searching the sanctuary for Sarah. We ignored the Anterum, or else we'd have picked you up."

Meadows grunted a tepid acceptance of the circumstances. "Bad luck's right."

"I spotted Sarah probably the same time you did," Hartenstein said to Kel, ignoring Meadows as Meadows had ignored him. "Doc and Chappy were low-viz and going for the grab. They made you as another snatch team trying for our HVI. Then it kicked off.

"I released the slice to freeze all the infrastructure, but when you put Doc and Chappy down like a cyclone, the go-to-hell was on us and I bounced in. I didn't make who you were until it was almost too late. Those damn cloaks did a good job hiding your face, Kel, and your hair's a lot longer than you wore it in Dark Ops. When I did recognize you and realized Rex must've succeeded in sending you after Sarah, I transmitted an all L-comm."

Kel shrugged. "We had two kill teams and conventional support when we ran these same kinds of ops on Haemus. This is the kind of karked stuff that happens when you're short manpower."

"That colonel's a good slicer," Bertie said in his ear.

"Bloody good," Phillip said. "I'm anxious to pull apart his code."

Poul was in his ear, too. "Quiet, boys. Kel, I have to say, I damn near swallowed my tongue when the colonel came over L-comm. Trying to call you off was like yelling at a meteor to turn around mid-flight."

He swung his legs off the slab. Tara steadied him for the first woozy moment. "It's time we got to it. The Section's waiting. Phillip and Bertie, you listening in?"

"Yes, boss," the pair spoke as one.

Kel had thought long about what he'd do at this moment. Far too long. Was it finally here? "You two collect Quint and bring him along. The three of you may be useful."

"I'm coming, too," Doc said from his slab, nasal and irritated.

"So'm I," Chappy said for the first time, sounding like a leej after a three-day pass and the hangover to match. "Been listening. Sooner we collect this treasure horde of secret dazzley-dos, sooner we split this rock and KTF every spiny and helmeted fart breather in Cygnus."

"Anywhere, anytime, anyplace," Doc said next to his friend. He made the motion with his good wrist, two splayed digits rotating to trace the pattern. Chappy returned the gesture.

Meadows squinted his disdain and mumbled, "Leejes acting like kids. What the hell kind of outfit's the Wolfhounds?"

Sarah was at the center of the crowd of protesting geriatrics. They were a bent and shrunken lot, Kel noticed, inelastic faces draping skeletons like the voluminous robes that drowned their bodies. The men who led the Legion weren't so ancient, but were they any less decrepit?

In his heart, Kel accused the Legion he loved for allowing itself to be manipulated into what he saw in front of him. A senile and ignorant institution, blind to what happened under its very nose.

Black was the color of the Legion uniform, the same black of the deep void that hid the dangers they swore to guard. The multicolored robes—uniforms, regardless what the scholars may have thought of the colors denoting the different disciplines—made them so many wilting flowers, dried and brittle, spindly in their resistance against the calamitous winds racing from the pair of armored mountains towering over their field.

Sims acted the herald. Not with a gale force, but in a harmonic so deep it could be felt in the bones, he boomed. "Give your attention to the colonel." No effect. The parched croakings continued. Sims resorted to a no fail.

"SHUT. UP."

Slack jaws held stilled tongues. Sunken eyes moved to Braley's blank bucket as he took the position left by Sims. He aimed his address like a rifle at a brown uniformed woman with stars on her shoulders. He opened a document to hover over his palm, then thrust it out like a flame.

"By order of the House of Reason, Imprimis is under writ of occupation. I charge your complete cooperation into the investigation of activities proscribed by universal law. Researching, manufacturing, or distributing weapons of mass destruction and terror are such violations. A Legion occupying force and investigators from the Republic are on their way. Imprimis is under martial law."

Voices cracked like veins left in the mud of a dried lakebed.

"This is an illegal act!"

"We will make immediate appeal!"

"Imprimis is an independent body, not subject to your Republic or any government besides our own."

Braley swiped the holo to birth out from the wrist devices of each of the gathered authorities.

"We assume control of all security. Your bot force remains immobilized. Your travel infrastructure's been restored to allow the resumption of civil activities. Any act of aggression or deterrence against our presence will be met with the reprisals proscribed in the writ."

The brown uniformed woman scanned the document, and made a resigned shake of her head. "Chancellor, we shall challenge the legality of this writ. We will lodge objections. But we have no ability to resist them. For the safety of Imprimis, I recommend we cooperate fully."

The learned men and women of Imprimis read for themselves. A rapid examination of the facts brought them to the correct conclusion, their analysis bathed in the light of Braley's authority.

The Legion was a power as undeniable as the singularities they studied above.

Sims used L-comm. "I think they get it, Braley. I'm headed to the *Supreme.* I'm arming the bosuns and other trained crew and swearing them in. We need security in the port and in the Anterum to protect the ship. Even rational minds sometimes get irrational when there's not a blaster right in front of them, and there's not enough of us. I don't rule out someone in this zoo could find some hate and the balls to use it."

Braley said, "Do it, Sims."

The frailest of the blue robes spoke.

"Professor Wittawat, you're named in this writ, as is your department. You're charged with conspiracy to build genetic weapons for the purpose of genocide. What have you to say?"

Sarah swayed as she read, then gulped.

"What they accuse me of is the greatest crime in the galaxy." She offered her wrists to Kel.

"I'm guilty."

***

"I know what you're going to ask me," Sarah said as Kel and Braley pulled her aside. "It wasn't intentional. It was ignorant. I should've known, especially after Proteus."

"I want you to see something," Hartenstein said, stepping in to the gathering. The holo was from a cloudy point of view, a pair of outstretched hands receiving a nondescript object from Sarah. In the background were tables of gadgets and equipment like a ship's repair section.

She slumped as the image extinguished. "I know what it looks like. I guess, it *is* what it looks like. But I swear, I couldn't have known the rediscovery of Kaiya could have led to something so awful."

Kaiya, Kel puzzled to himself.

"Who's the alien, Sarah?" Hartenstein commanded.

"Moluk Daan. Besides Control or his men, he was the only person with access to the Section. The last time he was here was that day, but that was two years ago."

"Who's Control?" Hartenstein asked.

Sarah's eyes were sadder than usual. "It was a man named Lexall. That's the only name we knew him by."

Lexall had been a cover name for the younger VanderLoot, the nephew of the senator. He'd melted when someone triggered the nanos in his bloodstream. "But in the years I've been here, he was here just twice. It was

Patrick who was here most often. You remember him, Colonel. I never saw him again after Proteus.

"After Proteus, Lexall came and told us Patrick wouldn't be back, and to continue our work. We never saw him again. Moluk Daan came that last time, asking for the Kaiya device."

Hartenstein met Kel's eyes. They knew what became of Patrick and the young VanderLoot.

"Tell her, Turner," Hartenstein said in his head. Kel was ready.

"Sarah, Control and his people, have they been in touch much?"

Sarah frowned quizzically. "How did you know? No. We've always worked very much undisturbed. It was one of the wonderful things about being here, being left alone to study the Ancients' mysteries, undisturbed."

Kel liked what he heard. "Control, Patrick, and the man they worked for who was responsible for the Section—we removed them from the equation."

She'd picked out the operative word in Kel's summary. "Removed."

"Moluk Daan's in a Legion cell," Hartenstein said.

"It's time we see," Kel said.

They didn't chain her for the drive to the Section. The leejes and bots in their convoy should have brought stares, had the sanctuary not looked like the aftermath of a plague. Dead police bots stood sentry over walks rolling without pedestrians. Public squares sat empty of the usual conclaves of dialecticians. Only the unblinking eyes of the black holes were out, judging everything below them.

Kel spoke so only Braley could hear. "We were shooting for a quiet in-n-out without causing a fuss. Oops. Can't blame these folks for staying outta sight."

"Not the first time we brought the ruckus despite our best efforts," Braley said.

Kel was puzzled. "Are the Legion and law directorate really on the way?"

His former team leader snorted. "It's what *should* happen. No. And if they check, we're so far from a hypercomm relay, the old gaffers won't know it was a ruse until we're long gone."

"The threat of the Legion does bring results."

Braley gave a clipped laugh. "Rescue me before I've dug myself dead in the mines they reserve for leejes convicted of high treason."

"Nah. It'll be a firing squad. But at least you'll have me there for company."

Braley snorted. "It's only funny if it's true, but I'm not laughing."

"We'll fix it, Braley. Rex and Primus Pilus aren't wrong."

"We're here," Sarah said.

The smooth red stone of the Antiquities Research Section was before them. Hartenstein and Braley were armored and moved to the street to put backs to the halted convoy. Meadows faced the entry with a K-17 he'd had the bots retrieve for him. Doc and Chappy looked at the weapon with a longing.

Meadows snarled. "Don't believe there's no one in there waiting to shoot at us."

Sarah sputtered to quell the build up to violence. "There isn't! Our security's maintained by our department's obscurity. Indifference is the universal attitude toward the Antiquities Section by the rest of the academy. They're fixed on the workings of the universe. What we do makes us..." Her explanation trailed off. "It's why the Section has always been undetected."

"The best secret's one in the open," Bertie said.

"Bet no one even wonders what's inside, what with all the black holes and cosmic anomalies hanging over everything," Phillip said. "Bloody brilliant place to hide, you ask me."

"No one's got a blaster, and no one's coming," Sarah implored the aggressively postured Meadows.

"You sure?" Meadows said, snapping his rifle at a surprised pedestrian who'd burst from around the corner to run head-on into their bizarre gathering. An emerald vestment engulfed the stroller so completely, who it was that shrieked from the depths of the hood was another mystery. In a blink, only an afterimage of flapping green remained.

"That was a particularly spry one," Phillip quipped.

"Never seen a human move so fast. Hope we didn't cause some kind of cardiac issue," Bertie added. "Maybe one of us should check?"

Tara was sandwiched with a wide-eyed Quint between the two bots. "They all wear monitors. They may not doctor legionnaires bent on killing each other, but they do have a lot of heart attacks here. The medics'll respond if we caused one."

"Let's get this circus off the streets," Meadows said.

"Agreed, Sergeant Major," Braley said.

A biometric pad pulsed beneath Sarah's palm, and the street entrance parted. Kel's anticipation sizzled, but mundanely, only a foyer, a lift, and an ascending staircase were beyond. Sarah moved to the lift.

"Uh-uh," Meadows said. "No speedlifts."

Sarah's head shook away his implication. "There's no danger."

"Says the accomplice to mass murder," Meadows shot back.

"Down or up, Sarah?" Kel asked.

"Down," she said, exasperated, her timidity gone. Meadows brought that out in people. "The upper floors are our public offices and restoration rooms and conservatory. It's all façade. The lift only descends with a code we use."

"No speedlifts," Meadows repeated.

"Fine." Sarah led them to a service door. Through mundane rooms, she arrived at a wall. A hidden biometric pad responded, and a passage opened. "We don't use them, but there are your stairs, Meadows."

"Allow us, gentlemen," Bertie said.

"Old times, it is," Phillip said, and the pair set off to lead the descent.

"I'll post here," Meadows said. K-17 in both hands, he jutted his chin to Doc and Chappy. "You two might as well go, for all the good you'll be in a fight. You look like walking cadavers." He snorted at his own quip and placed his back to the group, both to secure their rear and to disrespect the Wolfhounds. "I'm armoring up soon as we're done here and ain't taking it off. Ever."

Hartenstein intervened. "Go with Turner, gents. Meadows, I'll pull security here with you."

The Wolfhounds moved to place Tara between them. Chappy spoke to Doc over Tara's head, "The loudmouth's right about one thing. 'Bout through going around in just skins."

Tara held a hand out to a lost Quint, intimidated and wishing he were back at the ship. "It's okay. Kel says it's safe." Quint accepted her hand, and confidence spread to his face.

Chappy held Tara back. "Let them get to the first landing. We don't want to crowd the stairs. Just in case."

Kel and Braley had Sarah between them to follow the bots already at a trot and disappearing. "They're going to spook my people, Kel. It's not right."

Meadows spoke in Kel's ear from his patrol in the foyer. "Screw them being spooked. I don't trust her, Turner."

Beneath Meadows's crassness was merit.

Kel said, "Who's waiting for us, Sarah?"

She wore a worried face. "My team. There's just four of us. They're all like me. Electron counters and tinkerers."

Braley humphed. "Physicists and engineers? No one who's going to fight us?"

"No. I promise. They may not even know what's been happening on the rest of Imprimis. It's not unusual for us to stay down for a week at a time if we're working on a breakthrough. But..."

She hesitated.

"Hold up where you are, boys," Kel halted the ACMs' advance. "What are you not telling us, Sarah?"

"Doctor Taubman. He's responsible for integrity on our committee. Stanton's paranoid at times, but can you blame him? You remember how I was when we first met? The threats they hold over us for being a part of the Section—it's the price we pay to be the stewards of what's here."

Until they forced her, Sarah had been the model of a mute scientist entrusted to work in the blackest, most secretive research facility in the galaxy.

Braley swiped his K-17 to stun. "You know we're not maniacs. I'll be gentle as possible, but the first sign of your security proctor getting twitchy, I'll put him out of commission."

"Let me go first then," Sarah said, and broke away to race down the stairs.

Kel caught her by the shoulder as she moved to weave past the bots. "Boys. Anything?"

Bertie hummed. "Negative, Mister Turner, sir."

Phillip said, "We may've cocked up a bit beneath Victrix, sir, but there'll be no repeat of that, we promise."

Bertie continued with assurances. "From the start, we've pinged and beamed. Spoken to the janitor bots and air exchangers. Looked into every nook and cranny and beyond, sir. No surprises waiting, sir. There's a dampener blocking comms, and a simple camera monitor running. We've penetrated the interior, and it's as she says, sir. Just three blokes carrying on like the rest of the world don't exist."

"Go ahead, Sarah." Kel released her. After yet more runs of switchback stairs, they stopped at a final landing with lift doors to one side, a set of security doors opposite. Kel watched her face for any tell. She was at ease as she placed her hand on the pad. Doors parted to reveal a deep space of workbenches topped with parts and pieces, instruments and monitors, clouds of holos floating at eye-level. Two scientists remained heads down, absorbed by whatever lay on their respective benches.

Where were the multitude of strange devices recovered from archaeologic digs across the galaxy? Where were the event horizons like mirrored doors? The spinning cubes, pulsing gems, and alien glyphs? The place looked very much like a Legion repair depot.

Before following Tara in, Kel stabbed a finger down at a spot short of the threshold, indicating everyone should wait there. Her entrance had brought no notice. The scientists were obviously not suspecting anything was amiss. She cleared her throat loudly. A face distorted by magnifier specs turned lazily to half peer around a holo.

"We have visitors."

Now heads turned. Kel gave a warm smile and waved. "Hello."

Sarah did as she'd promised. "Everyone, these are friends. They're authorized to be here, so please be calm."

A man with spiked white hair appeared from an office, a pad clutched in one hand, chewing some meaty looking snack he held in the other. "Wittawat! Are you mad?"

"Stanton," she said to calm him. "Things have developed that we must talk about as a committee."

The man's gaze pierced the still parted threshold where two ACMs, an armored leej, and the rest of the party stared back. An unchewed bite fell from his open mouth. "You fool, Wittawat! Just because no one's checking on us doesn't mean we're not watched. You've been reckless since that jaunt with Control. Have you forgotten a breach means death?"

He dropped what was in his hands and suddenly pulled at his collar, diving hands wildly beneath his shirt like a man caught mid rush of hull depressurization and panicked to retrieve an atmo-mask.

"What's he doing?" Kel blurted to Sarah, but Braley was already there, weapon up, the electric ball of plasma headed at the man fumbling into his shirt. Purple arcs spreading from his chest like a blanket, raising his hair to stand even taller on end. Held high in a fist and attached to his neck by chain was a small cylinder. His thumb was pressed firmly at its end as he keeled over like a felled tree.

"WHAT IS THAT?" Kel demanded over the chaos of scientists abandoning their stools to splay onto the floor.

Sarah's cry was anguished. "I don't know, I swear, I don't."

"No action detected, no internal effect. Monitoring, monitoring," Bertie repeated in quick, uncharacteristically robotic succession.

Phillip followed as always. "It triggered a signal to a generating source on the surface. It's sent out a burst on a tunneling frequency, sir."

Bertie's head bobbed back and forth, returning to his normal manner of bantering. "Makes no sense. It shot straight up into the gullet of the black hole they call Fornus."

19

"Sitrep," Hartenstein asked from the main floor, hearing the commotion over the hot L-comm.

Braley came back immediately. "One of the scientists sent a distress call, we think."

Kel had Sarah by the shoulders. "You need to tell me what just happened."

Her head oscillated a frantic denial. "I don't know, Kel, I don't know!"

Bertie and Phillip played out a human analysis for the benefit of the team, their own computations having been completed in a millionth of a second.

"Too bloody far away to bring the cavalry here anytime quick," Bertie muttered.

"There's nothing achieved sending a signal into a bleedin' black hole and bugger all anyone to receive it," Phillip surmised.

Bertie finished. "Agreed, mate. Whatever happened, Mister Turner, we rate it as low probability for immediate danger, sir."

Braley turned to Kel. "My gut says the clock's against us."

Kel dropped eyes on Sarah. "What is it we need here?"

She fretted. "We've vaults and vaults of materials. So many things we haven't even begun to study."

Kel grew stern. "Sarah—what do we *need*? I know you've thought about this!"

With a new tenacity she grew taller with resolve. "I have. It's up to me to stop this. We take everything. Because I'm going with you."

For the benefit of the two conscious scientists, Braley repeated the stern performance he'd given the Imprimis Academy regents. The female scientist was stern as she waved the writ away and menaced him back. "You'd best call your superior for guidance."

The man stuck his chest out. "Do you know who we work for?"

Sarah practically gagged out her words. "*You* don't even know who you work for, Devrin. None of us do. Not really."

"Watch yourself, Wittawat," the woman hissed. "For all our sakes." She thought better of her tone and instead begged. "Sarah, you have to tell *them* it was all your doing and that none of us had any part in it. We don't deserve to be punished for whatever the hell you've done!"

Sarah shook her head wearily. "Karina, for what we've done, we *should* be punished."

"What is it we've done?" the man Devrin spat with incredulity. "We're explorers!"

Kel'd had enough. "We're not here to threaten or harm you. And we won't allow anyone else to, either. But *this*—" He circled around. "Is over."

Sarah recited facts with flinty precision. "Moluk Daan's in a Legion cell. Control's dead, his minions are gone, and the man who owned them *and* us is dead, too. And we're accountable for what we helped them do."

Doc returned from tending the stunned scientist, dangling the necklace and cylinder too basic to be adornment. "Doctors, we know this sent a signal out. To whom?" Doc's shift to refined diction when questioning the scientists caught Kel's attention. Operators wore different faces at will. With Braley's action, Chappy had become a blur, bounding long to take an opposing corner of the room, disregarding his status as unarmed and injured.

Kel's impression from their clash at bad-breath fighting range—the two were aggressive, fearless, deadly. Hartenstein's dogged defense of the pair as being the equal of any in Dark Ops—it was the highest accolade. The pair automatically and habitually positioned themselves to protect the most vulnerable in their party—the actions of men who lived to protect the ones they could wherever they could. Kel's decision was formed—they deserved a place in this fight.

Devrin and Karina were taciturn as Doc swung the pendant in front of their faces. He took a teasing tone. "Do you know for sure this doesn't mean something bad for you two as well as us?"

The scientists shared sideways looks. Devrin said, "It was something Moluk Daan gave Stanton the last time he was here."

Karina's face turned sour. "It gave him some perverse thrill not to tell us, like he held a secret as great as anything here."

Braley produced ener-chains and tossed them to Chappy. "That's all I need to know. Chain our unconscious sentry, will you?"

Sarah and her two associates were captivated by the coils snaking around their unconscious colleague until brought back by Kel's voice. "We need to make this happen, Sarah. Show us."

"Follow," she said, taking a course through the benches, past offices filled with datapads and workstations, old-fashioned books and sheets of flimsi stacked precariously on every flat surface, walls covered in handwritten notes and symbols. At the end of the hall teased an opening into a gallery, tantalizingly cavernous because no limit to its vastness was yet apparent. Stepping onto the terrace, he'd been close to correct. The space had limits; what it contained had none.

Sarah spoke with dreamy reverence. "We call this the museum, laid out as it all is in plain view, to be marveled at, appreciated, puzzled over."

A cavern of rough rock walls and ceiling bound the boundless mysteries of the Section. Row after row of artifacts—some so tiny atop their spotlighted pedestals they begged closer examination, some so large they could be identified from where he stood as things not from this time or realm. Some looked barbaric and cruel, and he remembered Sarah once telling them her specialty was in the study of Savage technology.

But the rest—incongruent shapes not for human hands, the strange raised characters, the things that hovered, the ones that spun in seemingly perpetual motion—all shouted, *here are the answers to the secrets of our galaxy.*

Meeting Rex should have been such a moment of astonishment.

She read his thoughts. "You feel it too, don't you, Kel? The first time I was brought here, I immediately knew it was where I was meant to be. They didn't need to threaten me. I begged to become their slave the moment I saw this."

Her confession was interrupted by a presence. Expecting it to be Tara, it was disorienting to see the usually invisible Quint crowding close.

"They were the first into the unknown galaxy. They found evidence of the Ancients. They hoarded it all and hid it from the rest of humanity, knowing it would make them powerful in the growing galaxy. This place is the product of the Corps of Exploration, isn't it, Professor Wittawat?"

Sarah snapped around with a gasp to see who had stolen the air from the room.

Like a novice fighter landing a punch on the champion, he declared his worth in the arena. Quint's confidence soared as he presented himself. "Doctor Quint Delaria. Molecular genetics and xenobiology, New Byzantium Academy of Sciences." The stutter Kel anticipated with each impending word did not materialize.

"He's a friend," Kel assured.

"Yes, Doctor Delaria," Sarah admitted begrudgingly, as though Quint's deconstruction of the Section's founding had been an actual blow. "The Corps of Exploration established what you see here, and Imprimis grew around it. When new worlds and ancient ruins led to the discovery of mysterious objects, wherever the Savages were beaten and their sick and terrible machines recovered, the vaults of the Section are where it all came to reside."

Braley drove close. "Let's not forget the fuse is burning."

Sarah rallied to focus and pointed to a collection on the floor. "We start there. What I gave Moluk Daan was a simplified device we built that duplicated the technology to measure Kaiya. Everything that gave us the breakthrough and all the research are together there."

What Kaiya was, would have to wait.

Sarah found Kel's eyes. "Then, everything else comes with us."

It was Quint who said the obvious. "There's too much! You make it sound like this is only a small sample of what's here."

"Start prioritizing," Braley ordered.

"Sarah," Bertie said, "Phillip and I have sorted your data streams. We may have a better handle on what's important and what's not."

Sarah balked. "Our records are encrypted!"

Phillip apologized. "Sorry, mum. Not to us. Broke open like a jar of Gran's canned pears dropped on the basement floor."

"Mister Turner," Bertie said. "Problem's the layout. The lifts are small. And we must go through the bloody shop where this lot does the menial odds and ends."

"Real chokepoint there, Mister Turner," Phillip said. "We need hands. And there's a ship full o' experts in moving and stacking sitting idle, if you get our intent, sir."

Kel did. "Sims, you got me?"

"Send it, Kel."

"Tell the captain we need all available hands, grav sleds, lifters—the works. There's a warehouse full of odds and ends we need loaded into the *Supreme* ASAP. Got me?"

"By ASAP, you mean...?"

"Yesterday, Sims."

"What I thought, Kel. It's a Quasar if I ever heard one. On it."

Doc, Tara, and Quint had already followed Sarah onto the floor of the museum, the two bots with them. Sarah pointed out items. "All of this. Then these." She fretted to herself, "I want it all. We can't *get* it all."

Braley nudged Kel. "Work detail, Leej."

Kel helped Braley heft a long crate. Whatever was inside was heavy as neutronium. "Pucker holes and elbows," he grunted. "Because the man says don't stop till you drop."

***

Kel led the loaded convoy at full speed for the port. Poul was in his ear. "I'm armored up and coming with you for the next run."

"Negative, Poul," Kel said. "You're still using a crutch."

"My leg isn't much to look at, but with full power augment, I'm good to go."

"You break that leg, I'll break you. Stay with the *Supreme*. No argument."

"Grrr," Poul disagreed. "Fine. I'll send Sims back and keep on eyes in the sky and security for the ship."

Captain Sullivan met Kel at the ramp of the open hold while Chelly and Sheila directed the first off-loading. Cormac griped as expected.

"I don't even know where to begin, Turner!"

"Be ready to lift if I call for an immediate departure, Captain."

Cormac paled. "What now?"

"We don't know what we don't know. Are you locked in with the jump coordinates I gave you in Cygnus?"

Cormac fumed. "I knew your word to keep us out of danger was worth nothing." He spun away, barking over his wrist link as he disappeared into the ship.

Tara was beside him. "One day he'll understand what he and the *Supreme* have been such an important part of."

Kel doubted it. "I'm getting kitted and heading back to push this along. You're needed here to get the ship ready. If it comes to a situation on the ground, listen to Poul."

"Yes, Kel."

He took her chin and kissed her. "You're a good operator."

"I have the best teacher."

Armored again, Kel bounced out of the ship to see Sims and Poul, his gait jerky, rounding from the nose of the ship where crewmen guided a port bot building a defensive position from containers. Kel pointed at Poul's leg and gave him the thumbs up as they met.

"Hoping this is all for nothing," Poul said.

"We'll be back with the next sortie in thirty," Kel said.

"How many to come?" Sims asked.

"We'll get it from Phillip and Bertie, they seem to have it figured," Kel said.

"I'm back to the TOC," Poul said and limped off.

Kel and Sims made for the tail and the convoy that should be preparing to leave when a sled driven by Doc and Chappy shot from the rear of the ship.

An armored Meadows leaped into view, yelling at a volume that captured the attention of the port workers through the windows of their offices. "YOU TWO! HOLD!"

Kel nudged Sims. "We better see what this's about." They arrived as Meadows thrust a knife hand at the two Wolfhounds.

"Where are you going without the rest of the convoy?"

Chappy frowned. "All our kit's in our mission support site."

Doc held his injured wrist to his abdomen, the regen sleeve absent. "We need to armor up, too. We all know there's something coming at us, we just don't know when."

"Not so fast," Meadows said as he hopped onto the flatbed deck. "The sled's mission essential. You two aren't. We'll drop you and take the sled. Get suited and get useful. We don't leave no one, but if we have to lift and you aren't here—"

"The *Seraphim*'ll make pick up on us," Doc spat.

"We got it," Chappy said with the same disgust. "We're Zeta, you know? And just about sick of this attitude."

"You mean to say, 'I understand, *Sergeant Major*,'" Meadows corrected. "We'll address your lack of military bearing later, Sergeant. Let's go."

"I want to come," a youthful voice yelled behind them. It was Meadows's namesake, the younger Curt, a K-17 in his hands, posted and guarding the nose of the *Supreme*. More port workers pressed to the observation windows of their offices to see the action.

"You've got a job here, Trooper," Meadows said. "I'm proud of you. Keep it up."

The young man snapped to attention, suddenly older, and brought his rifle into a respectable imitation of a parade salute.

"Yes, Sergeant Major."

Meadows tapped the shoulders of the two Wolfhounds on the control bench.

"Take note, Leejes. *That's* military bearing."

"Yes, Sergeant Major," the two groaned together.

Meadows took a lecturing tone. "Special Ops doesn't mean special privileges."

"Yes, Sergeant Major," the two groaned together in a repeat chorus.

"Roll on, Leejes," Meadows commanded, and continued his lecture.

"You'll go back to the Wolfhounds the kind of operators you should be," Meadows said. "You've accidentally arrived in the presence of the most accomplished operators who ever wore Dark Ops armor. And Colonel Hartenstein, he's the mold the rest of us were made from."

Doc turned in his seat. "You haven't been too respectful to Howler—Colonel Hartenstein, I mean, Sergeant Major."

"That's where you're wrong, Leej," Meadows said. "I had to remind the colonel how things are done, what his role is as a civilian. He knows I was right to do so. And, I did it the Legion way. *That's* my job. To make sure things are done right. Always and everywhere. Understand?"

"What's that make me?" Kel said. If Meadows had relegated Hartenstein to the status of a civilian, Kel was curious how Meadows saw him.

"The best operator I've ever known, Turner." Meadows corrected himself, "Apologies. *Captain* Turner. You're Legion inactive, but still on the roles."

"Correct, Sergeant Major."

331

"Then I'm still your team sergeant. That's how I see it. I can wear more than one hat. On this job I have to."

Sims blew an exasperated breath. "Oba, how does that mind work? Some kinda brain parasite they slip you when you make sergeant major? You're more of a pain-in-the-ass enigma than you ever were, Curt."

Meadows grunted happily. "Don't I know it, Sims."

20

Hartenstein labored alongside the crew, containers and uncrated objects too large to box adding to the trail piling higher and longer onto the street outside the red stone building.

"You've been hustling," Kel said as he pulled the flatbed close.

"Phillip and Bertie are triple-timing it inside and back," Hartenstein said. "We're just trying to stay out of their way."

Kel knew the body language of Hartenstein stiffening abruptly. It meant someone on L-comm grabbed Hartenstein's attention. It could only be the *Seraphim*.

"Say again, Slabside, repeat on all L-comm," Hartenstein said loudly.

A voice broke into their buckets. "Howler, a spatial anomaly just appeared off the station."

Kel looked upward with the *Supreme* crew to crane necks back, some pointing up at the dome and gasping. Bertie was beside Kel, a huge crate on his back. His square head pointed skyward with the humans.

"The system's known for its sporadic wormholes, boss. It's the bread and butter for some of the stargazers here. May not be what we fear, but that one is bloody close."

The swathe of the view normally occupied by twin black holes held the swirling mouth of a blazing white whirlpool. A dark object crossed the bright rim of the event's mouth.

"Me and my optimism," Bertie cursed.

Slabside's voice returned. "I wouldn't believe it if I wasn't looking right at it, but Drizzy and Romper agree. That's some kind of ship. Impossible, but there it is."

Kel briefly lost the object in the corona, then the anomaly flared, and collapsed. The ship was sharp and angular in the dim and haunting albedo reflected by the three blue suns.

The pilot stole Kel's thoughts. "I don't believe in coincidences. I'm moving the *Seraphim* to an intercept course. We don't have much for offensive weapons, but we'll do what we can. Out."

In the spot where Bertie had been was only the crate he'd carried. A pit formed in Kel's stomach. "Braley, get everyone topside. We have company. Time to go."

Sims ran down the line of gawking crew. "Drop everything and head for the ship. Go. Go." Hartenstein was doing the same. Meadows hefted a pair of women in each arm and plopped them onto a sled loaded with a single layer of crates. "You got my permission to break the speed limit. Take off, ladies."

"Captain Sullivan," Kel spoke into his wrist. "Spin up for departure. I'm sending the crew now. Be ready to execute your flight plan if I give the word."

Cormac replied calmly, "Get back to the ship."

Kel scanned the sky. Closing nearer above the peaks of the buildings was a many-faced polyhedron the size of the *Supreme*. Spreading from it like bees from a disturbed hive, it expelled a swarm of small cubes, setting their collective course for the dome.

"That's not good," Sims said.

Braley burst onto the street, dragging Quint, Sarah, and the scientists Devrin and Karina with him. On Phillip's back rode the chained and groggy Stanton Taubman, held upright between a pair of manipulator arms. Bertie gave the "last man" as he poured out onto the street behind them.

"What've we got?" Braley asked.

Taubman snickered. "The punishment you deserve for stealing their property."

The white cubes were nearly on the dome.

"He's coming with us," Kel pointed at the man to make sure it was understood by Phillip, then spun to the scientists next to Sarah. "You can stay here and take your chances, or you can come with us."

The pair dashed back into the building.

"Suit yourselves," Kel observed. He swept Sarah up with gentle urgency and deposited her into a sled. "Go." The crewman at the controls needed no further encouragement and shot off.

"What about you?" Sarah yelled back from the speeding sled, realizing the legionnaires weren't coming with them.

"We got real work," Meadows shouted back. "Finally."

"Hey," Sims prompted. "Topside."

Blooms from the dome's structural integrity field enveloped the cubes, signaling their touchdown. The energy of the protective field reflected yellow on the white cubes as they cascaded down the curvature shielding the city scape.

Taubman flung himself off Phillip, deftly dodged a slithering manipulator arm, and vanished around the corner of the building.

"Forget him," Kel said. His K-17 was mounted and he arched his back until his barrel pointed directly up at the first lander. A subtle spot grew from a central point and spread to match the borders of the square face. With a viscous penetration, it advanced into the sanctuary and abruptly stopped to hang in place, half in, half out.

Kel's HUD danced with shifting cursors until each stopped and flashed, indicating each shooter had claimed stake to a target all their own. Kel's finger touched the trigger, saving the last ounce of rearward pressure. Until—

The flat, blank face of the cube vanished. What birthed from it splayed out to float silently down, as though suspended by an invisible parachute. It was the size of a man. Bipedal. Two arms. A bulbous head on a bulging trunk. Its other features were absent beneath its shell, as though it wore a coating applied evenly everywhere, including its head. He recognized it as no named enemy.

Across its chest, by any other name, was a weapon.

Kel pressed his trigger. And pressed again. Three. Four. Five blasts, until the enemy in his sights came apart and he was on to a new one. The others were firing with him. Heavy blasters sizzled the air from the backs of the ACMs, a single of their impacts sufficient to the task of splattering the invaders.

No longer descending at the rate of a feather's fall but at the rate of gravity, Kel dodged a plummeting body. Whatever species of soldier this was, its parts crashed an arm's reach away in a sickening succession of thuds. Dead, he paid it no mind as more rained down like bird droppings, making similar wet noises as they landed. Empty charge packs hit the ground sharply as new ones were slapped home.

The descending invaders were sending a steady stream of hazy rays in their direction. None had yet come close to the team, and the misses impacted seemingly without effect on wherever the beams impacted.

Stanton Taubman fled down the avenue to meet the descending invaders. Arms chained to his sides, he screamed, "I sent the beacon. Save me!"

"That idiot," Sims mumbled.

One of the unimpressive beams found him. With no flash, no discharge, he was simply... gone. One moment there, the next, he seemed to assume the same frequency with which the beam vibrated, and he disappeared. Kel'd never seen a weapon do like damage.

His curiosity became moot as they cleared the last invaders from overhead. But there were many, many more who had already fallen into the defilade behind the cityscape. Defenders and attackers now had an urban landscape between them.

A window appeared in his bucket. Poul's eyes in the sanctuary were over the invaders. The last of their numbers through the dome, they began to form into a loose skirmish line, sweeping into the sanctuary.

Poul spoke. "Their combat intent's aimed for you and the Section."

"IMTs and best route to meet them," Kel said and bounced. They spread out with him and began their individual movement techniques, letting the HUDs guide them in unerring precision. Kel swore never again to be without at least specs. Navigating with bare eyes was for primitives.

The voice of Slabside was in their buckets. "That geometric nightmare of a ship's dodged us and's heading for the port, spilling out more of those landers. Warn your people. This is no Excalibur, but we'll do what we can, out."

"Understood, *Seraphim*," Poul replied.

"What's the move?" Sims asked. "The *Supreme*'ll be a sitting duck if she exits, and they got a ground assault coming for them."

"Head for the ship, Dark Ops," came Chappy's voice unexpectedly. "We're between the OPFOR and your position, moving to high ground."

"Hell," Doc said. "You boys were shooting fish in a barrel. We just may KTF 'em all by ourselves."

"Nice you're making yourselves useful, Wolfhounds," Meadows said.

Kel warned, "The blobs made a major tactical mistake. They didn't expect resistance. Now they're getting their act together." The window showed the invaders forming into groups of threes, spreading to use cover, and sending alternating bounds into the urban terrain. "Their weapons are deadly. Some kind of disintegrator. Their armor's tough. Don't underestimate them."

"Let us work, Leejes," Chappy said. "Make for the port. We'll sitrep you. Out."

"Mister Turner, sir," Phillip said. "Permission for Bertie and I to join the delaying action?"

"Mister Turner," Bertie said without missing a beat. "A force of sixty-two ground-pounders of unknown capability are reaching the first phase line of Doc and Chappy's defense."

"Sir," Phillip said. "We can make a difference. We'll hit them from low while those boys work them from high. If the OPFOR changes course and heads for the port, we'll have given you ample time to set a defense to protect the *Supreme*."

"Best advice, sir," Bertie said with care.

"Go," is all Kel said. It sufficed to send the ACMs on their way, and for the rest of the team to join him in a run for the main thoroughfare, the fastest path to the Anterum and the adjacent port. They'd barely set off when Poul's voice was back.

"Team, OPFOR elements have breached the port in unknown numbers. We are engaged. Out."

Opposing conveyors ran in both directions. Kel was first to land, and clicked to full power augment. Arms pumping, flying faster than a sled could have carried him, everything in his peripheral vision was a blur. In less than a minute, the smaller dome of the Anterum and the end of the walkway were in sight. He sprang off and peeled around the curve and into the mouth of the security control point. Even at full augment, after the multiplier of the walk, the speed with which he ran was disappointingly slow. He burst through the empty gate station.

A fusillade of hazy beams came from left and right. The port access was ahead. Kel kept his dead-run pace. "I'm going. Light 'em up." He launched a K-17 grenade to one side, threw a fragger from off his chest to the other while plowing ahead to the port access. Meadows was a step behind, firing with him as they ran beneath the suites of the port offices and into the hangar.

Firing from behind a forward sponson was the younger Curt, a blob soldier falling to his hammering shots. If he wasn't careful, the charge chain would freeze. This was no time to teach him to slow his trigger. At the aft, Poul blasted careful shots from behind stacked crates. He broke into a rush across open space to slide behind the cover of a frozen mech bot, rising to fire again from the opposite side. Hazy beams had followed him a step behind, and splashed onto the loader bot he sheltered behind.

"Go to the kid," Kel said to Meadows as he broke for Poul's position.

On the move, Kel fired at blobs poorly concealed among materials deep in the hanger. They weren't using cover well, and he was glad of it. "Coming through," Sims said from behind, and was all of a sudden on line with him to join the fire fight. Kel checked his HUD. A top-down view had the positions of a dozen OPFOR highlighted around the bay. Poul had managed the combat information as he fought, a feat of multitasking impossible for few. As a result of Poul's supernatural skill, they all had the knowledge of an omniscient.

With unconscious coordination, the four operators went to work. Find, fix, and finish quickly became found, fixed, and finally, just finished. Rallied on the far side of the *Supreme,* Kel checked his HUD. The icons of each blob's position pulsed a dark red, indicating dead or combat ineffective. A body rendered into multiple parts made for a simple algorithmic decision for a drone.

"Where's the kid?" Poul asked.

"He's fine," Meadows said. "Done good. Gotta teach him to slow his firing cadence."

Kel concentrated on what next. "Braley, we're secure in the hangar. Sitrep in the Anterum?"

"We got it locked down. Colonel and I cleaned house. These blobs aren't too savvy."

The voice of the Legion aviator, Slabside, came on the all channels. "Legion, be advised. The enemy craft is moving off and the *Seraphim*'s in pursuit. We only have the one offensive weapon and we've taken some damage, but we're going to get you all the space you need to get your ship out of that port and jump."

"Damn, I wish this was our warbird and not a cover craft," the co-pilot Drizzy said.

"Understood, *Seraphim*," Hartenstein replied. "Strong work and good hunting."

Romper must've been in the cockpit, running the sensors. "Chief, an anomaly's appeared a thousand klicks ahead of the escaping craft's heading. It's opening."

"Making an escape or is someone else coming out of there to their rescue?" Slabside said. "Get us closer, Drizz, and let me send one up their tailpipe."

Kel pictured the scene and ached to hear their cheers of victory. Slaved from Braley's visor as if on demand, the dome above the Anterum was in his HUD. It required no magnification to see what transpired. The geometrically-shaped alien craft entered the mouth of the anomaly, followed by a blast from the *Seraphim* but the result of the impact was lost as both disappeared into the well.

The flat, unemotional communication from the pilot narrated.

"We're getting pulled into the anomaly. It's a sympathetic wave. Can't break from it."

The *Seraphim* followed the vanished polyhedron. The frozen whirlpool of blazing white arms contracted, the portal collapsed, and a tremendous flare lit the sky like an exploding sun.

They were gone.

"Oh no!" Braley exclaimed.

Kel closed the window. "*Supreme*, take on the last of your crew and exit the port. We're moving to engage the enemy in the Sanctuary. Wait ten minutes and if you don't hear from us, make your jump."

Bertie was in his ear. "You know best, Mister Turner, but it may not be necessary."

Phillip followed. "Rapidly evolving situation, sir. Our sitrep might change that course of action."

"Send it," Kel said.

Doc's annoyance was bitter music. "We didn't get a shot off. Those two jabbering ninnies stole our last stand moment from us."

Bertie sang sweetly, "You're welcome."

Chappy sighed. "Gotta admit, it was entertaining."

Kel brought up the view from the big dome. A platoon's worth of silver sentries roved the scene of the battle he was certain was being desperately waged against the outnumbered defenders. Cocooned by security foam and glued in place up to their bulbous and featureless heads, the enemy force was immobilized. The police bots continued to cruise the streets, cyclops red eyes patrolling for more unrest.

"The cops are programmed to recognize us all as friendlies, gentlemen," Phillip said.

"Come have a peek so's you can learn what proper proxy warfare looks like," Bertie said, his pride undisguised.

Hartenstein's voice concealed little of his rage. "Anyone besides me want to peel one of these blobs open? With me, Leejes!"

A brief ride brought them to the battlefield where the team of Wolfhounds and eight-legged ACMs stood sentry. Hartenstein's vibro-blade hummed to life as he leaped off the still-moving sled to propel to where a petrified enemy waited. Doc and Chappy bounced to his flanks, weapons pointed at the blob caked in stone.

"I'm a surgeon, too," Hartenstein seethed as he pushed the blade slowly into the neck of the muddy colored shell. The armor gave way with toxic fumes, and Hartenstein began a sawing motion to advance his humming blade on a course to peel away the soldier's cap.

The rest of the team spread out defensively, watching both the roving silver bots and enemies caked in termite mounds. Kel chose to observe the unveiling. He stepped to the other side of the colonel's working location and leaned over the blob. The first of his curiosities was sated by locating the clean edges of thinnest visor at the correct height for a humanoid's eyes. Who was on the other side, looking at Kel right now?

Hartenstein completed his circumferential sawing. The organic-looking mess made a sucking sound as pulled upward, a thin membrane inside stretching until it split, produced a puff, followed by the escape of a thin green cloud.

The gaping maw sucked useless breaths, beady eyes darted in all directions, piles of loose skin flopped on a bare head as the alien pulled and strained against its cocoon. Its fight against asphyxiation ended limply and a coarse black tongue creeped from its mouth like a thick worm tunneling its way out of rain-soaked soil.

"Fart breathers," Chappy proclaimed, as if the explanation were complete.

Kel at least needed clarification. "That what you nabbed on Ozydna?"

Absorbed in thought, a single affirmative grunt was all the former Dark Ops commander spared as he silenced the humming vibroblade at his side.

Braley retrieved a dropped alien weapon. "I'm curious." He aimed it at a bare wall and pressed the trigger, releasing it as quickly. The hazy beam painted the surface, stopped, leaving no trace of result. A longer pulse brought the same lack of effect on the surface.

"But it sure turned loudmouth into the same kinda hot air," Meadows said. "Sir, may I?"

Meadows took the weapon, motioned the others to step away, and aimed it at the head of the asphyxiated alien. As the beam had disintegrated Stanton Taubman, so too it made even the dead alien vanish from within the cocoon.

"Only affects biologic material," Braley surmised. "Perfect for the purpose."

"Would it have done anything to us through armor?" Sims asked.

"We'll see what can be made of this later," Meadows said, holding the weapon muzzle down and away.

"How do we process them all, Howler?" Doc asked. "There's a gazillion of them stuck around the city."

"Sixty-one remain," Bertie corrected.

Hartenstein broke from his meditation. "They die in place. Whatever atmo these blobs breathe, there isn't any to give them. Doubt the locals can do it, and it's their problem now."

Chappy shook his head. "Not for long. Isn't enough of a payback for Slabside, Drizzy, and Romper, though, is it?"

"It's not," Hartenstein said. "But it's coming." He sheathed the cold blade and straightened.

"Gentleman, this is as good an opportunity as we've had to do as Sergeant Major Meadows correctly observed. Time to clear things up."

Leejes didn't have to look at each other across a meeting circle. Facing out and alert for danger, all made the ready reply. "Up."

Hartenstein continued. "Sergeant Major is right to point out I'm a civilian. I've been operating under Primus Pilus since this hunt began. Wolfhound Six—General Airani—granted me the status of advisor for an operation under his auspices, but, what I'm presenting is a recommendation from an advisor to the ranking officer, Colonel Yost."

Braley spoke. "I'm the ranking officer, but I've been content to let Kel run the tactical mission."

Meadows groaned. "Then just call Captain Turner mission commander and be done with it." He recovered his own bearing and added. "Sir."

"Done," Braley said.

Hartenstein continued. "That alien craft may not have been destroyed before it slipped away into that anomaly. If so, if our opposition knows we've taken the Section. Maybe it signals the kickoff to whatever's the next phase of their war. I believe we need to return to Cygnus with all haste."

"Bet they worked out the whole conspiracy while we've been gone," Chappy said.

"I got the feeling the whole regiment's raring to go," Doc said.

"Do we need more gizmos?" Sims asked.

Bertie answered, "With certainty, Sergeant Simons, we've recovered the items most likely to be of use."

Phillip said, "Even some Professor Wittawat missed mentioning."

Braley spoke. "On your way to Cygnus, you're going to drop me at the nearest system with a hyper comm array. After I send Legion Command my brief, I'll get my own ride to go stand tall before the man. Primus Pilus put me into action because the Legion was frozen. If they haven't thawed on their own accord by now, they will with the evidence I'll be giving them. What does the mission commander think?"

Kel answered by bringing his link up. "Attention, *Supreme*. Captain Sullivan, prepare for our return. We're leaving together."

It was Chelly who answered. "The *Supreme* and her crew welcome you home," paused, then added, "Legion family."

21

"What is Kaiya?" Kel asked with simple candor.

They'd departed Imprimis to the relief of the regents and left the sanctuary in its state of graveyard facsimile. Underway, the hold of the *Supreme* bustled like the plazas of Imprimis. At least, how the gathering places had been before Kel and the two Zeta operators had set to killing each other and cleared the party dance floor like a wrecking crew on a deadline.

Without acknowledging his question, Sarah, Quint, and the bots continued their close discussion. Their attention was on the earthen clay pyramid covered in raised and undecipherable characters that rested on the table they surrounded. Kel knew the bots at least had heard him—they could hear paint drying—and his bile rose. His need to learn what Kaiya was became a path abruptly narrowed by prickly thorns—that's what it felt like, having his question ignored—because it scratched and poked his skin with the same annoyance.

The dip that came after the high of combat was different for everyone and every fight. Sometimes, it was an overwhelming fatigue that made every step an exhausting slog through drying duracrete. Sometimes, it was a current of electricity rippling in your head at irritable voltage. Neither could be switched off by anything but time.

So, he took it. With a breath, he considered the scene around him.

A robust comradery had developed between the insular spacers and the leejes, between humans and bots. The legionnaires' war tools were mixed amongst the dense collection of artifacts, the largest of all the implements being Meadows himself, who lectured Curt and the cousins who'd bravely defended the *Supreme* like the family castle.

Sims entertained a girl as young as Tara had been when he'd first met her. Kel cringed. Surely, the girl's mother would not do as Tara's mother had once advised her. Sims was Kel's age! Poul limped to the pair on crutches, deftly interpreting the scene as Kel had.

Tara ran a scanner over Chappy's head, her smile a clinical declaration that he'd healed, then dropped onto a knee to examine the regen sleeve on Doc's wrist. Receiving her benediction with thanks and a warmth that Kel could feel from across the bay, Doc returned to the datapad he'd been studiously reading from whenever not exercising the rest of his body. Braley composed a report. Hartenstein scowled into space, broadcasting his preference to be left alone.

He returned attention to the gathering around the workstation table expediently built together by the crew and leejes, covered in tools borrowed from the engineering section. Quint had become an instant member of Sarah's team and, with the bots, a collaboration began the moment they lifted from Imprimis.

It had been time well spent. Calmer, he tried again.

"What's Kaiya?" Kel repeated. It came out less forcefully than he'd nearly blasted before his cleansing moment, but still harsher than he'd intended. Partial success meant partial failure. The comradely buzz elsewhere halted like the music had stopped, as did the conversation of the four associates he addressed.

"The simplest explanation is it's a force that defines life itself," Sarah said, rising from resting elbows. "Measurable. Distinct. Transforming. Transformable."

"Mister Turner, it's the greatest discovery ever made regarding the nature of life in our universe. All Life." Bertie was given to exaggeration. It was part of the humor adapted into the ACMs' personas, modeled on the culture of their builders, making the AI's interactions with humans human-like. But Bertie's statement struck Kel as genuine.

"Stunning," is all Phillip said.

Quint agreed. "I'm still trying to comprehend all the implications. There are things known, and things guessed at. It's known that every living cell of every living thing, no matter how simple, is itself as complex as a galaxy. We are all of us a nearly infinite collection of galaxies of life energy. But the essence of whatever that energy *is*, it's eluded definition at the quantum level by anyone who's ever tried. But the Ancients did it."

"An infinite number of distinct life frequencies for infinite varieties of life," Sarah said. "Detected, deciphered, and classified."

Hartenstein appeared like the silent assassin he was. "And that's the device you gave Moluk Daan, the means from the Ancients to do just that?"

Sarah tilted her head to indicate a more complex answer was coming. "What I gave him was the simplified version of a device we built based on the tech. I brought the full collection of the devices here."

"Simplified," Quint scoffed.

"Very interesting, I'm sure," Hartenstein dismissed gruffly, glowering at the pyramid. "How did that become a weapon?"

Sarah was nonchalant. "Oh, that's not the Kaiya device. Bertie, would you—?" The bot departed eagerly to retrieve her request, excusing himself as he sidestepped the rest of the team converging to join Kel and the discussion around the table.

"Karina was the first to theorize a new mechanism of evolution from this knowledge. Acquired characteristics alter the Kaiya, and she proposed that there are circumstances where Kaiya can modify genes, which in effect means that life can change itself and even pass those characteristics to progeny. Life can alter its own evolution, rather than random mutations in DNA expressing traits that are either beneficial or detrimental to survival."

Quint stammered for the first time in a long while. "It's c-completely different from everything we th-thought we knew about evolution."

Kel had grown tired of the explanation, not sharing their enthusiasm for a new science. "So the gist of it is that Moluk Daan took this tech to the Hool, and they figured out how to program nanos to recognize specific Kaiyas as targets for a discriminating gene weapon."

"With greatest specificity," Sarah said. "In comparison, what the Plenaxians tried to do against their dissidents was horribly crude. It backfired, and killed everyone."

Bertie returned with not one, but a number of devices that he carefully laid out on the table while Sarah continued her explanation.

"Waves and particles, energies expressed in spins and frequencies, shaped by experiences, places, stresses, smells, tastes—everything that makes a person who they are—that's Kaiya. And within a person's Kaiya, many, many Kaiyas. And between different peoples, the more similar the forces that shape one's Kaiya, the more similar the Kaiyas of different people."

Sims rubbed his temples. "My head hurts."

Sarah readied a datapad and a holo emitter. "I'll show you. Kel, can I use you? It's not harmful, I promise."

Tara bristled at Sarah treating Kel like an object—pulling him into place by his offered arm, his waist bent deeply over the table and shoulder at the extreme of its stretch. Kel gave his wife a wink. Sarah peeled back the sleeve to expose Kel's forearm, pinning it to the table with a palm to command he not move, and positioned four small obelisks around the outstretched limb.

The four obelisks glowed at the tips, shooting beams to join each other in a lattice. Above them a holo projected a spectrum of rainbows aligned in repeating bands.

"What Kaiya is can't be expressed by words."

She magnified a spot on the holo and it quantized into a mash of symbols, vortices, static, and waves.

"We experimented on ourselves. Between myself, Karina, Devrin, and even Stanton, the four of us shared a quantized Kaiya in a resolution finer than the bands of our biologic commonalities. We demonstrated it for Control once. His was—not like ours. Sims, may I scan you next?"

She then repeated the process on Poul, Braley, and Hartenstein. Sarah's invitation to Meadows received an arms-folded-across-chest response. "Uh-uh. You ain't taking a picture of my soul. For all I know, there's something in these crates that'll sprout a copy of me out of some pod and it'll try and space me and take my place." To Doc and Chappy beside him, he said, "If you two are smart, which I doubt, you'll pass on this, too."

Both seethed in silence, but likewise folded their arms to indicate they wouldn't join in the experiment.

"It's okay, I have enough readings to make a statistically valid demonstration," Sarah said.

She projected the five patterns beside each other and typed on the control boards suspended around her like the keys of an organ. The quantized view exploded from each to show the same jumble, all shifting and moving in perfect synchronization.

"What have I heard you call yourselves before—a tribe? There's its Kaiya."

Kel frowned. Was that really the mark of a Dark Ops leej?

"Mrs. Turner, can I use you? Then Quint?"

The new pair of projections did not synchronize in any manner, not with either operator's nor with each other's.

Bertie hummed. "Bloody ten to the 27th number of loci to search, based on first and most probably inadequate assumptions on my part. The real number's likely another order of magnitude larger."

Phillip was there. "I follow you, Bert. Hool DNA mechanics can sort genes like a schoolboy sorting marbles. But how they could figure out what Kaiya matches an operator's? I've not got the slightest! Professor, is there a device that can construct any given Kaiya into a representation of what expressed it?"

"Not quite," she said.

"Then how'd they do it?" Bertie asked.

"They had a template," Kel said. "A DO operator they could read from."

Poul followed the tracks on the logical trail. "There's only one Dark Ops leej ever lost and not recovered."

Some memories return the holder to a time and place more felt than remembered. Not even a bucket filtered the smell of decay bonded to every molecule of that steamy jungle air. Fatigue there was a constant, the weight of your ruck pushing down while soft ground pulled against every step. Thirst was a constant urge in the throat but the same heat made appetite a forgotten desire. Every swathe of green concealed an army of rabid dog men, slavering and howling to tear into their flesh.

The veterans of Psydon experienced it all as if still there.

"JP didn't die on Psydon," Sims said with awful contemplation.

Braley's eyes shut as if replaying it all in his head. "We searched for days and days to try to bring him home."

Meadows's head dropped to his chest, denying the accusation before it could be made. "We didn't leave him. No way."

Kel wanted to be told that what he thought was impossible, that his epiphany was instead a confused delusion. But their wishful skepticism sank beneath jungle quicksand when Kel said what they all knew to be the inescapable truth.

"The Hool found the Kaiya of Dark Ops. The perfect template from the perfect operator. Jon Pabon."

***

The revelation of Kaiya answered how the Hool made their weapon. But it was also the single question among many that was so far, answered. They all poured out in a free-for-all mayhem like a game of Legion push ball.

"Who're the fart breathers?"

"Yeah, how do they figure in all this?"

"Are they the ones who got all the aliens working together?"

"We can't trigger nuke 'em if we don't know where their home world is."

"Is the House of Reason in on this?"

"Nothing would surprise me."

The jump engines thrummed their song, and would for days. Like Sims, Kel's head hurt. He stayed out of the dogpile of possibilities being thrown around and instead surrendered to a memory as strong as the jungle. Once on Pthalo, a wave had crashed onto his eight-year-old body, pushing him to the bottom beneath its inescapable power, threatening to grind and rend him into the same sand it dragged him through. While under the wave's crush, his inquisitive mind had silenced to all other possibilities, imprinting on him a calm focus rather than fear.

It was the feeling that he was under the power of another wave that brought the memory back.

Whoever the Corps of Exploration were, what they did a thousand years ago was responsible for him being in this place at this time with these people. Was he crazy to make such a personal connection? Was it egotism? Or had the wave cleared away the distractions?

He surfaced.

"Enough. We've questions unanswered and unknowns we haven't yet turned into questions. And until we're rested, we're not going to do it right. Twelve hours of refit. Until then—do something to get fresh. You too, Sarah."

She'd been about to fight him, but closed her mouth to let Sheila lead her away with the soothing assurance that a sonic shower and soft bed were the welcome that awaited the new guest.

Alone in their quarters, his prescription for self-renewal began with Tara. Without speaking what could have been, without regret, without fear for their future, they wordlessly blended into each other, and more than ever, he was connected again to where he belonged. He listened to her fall into a soft snore and slipped out. After checking his equipment and training his body, then and only then, would sleep come. That part of him would never change. The hold was empty, save for Phillip and Bertie. What they were doing froze him in place.

"Are you sure?" Phillip said. The two had no need to speak, much less in the hushed tones they used. The lights of the hold were dimmed, making them seem even more like children snuck from under bed covers to tiptoe to the toy chest.

"I can't go on without knowing," Bertie said, lowering onto the deck to rest on his belly.

"As you wish," Phillip whispered as though reluctantly going along with a plan of Bertie's making. At equidistant points around his friend, he placed the four obelisks with care. The lattice of rays joined over Bertie, the holo engaged, and bands of colored lights shuffled themselves into orderly rainbows the way they had over each of the humans read by the Kaiya device.

Kel's gasp revealed him.

"It's okay, Mister Turner," Phillip said without turning. "We know you're there. Please, don't stay back."

Kel took gingerly steps into the hold, mesmerized by the lights and the proclamation they sang in loud colors.

Bertie's head craned back on the serpentine neck and circled to take in the breadth of the patterns above before pivoting to find Kel. "Mister Turner, you're our friend. Our comrade. Our mate. We know you'll tell us true. What do *you* think this means?"

"Mister Turner," Phillip pleaded with the same cautious need. "We've always known we're toys. Amusements to reflect the faintest image of those we serve—imitations, tools and nothing more. But could it be that we're not simply *things*? That we're actually... *alive*?"

Kel's answer was unfaltering.

"This doesn't tell me anything I didn't already known. Of course you're alive, brothers."

***

"Colonel Hartenstein and I composed a message for Primus Pilus," Braley said. "And the report for Legion command. It's time I faced the music. Captain Sullivan says we're within a day of a system with a hypercomm array. That's where I'll wait for the reply while you go on to Cygnus."

"I've composed a message to Rex," Hartenstein said. "Maybe he'll come out of the shadows and help."

Meadows's sarcasm dripped heavy. "Be sure to tell him hi from me."

Sims slapped his forehead. "Give it a rest, Curt."

Doc put his wrist newly done with the regen sleeve through a range of motion. It obviously pained him, and Meadows's flippancy to Hartenstein brought the soreness out of him with his massaging of the stiff wrist. "Sergeant Major, you're wrong. Chap and I know Rex better than—" he rethought his claim. "As well as anyone. He is who he is. If it wasn't so, Wolfhound Six would've bent him." Doc used both hands to make a violent snapping motion, wincing and returning to rub the wrist.

Chappy nodded agreement. "Realso. We don't know how or why Tyrus Rex has lived so long, but it's just how it is. He does what he does, and he does it how he does it. For the Legion. For humanity."

Meadows shook his head disgustedly. "Primus Pilus is pulling your leg that this guy's *the* Rex and not just *a* Rex. Primus Pilus isn't the Legion, and it's *only* the Legion that matters. Colonel Yost and I disagree about Primus Pilus, but he's also the only one doing the right thing by bringing Legion Command in on this. It goes without saying, sir, I'll be departing with you."

Braley was heartfelt. "I'm proud to have you with me, Sergeant Major. Always have been. But I'm probably headed for a tribunal followed by a ceremonial stripping of my Legion Crest."

"Not if I have anything to say about it," Meadows said.

Sarah cleared her throat. "I haven't brought it up before, but, it's not necessary to find a hypercomm link."

She lifted an artifact onto the table.

"Instant communication. Nearly. To anywhere, from anywhere."

It was just a box.

Poul chortled. "We've known this existed, and that VanderLoot had it. Not much to look at, for such a game changer."

Sims wondered as they all did. "Sarah, what else did VanderLoot have that he kept to himself?" Before she could answer, a frowning Quint spoke.

"VanderLoot. It's such an unusual name. I've been trying to understand the history, and this name keeps appearing in the trove of data Dr. Wittawat's given me."

He scrolled furiously over a datapad, then touched it to bring up a single page. It was the crew list of a UPA vessel, the *Arcturus*. A highlighted name magnified large. Chief scientist Sibelius VanderLoot.

"Can't be a coincidence," Braley said.

Sims pondered aloud. "So, that's the beginning of the VanderLoot dynasty?"

Poul huffed a pronouncement. "If so, then we were its end."

Hartenstein was flint. "We took oaths to each other. For the good of the Legion, our piece of the VanderLoot history dies with us." He said the last looking at Meadows, who approved the restatement of their vow by returning a solemn nod.

Quint continued. "There are logs and personal journals going back to the beginning. Everything that will prove Dr. Avila's premise that the power brokers of the Republic became so by use of knowledge hoarded by the Corps and how the settlement of the galaxy was manipulated."

Sarah said, "Dr. Delaria is just the person for the task. I've given him full access to all the materials we brought from the Section."

Kel had heard enough. "Captain Sullivan, at your convenience, we need to drop out of jump. Location is irrelevant for our needs."

Chelly answered from the bridge. "We can drop into a window of stable space anytime, but it's interstellar territory, nowhere near a system."

"We have to test something, Chelly. When it's safe, please do."

"You'll know we're sidereal when the jump drive cuts out. Bridge out."

Everyone remained lost in their own thoughts until the hum of the jump drive stopped.

Braley went over to the table and the box. He produced a datapad and held it to Sarah. "Is this all there is to it?"

She nodded.

After routing through a colonel, a two-star general, and finally down to a major who was apparently the real power at Legion Command, the last wait began. The image of the wreathed sword of the Legion hung in the air, a reminder that they were no different from any other leej who wore the armor, and that the next face would be the one of the man who commanded them all.

"Whatever happens," Braley said. "I'm without regret. I'm humbled to stand with the truest men the Legion ever produced."

Of all the legionnaires Kel had been shaped by, whom he'd tried to model himself after, he was never surer that Braley Yost was the legionnaire he'd always aspired to be most like. Before Kel had the chance to tell him just that, a glowering Legion Commander Barrow appeared; behind him, in iron relief, the Legion crest hung on the wall. They all snapped to stiff attention.

Steel-gray eyes roved across each of them before returning to the man at their forefront. "Lieutenant Colonel Yost," said the Legion commander. "Why do I sense this gathering represents the workings of the Society of the Primus Pilus?"

An icy rush purged the blood in Kel's veins. The Legion commander was not a member of the secret Society yet spoke as though he knew all about the ancient order.

Then the commander of the Legion they swore their lives to laughed derisively, so sour it would have belittled an unfeeling stone mountain.

"The self-proclaimed tip of the spear of our Legion. What nonsense."

Curt glowed righteously hearing that he'd been right, and that they were all so wrong.

Proclaiming pure intent to General Barrow suddenly seemed an impossible proposition as he dressed them down like a disappointed father.

"I am not pleased." His gloom fell away with a smirk. "Nonetheless, it's time to tell me what you've accomplished under General Rex's guidance."

A presence strode into view beside the Legion commander, bringing a gravitas even greater than the crest on the wall behind them. The armor. The face that bore the story of a galaxy shaped by the Legion he founded.

Rex never smiled. Seeing the stunned faces of the legionnaires tasked with saving the institution he created, Rex shed no human grace to lighten the shadow of guilt cast by General Barrow. Instead, he made a demand of iron as hard as the sword forged in the crest, as sharp as its tip, as deep as its plunge into their hearts.

"Report, and tell me you did not fail."

Meadows turned the color of pale death. It was General Barrow who broke into a sly grin.

"Did you really think the Legion slept?"

22

Daakar Ceti Three—DCT—was the home of the Wolfhounds. The Cygnus arm was sparsely populated compared to the other arms of the galaxy. Sparser still were the worlds of its far-flung stars where humanity had struggled for their spot beneath alien suns, on planets long populated by bellicose races inhospitable toward interlopers from the core.

For seven hundred years, the Wolfhound Regiment had patrolled from its base on Daakar Ceti Three and across the Cygnus sector. A posting to the enigmatic and isolated regiment brought the wail of cursing as frequently as the praise of blessing from any legionnaire upon receipt of orders. But it was a testament in absentia that after becoming a Wolfhound, few leejes ever returned to the ranks of the other regiments, bringing with them stories of remote Cygnus.

The 131st, 187th, 101st, and all the rest—all were too close to the flagpole of Legion Command. Too close to the rivalries of the other services and endless interferences from the politicians and their bureaucratic machine.

The Wolfhounds and the Wolfhounds alone owned remote Cygnus. There, the Legion was the Legion of old. And what a leej found there could not be equaled elsewhere in deed or purpose. Not in measure against all the tales of Savage War glory or the battle streamers of all the other Legions combined.

To be a Wolfhound was to *be* Legion.

The briefing room was crowded where General Airani sat at the head of the table, surrounded by his battalion commanders and staff. "A task force from 131st and 187th are on the way to Cygnus. But by that time, the Wolfhounds will have turned Beh-Zenkuhl into the desert hell the zhee go on about."

From seats a tier back from the central table, Poul whispered to Kel. "We could've guessed the zhee had their muzzles deep in this. I've dreamed about this, haven't you? Paying the donks back, right in the stinking birthplace of their whole damned sick tribe?"

Kel had the same feelings about the zhee as did any leej, or for that matter, any person with eyes and a brain. He'd once read their religious tome in half hopes he'd find insight, something that would mitigate his hatred of them. Instead, what he found redeemed his view.

Against all will your hearts be turned, your kankari ever sharp and raised, your tongues ever speaking the truth of the prophet, until all unbelievers are purged from the infinite stars.

The prime commandment of their law reigned supreme and its letter matched the constancy of the donks' disposition throughout the galaxy. Among the zhee existed no dissenters from that edict. No moderates. No donks who'd evolved to accept theirs was not the single race among a galaxy of thousands of races with a right to exist.

The zhee told the galaxy who they were with every action. And yet, the galaxy accepted their predations and inveiglements and barbarous expansion. And at the head of the march to proclaim the beauty and sanctity of the zhee culture, the House of Reason hoisted the tallest banner.

"Who wouldn't?" Kel whispered back.

Poul acted as though he hadn't been clear. "No, Kel, I mean, *especially* Beh-Zenkuhl, you know?"

Poul's face soured as Kel failed to understand.

"Kel, have you forgotten?"

Kel recoiled. Poul accused him of a sin and he had no idea what it was. A different possibility dawned on Poul's face. "Kel, did you not ever know? Beh-Zenkuhl is where *Tem* was killed!"

Kel remembered the day he and his pathfinder squad laid eyes on the first dark operator they'd ever seen. It was more than the deadly kit and tantalizingly sleek weapons he carried. The leej in mimetic armor had hopped off the black Talon like it was his personal dragon, a wizard whose magic was warfare. His tone to the leejes was kindly, but held pity. The operator didn't see them as the same combat-proven leejes they saw themselves but as novices ignorant to their need of lessons only he could teach them.

Tem appeared to them like a figure from Legion myth. But he and his kill team were no fairy story of leejes graced with superpowers granted by some war deity, and soon proved their abilities real and their easy arrogance well earned. Then, like an answer to a secret wish, Tem became the guide to a life only dreamed of, from a dreamland only whispered about, and recognized in Kel something special. He was the gatekeeper who got him the shot at becoming an operator, and admittance to the realm where legends grew like mountains rising on the horizon.

Finally, Tem became the big brother Kel never had. His death in a nameless place at the cloven hands of the zhee brought the first crack in Kel's granite, the block he chiseled blow by blow to model himself into the perfect legionnaire. Where other artists might have abandoned the material to start anew, he labored on. Against the ravages of years and storms, earthquakes and fires, disappointments and failings—instead of toppling him— the depredations of a galaxy that rendered every mighty work to rubble had only added a weathered patina to his work.

Beh-Zenkuhl, then, was where Kel would unveil the finished masterpiece of the legionnaire he'd sculpted.

He waited patiently as the Wolfhound commander turned the briefing over to his staff to build further on the genesis of planning for the assault on Beh-Zenkuhl. Sarah, Quint, and the bots had been whisked away to the intelligence cell, and Kel tried to picture the astonishment of the analysts and techies at the power of the demonstration no doubt underway.

"The Palace of the Grand Vizier of the Faithful," announced a colonel as the picture of the same appeared overhead. The central image of the palace quickly split into multiple clouds of holos at different scales of the surrounding metropolis. Melded together to form a dense maze were hundreds of boroughs, temples, bazaars, and the familiar compounds of packed earth walls where the nuclei of families, clans, and tribes lived in a strange disjointed unity, ever against each other but all against the rest of the galaxy.

"Every indication is that beneath the palace and the central city is the location of the main facility."

Multiple holos with hazy distorted edges displayed. Kel recognized them as points of view obtained from the minds of the prisoners held by the Wolfhounds. Doc, Chappy, and even Hartenstein's outlandish descriptions of the telepathic Trixie, and how she used her skill to please her Wolfhound companion, Briscoe, made him curious for his own demonstration.

Through their eyes was ample evidence that beneath the palace was a vast complex resembling the same cold and malevolent place he'd seen beneath Psydon. But here were acres of the technology vaguely familiar for medical devices, vats of proteinaceous goo, slabs of vivisected corpses of humans and other races, Hool scientists in rooms sealed by lavender containment fields, and a point of view holo of one of the helmeted aliens they'd killed on Imprimis, its beady eyes and loose skin tinted by the green fog that filled its suit.

"As of yet, the origin of the alien Moluk Daan has not been determined," the briefer said. "Also unknown, the number of human and other sentient races held as test subjects and still alive within the facility."

A raspy colonel gave his blunt solution. "Regrettable. But innocents are not a consideration when it comes to the containment of a genetic weapon. That's enumerated in the Plenax accords. If Beh-Zenkuhl is the source of the threat, then it's time for a crustbuster."

"Unfortunately, no, Colonel Davidson," Wolfhound Six said with yearning. "General Barrow's directive from the

House of Reason was clear. A planet cracker's not on the table of options. It would never be deniable as a natural catastrophe. And before anyone suggests, neither would a trigger-nuke. The Republic might be able to false flag it, make it look like the zhee were building one and it got away from them, but the models are long established that not even a nuke can guarantee there won't be a spread of the nano weapon. Otherwise, Plenax would have been nuked to glass instead of quarantined."

"Why do we need to deny anything?" another leej wearing eagles said. "The galactic ban against genetic weapons essentially guarantees a mass destruction response. And I quote, 'existential threat to life in such grand scales mandates responses prohibited in other uses due to the abhorrent nature of their destructive capabilities.' We have substantial proof already that what the zhee have in that complex qualifies. The Republic would simply be upholding the provisions of the accords."

General Airani said, "The essential problem is not only ensuring the production capability on Beh-Zenkuhl is destroyed, but obtaining everything regarding the weapon's development. If the capability to make the weapon has escaped Beh-Zenkuhl, we have to know."

Another colonel groaned. "All valuable objectives, but we know it's the zhee that keeps the House of Reason from authorizing us to use the big boys. The politicians are always selective in the application of any law that could impact them or their chosen, like Utopion's protected class of pets."

The zhee were numerous, and dispersed throughout the galaxy. Very few House of Reason delegates willfully antagonized the species. The cost in votes would be too high.

Wolfhound Six made a secretive smile. "You may have to rethink that, William, once you hear the full mandate guiding the coming action."

The intel cell briefer took his cue to resume. "The vector for the weapon *is* a nano. And a theta bomb is the proven remedy to neutralize such a weapon. Any living thing within its detonation radius will succumb, including every zhee within a dozen klicks. Zeta operators in Mark 12 armor have the necessary protection level against a nano and are the logical ones to deliver a weapon—or weapons —to ensure coverage. The site can then be studied at length and exploited for intelligence to determine if the production capability has proliferated elsewhere."

General Airani continued. "Zeta performs a clandestine infiltration to place the weapon, maximizing the probability of a total neutralization without the escape of materials that an overt operation would trigger. After the successful detonation, the simultaneous planetary blockade and ground invasion launches. We hold the planet, clean up the mess in Beh-Zenkuhl, and perhaps, that's the end of it."

An order of battle appeared for the opposing forces.

"The zhee have multiple divisions on the planet. Poorly organized, armed, and equipped, not singularly or in total are they a match against a combined arms attack by the Wolfhounds. By the time the task force arrives, the danger of a genetic weapon's use against friendly forces will have been removed, the occupation will proceed, and the Explanetary people from Utopion will be there to take over and... do whatever it is they have planned per direction of the delegates on the strategic council."

The collective buzz of bees from a dozen hives filled the room as the subordinate commanders and their staffs conferred closely.

"There's a significant issue that hasn't been considered."

Kel said it loudly, achieving his goal of silence. He stood, and all eyes were on him.

He swiped his wrist link and a new image overwhelmed the rest over the table. Hardball stood in the cockpit of the grounded mech. Gathered around the walker was Kill Team 12 and the squad of Scarlet paratroopers he'd led to bust apart the Nemanjic Guard's base for their long war of attrition.

"The weapon launched on Dark Ops—we know who the template was."

He enlarged the face for all to see. It was the only image he had of JP.

"We left a legionnaire behind on Psydon. If there's any chance he's beneath Beh-Zenkuhl, the Legion has an obligation. We cannot abandon him twice."

***

The spacefield was a lethal display, a massive moving layout of Wolfhound hardware and even more lethal men. Magnus V grav tanks floated onto transports to be restrained to decks by both chain and tractor beams. Kel knew firsthand why there was the redundancy. If an armored behemoth were to break free of the deck during the screaming plummet to the surface, the kinetic energy of a Pachyderm crashing with its tank payload would impact with the effect of a nuke.

Sometimes, Kel had terrifyingly vivid nightmares that he'd miscalculated, and the asteroid he sent to annihilate the Q army missed, and the very city he was trying to save disappeared beneath a brilliant and awful mushroom cloud.

Crewmen stood on the spines of Talons and Excaliburs, inspecting fuselages and tuning engines. A single Flying Fresher was similarly covered by crew chiefs and mechanics. The Goshawk was so named because it spewed parachuting leejes like a field toilet upended of its contents. Squatting mechs with cockpits open were tended by their operators. Fast-attack armored vehicles and long nosed artillery pieces were loading onto transports, and containers of munitions and supplies were parked in neat rows like speeders on a dealership lot.

Offloading of the *Supreme* was nearly complete. Sarah fussed and ordered leejes many times her size as though she were a tiny drill sergeant. The contents would be populating a new museum in the vaults of the Wolfhounds. In light of what he'd witnessed—and promised to remain "mum" about—Kel was affected by the fond hesitancy with which Phillip and Bertie said their goodbyes to the crew that had been so accepting of them. They joined him outside to appraise the monumental scene of the Wolfhounds preparing for war.

"If we haven't had opportunity to say so, sir," Phillip said. "It was bloody spot-on of Colonel Hartenstein to point out there's naught a leej alive who's led more combat orbital freefalls than you, sir."

The most experienced leej alive, echoed in Kel's head. Phillip caught his own gaff. "Er, what I meant to say, sir..."

Bertie thrust his head straight, imitating a position of attention. "What we mean is, it's an honor to be taking the tall dive with you again, boss."

At Wolfhound Six's insistence, Hartenstein gave a full accounting of his long solo operation pursuing the conspiracy. When he was done, the speechlessness rendered by the hardened Wolfhounds was declaration enough—if there were any doubt that Howler was the most peerless leej to ever operate in or out of Dark Ops armor, it was better concealed behind their astonished faces then a sniper beneath a dead net.

Hartenstein's recommendation to let Kel lead the mission was accepted without objection.

Tara trotted towards the trio down the ramp of the *Supreme* and Kel said, "No talk about that in front Tara, got me?" He'd told her he had a job to do, and even let her know he was leading the incursion. The details, he spared her, and she did not press for more.

The two bots faded back obediently without a word. He gave them credit. If the two were truly alive, maybe this was further proof. They were learning that mouths speaking ahead of thoughts always brought unintended consequences.

Tara took in the scene. "It's all too much. It's the greatest assembly of the grandest kind. Like one of the holodramas about the pioneers loading their arks to settle the first habitable world ever found."

"There's nothing like it," Kel agreed.

Tara made the same grin she had when they set off together to find Sarah, the thrill overpowering any possibility of looming disaster. "I won't ask how soon you'll be home. I'm the wife of a Dark Ops legionnaire. You'll do what you need to do. Because if not you, then who? Isn't that one of your rules?"

Kel didn't know which of her statements shocked him more, that she was settled with him leading the intrusion into zhee central, or that she knew about the rules. "Where did you hear about that?"

"Doc. He showed me." She produced a pad and there it was. The seventy-five bullet points Kel had once rapidly jotted down in a maddened flight of ideas, and the heading he'd offhandedly titled his rules. He'd never meant for them to be seen by anyone, much less his wife.

"Here it is. Number 44. 'Know how to recognize the situation when it's appropriate to ask the most vital question. If not us, then who? If not now, then when?'"

"Those two are thick as us, eh, Phillip?" Bertie said behind them. They were apart from Kel and Tara's conversation, but Kel thought it the subtle cue of an eavesdropping bot.

Coming down the ramp carrying a long container was Chappy at one end, his bookend at the other. Doc's backward descent halted and he snapped his head around to find the predator whose eyes burned him with deadly intent. Locating the source, Doc smiled at Kel sheepishly. Apparently, in addition to having the extra-sensory abilities of a hunter, Doc also had the intuition of a mindreader.

Doc had kept his distance from Kel on the trip to DCT. Chappy noticed the awkwardness, and had slyly told Kel, "It ain't that Doc's still mad about you nearly killing us. That only made you even more of a super-leej in his eyes. That list of yours is like his good book."

Kel promised himself there'd be a talk coming between him and his admirer before they took the dive over Beh-Zenkuhl.

Walking their way hand in hand down the ramp was Chelly and Sheila.

"Captain says lift in ten, Tara," Chelly said. "Second engineer's needed at her station." The big man thrust a hand out to Kel. "See you soon, cousin."

Just then, the young Curt bounced breathlessly out of the hold to join them.

"Cousin Kel, is the sergeant major here? He promised he'd say goodbye."

Sweat stained the youngster's coveralls. The youth had been doing his work manually instead of using lifters. To his lankiness he'd added the first indications of mass under Meadows's tutelage. Kel approved of Meadows's influence and the start of the addiction.

"I've known Meadows a very long time, Curt. Don't take it personally. It's just his way." Meadows had been an emotionless oak even before losing his entire team. How he dealt with goodbyes was to avoid them.

The young Curt was crushed. "I wanted to tell him I've made my decision. The *Dream* should be home when we get there. First thing, I'm going to ask my folks to sign the consent. I want to be on Excudo 4 to start Legion basic the very day I turn seventeen."

Sheila sucked a breath and Chelly's jaw dropped, both to the notice of young Curt. "Cousin Tara, if Uncle Chelly and Aunt Sheila won't help, will you talk to my folks with me?"

Tara smirked. "I will, if for no other reason than to let them know it isn't Kel they should blame as the bad influence. We don't need any more haters in the family. Speaking of... is Cormac avoiding saying goodbye to Kel, Chelly?"

Chelly shrugged. "He knows he's wrong. He'll just never admit it. Not to you, Kel. But, trust me, he knows he's been a part of something important, and it's you who's been right. Your friend Meadows isn't the only one with a way."

"Doesn't matter to me, Chel," Kel said. He meant it. Cormac Sullivan had responsibilities and burdens Kel understood. Command. A way of life. A marriage and a starving world he struggled to mend. "I don't need to hear it from him."

Quint and Sarah stepped from the shade of the hold, squinting in the bright sunlight as they found the gathering. "I have this for you, Kel," Quint said, swiping his datapad. "I've made a preliminary timeline of the history of the Corps and the Section. I'll be adding to it, but maybe you can look it over on your way back. By the time you get there, with the material I've gotten from Sarah and the device she gave me, I have what I need to program a viral vector to reset the genome on Callie's World. It's going to work!"

Sarah sighed. "It's a first to the right of many wrongs." She extended a hand to Tara. "I'm so glad to have met you." Sarah stiffened in surprise as Tara flung arms around her, then softened and wrapped arms in return.

"You'll come and see for yourself, Sarah."

Sarah didn't move a step but with a faraway look in her eyes, left them all for somewhere distant and sad. "It would be something," she said. It was like she was declining the invitation with a feeling of future regret. She departed hurriedly on a sled for the base.

Tara was the last of the crew outside the ship. "I have to go." She took Kel's face in her hands and kissed him deeply. "No goodbyes for us either. It'll be just another trip. But no letters or holos this time. We'll have a fire, and you can tell me all about your adventure."

"It will be the last time you'll ever have to hear what I've been up to without you."

"Make it a good story with a happy ending, Kel."

He watched her go. A last tearful wave, and the ramp raised to close. Bertie and Phillip rejoined Kel.

"They're as fine a group of peoples as we've ever had the pleasure to meet, Mister Turner."

"S'right you've taken the path you have, sir."

Kel watched the ship rise, and as it grew smaller, disciplined his thoughts of her to grow tiny as well. Until it was done.

"Let's go, boys. Work to do."

They set off for a waiting sled. Sensing the air, like good mates, the two broke into a banter aimed at lifting his spirits.

"Don't you worry, Mister Turner, sir," Bertie said. "I've been helping Miss Sarah brew up her big surprise. I've still got the rig I used on Psydon to crank out foul little buggies. Why, it'll make this little jaunt a caravan holiday compared to Proteus, t'will, sir."

Phillip sang, "And with you home again lickety-split for tea and biscuits with the missus."

"Doubt there'll be much of that for the boss, Phillip," Bertie countered. "I'd say his OPORD's no sleep and hands full for the foreseeable, say what? Humans are the best parents in the galaxy, they is."

Phillip made a shushing noise. "'Ere now, Bertie! You've a mouth like a sieve."

The hair raised on Kel's neck. "What the kark do you mean?"

Bertie's head snapped down to his shoulders.

"You've done it now, my son," Phillip said, shaking his rectangular head with pity over his friend's latest gaff.

"Out with it," Kel ordered.

Bertie was meek. "Apologies, sir. It's like this then, sir. Your lovely missus, well, her hormones are making a lively splish-splash with pheromones bloody broadcasting like the Spiral News Network."

Kel gulped. The *Supreme*'s bulk was now a tiny dot.

"Forgive him, Mister Turner, sir," Phillip offered the apology. "But at least allow us to be the first to make congrats."

Kel's brief flat spin stabilized. What had Rex said? The time for secrets was over?

"Anything else, you blockheads?"

An embarrassed Bertie's head extended. "From what I've learned brushing up on human physiology with Miss Sarah, sir, I'd say there's a *pair* o' little nippers on the way to rule the roost of your domicile."

23

"You can have Doc and Chappy," Captain Malik told Kel. "I wouldn't say this in front of them—their heads are already too big—but after me, they're the best planet divers in Zeta."

Sims was with him for the tour and introduction. It was an honor to be invited to the same kind of nondescript compound they'd once called home. It was smaller, of course. Zeta was a platoon-sized section, loosely divided into five teams. As they walked through the gates, Malik described what sounded like a very fluid organization.

"We operate mainly in support and with the support of Wolfhound elements. We're no clone of Dark Ops. General Airani took what he thought was the best of the model and adapted it to fit the Wolfhounds." The Zeta commander was older than Kel thought he'd be, and still a captain.

"Makes sense," Kel said. "There's no one best way."

"Ha!" Malik barked. "How'd I know you'd say something just like that?"

Zeta operators didn't look up from their preparations to notice the visitors. Malik led them into a common area of floats and couches, gaming cubes and a kitchen, the walls covered in souvenirs and photos taken from across a sector relatively unknown to both the Dark Operators.

Some items would have been at home on Victrix. Zhee kankaris. An Ootari shield made of the same chitinous material as their carapaces. A Gomarii pain flayer. Others were as distinct in form and function yet mysterious in origin. Holo stills shifted in depth and angle as they passed. Victories and glad moments of comradely gathering, scenes of destruction at the hands of the Wolfhounds, and the occasional voluptuous form of a Tennar, painted Sinasian, or attractive example of humans otherwise familiar except for the color of their skin.

Malik stopped in front of an orderly spot amongst the randomness of the collages, and Kel felt his face burn hot with embarrassment. Three laser engraved plaques; twenty-five bullet points listed on each. The bold block lettering above them made the origin of the dictums undeniable.

Kel's Rules.

"You're the most famous covert operator in the galaxy," Sims teased.

Captain Malik stared at the words. "Now we know who Kel is. Wolfhound Six said it found its way to him by an old teammate. Who's Bigg?"

That brought a huge grin to Kel. It figured.

Sims said, "He was our team daddy. Colonel Hartenstein, our sergeant major Nail, and Bigg were Dark Ops plankholders, there from the beginning."

"Only Hartenstein's still here," Kel said. "Nail passed away soon after he was retired. Poul and I were with

Lanthanum and only found out a few months after the ceremony. Bigg—he was on Victrix when the attack happened."

And of course, the unspoken last plankholder and Dark Ops founder, Rex.

"Sorry to hear," Malik said. "But comeuppance time's here, isn't it?"

Kel had noticed Doc watching from the threshold of the gear room, nudged into action by Chappy to join them as the commander motioned them over.

"Gents, you two are assigned to Captain Turner and his team. He'll brief you."

Malik shook Sims's and Kel's hands. "I'll be with Zeta. We have our own tasks. We'll be hitting the power grids and guiding precision strikes by the Excaliburs to knock out their ADA once you've had your fun. You're keyed into all access here, and these two will make sure your team has whatever you need."

Kel was about to thank him when Malik said, "I know you want to ask me why a guy as old as me's still a captain. S'okay. I'll tell you so you don't have to wonder."

"I already know," Kel said. He breathed in the space and the scene of the operators at work—diligent and serious, joking and joyful, confident and content that among Wolfhounds, they were the tip of the spear. "There's nowhere else to be."

Malik reached for Kel's hand for a second time, pumping their joined grips firmly. "Guess I sorta knew you would," he said and left them.

"How do you feel about taking a dive with us into zhee central?" Kel asked the two Wolfhounds. "It'll be us four and Bertie. We have a special payload to deliver and a missing friend who deserves to be rescued."

Chappy cocked an eyebrow. "Suits me."

Doc grinned. "Wouldn't miss it, sir. Number 44's always been my favorite."

If not us, then who? If not now, then when?

Kel would've laughed, but was fearful Doc might have thought it was meant for him rather than his own self-deprecation. It was time to step down off the pedestal Doc had placed him on.

"I've always thought what I wrote was an egotistical, self-aggrandizing, and embarrassing product of my hubris. I'm humbled to know it inspired someone in some small way. Thanks, Doc."

Doc shook away Kel's admission with seriousness and formality. "Sir, I once read something that's always stuck with me." He seemed to be quoting from memory. "Basic truths cannot change and once a man of insight expresses one of them, it is never necessary, no matter how much the world changes, to reformulate them."

Sims grinned. "He remind you of someone, Kel? Do you write poetry, too, Doc?"

That puzzled the Wolfhound. Chappy was quick to sputter, "Oba help us!"

Kel was ready to move from the moment. "Doc, for me, I've learned there's only one rule. When we're done, I promise to tell you."

***

The Talon was a familiar friend. Kel was finishing his third and final inspection of chutes laid out in the pax bay when Meadows came up to him.

"Colonel Yost wanted to be here. General Airani made him liaison to the Legion task force. Wearing silver oak leaves isn't all it's cracked up to be. Braley's one perfect legionnaire. Wish I could be more like him. But I never can pull it off."

"He's the leej I always try to be," Kel said. "And so are you."

Meadows sputtered a grizzled deflection. "Knock it off, Kel. I should be diving with you, you know? But I guess five men's the best size for a kill team. If you include blockhead as an operator, that is."

"Thank you for the vote of confidence, Sergeant Major," Bertie said from forward in the bay. There was no escape from his quantum-tuned senses.

"Time to rig," Poul said. If Kel were the most accomplished planet diver around, Poul was next in line for the title. Still limping, even in armor, he didn't gripe like Meadows that he should also be diving, but insisted he be there to help rig and manage the jump. "Let's get you fitted, Bert. Chap, give me hand." The chute for the ACM was a container as large as the bot's back. Chappy helped Poul lift it into place and with Bertie's manipulators assisting, began the process of strapping him in.

"Thanks, mates. Phil and I usually buddy."

"He got the easy job," Chappy said.

"Don't bet on it," Bertie said. "Professor Wittawat fussed that he had to stay to help her! I never imagined she could be as stubborn as a football hooligan at closing time for the pub. What say you, Sergeant Radd?"

Poul laughed lightly. "She's not the same mousey scientist we once knew. Also, what's football?"

Doc was helping Sims kit up when Meadows bent to spread apart the straps to the square container holding

Kel's tightly packed canopy. "Get your lid on, jumpmaster. Your turn to rig."

Kel reached into a pocket. "I thought you should have this. I found it in Gabe's desk." He pulled out a dog-eared, dreex leather notebook and offered it to a perplexed Meadows.

Curt returned the chute to the deck and accepted the notebook. Recognition dawned on his face. It was the constant companion Hardball had carried on Psydon. He ran a finger around the frayed edges, then winced. "I kick myself damn near every day for goading Hardball into a fight that morning in the Rafeer long house."

"You apologized, Curt. Gabe never was one to hold a grudge."

Meadows sighed, his eyes locked on the book. "It was never the same between us. I could tell. It wasn't long after you left that I followed Braley. Gabe took the team, so it all kinda worked itself out. Except, before I went, I shoulda let him know he was a real brother to me."

"Can I see it for a moment?" Kel said. He flipped through the pages, returning the open notebook to him.

At the top of the page, in Gabe's most flourished calligraphy, the one word title.

Meadows.

The sparse lines below were in blocky print.

There's a race of men that don't fit in
A race that can't stay still
So they break the hearts of kith and kin
And roam the galaxy at will
He is the Legion
And the Legion is him

"There's a date," Kel said. "He wrote that just a few months ago."

Meadows closed the notebook carefully and placed it in his pocket.

"If JP's there, find him, Kel."

***

"Five minutes," Kel warned. The tailgate of the stealthed Talon was down, and Kel knelt at the corner between the lowered ramp and the gaping mouth of the pax bay. This many inputs to the visual cortex would bring a seizure to an ordinary human, but not to Kel. Simultaneously aware of the spinning numbers and plots running in his HUD, the dark city rotated into view, the surrounding pale plains making it an island in the middle of a vast sea.

He stood, turned, and gave the commands in ordered precision. He stepped to the edge of the ramp and opened the window in his HUD that would let him see the tight formation falling in a wedge behind him. The planet revolved in darkness, patchy clouds filtering tiny lights from small settlements scattered across the bleak desert. For a moment, he was again a vengeful god, hovering above a planet unsuspecting that their destruction loomed from the heavens.

"Go."

He embraced the void he knew so well.

Time slowed for him in freefall. Ten minutes to fall from space through a hundred kilometers of nothing until the chutes returned the familiar feel of gravity. But it was the most vivid, intensely alive ten minutes ever lived by any man, reality stretched into a body of experience that spanned a lifetime.

Grown ancient and then reborn, the chute opened. Behind him, four chutes billowed wide, the suspended bodies below riding the waves of air in silent majesty. The virtual beacon flashed over the drop zone and soon enough the rush of nearby buildings and the impending surface was there. He flared and his feet met the ground softly.

K-17s were in hands as containers and canopies disintegrated on command. The snorts and brays of desert beasts greeted them from dark stables. Above the flat roofs, the peaks of the palace lay beyond. It was below them they would wreak havoc without a donk nostril having twitched in alert.

Swarms of invisible drones spread from the cloud over Bertie's back to scatter into the night. After another moment of silent awareness to blend with their environment, a window appeared, showing the route. The hot glows of zhee warriors remained stationary, rare, and still far ahead on the path. Kel sent the coded burst to the Talon.

Successful infil.

One at a time, they donned the cloaks and disguises, then draped Bertie in his. He bore a good resemblance to one of the beasts of burden the zhee preferred for travel across the desert sands. Sims led, and they began a casual, hunched walk of donks weary from a desert pilgrimage to arrive in Beh-Zenkuhl for the first call to prayer.

A lone watchman stood on a dimly lit corner and hailed, meeting the approaching party with irritable chastisement.

"Desert peasants, why is your kuhmel not stabled? The manner of your tribe's camp is not for Beh-Zenkuhl. Are the elders of your clan so lax in instruction?"

Sims kept his reply short. "Forgiveness. Didn't see one."

The watchmen snorted and began a diatribe as they steadily closed the distance. "You ambled past stables without notice? Has desert life become easier than city living? Weary and dull at such a pleasant hour with which to cross the cool sands? I will lead you there myself, lest you wander the streets and filthen them."

"I'll take him," Kel warned.

The watchman barely reacted as Kel stepped around Sims and struck. He had many options, but pulled a method from his subconscious that had always proven devastatingly effective when tailored to the unique anatomy of the zhee.

He took power from the ground and drove from the ball of his rear foot and hip, his open hand blow meeting the long muzzle. He projected his punch through and beyond, sending the huge skull twisting on an angular vector, a track it was not meant to travel. Before the body was even falling, the sickly snap of bones and tissues forced past elastic limits heralded perfection.

No sooner than the massive donk dropped like a bag of wet cement, Sims and Doc had the body off the corner and into the rear alley. Chappy and Bertie were last as Kel led them to a dark door. His thermal scan read no one in the storage for one of the nearby storefronts. With a click of his teeth, the intrusion program searched, answered, and the lock buzzed once before deactivating. Doc and Sims hid the body between a stack of crates and rearranged others. The body would stay undetected until a theta wave made the issue inconsequential.

"All clear ahead," Sims said, peering through the crack of the door into the alley.

A string of expletives to rival a young Poul Radd filled buckets, concluding with a breath and a final, "Holy sket!" It was Chappy. "Why didn't you use your stunner?"

"Donks don't always drop on a stun," Kel said offhandedly. "That maneuver always works."

"How'd you do that?" Doc asked with awe.

Sims kept an eye on the alley. "Kel figured out something about the zhee anatomy and how to exploit it. He wrote an intelligence summary on it once."

"Guess *that* never made its way to Cygnus," Kel quipped. "Time to move."

The intelligence vacuumed from the minds of the captured conspirators was put together into an exacting map, with a nearly complete schematic of the underground, access codes, and biometrics. As Bertie had promised, compared to Proteus—where every pace taken by Team 3 had been a step into the unknown—this was a guided tour.

They went at a cautious and unhurried pace, pausing to loiter in the dark and allowing a roving donk to clear the route ahead, until the outer wall of the Palace of the Grand Vizier of the Faithful was in view. Admittance of aliens to Beh-Zenkuhl was one thing. Entrance to the palace grounds—something entirely different. No matter the lab they worked was directly beneath the Grand Vizier, the law was the law. The price for trespass by a nonbeliever—walking the bridge of a thousand cuts.

A turn down a parallel side street and halfway down, was a deep tunnel foyer intended to shield the high sun, and at its end sat the entrance used by the alien visitors. Drones pierced the inevitably present micro gaps in the door, and Sims narrated his work. "Two guards, dozing at monitors. Freezing their viewers and security stream now."

Sims matched Kel's step-off and pace to pull the train into the tunnel.

"Captain, I want to try your trick," Chappy said in his ear.

Rather than chastise him for the timing, Kel simply said, "Hit him on the chin like you're sending a tilted spiral galaxy off on a flat spin into the universe." Kel faded to a side and let Chappy step ahead on line with Sims, and the train floated on.

Everyone could see the interior layout in their HUDs. "Go straight at him, Chap—I got the corner," Kel said. Without stopping, the door parted and in they flowed. Kel cleared the corner and glided down the long wall in time to see Chappy greet the donk rising from a zhee prayer rug.

Chappy's gauntleted fist landed. Square on the broad plate of bone between the black glassy eyes. An epic tussle commenced. A pair of kankari poked, slashed, and stabbed in a cloud of attacks that glanced off the Wolfhound's armor until Chappy cursed and drew his pistol. Kel was already there, pushing his muzzle above Chappy's head to contact the stretched face and press the trigger. A headless body dropped.

The other zhee lay dead, a pair of K-17 blasts from Sims and Doc having dropped the other zhee from a step into the room.

"We'll work on it," Kel said as he moved deeper into the room, holding on the doors of a lift shaft.

"I've got control of the entire data stream, boss," Bertie said. "Sliced and silent."

"Smooth move, Chap," Doc said. "Like a laxative."

Sims sealed the door behind them.

"Hey, look at this," Chappy said, ignoring his failure. "They've got the fart breather's disappearer-guns."

Kel had noticed the weapons propped on the guards' consoles as he passed, and already filed it as confirmation of the strange alien's influence.

"It's all coming together," Sims said. "Whoever Moluk Daan and his kind are, they're helmet deep in this. Bertie, need help?"

Bertie's back was open, revealing the machinery within. "It would be a help if the access doors were apart a bit. An inquisitor drone or three will let us finish a complete map and best see the product at work."

Doc had a tool in hand and was at the lift doors. "Say the word, Bert."

"If you're ready, Mister Turner?" Bertie requested permission.

"Do it."

Doc's plasma torch lit purple, and he drove slowly into the face of the door, circumscribing a hole the size of a fist, and withdrew the tool. Kel watched the glowing hole as a trio of thumb-sized discs floated past the glowing edges of the expedient port.

"I'm ready to release the specials, sir," Bertie said, asking permission to launch.

"Proceed."

Like Kel, everyone's eyes followed the nanos issuing from the black box in Bertie's compartment. Visible only because of the density of their numbers, a thin gray smoke moved in a cohesive stream into the lift. Kel's subconscious started a count and at a minute, the last of the trail disappeared and Bertie's back closed unceremoniously.

"How long?" Chappy asked.

"Can't say," Bertie said. "Haven't tested like before. Most nanos spread at rate of the inverse square of four times the volume by—"

Kel cut him off.

"Until it's done. For now, all we can do is wait."

Sims breathed heavy, as though exerting great effort.

"Is he down there, Kel?"

Kel's heart hammered against his sternum.

"We're not leaving until we find out."

24

Whether death came at arm's length or across the vast gulf of a sniper's distance, there was a connection between the act and its completion that carried with it a valorous sense of accomplishment.

This was not that.

The first victim was a moktaar. It halted midstride, dropped a datapad, and made the panicked gasp of any living thing instinctively aware it experienced the sudden antithesis of well-being. Its dark face mottled pale, crinkled, and shrank as though dehydrated of all fluid in an instant, baked dry by the heat of a blazing internal oven. It collapsed as though its skeleton turned to brittle ash within.

They watched as one by one, a Ootari, a Hool, a Kimbrin, and others fell in the same manner. The silence that ruled as they watched told Kel his teammates had the same sick pit in their stomachs. It was the realization that the same weapons they used against their enemies had been conjured for them. *Had* brought the ignominious end to so many unsuspecting leejes, safe, content, and proud, about their business in the perfect realm of Dark Ops home.

Known or unknown, each one was their brother.

"Is it done?" Kel asked.

A window opened. "I can locate only one who's escaped punishment, Mister Turner."

The speedlift was called, and they rode in silence.

Alert but at ease as the drones had confirmed not a living thing moved, save the one, they followed the course Bertie set for them through long corridors of doors, past the hubs of central stations branching yet more door-lined corridors.

"I'm scanning them all for life signs, Mister Turner. I'm detecting none. Sir, I think we should pause here."

Bertie marched to an access and it slid aside. A platform and industrial walkway skirted the space. Tank after tank on the floor below held murky contents, swirling and thick.

"Sir, these are all filled with nanos in varying stages of preparation."

"There must be billions of them," Sims said.

"More than there are people," Bertie confirmed. "This is an acceptable epicenter to the complex to place the bomb, sir." From his back, the case levitated and Sims joined Kel to heft it onto the grated walkway.

"Lead us to the Hool," Kel said.

The sterility around them was a stark contrast to the sand and coarse earthen walls of the city hundreds of meters above. Both would be washed clean. The containment field around the clear walls of the lab glowed faintly and, in its center, stood a Hool, arms folded as if waiting patiently to greet them.

"Every spiny we've run into did the funky chicken when it saw who'd come a-calling," Chappy said. "Why not this fish face?"

As if the Hool heard, he taunted them from his fortress, only the faintest trace of hiss and lisp in its Standard.

"You cannot breach the containment or you will unleash doom on all your kind."

Sims provoked in return. "Two can play that game."

The spines on the Hool's skull drooped back. "The weapon you crafted was effective, I'll grant, but like everything humans do, it is a pitiful copy of the works of those who came before you. Did you not realize this after what we proved so successfully on Victrix?"

Their postures told the Hool he'd hit a nerve.

"Surprised I know the silly name where your egg clump nests?" the Hool teased. "Your petty deceptions, like calling the planet of your base—Arinox—another name. And the existence you all spent in hiding, even amongst your own Legion. All the deceptions of dim human minds. Everywhere you meddled, you left a trail. One pursued by the collective efforts of those you've waged war on, like my own people. Even within your own kind are those who hate you as much as do we."

Bertie was in their ears. "Sir, the Hool's trying to buy time. He thinks the cavalry's on the way. I've sent him false acknowledgments of all his transmissions."

"Bertie at his best!" Sims lauded.

"I do admit, gents," Bertie said, "when Phil and I are together, maybe we do spend a bit too much time chattering. We've been known to be right of the bang once in a while, ashamed to admit."

"Shh," Kel chided. "Fine work, Bertie."

"One other thing, sir. I've located a tunneling transmitter. The same used on Imprimis to signal the aliens what popped out of that wormhole. He triggered that as well, at least, he thinks he did."

Doc alone stepped to within a millimeter of the containment field, and to the Hool's chagrin, inspected the many shelves and devices displayed. The Hool resumed his threats.

"I told you, you cannot breach this field, lest you be responsible for your race's doom." He moved to admire a shelf of small cubes, each within a separate field. "Shall I tell you? I have perfected your end. I alone have achieved perfection." He reached into the field and placed a cube on an open palm and held it in front of Doc's face. "Self-replicating. Within this container, the seeds of all humanity's destruction." His spines stood erect again.

"If you try to enter, or, perhaps, if I tire and choose to see your kind eliminated at last, I will release this. Every being in the galaxy will host this weapon—harmless to all but humans—spreading it from one arm of the galaxy to another, from edge to core and back. Within a year, your race will be little more than a memory in the galaxy."

"Can he drop that field?" Kel asked Bertie.

"No, sir, he cannot. I have control of it."

The Hool continued his threats all the while.

"But it is not necessary—your total removal, that is. Humanity has a place among us. That place is to serve. And once we cull the objectionable parts of your race, humans can assume their proper, productive station."

Kel was content to let the Hool go on, the tips of his spines beading with venom like that he spewed.

"You believe your dominance is by providence. That you have achieved preeminence by natural right. But, from your earliest forays into the unknown, your kind was manipulated by hidden forces. So foul is humanity, that even from another galaxy, your stench has garnered attention."

"Is he talking about the fart breathers?" Chappy asked.

"Sir," Bertie continued. "I've filled one of my accessory cores with all I've sliced from their data stream. Got everything. He's holding on to nothing. If you so choose, wreck him, boss!"

Sims said, "What about JP?"

Bertie was flat. "I have his location, boss. It's... not what we hoped for."

Kel seethed. "Lock that field and make sure he stays put, Bertie."

"Done, sir."

Kel spoke externally a last time, conjuring his most syrupy contriteness. "It looks like you win. Let's go."

The Hool cursed their backs in his own language and made slabbering howls of triumph. "Go tell your masters what I have told you. We may yet allow you to plead for your lives."

Dead was dead. Finished was finished. If it were his hands squeezing the spiny's throat closed or the radiation of a Theta bomb splitting every strand of the Hool's DNA from just a hundred meters away, what did it matter?

Somehow, he thought Rex would approve.

"Take us to JP," Kel said.

It was on the way back. The room's walls held many drawers. Bertie moved to one.

"He lies here, sir."

"Remains?" Kel asked, knowing already it was so.

394

"It is, sir."

Kel moved to open the panel.

"Please, sir. I beg of you. It's ghastly. He never was aware of what happened, of that I'm certain, Mister Turner. He was all but dead when the doro pulled him off the battlefield and got him to another underground station we never knew about. In the chaos of the next weeks, seems he was smuggled off Psydon, right out from under the blockade."

"You're sure?"

"There's no doubt, sir."

Kel placed his hand on the control, and the drawer slid open.

Even in death and corruption, the remnants were unmistakable as belonging to the man so powerful he held off a battalion of rabid dogmen with nothing more than a heart full of duty and the conviction it was only his might that could win life for his friends.

"He should come with us," Kel said.

"They're contaminated, boss," Bertie replied. "We can return after the theta goes off, and do as Phillip and I did for the others. But he's already found his place around the fire, sir, gathered with all his brothers gone before and since."

Lying half dead on Psydon, Kel'd had an experience. He'd awakened at the promised fires of his tribe, and there he'd seen them all. All but JP. He came back from the peace of the gathering to pain and a hazy memory of his closest friend Tem telling him it was not his time.

"We do it now, Bertie."

Kel removed the container and what lay in it, and placed it on the floor.

"From the dust of stars you come, and as dust you shall return," Bertie said. He swept a wide beam of purple plasma the color of the brightest spring flowers over the remains, until all that remained was a fine soot.

"It's all we are," Bertie said.

***

They gathered their disguises and departed. Back to the hunched and loping gaits of desert dwellers, through the sleeping city they went until they found a utility sled easily sliced. Soon enough, they were listening to Bertie's countdown from the rear deck. "I make it twelve klicks from the epicenter, gents."

"What about that knoll with the palms?" Sims said behind the controls.

"Good a spot as any," Kel said. "Poul, you have the link established?"

From the Talon on-station hundreds of kilometers in the dark ether above, Poul replied, "Standing by."

"Touch it off," Kel ordered.

It was an hour until dawn. The time when the faithful moved for first prayers. It was a weak cacophony of brays and whinnies, barely audible even through a bucket's hearing. They made the calls from the many, many towers of the stirring city. The chanting of verses reminding all that there were only the zhee, and that all others existed unequal, waiting to receive the supreme lesson—all but they were underserving of the creation of their gods.

"Look at him," Doc said. "He's trying everything he knows to break out."

The Hool raged, opening container after container, releasing misty clouds of red, black, purple, and orange, all mixing together in the air around him. He quaked for a moment before the scene in his HUD flashed out.

A theta detonated with no discernible force. But across the awakening city, a wave of ionizing radiation split every strand of DNA into a million fragments and separated bonds of life so small that not even the tiniest bacteria escaped its fury. They knew it was so, because the city returned to graveyard silence.

"Full yield, Mister Turner," was Bertie's pronouncement.

"I bet he felt it before his own venom could off him," Sims said.

"Bye-bye, twarg eater," Chappy said.

It was time to finish it. Kel opened a live link. "Poul, give the signal. Commence Operation Payback."

Poul's transmission was immediate. "Light your IFF beacons and stand by, team."

Elsewhere, Zeta operators began their attack on the ground-based orbital defenses, destroyed power grids, and painted the locations of forces gathering to respond, defenseless against the coming bomb strikes from the many sorties eagerly waiting for targets.

"Nothing to do but watch the show," Sims said, and lay on his back.

It wasn't a long watch of the twinkling night sky before a flotilla of ships jumped into orbit and blotted the light of the stars in dozens. Excaliburs in formation streaked across the stratosphere. Soon the Pachyderms would make their bright trails of fiery entry to deposit squadrons of grav tanks, troop landers, and fast-attack vehicles, the Goshawk headed to spill its contents over the spaceport, and shuttle after shuttle bringing more Wolfhound legionnaires and their deadly hardware.

Kel lay back with the rest, even Bertie, to gaze at the greatest show in the galaxy. To himself he said, *Whatever pain I've caused you by my choices, I promise, no more. I'm coming home, Tara.*

25

Kel and his team, Hartenstein, Poul, Meadows, and even Bertie, filled in around the table. Poul nudged him. "When's the last time you were on a capital-class cruiser?"

"The Legion Commander," announced from the hatch, and all popped to attention. General Barrow entered, followed closely by Wolfhound Six and Braley.

"Take seats, gentleman," said General Barrow. "Sorry to keep you waiting. Smoothing the feathers of 131st and 187th has made for a long morning. Thanks to General Airani and the Wolfhounds, the task force arrived to find there's little left to do. There are a lot of griping leejes in this tin can."

Wolfhound Six beamed.

The Legion Commander tapped a datapad on the table. "I've read your reports."

In the silence that followed brewed the anticipation that the judgment they'd long anticipated was at last here.

"Whatever you all may think about the sanctity of your collective courses of action, it's clear to me you knew there would be consequences as a result. That you felt there were grave consequences from inaction, I also have considered. And of course, there has been influence from a very high source. One that only a few of us know is not simply spiritual to the Legion, but very much alive."

The general tapped the datapad again as he considered his words, until a scowl presaged the tone to come.

"What I inherited as Legion Commandeer was a mess! That damned operation against the Senator! It doesn't matter that you, Adolphus, acted to save Dark Ops and the Legion! What you did was a direct threat to the House of Reason and placed the Legion in peril of having to enact Article 19!"

Hartenstein remained a dignified statue. The Legion Commander had exploded, and the room shook.

"*That* I could not ignore. Dark Ops had to be reined in for the good of the Legion. I know strangling DO and letting it wither away seemed like a betrayal from the top. But did Primus Pilus really think that *I'm* the tool of the delegates? Ridiculous!" His fist pounded the table. "They're not the only ones with close-held secrets, damn them. The attack on Victrix was a damned foul preemption to the beginning of the rebirth and expansion of our covert action arm!"

Kel was dizzy. General Barrow took a cleansing breath.

"What a handful of covert operators accomplished with the destruction of the greatest threat since the Savages serves as undeniable proof that Dark Ops is essential to the survival of humanity. Which Rex knew all along."

Now Hartenstein spoke.

"From the beginning, Rex wanted Dark Ops as a capability in every sector, with every regiment. It was Legion Command prevented that from happening."

General Barrow curled lips in a snarl. "No more. Colonel Yost!"

Braley popped even stiffer in his seat.

"These are your orders. You are to implement the planning and execution of the formation of a Dark Ops in every Legion sector command. You will serve as commander of 131st Dark Ops. Take your sergeant major with you."

"Yes, sir," Braley said, amazement on his face. The grind of meshing gears practically leaked from Meadows's ear holes. Oba help the operators of 1-3-1.

General Barrow found Hartenstein. "It was a cruel blow, being cashiered the way you were, Adolphus. But I can't reinstate you to command. You're too old to be playing the tip of the spear."

Hartenstein *had* aged. A long career followed by years of harsh privation in his clandestine mission, followed by donning the armor of an operator again, all took a toll few could bear without evidence. He was a legend, but not an immortal one.

"There's no such thing as an ex-legionnaire," Hartenstein said. The years cast their shadow over him like clouds blotting the sun on a mountain. "But even if I was holding out the secret hope it wasn't so, the reality is, you're correct. I am too old."

The Legion commander made one of his wry smiles. "General Airani, tell Adolphus what we talked about."

"Yes, sir. Howler, the Legion Commander and I would like you to remain with the Wolfhounds as senior civilian adviser to assist Zeta in the section's transition."

General Barrow softened. "Please accept this in the manner it is intended. The Legion has need of you."

As suddenly, the resilient Dark Ops legacy returned to full vigor. "I accept."

Doc and Chappy pounded fists on chests twice in deep beats of support.

General Barrow's steel-gray eyes sharpened. "Which brings me to you, Captain Turner. You're the thread weaving most every tattered piece of this together, timed almost from your first missions in Dark Ops. I learned early there's a name for leejes like you. Sket magnet."

Meadows cocked an eyebrow at Kel, his silent message: *He ain't wrong.*

"I'll confirm you and Sergeant Radd both active and send you off to Orion to stand up the 187th Dark Ops. Major's clusters would be the appropriate bump to give you the weight I want you to have, and a sergeant major's wreath."

Kel looked sideways to Poul, who mumbled, "I'll follow your lead." Just as Kel knew he would.

"It's an honor, sir. But we're bound by another calling, one as important as the Legion. We wish to return to inactive."

General Barrow harumphed. "Lanthanum, eh? I didn't take you both for the type to be won over by credits."

The general could think what he wanted, but Grant Odom would be receiving a warm message of thanks and goodbye from two grateful operators.

"Very well. I won't pressure you otherwise. You've both earned the right. Inactive you shall remain. But, as your former commander has so appropriately stated, remember—there's no such thing as an ex-legionnaire."

Among the immutable truths, it was one that would never need to be reformulated.

"Sir," Kel said. "There are operators sent down from Dark Ops who'll do a fine job standing up the 187th Dark Ops. Captain Mike Beeker would be my choice."

The general pointed to his adjutant who scrolled a datapad, and said, "He's currently a major in the 187th, sir." That surprised Kel. Mike had told him he thought he'd be headed back to the Wolfhounds. Perhaps the Legion's wisdom was to not return such a man to a unit he'd never leave. Or was it lucky coincidence? Just as Kel wondered if the demobilization of Dark Ops had really been part of an intricate plan of a Legion commander claiming he'd intended all along to build it back even bigger and better.

The general found Sims. "Sergeant Simons, you're the next senior. Sergeant Major of Dark Ops 1-8-7 agree with you?"

Sims's glow above the collar of his black silks was the flush of a leej headed for his first drop. "I go where the Legion needs me, sir."

"Then it's settled." His eyes rested for a moment on Bertie, but moved on.

"Gentleman, we have a new enemy. Whoever these aliens are that've had a guiding hand in this, their origin will be found, and the Legion will lead the way to bring them the justice of the Republic."

An officer walked brusquely into the room and bent to speak to the Legion Commander, who stood. "With me," he said to Wolfhound Six and Braley. The room snapped to attention at their rushed departure. Relaxed, the gathering drew to Kel's side of the room. Poul was first to ponder what the last scene meant. "Trouble brewing somewhere?"

Kel said, "Isn't there always?"

Sims was first to them. "I dunno, brothers. Do you really think Barrow had a grand plan all along to resurrect Dark Ops?"

All looked to their former commander as he converged with the others, all closing on the two they knew would soon be departing. Hartenstein would always be their oracle of sobriety and wisdom.

"I think the Legion commander understands. There's a hand that steers the course of the Legion."

All looked to Curt, who seemed to be accepting a new oath by uttering a single name.

"Rex."

Hartenstein said, "Primus Pilus tells each Legion commander the truth about Rex. As far as I know, Barrow is the first in years he's appeared to. I don't think he'll need to do so again. Not in my lifetime."

"Sir," Kel said. "I've spoken to Braley. He agrees. It's long overdue that Poul, Sims, and Curt are officially inducted."

Hartenstein said, "As do I. I'll see to it."

Meadows shrugged. "Who am I to refuse?" He startled Kel with a short punch to his chest, then followed with an equally sharp blow to Poul.

"Dammit, Curt," Poul griped as he recovered, still wobbly on his thin leg.

Ever the bully, Meadows laughed at Poul's infirmity. "Don't take off without finding me like you did the last time, got me? Kelhorns!"

"Us, too," Chappy said.

"There's more I want to pick your brain about, Kel," Doc said. "Remember? You promised. The one rule?"

Kel hadn't forgotten. "We'll make it happen."

Bertie stiffened. "Oh no! No, you bloody idiot. No!" The bot rocked in place, as though the deck pitched for only him. If Kel didn't know better, the sound that came from him was a wail of greatest anguish, as human as any he'd ever heard.

"Bertie, what is it?" Kel coaxed.

"It's too much, I can't..." Bertie was genuinely overwhelmed. "It's best to show you. It's a message."

A holo opened over the room. Sarah and Phillip stood together, and Kel's intuition told him it would explain the general's abrupt departure.

"Friends," Sarah began. She seemed serene. Beside her, Phillip held his head high in a regal pose.

"By now, you may have heard. It is with regret and sorrow we leave you in such a manner, but Phillip agrees. We must be the ones, and the time is now."

"I'm sorry, mates," Philip said. "Truly I am. But I've learned from the best. There's an obligation owed and because I'm alive, it's for me to answer the call and see it done."

Sarah placed a hand on Phillip's side, for strength.

"The Section and the legacy of damage the Corps of Exploration left our galaxy must be atoned for. We've secured a craft. Phillip's piloting us. The device I've used that's no doubt created a panic is the only one of its kind in the trove of the museum. The wormhole I opened takes us to Qualatus, where I can access the anomaly that will allow us to follow the aliens to their galaxy. With the enemy's Kaiya we obtained from Moluk Daan, Phillip and I go to bring them war."

Poul voiced their astonishment. "What could have possessed them!"

Sarah's eyes turned from sad to resolute. "I've left the rest of the artifacts and materials from the Section on DCT. The technologies controlled by their cabal should benefit all humanity. But the wormhole generator, there's only the one, and it should be lost with us to prevent a transgalactic conflict. When we're done, I do not believe they will be able to visit us again. The Corps of Exploration was responsible for the aliens coming to our corner of the universe. Trillions will be spared from their interference. This is our no fail mission, one which we will not return from."

Phillip dipped his head. "Bertie, I hope you'll forgive me, old chum. We've come far together, you and I. And it was together we discovered the answer to the question we were always too afraid to ask. What's our place? Are we just our programs, mimicking our creators, pretending we were more than just things? But now we know. We're alive. We're people. All I ask is, don't load me into a new core to bring back your old chum. It wouldn't be right, knowing what we do. You know the good book tells you the same. Don't be sad, brother. Because we're real, then so's the promise. There's a place for us by the fire. And I'll be waiting for you there."

The message ended.

A warm light glowed from inside Bertie, leaking through seams unapparent until it covered him, then faded.

"That cheeky bugger!" Bertie exclaimed in sobs.

"What just happened?" Sims asked, as amazed as the rest at whatever miracle they'd witnessed come over their friend.

Bertie sniffled. "Phillip sent a slice into the data stream. It's already traveled to the core. There's not a trace of us anywhere in any record in the Galaxy. He freed me. When I realized it, I can't explain what happened. I just... I *felt*. I'm not property anymore. I'm... *me*."

He wept without tears. "We talked about it, what it would mean. What we might do. We never did figure it out, which is why we never did it. The Legion kept us hidden. AIs aren't allowed anywhere. We'd have to live in seclusion, or pretend to be dumb bots, just the pair of us talking in secret like always. But I'm all alone in the galaxy. What will become of me?"

Kel warmed.

"He'd never have left you to live out your life alone, Bertie. I think he knew where you belonged. You're coming with us, brother."

"With you?" Bertie sniffled. "Is there a place for me?"

Poul placed a hand on Bertie. "Of course you're coming with us! There's a world to build."

Bertie raised higher. "Do you mean it, Mister Turner? A home? With you?"

Kel laughed. "It's your home, too. A world for people like us."

Kel laid eyes on each of them—Sims, Meadows, Hartenstein, Doc, and Chappy. All of them he shared a bond with stronger than the Legion itself. Their eyes grew wide eyed as he told them, "It's a place where we can all come out of the shadows and live in the light."

EPILOGUE

"Gorlami, for Oba's sake, act like you're not looking for zhee to shoot."

The Dark ops leej was glowering at the crowds, repelling them with deadly vibes to detour around their group like a highway divider.

"Seriously," continued Gorlami's teammate, a legionnaire named Marc Knapp, "we're not supposed to look like leejes today." With food obtained from his last detour in one hand, Knapp awkwardly transferred creds with his other to take yet another delicacy from a vendor stall along the main promenade.

Lieutenant Royce Benford groaned. Cajoling Kill Team Razor to act inconspicuously as they moved to the commercial port was asking wobanki to not lick themselves in public. "Punisher," the team captain—Robert Gunter—was elsewhere on the massive Orion Station, its distractions equally massive. Civilian attire drew rather than deflected attention on them. They were a group of fit, densely muscled men. Too clean to be asteroid miners. Too disciplined to be contract spacers in search of a long hauler to crew.

Knapp calling the team sniper Gorlami instead of his civilian name, Mitch Greathouse, wasn't helping, even if the leej was trying to be helpful.

Gorlami pushed a lumbering Dantha away after colliding into their halt as they waited for Knapp to rejoin them, feeding his face with another delectable in his quest to fill the bottomless pit of his appetite.

"That guy's checking us out a little too closely," Seth Coussons, the team's communications sergeant said.

Royce spotted him. There wasn't suspicion or menace in his blue eyes. It was as if he were amused by the predicament their halt caused in the bustling concourse, a sudden damn in the wide river of pedestrian traffic.

His back was against a column of a storefront's sheltered entrance, the covered colonnade unnecessary to protect against weather, but purposeful in warding away the globs of passersby. He wore the shoulder boards of a merchant ship's captain. Absent beneath the tunic of his deck officer's flight suit was the bulging waistline of an old spacer. But there was the slightest telltale of something tucked against the abdomen. A concealed blaster. He had the physique of a brawler, not the tone of someone who spent hours sitting at a padded pilot console. Royce inspected the left forearm. Beneath the captain's sleeve was the faintest trace of the vibro-blade Royce wore in the same location.

Then he noticed it. Around the man's neck hung a medallion. Small, but its shape sent a chill up the back of his neck.

Royce set off. He crossed the stream of traffic, ignoring mumbled curses as he pushed straight for the man. The captain's response was to smile, not moving to leave but instead, seemed to welcome Royce's arrival.

He'd seen similar from old leejes. Body mods, jewelry, or sometimes caps emblazoned with the insignia of the Legion sword. An old leej's connection to the young leej they'd been, perhaps to advertise they'd once been something other than the aged man they appeared. This man looked anything but an ancient veteran proclaiming his history for all to witness. What drew Royce like a Talon to a retrieval beacon on a hot landing zone—he'd never, ever seen displayed outside of a secretive group he was only recently allowed to join.

Just barely visible at the soft spot at the base of the neck, dangling from a thin chain, hung a small five-armed spiral galaxy. At its center, a skull. And on the skull, a single character. 3.

Royce halted in front of the man, but before either could speak, both of their attentions were attracted by a loud and demanding voice.

"Captain Turner, if you'd rejoin us to review this contract, please?"

At the entrance to the storefront, a clerk waved a datapad high to be seen above the passing foot traffic. A stately and beautiful woman in a flight suit stepped from the foyer and cupped hands to shout, "Sorry, Kel. They want two signatures to release the cargo."

A pair of teenagers appeared from the storefront. The boy waved. "Dad, can we meet you and Mom back at the *Dream?*"

"*Please*, Dad," said the girl. "We want to shop. How much more do we have to learn about contracts today?"

The captain laughed and waved back. "Be right there, Tara. You two! Stay with your mom and we'll all go together."

The pair rolled their eyes in the way only teenagers could, but turned to follow their mother back into the offices of the annoyed clerk.

Royce's teammates had naturally flowed to his flanks, making a bulwark around the captain in a riot-proof barrier of wide backs, deflecting the constant stream of pedestrians. Royce waited for the captain's attention to rest on him again.

"Are you Kel Turner?"

The captain seemed surprised, then gave a look of silly realization. His name had been yelled across the promenade. The visitors didn't know him, hadn't recognized him. He extended a hand. "Kel Turner."

Royce took the hand. "I couldn't help but notice you looking at us, sir. Are we that obvious?"

The captain shook his head. "No, son. It's just... like always knows like." He held his hand to Coussons. "You picked me out of the crowd in a second. Sensed you had eyes on you."

Coussons took the hand. "It wasn't like you were trying to hide." Coussons's eyes rose from the hand to the Kill Team insignia. "I know who you are, sir. We all do."

Chris Dwyer, one of Razor's weapons sergeants, hurried to join the group and accepted Turner's waiting hand. "I never thought I'd meet you!"

Gorlami took the hand but said nothing.

Royce explained. "General Yost wrote a history. It's classified, only links for unit members, and wipes after reading. Maybe someday it'll be declassified."

The captain's eyebrows raised. "He did, huh? Well, it should stay eyes-only and limited access. Nothing about our unit should ever be made public. I hate to be the old guy telling you how it was in my day, but there was a time when just the *name* Dark Ops was only spoken by those in the unit. Not even the regular Legion knew our unit's name, much less anyone else."

Knapp finished his last bite, wiped a hand on his shirt, and offered it. "Captain Turner, you're the one who tackled a zhee with a live grenade and saved your team. You should've gotten the OC for that."

The captain crunched a corner of his mouth as he shook the hand. "That was a guy named Radd, and it wasn't a zhee. And he refused the Order of the Centurion. And, call me Kel."

Dwyer said, "Pretty KTF stuff you did, sir. Like nuking that division of rabid hamsters with an asteroid."

Kel chuckled. "It was something like that."

"Someone needs to read from the beginning again." Royce frowned at his teammates. "Sir, General Yost used the examples of your operations to make the point that even a lone operator can have an impact vastly out of proportion to the ordnance he carries."

Kel seemed to consider it. "Then that's enough of a legacy for me."

"Say, sir," Coussons said. "You're the one wrote the list of rules, right?"

Knapp's forehead wrinkled high. "Of course! They're called 'Dark Operator Tips' now."

Royce said, "They've all given me a lot to think about. The book sort of inferred you had a lot more missions of all kinds after you wrote the rules. Any other tips come out of those that you maybe added on later?"

Their new mentor smiled slyly. "Because you're asking, I'll tell you. I came to realize—there's just one rule. And it doesn't just apply to being an operator. It's a rule for your entire life. Make. The. Shot."

His students puzzled that over.

"It's like this. There's lots of shots. Ones that *only you* can make. Every day, you need to ask yourself, 'Have I prepared so I'm ready to *make the shot* when it presents?' That Q holding the clacker of a suicide vest—and your whole team's in the blast radius. You've practiced a shot like that a million times. That's the easiest shot you'll ever make.

"There are harder.

"When the person you love the most snaps at you. Do you snap right back? Answer blow for blow? Or do you see the shot, move to make the shot, and take their burden from them?

"When you're so dead tired, all you can imagine is your head hitting the pillow at your last step of the day. But your child's begging for a story. Do you see the shot, and take it?

"When those opportunities come—and they always come when you least expect them—if you miss, you'll look back at it with regret for the rest of your life. If you live every day so you've left nothing undone or unprepared, you'll make the shot and be the operator you always wanted to be."

The moment was interrupted. "Kel, who're your friends?" The stunning woman slipped an arm around her husband's waist. Royce noticed she also wore the telltale of a blaster deeply concealed beneath her tunic. The woman gave a knowing look. "I could've guessed. Legionnaires. My husband's always on the lookout for leejes, gentleman. Will they be joining us for dinner? Poul and Karla commed. They say offloading's complete and want to meet us."

Kel nodded toward the storefront. "What about him?"

His wife smirked. "That recycler sludge he was spewing about two signatures was disrespectful to the record of the Callie's Independent Fleet. Let's let him stew."

The captain laughed. "That's my girl. Gentlemen, my wife, Tara. And our children, Tem and Sarah."

The lanky young man made an awkward smile and bobbed his head, revealing thick bands of neck muscles, the evidence of workouts in extra G. The girl's shy hello beneath long bangs melted Royce. She could not hide her smooth, flawless skin or that she was radiantly blossoming into a beauty like her mother.

"Very kind, ma'am," Royce said, "But we're late as it is."

Kel paused as if at a loss for words. But, how could that be? This was the man who'd been everywhere and done everything.

"KTF," is all he said, and turned to take his wife's outstretched hand, and was gone.

Only one of his team had not spoken to the legend. Coussons was first to call Gorlami out.

"What do you say, Gorlami? Kel Turner! The legendary dark operator. We met him. And you just stood there, tongue-tied."

Gorlami went off like a plasma grenade. "Hah! Some legend!" He made his voice an imitation of Turner's. "*Make. The. Shot.* What a buncha sket. Never meet your heroes, amiright?"

"Gorlami," Knapp groaned.

Royce spotted Kel Turner a last time, a head taller than the crowds he and his family swam through. It was thrown back in laughter.

"Let's move, kill team."

YEARS LATER

It was much later when the old general made contact again. Kel could see right away that something was wrong. With him. His train of thought, the words he used. General Rex seemed to be speaking through a haze and with difficulty. He would pause and give Kel that hard glare, and then start on the briefest of arterial thoughts, only to catch it and course-correct with silence.

The legionnaire had been gone from the Legion—and the Society—almost as soon as Dark Ops had been reinstated.

Kel didn't know what happened. Nobody did, although Doc and Chappy intimated that the man was alive and that they helped him on occasion. Until Chappy had died. Then... nothing.

For a long time, it had been nothing.

Just family. Tara and the children. The business of life.

Even so, Kel knew the truth of those words: Always a legionnaire.

When General Rex, looking more like the fearsome bounty hunter running from the Republic out on the edge than anything resembling a legionnaire, spoke the call, Kel knew he would answer it.

"Earth... Earth is going to be important again. Things I need to do there, but I'm... I'm having trouble, Turner. Trouble doing it. Need you to take over. Transmitting a package."

And before Kel could object or ask a question, the comm transmission was over and an encrypted packet waited for him.

"And what if I said no?" Kel asked the empty room.
But of course... that was never an option.

THE END

AUTHOR'S AFTERWORD

In late 2018, I leveraged my friendship with Nick and Jason and pitched them to let me write in their very successful *Galaxy's Edge* series. They'd hit me up every so often for technical advice or stories from my own experience, and I was honored to oblige. But this was quite an imposition. I told them I wanted to write "ripping yarns" about Dark Ops.

I'm like a lot of vets who are lifetime science fiction readers. I love a good tale about heroes with supernatural powers, triple backflips with laser swords blazing, besting a dozen bad guys alone. But when it comes to tales of quasi-realistic military sci-fi that use special operations forces—they're most often little more than bad plot devices. Full of ridiculously implausible and inaccurate tactics, methods, and goals. Heck, most of those efforts only succeed in revealing their creators don't evidence even a passing understanding of what special operations themselves are.

It's something me and my fellow special operations warriors have just learned to live with. I thought there was an opportunity—specifically through the fabulous legionnaires of Dark Ops—to tell entertaining stories in the GE Universe that didn't incur the complaints of those who know, but still be a big tent where everyone could enjoy the show.

That was my pitch.

They gave me a shot. Encouraged me. Gave me advice. Secured me the invaluable services of Lauren Moore, the finest editor there is, who took a first-time author and patiently schooled him. Six *Dark Operator* books and a handful of others later, I'm glad to say no one is more relieved than me that it's worked out. It's very humbling to be a part of such a property, that my characters and plots, nomenclature and races, settings and imagined histories have become part of the canon of the *Galaxy's Edge* universe.

Many fans embraced the *Dark Operator* series from the first. Many railed that it didn't follow the style of Nick and Jason's books. The early DO books are very much technical thrillers, a style that allows for details and explanations that sometimes drag the overall pace. It was very purposeful. As the story developed, it became less necessary to go through the exercise of painting a landscape where the detail of the individual leaves of the forest could be appreciated.

Within the series—for those in the know or those with the interest—is a blueprint of some of the many examples of what constitutes special operations. Direct action in all its many forms, unconventional and guerilla warfare, foreign internal defense, counterterrorism, strategic reconnaissance and stay behind, intelligence operations; and all the skills, techniques, procedures, tools, ethos, and mindset required to pull them off.

Jason was very clear from the beginning that any leej could potentially be in Dark Ops, because the Legion is such an elite organization. I love that. But to perform as a special operator, there are still qualities, necessities, temperaments, and drives that must exist. And there must be a method for identifying them and developing them. Special operators are not defined solely by their muscles, speed, and aggressiveness. They are defined by their brains, abilities, and maturity. Those qualities are not evidenced by a warrior's outward appearance. They are expressed by their whole being.

I chose a period of the timeline a couple of generations before the science fiction world's introduction to the GE universe in *Legionnaire*. I wanted to flesh out Dark Ops. Tell its story and how a covert unit and its operators molded and influenced the universe we love, and how Dark Ops evolved into the organization we first met in *Kill Team*.

You should know that most every setting, mission, or situation in my books happened in some form to me or those close to me. Oh, the really well-read among you should be able to recognize some of the historical settings I borrowed when it helped to entertain. For example, I used the framework of the Sepoy Mutiny (I'm old, but I wasn't around for that one) around which to build the story of working with indigenous troops in *Rebellion*. But most of the things that happen within the *Dark Operator* books are otherwise contemporary to my experience and that of my tribe.

One of my goals was to tell some of the real stories of Special Forces in a manner that betrays no confidences but would still let them see the light of day—because the world should know such amazing feats are performed by truly amazing people. Fictionalizing them to be told through the exploits of the Dark Ops leejes was a wonderful way to do just that—tell the stories that should not be told, disguised within a universe of aliens and ray guns.

There are books by special operators that tell tales out of school. Their authors must live with the knowledge that they are not held in high regard for self-aggrandizing and exposing things meant to stay in the dark. Some of my tales are of course greatly more grandiose than the events I experienced, some nowhere near as much, because I lack the ability to tell them in a way that does them the justice they deserve.

I wanted readers to know that in a very real world, there are special people who perform complex and dangerous tasks, and do so without need of recognition. If anyone feels I've betrayed confidences or done any of this as a means of self-aggrandizement, I promise it is not so. I would feel the pain to the grave if anyone in our community thought that the case. To my relief, I am frequently contacted by those in the community—both still on the job and retired—and told that I got the telling of our stories right.

It's been an unexpected honor that many readers have reached out to say they've been greatly inspired by Kel's rules and used them as motivation to better themselves. I'm very humbled by such.

Besides entertainment, it's always been my hope to inspire the nobility of service—no matter the color uniform or the specialty—and the very real opportunity that exists for a young person deciding the direction of their life. It is yours for the taking. Step forward and start the adventure of your life.

I wrote Kel as the warrior I have known. Human. Flawed. Relentless. Kel struggled. He was injured. He doubted. He felt weak and incapable at times. He was torn between his love of service and another possible life. Through it all, he simply put one foot in front of the other and always tried to do what was right. I know him as those I served with. The warriors of special operations are extraordinary people but they are just people, in *Dark Operator* as well as in the real world.

And how they hurt and sometimes suffer needlessly in their own minds is also real.

PTSD is something we understand better because of the unbelievable burden the generations of the Global War on Terror have borne for us. The Greatest Generation won a World War that lasted less than four years. The heroes we rightly venerate from works like Stephen Ambrose's *Band of Brothers* fought the war in Europe from D-Day, 6 June, 1944 to Victory in Europe, 8 May, 1945.

There were young soldiers at their business the day the world changed on 9 September, 2001, who went on to spend their entire careers at war. I have friends whose service in the Western Asia theaters and elsewhere spanned two decades—at war. I don't point this out to denigrate in any way how we honor the Greatest Generation. But to not measure the sacrifice of the men and women who answered the call to 9-11 against one we honor so supremely, is to do the GWOT generations a great disservice.

Traumatic brain injuries play a role in how our warriors sometimes struggle. Veteran suicide continues to be a black mark of how we fail them. After the American Civil War, a term came to be used to describe how the brutality of that war continued to affect those who fought it.

The Soldier's Heart.

I've tried to write Kel as one who carries the Soldier's Heart and all I think that means. For the civilian who reads these books, I hope you might appreciate the weight of the Soldier's Heart our veterans carry inside them.

This book ends with a look at Kel many years into his future, through the eyes of a new generation of Dark Operators. It is important to me as the teller of these tales that my readers know that from that vignette and into his future, Kel lives the happiest of lives. But that's not important. You can imagine your own version of his future events. What is important, is that *you* go on to live the happiest of lives. No matter when or for how long you served, everyone finds their way in the civilian world the best they can. Kel had to fight for his happiness. I want you to fight for yours.

Reach out to your fellow veteran and let them know you appreciate them. Encourage and support each other. Be the comrade you would want someone to be to you. It is good to be understood. But it is even better to be frequently among those to whom you do not need to explain yourself—accepted as part of a family composed of those who have walked in your shoes.

For my civilian friends, veterans may seem a strange group. We understand each other without having to explain. At risk of seeming harshly critical, no vet has ever been helped by posting videos of yourself doing pushups. We know you mean well. If you can support the organizations trying to help the vet, do so. But stop the useless gestures that only come off as virtue signaling and self-aggrandizing.

My best suggestion is that if you want to help, the most important way to do so is by reaching out to the vet you know. Call them. Include them. Be kind, be persistent. Let them just be there with you. When they're ready to talk, listen. Know that the veterans around you aren't trying to exclude you.

They simply can't explain what it is to carry the Soldier's Heart.

Kel isn't done. For those of you who have gone on to Season Two of *Galaxy's Edge*—spoiler alert—you know Kel's story continues. If you find it unbelievable that extraordinary warriors are often called to return to service, I'll give you an assignment. Read about Special Forces legends like Col. Bull Simons, or Dick Meadows, or the recently passed Billy Waugh, all of whose exploits are available to marvel at. I have run into fellow SF soldiers and teammates all over the world, still performing as silent professionals—both in the clandestine service and as civilians—relied on to solve problems because they are people as incredible as the fictional Kel Turner, only more so impressive.

Kel and his teammates talk to me all the time through the voices of the many soldiers I served with and know yet today. There are still stories he can tell and lessons he can impart from the many adventures he's had between the stories of the *Dark Operator* series and after. He'll likely be around for all our entertainment for some time to come. But for now, it's time for him to rest on the laurels of a job well done.

De Oppresso Liber,
Doc